MARIUS' MULES XIII

CIVIL WAR

BY S. J. A. TURNEY

1ST EDITION

"Marius' Mules: nickname acquired by the legions after the general Marius made it standard practice for the soldier to carry all of his kit about his person."

For Bev

Cover photos courtesy of Paul and Garry of the Deva Victrix Legio XX. Visit http://www.romantoursuk.com/ to see their excellent work.

Cover design by Dave Slaney.

Many thanks to the above for their skill and generosity.

All internal maps are copyright the author of this work.

* * *

Also by S. J. A. Turney:

Continuing the Marius' Mules Series

Marius' Mules I: The Invasion of Gaul (2009)
Marius' Mules II: The Belgae (2010)
Marius' Mules III: Gallia Invicta (2011)
Marius' Mules IV: Conspiracy of Eagles (2012)
Marius' Mules V: Hades' Gate (2013)
Marius' Mules VI: Caesar's Vow (2014)
Marius' Mules: Prelude to War (2014)
Marius' Mules VII: The Great Revolt (2014)
Marius' Mules VIII: Sons of Taranis (2015)
Marius' Mules IX: Pax Gallica (2016)
Marius' Mules X: Fields of Mars (2017)
Marius' Mules XI: Tides of War (2018)
Marius' Mules XII: Sands of Egypt (2019)

The Praetorian Series

The Great Game (2015)
The Price of Treason (2015)
Eagles of Dacia (2017)
Lions of Rome (2019)
The Cleansing Fire (2020)

The Damned Emperors Series

Caligula (2018)
Commodus (2019)

The Rise of Emperors Series (with Gordon Doherty)

Sons of Rome (2020)

The Ottoman Cycle

The Thief's Tale (2013)
The Priest's Tale (2013)
The Assassin's Tale (2014)
The Pasha's Tale (2015)
The Knights Templar Series

Daughter of War (2018)
The Last Emir (2018)
City of God (2019)
The Winter Knight (2019)
The Crescent and the Cross (2020)

Tales of the Empire

Interregnum (2009)
Ironroot (2010)
Dark Empress (2011)
Insurgency (2016)
Invasion (2017)
Jade Empire (2017)

Roman Adventures (Children's Roman fiction with Dave Slaney)

Crocodile Legion (2016)
Pirate Legion (Summer 2017)

Short story compilations & contributions:

Tales of Ancient Rome vol. 1 – S.J.A. Turney (2011)
Tortured Hearts vol 1 – Various (2012)
Tortured Hearts vol 2 – Various (2012)
Temporal Tales – Various (2013)
A Year of Ravens – Various (2015)
A Song of War – Various (2016)
Rubicon – Various (2020)

For more information visit www.sjaturney.co.uk or
www.facebook.com/SJATurney or follow Simon on Twitter
@SJATurney

ROME

ITALIA

CAMPANIA

LILYBAEUM

SICILIA

UTICA

CLUPEA

NEAPOLIS

SYRACUSAE

HADRUMETUM

AFRICA

THAPSUS

THYSDRUS

CERCINA

ITALIA AND AFRICA

SHOWING IMPORTANT
LOCATIONS

PRINCIPLE AREA OF OPERATIONS IN AFRICA

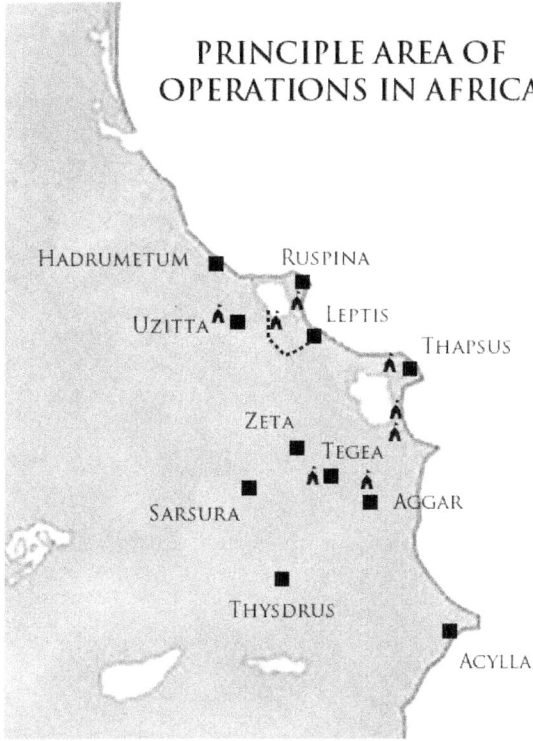

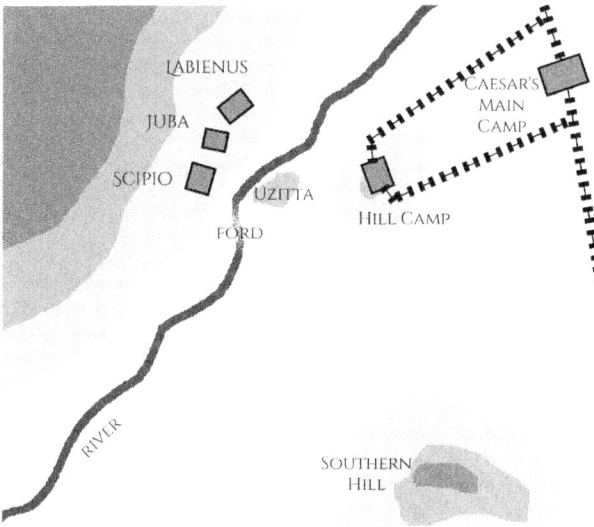

HADRUMETUM

RUSPINA

UZITTA

LEPTIS

THAPSUS

ZETA

TEGEA

SARSURA

AGGAR

THYSDRUS

ACYLLA

LABIENUS

JUBA

SCIPIO

UZITTA

FORD

CAESAR'S MAIN CAMP

HILL CAMP

RIVER

SOUTHERN HILL

UZITTA

"Neque enim Africam aut Italiam, sed orbem terrarum victoriae praemium fore; par periculum praemio quibus adversa pugnae fortuna fuisset."

The reward for victory was not just Italy or Africa, but all the world. Yet for those that lost the battle, the risk equalled the reward.

- Livy's History of Rome, Book 30, 32.2

"Neque enim Africam aut Italiam, sed orbem terrarum victoriae pr aemium fore; par periculum praemio quibus adversa pugnae fortun a fuisset."

The reward for victory was not just Italy or Africa, but all the world. Yet for those that lost the battle, the risk equalled the reward.

- Livy's History of Rome, Book 30, 32.2

CHAPTER ONE

Lilybaeum, Sicily, 20th December 47 BC

Marcus Falerius Fronto stood at the parapet of the wall, looking out over the port and its shimmering, glistening black waters. To the north of the city proper a great natural harbour dotted with inhabited islands stretched out along the coast. Scores of ships of varying sizes lay calmly at jetties, rocking only slightly in the protection of the sheltered waters under a troubled sky. Even at night, winter was insistent it be remembered, and the thick black clouds dashed across the sky as though pitted in a race. Fronto's eyes slid towards the harbour entrance. Beyond, he could spot the open sea, churning with white-caps.

Even men who were at home on the rolling waves said it was madness travelling in mid-winter, and the waters around Sicilia and southern Italia were notoriously bad any time past early autumn. Fronto could feel his stomach knotting into a cramped-up ball even thinking about floating out onto that roiling surface in a timber death-trap. In some ways he felt that at his age he should really be sitting in that vineyard near Tarraco and sipping wine on a veranda rather than campaigning, but the age argument held no water when the general was older than he, and yet the old man was twitching to be off.

Indeed, as the six legions, the cavalry and the various auxiliary units had arrived at this staging post, they had each been directed to quarters aboard ships in the harbour. No great legionary camps lay around Lilybaeum. Caesar wanted his army ready to sail at a moment's notice. Fronto was grateful to be quartered in the command tents on land, and could only imagine how horrible it was spending night after night aboard those gently rocking ships, waiting for the off. He shuddered and shifted his gaze from the water to the town. Footsteps drew his attention a moment later and he turned to see a soldier in light kit hurrying along the wall towards him. No guesses required as to what the man wanted.

'Commander, the general requests your presence in his tent.'

Fronto nodded and waved the man away. Of course he did. The only people up at this time of night were sentries, thieves, owls and the general. And old soldiers who no longer slept so well in camp cots and were prone at the moment to nightmares about drowning. Stretching, he turned and began the mile long walk from here to the general's accommodation at the sea edge of the officers' compound. Caesar's headquarters was not in its usual position at the heart of the legions, not because of their unusual position aboard the ships in the harbour, since the general had positioned himself long before the legions had arrived. His tent was pitched so low on the beach that Fronto had half expected it to be washed away on the first night. But it was not a love of the water that was responsible, either. The choice had been a deliberate statement of intent.

They had left Rome on the tenth of December, with only a cavalry force of Gauls and Germans led by Galronus, crossing to Sicilia and arriving at Lilybaeum on the seventeenth. Over the next few days six legions had arrived, along with sundry auxilia and cavalry, and had found the general lodged so close to the water that it looked as though he planned to swim to Africa on the morrow. Each had been directed to on-board accommodation. No man arriving in Lilybaeum could have questioned Caesar's intentions.

The remaining great bastion of opposition to Caesar lay only a short sail across those rolling waves: Africa. Oh there was still minor resistance in Hispania, too, but that would be easy enough to control, for Africa was where all the men of import had gathered now.

Fronto moved from the walls and began to stride across the beach. Over the past few days, he had attended a private meeting with the general every night, and it was becoming somewhat wearing. There was nothing really to discuss, after all. Disposition of troops and ships had been settled upon their arrival, and planning the campaign ahead was somewhat difficult to say the least and had been constantly put off. In Fronto's opinion it was more that the general, who was a martyr to insomnia anyway, simply needed someone he knew of old to talk to. Someone of an age and with at least a modicum of intelligence. And that was Fronto.

Over the years there had been plenty of people Caesar had confided in, apart from Fronto. Labienus, of course was a prime example, though now that great lieutenant of his sat in Africa awaiting them, a sizeable force of horsemen at his command who he had taken with him when he'd gone over to Pompey's side. Marcus Antonius had always been the general's close friend, but for the past few years the man had remained in Rome as 'Master of the Horse' and more or less kept control there. Cassius, who for all his ethical opposition to Caesar had proved to be a loyal and talented commander, had simply refused to go to war with any more Roman armies and had bid them farewell in Rome and retired to his estate until all of this was over. Sensible man, Fronto thought. Then there was Brutus, a close relation of Caesar's, and therefore too valuable in other roles to bring here. Brutus now controlled all shipping and logistics across the east, ostensibly to prevent any resurgence of opposition, though many whispered that he was assigned to keep a protective eye on the queen of Aegyptus and the son she had now had with Caesar.

Really, all the old guard were gone now. Of those who gathered for the morning briefing, apart from Fronto, the only men who had been with them over those days in Gaul were Aulus Hirtius, who was more secretary than commander anyway, and Lucius Munatius Plancus. Fronto remembered Plancus from those earlier days, when he had been an exceptionally average officer. Whether it was that age had matured the man, or perhaps simply being placed among all these untested youngsters, Fronto had grown to appreciate Plancus now, who had arrived with one of the legions, unexpectedly to put his sword once more at Caesar's command.

That was it. Fronto and Plancus. Oh, and many others, but no one else of great note. There was Rabirius Postumus, a rodent faced man with a chequered past, who'd been imprisoned in Aegyptus a few years earlier for complicity in financial mismanagement by Gabinius. Publius Vatinius, florid of face and inscrutable of expression, whose history held a plethora of accusations of extortion, theft and threats of violence. Sallustius Crispus, a shrewd man, and a clever one, but more bookish than martial, and whose history included strong support of Pompey. Publius Saserna and his brother Quintus, scions of the noble Hostilii, but very young and with little in the way of military experience. Gaius Messius, only here on the recommendation of Antonius, whose client the man was. Likewise, Lucius Cispius, a man with a very bucolic country drawl who was here on the strength of his links to Brutus, given that he had served under him all those years ago in Gaul against the Veneti ships. And finally Nonius Asprenas, who seemed to be here simply seeking military experience to further his political career. Not an auspicious high command, in Fronto's opinion.

Reaching the small gathering of tents on the beach, he nodded to the praetorian soldiers on guard and, being waved on, strode over to the tent close to the waves. The whole place had that shoreline smell of dead fish, brine and seagulls which made Fronto's stomach turn over a few times. Rapping on the timber frame of the door, he waited for the general to call him, and then made his way inside.

The tent's interior was lit by two oil lamps and a brazier, and the smell was acrid and thick, of hot coals and, for some unknown reason, goat's cheese. Still, it was a marked improvement on the smell outside. The general stood behind his campaign table, hands clasped behind his back, face folded into a frown as he pored over a map of Africa, also showing Sicilia and several smaller islands. Wax tablets and vellum lists in Hirtius' scrawl littered the table. No sign of a plate of cheese, which further confused Fronto as he breathed that smell in again.

'You sent for me?'

Caesar nodded without looking up.

'I shall wait no longer, Fronto.'

Not what he wanted to hear, though far from unexpected. Without waiting for permission, Fronto crossed to a cabinet and poured himself a cup of rich wine, cutting it with minimal water. These days, he tended to water it well, but if he was going to be going out on those waves tomorrow, who cared what he was throwing up. Might as well be hungover and seasick as just seasick. Besides, the mix of dead fish and goat's cheese was starting to make him feel queasy anyway. Caesar gave him a pointed look at his presumption, but said nothing as Fronto wandered back to the table and slumped into a chair opposite the general, taking a sip. One advantage Fronto had noted to being the senior officer and only here under sufferance was that Caesar gave him an unprecedented amount of leniency.

'Shall I reiterate all the reasons not to go, General?'

'You really need not bother,' sighed Caesar, but Fronto was already counting off on his fingers.

'Numbers. Latest intelligence puts their main force alone at ten legions plus thousands of cavalry, without the various other armies floating around and potential allies in Numidia.'

Second finger went up. 'Command. Your officers are largely untried, while what awaits us is the cream of Rome's tactical might.' Third finger. 'Season. No one fights in winter. Africa is not Aegyptus. It doesn't smoulder all year round. Across that strait it still rains and snows and is cold.' Fourth. 'No sailor would advise you to sail at this time of year. It's just too unpredictable.' Fifth. 'Lack of information and planning. We have no set plan of attack, and don't even know their dispositions.'

He looked irritably at his five spread fingers and at the cup in his other hand and then stuck up a foot. 'Sixth, we have no idea what's happening in Numidia.' Other foot. 'Seventh, Italia is still unsettled, and you don't know how much you can count on the legions.'

He stopped. He had a feeling there was an eighth, but he'd run out of appendages anyway unless he put his wine down. That last point had made Caesar's face wrinkle in distaste as he looked up and away into the distance beyond the tent walls.

Mutiny. More than once Caesar had been forced to impose his will on troublesome legions, the first time only a year into the war in Gaul, but mutiny was never well received, and this one had been particularly unpleasant. Upon their return from Aegyptus, they had been launched straight into trouble. Antonius had handled Rome in his usual heavy-handed manner, and there were a lot of bruised egos to sooth. And barely had that been achieved before several legionary detachments resting in Italia had openly revolted against the general.

In truth, Fronto could see their point, and it had been coming. Caesar had been promising them the spoils of war since Pharsalus, and while he'd gone on to campaign in Aegyptus, the legions who'd been sent back to quarters in Italia had received nothing. More than a year had passed now since those promises. Moreover, there were sizeable numbers of men who were due to be pensioned out but had not been, for they were still awaiting their share of the booty. What had truly rankled the most, though, and had drawn Fronto's displeasure, was that the glorious Tenth, Fronto's old command and Caesar's favoured legion, had been at the centre of the mutiny. Officers Fronto felt he should be able to rely upon had stood against them.

The matter had been settled swiftly, though, and with Caesar's usual flourish. They had demanded their money or they would disband and abandon the general. Caesar had fixed their spokesmen with a bored look, and had nodded and wished them well in their future careers, whatever they might be. He had turned and was riding away before the legions, their gambit having failed so drastically and so immediately, had collapsed and acquiesced.

In the end, Caesar had accepted them back into his service, and had promised them that their long awaited prizes would come, but that the crushing of the enemy forces in Africa had to take precedence. Notably, though, the six legions clustered near the shore at Lilybaeum did not yet include the Tenth. Whether they would rebel once more or actually answer the summons to war remained to be seen.

'The numbers do not concern me,' Caesar replied. 'We have fought superior forces before and come out on top. Wit makes a great deal of difference in the game of war and can counter a considerable imbalance. Moreover, while time will undoubtedly see further legions reach us, the same will be true of the opposition. The majority of my officers are an unknown quantity to me, but there is only one way to solve that, which is to watch them in action. I am not afeared of campaigning in winter, for we have done so successfully before. Remember the thick snows of the Cevenna Mountains in Gaul as we marched towards confrontation with the Arverni? Africa's conditions will never reach that level of difficulty, so I do not concern myself over them. Moreover, our opponents will not expect an invasion until spring, so we gain an element of surprise with a winter campaign. I will grant you that the sea could cause issues, but the crossing is not long, and we shall make copious libations to Neptune in the morning. As for what we leave behind, I have done all I can realistically do with the legions in Italia, and we must rely upon Marcus Antonius to maintain Rome in our absence.'

The general tapped the map. 'That leaves only the matter of our opposition and their disposition. Our erstwhile opponents from Ilerda and Hispania face us once again. I should perhaps have made an end to them at the time, though hindsight is always advantageous. Piso is bright enough, but we will have to hope that the fractures in command between Petrieus and Afranius once more cause them trouble. I am unaware of their positions, though last reports put them at Clupea with a small cavalry force. Considius is not a renowned commander, but as the former governor of the province, he knows the land and the terrain and people better than the others. The second most senior officer is Labienus. I do not know where he is currently to be found, but I understand that he commands a highly mobile force of cavalry, and so wherever he is, he could be elsewhere in a trice. He is one of my main concerns, for Titus knows us well, and personally, he commands a force that also knows us well, for they fought with us for years, and he is a clever man.'

Fronto nodded. The last thing he really wanted was to come up against their old companion in battle once more. Labienus had been a friend. Facing him was troubling on many levels.

'The man in overall command is Scipio. He will have the bulk of their army with him and reports place him in the region of Hadrumetum, to the south. Scipio you know. He will be our main military opponent. But it is none of these men that troubles me as much as the last – even Labienus with his knowledge of our ways and abilities or the great

Scipio with his huge army. My main worry is the man who pulls the strings to make them all dance.'

'Cato?' Fronto mused, taking another sip.

Caesar nodded. 'My old senatorial opponent, and the greatest politician among our enemy. There are still elements of Rome we claim to control who might easily be persuaded against us on the grounds of Cato's reputation alone. And it is a reputation well deserved, too. He may be no great military tactician, but in the matter of overall strategy he will prove to be very shrewd. He is extremely clever, and he is the one who will place those officers on the board and move them about to confront us, all from his seat at Utica.'

'You paint a somewhat bleak picture, General.'

'I reveal what is visible, rather than painting afresh. Two important centres of power await us. The enemy rule from Utica in the north, where Cato holds court, but the armoured fist is in the south with Scipio, near to Hadrumetum. The question is where to strike first. Neither lends itself readily.'

Fronto nodded. 'At a glance, Utica is a tempting target. To move swiftly, seize the centre of control and take Cato. Forces there are likely to be few. But the enemy know that too.'

Caesar nodded. 'It will undoubtedly be defended sufficiently to hold us until Scipio arrives with his army, and is closer to the Numidian king, who yet might well find an opportunity to involve himself.'

Fronto looked west across the map to the lands beyond Africa. 'What is the latest on Numidia?'

Caesar huffed. 'Sittius does a commendable job over in far Mauretania in keeping the Numidians busy. He continually stirs up trouble against them. As long as he is a thorn in the side, the Numidians will keep to themselves, I hope.'

Fronto nodded. Sittius was a notorious mercenary and at other times might well have become an enemy of the republic, selling his services to whoever had a cause and a vault of gold. Right now, though, that happened to be Caesar, and the man had proved his worth so far in keeping King Juba out of the game.

'If Sittius slips up, though,' Caesar noted, 'then Juba and his army could suddenly appear in Africa, supporting the enemy. Cato has well and truly bought the Numidians, and they have a large royal force. Four legions' worth or more, plus their infamous other units.'

'I don't like the idea of facing elephants.'

'Who does, Fronto? Still, as you say, Utica is the tempting target and doubtless the enemy will expect us to make for it. Cato may be sitting openly in Utica as bait, drawing us there. I fear that we would commit to taking Utica, find it a much tougher proposition than anticipated, and be trapped there in a siege as the Numidians come at us from the west and Scipio and Labienus from the south. I think we have to rule out Utica in the end.'

'Hadrumetum, then? Or Clupea?'

Caesar looked across the map. 'It is tempting to take Piso on at Clupea. It would be the easier opening. But Clupea is somewhat peripheral, far from the centres of power, and there is no guarantee that Piso and his force has not already moved on since our last reports. I fear we must make for Hadrumetum and pray we have sufficient force to take on the army there. If we can break their military's back in the south, we can then march north and west and head for Utica, taking out Piso and his Spaniards on the way. Then we are at liberty to deal with Utica and Cato, and if we are triumphant and the sole military power in Africa, then Juba might think again about his alliance with Cato and stay safely out of the way.'

Fronto fixed Caesar with a look. 'You know that this won't be like Cassius. No one here is going to capitulate and accept a deal. The commanders from Ilerda know you won't grant them clemency a second time, so they will fight to the end.

Labienus will oppose us with his last breath. Scipio cannot afford to consider surrender, and Cato will never stop.'

'I will not kill Cato,' Caesar said quietly. 'Just as with Pompey, while Cato is opposed to me, he represents the very heart of what it is to be Roman, and he is renowned and respected across the republic. He will be captured and subsequently allowed to retire into private life, just as Pompey should have been.'

'So we head for the south?'

Caesar chewed his lip as he examined the map once more. 'Almost certainly, though we must approach this entire campaign with a mutable strategy. We know so little about dispositions we must be prepared to change our plans, and I would like our enemy to remain at least as uncertain about our intentions as we are. I shall not have final orders given to each commander. Instead, we shall head for the African coast, assess what we find and there make our final decision.'

Fronto shivered. 'I'm not a fan of the uncertainty.'

'I understand that, but I am resolved.'

'I still say we are better waiting for spring.'

'Your concern is noted yet again, Fronto. The legions will embark in the morning and sail immediately for the island of Aponiana, which lies some ten miles west from the coast. There they will anchor for a few days. Perhaps in taking a very visible step in the direction of Utica we can make the enemy believe that is our final goal. Then we will veer off and make for the south. You will accompany the ships of the Fifth legion to Aponiana, that being the only veteran unit of the Gallic wars currently with us.' Another look of bitterness crossed the old man's face over the recent mutiny of the Tenth, though it quickly passed. 'I have a few matters still to tie up here with the governor and a number of dispatches I must send, and then I shall follow on and meet you at Aponiana. Following this, we shall move as a unified fleet and make for the African coast. I will leave word with the governor here that any other ships that answer our call are to wait in port for other legions to arrive and ship them over at the first opportunity.'

'I would like to make sure that the cavalry remain close to us and to the Fifth, General.'

Caesar threw him a sly smile. 'Watching over our friend Galronus of the Remi, are we?' The general chuckled. 'But yes, I highly value the Gallic cavalry and their commander. And if we are to face Labienus and his horsemen, I would like someone capable of dealing with them by my side. Very well, Fronto, will you see to it that the order is given? You embark and sail at dawn.'

Fronto nodded and rose from his seat, sinking the last of his wine. 'I shall pass the word, General. Sleep well.' Caesar's attention returned to his map, and with a sly grin Fronto crossed to the dresser, replacing his cup and subtly palming the small jug of very expensive wine before turning to leave.

Departing the tent, Fronto took a deep breath and immediately regretted it. Even now the mysterious aroma of goat's cheese was gone, the stench of brine and dead fish assaulted him afresh. Gagging, he strode away from the tents and back along the coast, heading for the town. Shops and taverns were naturally closed for the night, but the place he was bound for would be open.

As he passed swiftly by the tents of other officers, trying to breathe shallowly in the hope that it would somehow diminish the strength of the aroma, a familiar figure came from the compound at a tangent, passing by the legionaries on guard.

'Why aren't you asleep?' Fronto grunted.

'Why aren't *you*?' Galronus replied.

'Old bones, bad moods and the anticipation of sea travel.'

'You've been to see the general?'

Fronto nodded. 'We sail tomorrow. All six legions and the cavalry, heading for that island you can see off the coast. We're to anchor there until the general catches us up.'

'Why set off without him?'

'Potentially an attempt to throw the enemy off balance, suggesting a target for which we're not truly aiming, though I suspect that's only half the reason. Knowing Caesar, he's planning to do things he knows I won't approve of, and he's sending away witnesses first. Anyway, we're off in the morning. From Aponiana we're bound for Africa, and probably Hadrumetum, but that's not carved in stone yet and he's keeping his options open.'

'Sailing into the unknown. Perfect for you.'

'That's why I'm going where I'm going right now.'

'Which is?'

'Temple of Neptune. Best to have appropriate gods on our side ch?'

Galronus fell in alongside and walked with him. They moved in silence up into the town, through the gate and to the small rectangular temple that stood on the headland and overlooked the harbour. Braziers burned beneath the six-columned portico, their coals glowing like Vulcan's forge, the acrid smoke easily whipped away by the winter winds. Golden light issued from the doorway even at this time of night, and Fronto walked inside, bowing his head as he entered. Galronus followed at his shoulder, head high, eyes straying across the temple's interior, taking everything in. He muttered something in his native language.

'What was that?' Fronto murmured.

'Just introducing myself. Neptune is your name for Nodens, but down here he might not recognise me.'

'Just when I think I understand you, Galronus, you get weirder again.'

There was no sign of an attendant, and Fronto wandered over towards the far end of the temple. The brightly-painted statue of the god dominated the wall, more than twice the height of a man even while seated on his great marble throne. He was naked and well-muscled, the tips of the trident in his hand lost in the shadows of the ceiling and the folds of a sheet draped discreetly over his lap.

Fronto found himself looking at the god's neatly-draped lower half and grinning most impiously.

'What is it?' Galronus whispered.

'I was just wondering how different the statue would look if Amphitrite walked past naked. His lap might resemble my tent more than a sheet.'

As Fronto chuckled at the thought, Galronus rolled his eyes. 'He looks quite like Nodens, though he would be better dressed for winters sea than this one.'

Fronto strode to the altar below the great statue of the god. A quick read of the inscription on the altar, highlighted with red paint, claimed that it had been set here by a Marcus Valerius. He smiled wryly.

'A relation?' murmured Galronus.

'Presumably, in the distant past. I guess my family have always hated the sea.' He looked up at the statue and held up the jug of wine. About three cups left in it. Perfect. 'Great Neptune, father of the oceans and guardian of all ships, look to us on the morrow and on our crossing with favour.' He poured a third of the cup, then straightened again. 'To the fair winds, blow us swiftly to our destination.' Another third. 'To a calm and waveless sea.' The last of it.

He stepped back, lowering his jug. Galronus frowned.

'Did you hear that?'

'No, what?'

'Wait.'

Fronto did so. He could hear nothing. 'What was it?'

'Sounded like a deep rumble.'

'Probably the sea.'

Then the thunder clap struck again, directly overhead. Fragments of plaster and clouds of dust showered down over them. Fronto felt a chill run through him and his eyes rose to the great statue. For a moment he honestly thought Neptune was crying, but then he realised it was a trickle of black dust, fallen from the roof beams, which had settled beside the statue's nose. Better, but still in no way a good sign.

'What did you do?' Galronus hissed in a worried tone.

Fronto shrugged. 'Nothing. Unless…' he flashed a guilty look at his friend. 'I might have borrowed the wine from Caesar.'

'Borrowed without asking?'

'Sort of. I think Caesar expects it, though, so it's fine.'

'I'm not sure that Nodens… that *Neptune…* agrees.'

Fronto shuddered. He didn't like the thought of heading out to sea following this. 'I shall find more wine. Legitimate wine, and make fresh libations in the morning before we sail.' He looked up. Another boom of thunder echoed from nearby. 'It might be nothing to do with the displeasure of gods. Might just be a storm. It is winter, after all.'

But as they left the temple and it began to rain, he was less inclined to believe himself.

CHAPTER TWO

South of Sicily, 27th December 47 BC

The storm had come from nowhere, and the officers and men on the trireme *Aias* reacted with shock and horror, all except Fronto and Galronus. Fronto had been eyeing the sky intermittently from the moment they departed Lilybaeum, expecting this at any moment, and Galronus had been throwing him black looks repeatedly. Neither of them had spoken to anyone else about what had transpired in the temple of Neptune and, despite the fact that the next morning seemingly endless offerings had been made to the god, including fresh ones from Fronto, and a white sheep had been ritually opened with only positive signs, neither felt it would be a good idea to disseminate the information.

Clearly Neptune had been displeased at Fronto's offering of purloined wine, the incident just the latest in a protracted line of problems he'd had with temples, ever since the days of his youth.

They had sailed the next morning into a relatively clear sky with high, scudding clouds, and each man on board the fleet had been positive and optimistic about the journey. All the signs were good. Fronto had even managed half an hour before he'd ended up leaning over the rail and making sounds like a seal being turned inside out. They had reached the island of Aponiana swiftly and settled in, awaiting the arrival of the general. The small settlement on the island had been an enthusiastic supplier of goods, luxuries and girls to the fleet, and all had continued in good spirits. Not so much for Fronto, who pointed out to Galronus that the bay in which they were harboured was known as *Sinus Sanguinus* – Blood Bay – after a battle two centuries ago that had turned the water red for days. It seemed an inauspicious omen. Though all had gone well so far, Fronto had continued to feel as though the sword of Damocles hung over him.

Caesar had joined them on the morning of the twenty fifth and they had immediately departed Aponiana and headed west as though making directly for Utica, only turning south once they were out of sight of shore, against the possibility of Catonian spies in the city or port. At the end of the first day they had overnighted on the small island of Cossyra and the fleet had celebrated, for they were but a day from the African coast and all was well.

Fronto had sat in a corner with Galronus, glowering and continuing to feel breathtakingly ill.

The next morning they had departed Cossyra, once more sailing due west, heading for the peninsula upon which they would find the city of Clupea, where Piso and his men had last been reported, perhaps halfway between the political hub of Utica and the stronghold of Hadrumetum. Caesar's plans were still uncharacteristically vague, in that his intent was to examine Clupea and decide on the spot whether to land and begin the campaign or whether to continue moving on south.

Fronto had watched the skies with nervous eyes, certain that they'd not reach Africa without some dreadful incident, Neptune's thunderous displeasure still ringing in his ears, and yet he'd still not anticipated the storm when it arrived. Simply, the winds were extraordinarily fast, and the sailors had all been pleased with the alacrity with which their sails were carrying them west to the coast. Then, seemingly without warning, there had been a change. The wind doubled back on itself, swinging round and coming at high speed *from* the west instead.

Sailors had cursed across the fleet as the forward momentum all but ground to a halt and oars were run out, every ship now having to drag itself west by muscle power, straight into a headwind. The sails had been furled to prevent them acting against momentum but the seas, which had been surprisingly clear and calm thus far, had begun to buck and writhe, the waves coming higher and higher with each iteration, triremes plunging into them, rising at a worrying angle with each man holding on for dear life, cresting, and then plunging down the far side into the trough of black water only to come face to face with the next wave.

The sky had turned black in less than fifty heartbeats, the powerful winds blowing the storm from the mountainous highlands of Africa out across the sea and directly at the fleet. Sailors had begun to rush around in panic, the passengers on every vessel securing themselves and trying to stay safely out of the way. Fronto had lashed himself to a rail with his belt and tried to ignore the 'I told you so' looks he was getting from Galronus.

The storm had hit so swiftly that the fleet was not been prepared, and in no time Fronto was near-blind in the howling winds and battering spray, and hadn't a clue what was going on. All he knew was that the crew were praying as they ran this way and that, occasionally unlucky men were being swept over the edge, the oars had been withdrawn because their use was like trying to stir honey with a wheat stalk, and the ship was being thrown about like a child's wooden boat in an aqueduct channel.

He concentrated on staying on board and not drowning, to the extent that he'd almost forgotten to throw up periodically. Every buck and dip of the Aias seemed to be more and more vertiginous, and men slid past him along the soaked deck, crying out and cursing and praying. Every movement of the ship seemed to send a freezing, choking wave smashing into Fronto that would have hurled him across the deck had he not been tied to the rail. He lost count of the bruises and abrasions he took from being battered repeatedly against the timbers, and the salt water spraying the grazes and cuts simply added an extra instrument into the melody of pain. He had no true idea how anyone else was faring, though on the odd occasion he caught a glimpse of Galronus just along the rail, the Remi officer was still glaring at him, so he seemed to be alright at least.

To Fronto it seemed as though the storm lasted at least three or four hours, and so the reasoning part of his mind that was barely functioning in the circumstances divided that down and decided it had probably been an hour at most in reality.

It ended gradually, the pressure lessening, the ship's motion calming, the waves coming lower and lower. By the time they were moving relatively flat and the oars were deployed, a headcount was performed and it seemed miraculous that they had lost only three sailors and four soldiers. Fronto celebrated the return to normal by emptying his stomach over the side with a horrendous noise.

Eventually he untied himself and tried to rise, shakily, to his feet. Galronus had survived intact and came over to lend him support until his knees decided they could straighten safely. A tribune from the Fifth who was standing in conversation with the ship's captain nodded, then turned and headed straight for Fronto. He came to a halt and saluted, a gesture which Fronto returned with a half-hearted attempt at best.

'What's the damage?'

The tribune winced. 'We're several miles off course, sir, though the trierarch is attempting to bring us back. The storm has split the fleet. We can see another nine ships only, and are attempting to signal them to find out if they can spy out others. The fleet must be truly wide spread.'

If they survived at all, Fronto mentally finished the officer's uncomfortable sentence for him.

'It is the trierarch's intention to make for the coast directly,' the man said, 'which should be Clupea or somewhere close by to the south, gathering those we can find as we go. It is his hope that everyone will know to do the same.' The tribune gave Fronto a helpless look. 'I didn't want to disabuse him of that notion, sir.'

Fronto nodded, sagging. In one of Caesar's most disastrous decisions of his career, he had kept the planning for this campaign deliberately vague and flexible. Neither the trierarchs of the ships nor the officers of the legions could be confident of where they were expected to disembark. With luck, the majority would settle upon Clupea, but there was no guarantee.

'Some of them will likely head south, hoping to find Hadrumetum, and others might even make for Utica, if they were blown sufficiently northwards,' he grunted. 'What a shit shambles. If I told him once I told him a hundred times to wait for spring. Alright. Let the men know the intention and liaise with the trierarch. I'll be over in a bit, once I've emptied what's left of my guts.'

Cheeks bulging, he ran over to the rail once more. Galronus wandered to his side as he retched helplessly. 'This campaign might be over before it begins,' the Remi noted.

Fronto tried to nod, but discovered he was too weak. 'If this is all we have then even if the general made it, we don't stand a chance. Even Piso with his minor cavalry unit could crush us. If we reach Clupea and nothing's improved, we may have to simply sail back to Sicilia.'

The two men stood at the rail for the next hour, discussing the disastrous results of insufficient preparation, and eventually were interrupted by pounding feet. They turned to see that same tribune come to a halt.

'Sir, we've found Caesar's ship. She's survived, though with a ripped sail.'

Relief flooded through Fronto, though when he thought hard about it, he wasn't entirely sure why. Adding Caesar to their small force wouldn't make a grand difference. On the other hand it would move world-changing decision making back out of Fronto's hands, for he would no longer be the most senior officer in the fleet, and that could only be a boon in the circumstances.

The two friends and the tribune crossed the deck once more and reached the far rail where the trierarch was signalling another ship with waving arms. That second vessel was angling to come alongside, and Fronto recognised *Celeriter*, Caesar's ship. He straightened automatically at the rail and saluted as the figure of Caesar in his remarkably unblemished red cloak came into view. The Celeriter pulled level with Aias, two and a half oar-lengths apart, and Caesar waved to them.

'Fronto, by the gods it's good to see you.'

'Likewise, General. What's the situation?'

'My trierarch tells me we're less than three hours from Clupea now. We've managed to bring together twenty-seven ships, one of which is a cavalry transport, the rest vexillations from various legions along with a few auxilia.'

Fronto made a quick mental calculation and his spirits sank. 'Three thousand men?'

'And one ala of cavalry. We've managed to secure less than a sixth of the army.'

Fronto sighed. 'It might be better to turn back now, sir. We could make landfall at Cossyra by nightfall with the wind behind us, and we're unlikely to run into that same storm.'

'Nonsense, Fronto. We press on.'

Fronto stared. 'General, we were looking at a difficult enough task with six legions. With one, we might as well strip naked, paint ourselves red and jump about asking them to shoot at us.'

'Colourful, but hyperbolical, Fronto. Other ships will have survived the storm and in time they will find us. Moreover, other legions converge on Lilybaeum, as do other ships. Reinforcements will come. All we need to do is gain ourselves a foothold in Africa and secure it until the others join us.'

'And what happens if four of the legions are currently at the bottom of the sea, General? What happens if the other legions in Italia mutiny again and decide not to sail on a fool's errand? What happens if the rest of the fleet has decided to sail for Utica, or back home?'

'Have faith, Fronto. Venus will not let this come to naught.

'Yes, I'd forgotten how handy the goddess of love can be at a time like this,' Fronto replied bitterly.

'We still have a legion, the finest military minds in the republic, and an excellent cavalry unit with a fine commander. Empires have been built with less.'

'And lost.'

Caesar's expression hardened. 'I am still confident, Fronto, and the confidence of officers has a marked effect on the confidence of their men. I cannot do this with my most senior commander moping around and doom-saying. I need the Fronto that took Bibrax, that secured Ilerda, that made an impossible landing on Pharos. I need my best men if I am to pull this off. Are you with me?'

Fronto felt a wry smile cross his face. No wonder men across the republic marched into the maw of Cerberus just on this man's say. *Persuasive* was not the word.

'So what do we do, sir? What is the plan. And now we *need* a plan. We cannot risk a repeat of what happened last time, or we'll be going to war with three men and a sickly goat.'

Caesar smiled. 'We must still be flexible. More than ever, in fact, now that we have a smaller force to work with. Critically, the men will be suffering a lack of confidence similar to that you just displayed. An initial success could make a great deal of difference. That could come in the form of either victory or successful defiance. We make for Clupea and examine the force there. If we can take them and secure the place, then it would do us well to do so. Beating Piso and his Iberian friends would give our men heart and perhaps secure us a landing site. If we deem the battle too uncertain, we continue around the coast until we reach Hadrumetum and there we force a landing and form a beachhead. That will also give our men heart and allow a site for further landings.'

Fronto shivered. 'Clupea is too minor to be of real value, and as a landing site it puts us too far from any field of operation, but yes, if we can pin down Piso there and win, I agree it would be worth doing. I am, to say the least, nervous about Hadrumetum. If Scipio is in the area, he could have ten legions or more. Trying to hold a bridgehead against ten to one odds is a dangerous proposal.'

'What is the supply situation, General?' Galronus cut in.

Fronto didn't like the bleak expression that momentarily flashed across Caesar's face before he replied. 'None of the support vessels have made it so far. We have only what is on board our ships, which should sustain us for two to three more days. After that it becomes a matter of foraging.'

'In winter?' Fronto sighed. 'In unknown, enemy-held territory. Damn it.'

'To Clupea,' Caesar said encouragingly.

'To Clupea,' agreed Fronto.

The fleet gradually pulled itself closer together and closed on Africa. An hour after the shouted conversation between the two ships, the coast came into sight against a grey sky, the peninsula rose as a dark brown and grey mass, and finally Clupea resolved as a shape against it. A small harbour town lay by the sea with a hill rising behind it, crowned by an ancient acropolis.

'Can you see anything?' Galronus muttered as Fronto peered myopically at the coast.

'You've got better eyes than me.'

'But you know what you're looking for.'

Fronto bit his lip. 'There will be a garrison in that stronghold on the hill, but I can't see Piso being up there. Unsuitable.'

Galronus nodded. 'Cavalry need to be down on the flat. Assuming the information we have is correct and relatively up to date, of course. By now Piso could be leading a legion and a hundred miles from here.'

Fronto shook his head. 'I think Piso, Petreius and Afranius are carefully positioned. The main infantry force is in the south, and the decision makers in the north. To garrison the middle ground with highly mobile cavalry makes sense, and keeping these three generals who know one another's abilities working together also makes sense, despite any conflicts we've experienced between them in the past.'

'I see movement,' Galronus said, pointing.

'I don't,' Fronto replied, peering off in that direction, though it did not take him long to spy out what Galronus had spotted. A swarm of dark shapes, like a massive colony of ants at the water's edge on the southern edge of town. 'Tell me what that looks like to you'

Galronus squinted. 'Somewhere between two and four thousand cavalry, I'd say.'

Fronto nodded. 'I'd say that clinches it. We can't take them on. They'll butcher us as we land with such adequate warning. We'll not beach enough men in time to face them safely. Clupea is not an option.'

He crossed to the ship's starboard side and waved to attract the attention of the general. As Caesar turned to him, the old man cupped his hands around his mouth. 'Piso's cavalry is ready for us. I cannot see a safe landing point.'

Fronto bellowed back. 'They'd destroy us as we beach. Clupea is worthless, and victory impossible.'

'Then let us move south as planned.' At a signal from the general's ship, the vessels of the fleet began to turn to port, gradually bringing them parallel with the coast. As they moved south-west, away from the fortress of Clupea, they kept their eyes on the land nearby and noted that large force of riders departing the city in the same direction.

'They are not Gauls of any tribe,' Galronus said, squinting west, 'nor Germans.'

'Your eyesight is impressive, Fronto murmured. 'What are they, then?'

'I don't know. They're dressed in white. A lot of spears. Some are clearly armoured in bronze from the gleaming.'

'Probably native African levies. Labienus commands the Gauls and Germans and he's supposedly south somewhere. The Numidian horsemen have a fearsome reputation, and they know the terrain well, so any local levies are likely very similar – a force to be wary of. At least they're not elephants.'

'What's an elephant?'

Fronto turned to Galronus in surprise. Sometimes his Remi friend seemed so Roman that Fronto forgot to adjust his thinking. 'Elephants. Big bastards. Four times the size of a horse. Feet can crush a chariot. Weigh about the same as a trireme. They've got a snout that's ten feet long and they can use like a hand, and they have tusks as tall as me.'

Galronus stared at him.

'I know. Horrible. And the Africans tend to ride on their backs and use them as mobile archery platforms. If they charge you, you're screwed. But they can be a bit unpredictable. Commanders are often nervous about fielding them because if they get spooked, they can easily turn and trample a path through their own lines. It's a damn shame we don't have a ship full of hogs.'

'Hogs?' Galronus was starting to look as baffled as he was unhappy.

'Old countermeasure for elephants in war. Grease up pigs, set light to them and let them go. Squealing hogs panic elephants.'

'Probably panics the pigs a bit too.'

'Anyway, with luck we should be safe from elephants. The Numidians use them, but at the moment King Juba is uninvolved, at least as long as Sittius is keeping him busy in the west.' He frowned, chewing his lip. 'Look at the cavalry again. Are they keeping pace with us, do you think? Just easy? Or are they going as fast as they can?'

Galronus peered off west at the coast, judging the speed of the mass of horsemen. 'I would say they're going as fast as a column of horsemen can hope to, assuming they intend to maintain their pace for a while.'

Fronto nodded. 'I don't think they're shadowing us. I think they're riding for the main force near Hadrumetum to warn them that we're coming.' Cursing under his breath, he rushed over to the side rail once more and waved to Caesar. When the general turned to him, he pointed at the coast. 'Piso rides for the main army to warn them. If he gets there ahead of us, we lose any hope of surprise and we'll stand no chance of forging a bridgehead.'

Caesar looked away to the coast, and then back to Fronto. 'Then it becomes a race.'

'We're still bound for Hadrumetum, General?'

'We are. The cavalry will be forced to stop regularly and rest their horses, so we have the advantage.'

Fronto frowned. 'Only if we don't stop. I remember looking at your map. Hadrumetum is more than seventy miles from here. Ninety or even a hundred if we hug the coast.

We'll have to sail through the night to be certain of getting there ahead of Piso.'

'I would have liked to sail due south and cut off many miles, but given the storm we have already endured, we had best not risk open water through the night. We shall stay in sight of the coast and follow it round, but sail through the night to gain over Piso's cavalry.'

Fronto nodded unhappily. A night aboard with no respite for his guts, and that also meant a third day without food. His stomach was already growling with deep hunger, but there seemed so little point in filling it when he would only end up spewing it over the side of the ship later anyway.

Fronto settled in to watch with Galronus, leaning on the rail. Mercifully, the waters remained relatively calm this close to the shore, and the ship was quite stable. Moreover the winds had died down somewhat and swung around so that they now came from the north, billowing into the sails and adding much needed speed. They watched as the sun slid through the afternoon sky, and as evening loomed, the trierarch pointed off to the west. Already the cavalry were lagging, starting to fall behind, but what the captain was indicating made Fronto draw a worried breath.

They were passing another coastal town that the trierarch told them was Neapolis, and a second force of men was emerging from the edge of the built-up area. The sun was sinking fast now, and the increasing darkness made it hard to make out too many details. Fronto turned to his friend.

'Can you make anything out?'

'Mixed cavalry and infantry. About five hundred horse and a couple of thousand infantry, I'd say.'

Fronto sucked air through his teeth. 'That has to be either Afranius or Petreius, then, joining up with Piso. On the downside, that almost doubles a force we already dare not take on. There are now more of them than us. On the upside, the infantry will slow their pace. We gain the speed advantage now.'

'Excellent,' Galronus said. 'We will reach Hadrumetum with adequate time to land and fortify.'

'Wonderful,' Fronto added in a much more scathing tone. 'We'll have plenty of time to hide in a sandcastle from Scipio and his ten legions before Piso and his thousands of riders reach us too.'

Galronus gave him an infuriating encouraging grin, and the pair went back to watching the coast. Neapolis was the last place they saw Piso's riders. The two enemy forces met outside the town and combined, but the daylight was almost gone now and by the time the enemy force began to move once more the fleet was too far ahead to be able to see them in the poor light.

The night was unpleasant. Fronto hated sailing by day, let alone in the dark, though at least the water remained blessedly calm this close to land. By the time he awoke with the dawn to the calls of sailors, they had come most of the remaining distance. He rose from his blankets, blinking and looking about, and spied the angle of the sun, which was now to the left of the bow. That meant they had come right round the enormous bay, from Neapolis where they had been sailing southwest to a point where they were now heading southeast. They had to be almost there. Turning to look back, blinking, he could see no sign of the cavalry. They were coming, but had been left well behind during the night.

'Morning sir,' the tribune from the Fifth said, coming to a halt in front of him and saluting.

'Good morning. Any news?'

'Good and bad, sir. A few of the ships seem to have gone astray during the night, but they can't have gone far. On the bright side, if you look ahead, those walls in the distance are Hadrumetum.'

Fronto nodded. He could have anticipated losing a ship or two in the dark, but the man was right, and he wouldn't worry about it. As soon as the sun had come up, the missing vessels would have a good guide to rejoin Caesar's fleet, and they couldn't have gone too far. Ahead lay Hadrumetum. Would it be the stronghold they had expected?

He moved to the bow, where Galronus was peering off ahead. Fronto examined the place. It had strong walls surrounding a sizeable town, with a certain level of extramural settlement. A busy-looking large port sat outside it, though the only ships he could make out seemed to be fishing vessels and cargo ships.

'If this is the hub of the enemy forces, they're hiding it well,' Galronus noted.

Fronto nodded. 'There are not ten legions here. Quite apart from expected naval support and signs of auxilia, there wouldn't be space for them in the town. They'd have to be camped outside. Ten legions take up a lot of room. We'd be able to see them. Scipio might be in this area, but he's not specifically at Hadrumetum.'

'What does that mean?' Galronus mused.

'That,' Fronto said, taking a deep breath, 'means that Caesar will see a valuable strong point and want to seize it while it's poorly defended. And he'll be right. If we can take Hadrumetum while the main force is still somewhere else, it can be held with minimal effort and will make an excellent landing place for any reserves that come.'

He dashed to the other side of the ship. 'Caesar,' he bellowed, waving his arms.

'Fronto?'

'Scipio's army is not here.'

Caesar nodded. 'Depending on garrison size we may be able to secure it. We shall spend an hour, just a single hour, sitting just outside the port. That will give stray ships time to join us and give the defenders of the city plenty of time to take in what they're seeing and start to panic. With luck we can frighten them into capitulating without a fight.'

Fronto nodded. He hoped so. Hadrumetum had the look of a solid fortress.

The fleet anchored five hundred paces from the port, and Fronto spent the hour, along with Galronus and Caesar and every man with an ounce of tactical ability, watching the city and estimating the difficulties of what was to come.

Within the first half hour two of the three missing ships hoved into view and joined the fleet at anchor, and Fronto was surprised at how relieved he was to see Plancus aboard one of them, waving at him in relief. Also during that half hour the city burst into life, becoming a hive of activity. The port became abuzz, merchants and fishermen rushing to their vessels. Initially, they dithered, uncertain as to the reception they might find if they tried to leave the port, but much more certain that they didn't want to be occupying a valuable jetty when that fleet decided to move in. Finally, one wide-bellied merchant vessel made a run for it, racing east along the coast out of harm's way, and when Caesar's fleet watched it go, making no attempt to stop it, suddenly every ship in Hadrumetum's port was running for its life.

Behind the port, the city's gates remained resolutely shut, and Fronto could see soldiers taking up positions around the parapet, artillery creaking on every tower as their crews prepared the beasts. On the far side of Caesar's ship, that of Plancus had now come to a halt, and Fronto could see the man in discussion with Caesar. As the conflab ended, the general crossed to Fronto's side. 'Plancus is trying to estimate the defence strength. He worries that there could be upwards of three thousand. I am more inclined to see a caretaker garrison of a thousand, though it is difficult to determine based upon the manning of walls.'

Fronto peered at the city again. 'I would say a thousand is wishful thinking, General. The main force might not be here, but Hadrumetum is still strategically vital to the enemy. They would leave it with adequate defence. Three thousand would require a great deal of accommodation and support, though. I would be inclined to suggest somewhere in between.'

'Plancus believes we might be able to talk them down.'

'I hope he's right,' Fronto replied, 'but again I fear that may be wishful thinking. If they surrender Hadrumetum to you with the small force we have, they will worry what Scipio will do when he arrives with his huge army. They must know they are better off siding with Scipio and defying our three thousand than going over to us and defying his fifty thousand.'

'Whatever the case, I am determined to make a stand. The last stray ship is now in view. Unless the rest of our scattered fleet finds us, this is all the strength upon which we can currently rely. I want every ship docked in port and the men entrenched and fortified on the shore in half an hour. Pass the word to the tribunes and centurions that there will be no violence or looting until such an order is specifically given. If there is even a chance to win these people over, then we must seize upon it, and we therefore cannot afford to aggravate them before any negotiation is underway.'

Fronto nodded and looked about. This was it. They were about to set foot in Africa at last. Three thousand infantry and a hundred or so cavalry, building sandcastles while a fortified city with a two thousand strong garrison watched them, all the time waiting for Scipio to turn up with fifty thousand men, or Piso with his five thousand. It was like playing a game of dice with two clever gamblers, but all you'd been given was a coin to flip. With a sigh, he gave the order for the trierarch to put into port.

CHAPTER THREE

Hadrumetum, 28th December 47 BC

The three senior officers reined in, a small detachment of the general's praetorian horsemen following them back into the camp. Already, the army was managing to throw up a reasonable set of defences, hacking out a narrow ditch in the stony, sandy soil on the headland facing the town and dominating the port, and using the spoil to create a rampart. That would have to be all, for the place seemed to be largely devoid of trees, and the supply ships containing everything the army required for serious fortification had been scattered and lost in the storm. Galronus had led out a team of scouts to scour the area for anything of value and on a general reconnaissance.

Caesar dismounted and stood on the highest section of the rampart, Fronto and Plancus joining him. They had circuited the entirety of Hadrumetum during that first hour, as soon as the army and the horses had disembarked and while the force, formed from detachments of six different legions, began to set up camp before the walls and just out of missile shot. The outcome of their observations was not encouraging.

'No visible weak points,' Fronto muttered.

'Solid defence and ramparts with ample artillery and undoubtedly stocked with sufficient ammunition and supplies to enable them to withstand a lengthy siege,' Plancus added.

'A siege that we do not have the leisure to conduct,' Caesar concluded. Piso's force that approaches around the coast is sizeable enough to overcome us if utilised well in the field, especially added to the garrison of Hadrumetum. The last thing we can afford is to become trapped between the sea, the city and the army of Piso. Even if he is too uncertain to attack us, all he has to do is hold here until Scipio arrives with his legions, and he must be close. The vultures gather around us and we are a lean carcass, gentlemen.'

'Then our only options are to decamp and move to somewhere safe or to negotiate,' Fronto said, giving voice to what they all knew. Currently their three thousand faced perhaps two, but when Piso arrived they would face seven thousand or so, and if Scipio joined them it became near fifty thousand. A staggering number for the tiny force on the headland. Not for the first time in recent days, Fronto wondered whether Caesar, the great tactician of the Gallic and Greek campaigns, was starting to lose his edge. Aegyptus had been a shambles that they had only escaped through foolhardiness and blind luck. Africa looked like being even worse.

Plancus turned in the saddle. 'None of us want to run away, Caesar, so let me attempt to negotiate. The garrison commander will likely dismiss any missive from you, for you're the enemy's commander, and Fronto...' he flashed an apologetic look across. 'Fronto is not the most diplomatic.'

Fronto nodded, happy to take no offence at what was really a well-known fact. Caesar nodded wearily. 'Permission is granted, Lucius. Pen your missive now. I am willing to grant a commission on my staff and/or a place in the senate to their commander and to bestow the status of colonia with full citizenship on all occupants of Hadrumetum, both civil and military. I can offer little more, but that represents the dream of most men.'

'Let's hope it's enough to overwhelm the threat of Scipio and his army,' Fronto grumbled. He turned to locate the nearest officer. A centurion was busy overseeing the ditch a few paces away. 'Centurion, did we take prisoners in the port?'

The man nodded. 'Of a sort, sir. They are being detained, but fed and watered until it's decided what to do with them. Not sure whether they're the enemy or not, sir.'

'Quite. Find someone well dressed and bring him to the general's tent, will you?'

Caesar cocked an eyebrow at him, and Fronto shrugged. 'Better to send a messenger they won't just shoot from the walls.'

The three men turned and walked their horses to the headquarters at the camp's centre, where Caesar's equisio took the reins from the three beasts. The three senior commanders' tents had been raised immediately and the praetorians had formed a defensive ring around them. The standards and flags of the legions stood here, gleaming, pronouncing the presence of six legions, which was a little misleading and a bitter reminder of the truth of it.

Plancus went to work carefully constructing an offer of peace, asking for alliance and free entry to Hadrumetum in return for Caesar's exceedingly generous terms. Citizenship would effectively enrich every living soul in the city, granting them privileges above almost everyone else in Africa. He had finished it, passed it to Fronto and Caesar and received the latter's blessing before there was a knock on the tent and the centurion arrived with a civilian in tow.

'Please, come in,' Caesar said to the man. 'I can only apologise for your detention and that of your compatriots. We are uncertain as yet of our reception in the region, despite that we are here at the behest of the senate of Rome to bring peace and unity. I would ask you to be part of that settlement in taking an offer of peace to the commander of the Hadrumetum garrison. Do you happen to know who that is?'

The man, clearly frightened at being in the presence of the great and feared Caesar, stuttered his answer. 'H- he is called Considius, Consul.'

The general harrumphed quietly. 'That diminishes our hopes. Considius was one of the men who brought Curio to heel last year and caused this mess. He governed here almost a decade ago and he's been consolidating here for several years now. He's a Pompeian to the core.'

'We can but try,' Fronto urged him.

'True. Will you deliver our offer to Considius Longus, friend?'

The man, probably some middle man from the port authorities, nodded vigorously, probably more at the prospect of freedom and being able to return to the city than through enthusiasm for the task. Caesar sealed the letter and instructed the centurion to see the man out into the open near the city.

'And now the tense wait.'

The three men paused long enough to allow the messenger a head start and then left the tent and strode through the camp in his wake to the gate facing the city. There they climbed the low rampart to gain the best view. The centurion stood at the gate nearby and the erstwhile prisoner was already closing on the city's nearest gate. They waited, nerves taut, as the gate opened and the man disappeared inside.

'At the very least he must consider it,' Plancus murmured.

'Or his soldiers and civilians get to hear of the offer and revolt against him,' Fronto added.

Caesar remained silent as the three men stood and waited.

The answer came after little more than a quarter of an hour. The messenger appeared atop the gatehouse, screaming as he was thrown out into the open-air, shrieking briefly as he fell before landing with a distant, barely-audible crunch on the stony ground.

'It would appear that Considius has rejected the offer,' Caesar said darkly. 'Gentlemen, we are in a somewhat perilous position. Conference in the principia, if you will.'

Returning to the commander's tent, Galronus was waiting for them outside and the three men greeted him wearily. 'You've heard about the message?' Fronto asked his friend. The Remi nodded. 'It's the talk of the camp already, sadly.' The four men made their way inside. Fronto was grateful to note that some helpful soul had provided a plate of fruit and jars of wine and water. Pouring drinks for them all, he sank into one of the seats and munched on an apple, cup in his other hand.

'Thoughts,' said the general, sipping his wine and then placing it back on a table.

'Piso will be here soon,' Fronto said. 'No longer than two days, I would say?' he looked to Galronus for confirmation.

The Remi horsemen, the most au fait with cavalry among the officers, shook his head. 'That is true if the army remains mixed. It is my belief that as they close on Hadrumetum, the commander will split his force. If he is sensible, he has left the infantry to follow on in his wake and rides with the horse to join with local forces. I would not be entirely surprised to see him arrive by sundown, tomorrow morning at the latest. If he is not, then he has no grasp of the value of cavalry.'

Plancus chewed on a grape and huffed. 'How went your scouting?'

'The season is poor for foraging. Harvests are all stored in towns and cities. There will be poor pickings here. Construction materials are more abundant a mile or so inland, especially eastwards along the coast. There is no clear sign of a massed enemy force within three miles of Hadrumetum. The nearest other towns are, in an arc around Hadrumetum, Themetra to the northwest, Gurza, Uzae, Uzitta and Ruspina on the coast to the southeast.'

Caesar drummed his fingers on the table beside him. 'We cannot readily abandon our position here immediately. The men have endured a troublesome journey by ship, slept fitfully aboard last night, and are facing uncertain days. In order to preserve even a modicum of morale, they must be allowed a full night of sleep on land before I ask anything more of them.'

Fronto nodded. If the mutiny of the legions earlier in the winter had taught them anything it was to respect the needs of the men. 'But we cannot assault the town with the small force we have, and we do not have the leisure to besiege it. It is not a matter of whether we move out, but when.'

Caesar sighed. 'We must trust to the gods to preserve us for this night in our perilous position. We will move out at first light and seek more secure positioning.'

'But where?' Plancus mused.

'It will need to be near the coast,' Fronto said. 'On the assumption that other ships survived the storm and that reinforcements are coming from Sicilia they need to be able to land and join up with us.'

'Besides,' Galronus reminded them, 'Scipio is roaming around somewhere inland with ten legions.'

The general continued to drum his fingers. 'We need a position of strength, a Hadrumetum of our own, where fleets can land and walls will save us from immediate harm. Africa has been in enemy hands for over a year, but there must be towns and forces here that would go over to our side, especially since we can legitimately claim to be the rightful force of the republic, appointed by the senate. As we did that year in Italia, let us face the enemy with sharpened steel, but attempt to draw any who do not immediately oppose us into alliance.'

A chorus of nods met this. To gain allies in this land would change the game significantly.

'We travel east. Scipio is likely to be operating to the western side of Hadrumetum, since the power in the province lies in that direction. Galronus notes better foraging and materials to the east, and there are towns along the coast we can approach with attempts at alliance. We make first for Ruspina, some ten miles along the coast and attempt to secure the town. If we cannot do so, we shall move on without pause. Leptis lies ten miles beyond that, Thapsus another ten and then Aphrodisium. Beyond that the coast turns south and the chances of stray ships or reserves locating us decrease drastically.'

'So we essentially go from town to town, knocking on doors and asking to be let in,' Fronto said in a wry tone.

'More or less,' admitted Caesar. 'It is not ideal, but we make what we can of how the dice roll.'

* * *

The morning came cool and crisp, the sky a pale steel colour with high cloud and the scent of brine on the breeze. Fronto packed the few things he had unloaded the day before and dressed, mustering with the other officers outside among the praetorian horsemen. The camp was already being abandoned, tents being struck as men prepared to move out. Fronto sighed at their poor situation once more as the four officers sat on their horses nearby watching the last of the camp clearing.

A simple count showed that there were far too few tents for the army. Clearly many of the tents were still among the lost ships, and some had shared their tent with more soldiers than usual, cramming themselves in against the winter cold, while others had slept beneath temporary shelters formed of awnings held up by pila, others simply lying on the cold ground wrapped in their cloaks.

The four men watched the army as it finally departed the camp, as did the defenders of Hadrumetum, lining the city's walls. At least they did not jeer, which would have had such a deleterious effect on the men's morale. The officers, right down to optio and decurion level, were making sure to treat this as a tactical decision to relocate to better ground than simple flight.

Fronto watched wearily and his head suddenly shot round at a new sound cutting through the air. A call had gone up from the city, followed by two other cadences, each repeated across the walls. Something was happening.

'That can't be good.'

'No,' agreed Caesar, who turned to a tribune sitting astride his horse nearby. 'Have the men move at pace and a half.' He turned to Galronus. 'You might want to take personal control of the cavalry,' he suggested. The Remi officer nodded his agreement and rode off. As the three remaining senior officers turned to look at the city, the majority of the manpower was disappearing from the walls.

'If they mean to take us on,' Plancus noted, 'then there must be more men in there than we estimated.'

'Or they're not alone,' Fronto added. 'Scipio? Or Piso?'

The answer came in a heartbeat. A honking, booing horn blared in the distance and the three men turned to look northwest along the coast. A dark cloud hung over the early morning landscape, dust raised by the passage of many horses.

'Piso's cavalry. We need to move.'

The three men geed their horses into a canter and rode for the column. As they reached the rear, Fronto was pleased to see the flag and standards of the Fifth at the rear. Whether by some tribune's design or by pure luck the most veteran legionaries in the army were the rear-guard. Fronto veered off, catching sight of a centurion's crest, and waved at the man. 'We're about to be hit in the arse end by a force of cavalry and possibly infantry too. The moment they close, the entire column needs to halt and you need to deploy in contra equitas formation. Got it?'

The centurion saluted and began to bellow the commands across the column, where they were picked up by other officers and relayed.

'Are we really going to stop and face them?' Plancus murmured.

'You would prefer to try and outrun horses?'

'I suppose you're right. But unless we're very lucky, we could be cut to pieces in the next hour.'

Fronto turned. The city's garrison had flooded out towards the port, through that great gate, though they seemed more intent on attempting to secure the abandoned camp and the ships in the port than on chasing down the retreating army. Fortunately Caesar had ordered his ships to set sail and shadow them along the coast, and the fleet that had landed them at Hadrumetum was now already pulling safely out to sea, out of reach of the city garrison. Of course, somewhere out there Cato had deployed his own fleet, but that was a worry for another time.

The cavalry were coming closer and closer.

'Where has Galronus got to?'

Caesar pointed east. 'Much of our cavalry was at the van, scouting ahead. Our Remi friend will have to call them back and form them up to be of any real use.'

The officers moved a little further forward along the column, out of the zone of direct danger, for the enemy horse were approaching at worrying speed. 'There are maybe a couple of thousand horse there,' Fronto noted.

'The men can deal with that,' Plancus said.

'But they will keep us immobile while the garrison catch us up. There's a couple of thousand of them too. Together they outnumber us, and Piso and Considius are no fools. We've got a real fight on our hands.'

Sure enough, as they watched, just visible around the periphery of the cavalry force and its dust cloud, the Hadrumetum garrison, frustrated in their attempt to board Caesar's ships and finding his abandoned camp empty and useless, had turned and were now marching along the coast in the wake of the horse. Soon Caesar's force would be embroiled in a struggle with a force of at least equal size.

The army continued to move. They would be less than a mile from the town and still more than ten from Ruspina when the enemy caught them. Fronto ground his teeth, deep in thought, trying to form any kind of plan other than simply waiting to be caught and fighting their way out. He had nothing.

Now, he could see what Galronus had seen earlier, the form of the horsemen. They were clearly natives, their skin tone en masse much too dark for Gallic cavalry, the majority in white tunics, some with bronze cuirasses, occasional figures in bright blue and red, presumably officers of some sort. That they were close enough for such detail to be visible said much, and moments later the call went out across the column for the infantry to halt, the men of the Fifth immediately turning to face their pursuers. In an age-old formation against cavalry, the lines of legionaries braced themselves, three rows of shields gradually angled from straight through to forty-five degrees, pila jutting out between every shield and creating a lethal hedge that few horses would be willing to charge. Of course, that would only buy them time, and the infantry were coming too.

Fronto found he was holding his breath, the tension gripping him. He, Plancus and Caesar were far enough back that they would be out of immediate danger, but once the horses of the enemy shied away from those spear points they would race along the column looking for somewhere they could make an impact. They would inevitably find one, and before then the three officers would have to ride ahead and stay out of the fight. It was one thing to involve oneself in the battle, and both he and Caesar had done precisely that more than once, but three men on horses facing the pursuing cavalry was a different matter entirely.

A new honking suddenly drew his attention, and his head snapped round. Galronus was bearing down on him at the head of less than two hundred Gallic and German cavalry, Celtic horns booing at them. Blinking, Fronto joined Caesar and Plancus in dancing their horses out of the way, for far from slowing as they neared, Galronus and his men were urging their horses forward with increasing speed and whoops of violent anticipation.

'Surely not?' gasped Plancus.

'You fought the Belgae,' Fronto grinned. 'When did you ever see them back down from a fight?'

Indeed, as the leading riders hurtled past, spears and swords brandished, braided hair flying in the wind, Fronto caught sight of Galronus' expression for a moment and actually pitied the poor bastards who were about to be on the receiving end of that fury.

Turning as the riders passed, Fronto sat with his two fellow officers and watched as the small cavalry detachment that had made it as far as Africa charged a force ten times their number. The most damnedest thing happened then. The African riders had been closing on the legion, preparing to drive on their mounts and attempt to break a formation designed purely to hold them out, but as less than two hundred Gallic horse suddenly emerged from the rear of the column, riding back along the right flank with murder in mind, they baulked.

Galronus and his men passed the rear-guard, swords waving and circling in the air, spears couched ready to kill, and the enemy horse slowed in sporadic bursts, conflicting commands ringing out as the horsemen variously decided to turn to this new threat, to continue to charge the infantry, to turn and run or to stop and brace. The result was a shambles.

The enemy officers were still trying to pull together their disparate and shattered force when Galronus' riders hit them like a spear point into flesh. Fronto watched with wide eyes. He was used to the Germanic and Gallic cavalry and had seen them in action often enough to know how effective they could be, yet he'd rarely seen anything on this scale. As they had closed they had, seemingly without the need for a signal, pulled into a wedge formation with his friend at the very tip. The wedge hit the uncoordinated enemy so hard that they plunged deep into the mass of white-clad riders almost to the extent of being lost among them, swords rising and falling, spears jammed into torsos and simply abandoned as their wielders snarled and pulled swords from their sides, going to work with a second weapon.

For a long moment, Fronto worried that his friend had gone too far, the Gallic horse being no longer visible, enveloped entirely by the enemy. Then, suddenly, they broke. With a series of surprisingly panicky sounding calls, the African horsemen burst apart like a dropped melon, scattering away from the nightmare that had descended upon them and turning, fleeing west.

Fronto stared in surprise as the Gauls and Germans came into view once again, whooping and bellowing as they cut men down even as they turned to run. In moments, the Africans were running, two thousand men fleeing in fear from a tenth their number.

Well, not quite two thousand. Fronto eyed the open-air graveyard of men and horses amid which Galronus' men sat. Remarkably few wore the dark, iron chain shirts of Gallic riders, and the number of white tunics and gleaming bronze shirts among the mounds of quivering horse flesh was impressive. Clearly Galronus and his men had killed with impunity, laying about themselves with wild abandon, while the enemy had done little to fight back, more intent en masse in getting away.

Better still, the veteran Gauls were well-trained and experienced enough not to follow the fleeing horse and imperil their impressive victory by pushing it too far. As the Remi and his men formed up and began to trot back towards the column, occasionally pausing to thrust a spear down into a wounded man on the ground, the enemy cavalry continued to flee the field, making for the gates of Hadrumetum.

Fronto chuckled. As the legionaries disassembled the contra equitas formation and came to attention once more, they watched the Hadrumetum garrison, stunned by the failure of the horse, turn and follow them back into the city.

'Well fought,' Caesar smiled as Galronus reined in before him, blood-spattered and grinning like a lunatic. Behind him, the cavalry split into three groups, one riding ahead to act as scouts once more, the others falling in on either flank at the rear. 'A most entertaining engagement.'

Galronus swept into a bow in the saddle, grinning still. 'I think the army may have gained a little heart this morning, General.'

'I do believe so,' Caesar smiled. 'Let us press on to Ruspina and not risk our good fortune by remaining any longer than we must in this place.'

The others nodded their agreement and rode ahead to the front of the column.

* * *

The city of Ruspina was an immediately daunting sight. Sitting at the crest of a headland that marched out into the sea, it dominated its surroundings. Though it was considerably smaller than vast, metropolitan Hadrumetum and lacked some of the height and strength of its walls, Ruspina would be a nightmare to attack for entirely different reasons. Protected on three sides by sea and walls, the landward side offered an approach of only a single mile width, the rest of the headland cut off by what appeared to be a salt lake and multiple salt pans which would be impossible for any kind of assault. Simply, Ruspina would be a difficult proposition.

Fronto sat before the edge of the nearest salt pans and looked across them. The army was tired, and the afternoon was wearing on rapidly. It had been a slow journey from Hadrumetum. Four times in total the African cavalry of Piso had chased them and made to bring the column to a halt, though each time they had failed. Having clearly lost heart in the first engagement, their enthusiasm for battle shrank with each follow-up, while the mettle of the Caesarian force continued to improve. The second time they came, the contra equitas held them off, the riders wheeling and threatening with no real pressure and breaking once again, riding off into the distance the moment Galronus and his riders put heels to flanks and began to move. Again and again, with little danger coming.

For the last four miles they had seen nothing of the enemy, though the column had moved slowly anyway, against the possibility of another repeat. Though the elation of the unexpected success of their first engagements in Africa remained uplifting among the men, the tension was beginning to be felt over what they might come to expect at the end of their march.

'What's the plan, sir?' Fronto asked.

Caesar scratched his neck. Until we know whether they are friend or foe there is little we can do. We make our way along the land approach and make camp out of missile range of the walls of Ruspina. Then we shall consider our next move.'

Riding on, they walked their horses past the legion as it came to a halt and began to make camp. The ground was low and unpleasant, but adequate for the task and , leaving the men to it, Caesar, Fronto, Plancus and Galronus found a good position to examine the city. If it was garrisoned against them, then it was a small one, for there were few figures visible on the walls.

'What do we think, gentlemen?' Caesar asked.

'One wonders if a naval assault might be easier,' Plancus mused. 'Our ships are out there, visible even from here. We could board along the coast out of view.

'The way the city is planned, it seems likely that a similar level of defence awaits any sea attack as here. I fear we lose a certain edge from the ships.'

'The walls are not as high as Hadrumetum, and I can see little artillery to speak of,' Fronto said. 'A direct assault is not beyond reason.'

They sat watching and Galronus, ever eagle-eyed, suddenly thrust out a finger. 'Look.'

They did so. The gates had remained open, a mile away from their camp, but now, suddenly, a small group of riders emerged from the shadowed doorway and began to ride towards them. 'Try to look imposing, gentlemen,' Caesar said, as the praetorian riders that had accompanied their general as always fanned out protectively.

The riders came at walking pace, slowly wending their way along the track from the city gate, and the waiting Caesarian party gradually grew as the tribunes from the various legions present made their way forward and added to the gleaming cavalcade of command. The riders were a mix of civilian and military, which Fronto hoped boded well. The two at the front were clearly in charge, one in an officer's uniform, the other in an expensive looking tunic and cloak, a gold belt around his middle.

As they came to a halt close enough to converse but out of spear reach of the praetorians, Caesar inclined his head politely.

'Greetings, Consul,' the civilian announced. 'I am Marcus Florus Evenus, representing the ordo of Ruspina. Each man you see here represents a significant group within our ancient city. I presume I have the honour of addressing the Consul Gaius Julius Caesar?'

'The honour is mine,' Caesar replied with a nod.

'Then please allow me to welcome you to Ruspina. I hereby place our wellbeing and honour in your hands, Caesar. Ruspina's people are loyal sons and daughters of the republic and her legitimate senate-appointed dictator. Give the word and I shall have our granaries and stores opened to support your force...'

He paused, brow folding as he looked past the general. 'This is not the *entire* force, I presume, Consul?'

Caesar shook his head confidently. 'By no means. Five legions are close by at sea, and four more are waiting to embark in Sicilia. We are but the beachhead so to speak.'

The man nodded, clearly relieved. Fronto wondered how he might have reacted had Caesar not bent the truth a little in the telling. 'Your ships are welcome in port and though we do not have adequate room in the city to house your army, comfortable quarters will be made available for yourself and the senior officers.'

The councillor continued to gush at Caesar and the two engaged in detailed plans, but Fronto allowed it to wash over him and sat back in the saddle, drinking in the result of their day. They were to be settled at Ruspina and in no danger. Against all expectations, they had won their first battle in Africa and had secured a safe port for the fleet. Caesar's plan might have been half-formed at best, but it seemed to be working.

CHAPTER FOUR

Leptis Minor, 1ˢᵗ January 46 BC

Galronus stood at the rail of the ship as the small fleet neared their destination, his heart pounding. It had been too much to hope that the rumours were true, but now, seeing it with his own eyes, he could hardly deny it. They had found at least some of Caesar's fleet.

The army had been encamped at Ruspina for only a day when a deputation had arrived from nearby Leptis Minor, some eight miles from their position. Not only had the ordo of Leptis given their city and support to Caesar in the same manner as Ruspina, but best of all they had brought the tidings that a sizeable fleet of ships bearing Caesar's legions had landed on the shore outside the town.

There had been something of a debate among the officers in the wake of the news as to whether to trust these new arrivals, for the news was almost too good to be true. Plancus had pointed out, quite rightly, that they had only the word of half a dozen men, all of whom could easily be in Cato's pay. Currently they were in a favourable position at Ruspina. If they decamped and went to this Leptis, they might just find Scipio's legions waiting for them, while they had also opened the back door to Piso and the Hadrumetum garrison. If it was a trap it would mean the end of the campaign and likely all their lives. Caesar had nodded, taking it all in, but had in the end pronounced that the entire campaign was already in the hands of the gods, for they could not hold for long with the men and supplies they had. He needed this to be true, and consequently, he had to trust that it was no trick.

The general had loaded his cavalry aboard the ships in port and departed for Leptis, leaving the infantry fortified at Ruspina under the command of Fronto and Plancus. The beachhead they had struggled to secure would therefore remain safe, and only the general's cavalry would be at risk in seeking this potential support at Leptis.

Throughout the two hour journey aboard the ships, Galronus had fretted, gripping the rail. Caesar had done what he could. He'd gone by ship rather than land, which meant he could check the truth of the fleet rumour without risking being trapped by armies, while allowing him a swift method of flight should everything go wrong. He'd left the bulk of his force commanding Ruspina to maintain their safe port, for which the horse would make only a negligible difference anyway. And he'd brought east with him the Gallic cavalry, the most manoeuvrable and speedy element of his army, should he need them in the event of a trap. Still, sailing into the unknown was not to Galronus' liking.

Thus, as the town of Leptis Minor came into view, and beyond it a mass of triremes at anchor along the coast, the Remi officer felt a huge weight lifted from him and breathed deeply. Still, he did not cheer until they had come close enough to confirm that they were definitely Caesar's ships and not some fleet of the enemy. When it was confirmed, and the bull pennants of Caesarian forces had been identified, finally it felt settled.

He glanced across at the general, who stood with Aulus Hirtius and the Leptis deputation near the stern. Only those who had been with Caesar for years through the best and the worst, and who knew how to read the nuances in the man's expression, would be able to tell how relieved he truly was. He maintained his implacable granite exterior for the look of things among these civilians, but that tiny change in his visage was the equivalent of an explosive release of breath.

Still Galronus leaned on the rail as the lead ship made for the harbour of Leptis, pondering what this meant for the coming days. With the force that must be waiting here, Caesar would no longer be in critical danger every hour, and might well decide that it was time to play an offensive rather than defensive game in Africa. Musing on matters, he watched Leptis slide ever closer. As they neared the harbour, Galronus realised why the fleet had anchored offshore nearby. The facility was of a reasonable size for a civilian fishing port, but nowhere near enough to host a military fleet.

Caesar seemed to have accepted this also, for orders were now sent out and the bulk of the ships carrying the cavalry made for the near shore, on the other side of the city to the extant fleet, just Caesar's own ship continuing on into the harbour. Nearing the jetty, the oarsmen lining up carefully, Galronus could see a small party of men in officer's uniforms riding into the port and making for the jetty. Closer and closer they came, finally near enough for the Remi noble to make an attempt at identification. He didn't know the men specifically, which was no surprise with this new officer corps, but he did recognise them as men he had met in Sicilia, so they were definitely Caesar's legions.

The general crossed to him as the trireme lined up and slid in alongside the jetty, oars shipped. 'Let us see what awaits us,' he murmured.

The officers at the port had dismounted and strode along the jetty towards where the ramp had been run out. Caesar was the first to disembark, Galronus at his back and then the members of the city's ordo. The man at the head of the group bowed his head.

'General, it is truly marvellous to see you. We had feared you lost in the storm, even when these fresh rumours reached us yesterday.'

Caesar returned the gesture. 'Asprenas, well met indeed. We made for shore near Clupea with a small group of vessels and hugged the shore as far as Ruspina. We have already engaged the enemy on the most minor of scales, but since we number less than a single legion, we have been unable to attempt anything more major than running skirmishes. We are encamped at Ruspina along the coast, close to the enemy fortress of Hadrumetum.'

Asprenas, a former consul, straightened. 'We heard the rumour yesterday that allied forces had landed to the west, possibly under your command, but we are only freshly arrived and, knowing how strong the enemy are in the region we decided it would be prudent to scout before marching anywhere upon the strength of rumour. The city's ordo decided to send a deputation in the belief that you were there, and we decided that we would wait until they had confirmed the truth of the matter. Had it been a trap and the army been Scipio's, half a dozen civilians could walk in and out where we would be committed to battle.'

Caesar nodded. 'We were similarly uncertain of the rumour of your ships. It appears, however, that the good citizens of both Ruspina and Leptis are loyal and beyond reproach. How many men do you have here?'

'Just shy of fifteen thousand, sir. Two full legions and sundry vexillations from others. Also many of the staff officers.'

Caesar's brow folded. 'Then we are still missing almost two legions from the crossing. Have you any news of them?'

Asprenas sagged. 'My trierarch tells me that your ship was to the left flank of the fleet as we crossed, and we formed much of the centre. The missing ships must have been on the right flank. If you hit the coast near where we were separated, then the others can only have sailed northwest. Perhaps they made for Utica or Carthage.'

'Carthago delenda est,' Caesar said with a sigh.

'Quite, sir. Or at least *Cato* delenda est.'

'Still,' Caesar replied brightly, 'together our force should number four legions. We must still be careful, for a direct conflict with Scipio's army would be disastrous, but now at least we have an army sufficient to begin a campaign.'

The general looked at the dozen or so officers on the jetty. 'My apologies for this, gentlemen, for I know that you are freshly arrived and must be looking forward to at least a time of organisation and consolidation, but I am afraid that we need to move instantly to secure our position and even to improve it, and I need several of you to depart immediately on individual missions.'

His pointing finger fell upon one of the men. 'Postumus, take a fast and sturdy ship and return to Lilybaeum. Secure whatever ships have been gathered there and whatever forces are ready and bring them to Ruspina, whether they are fully assembled or not. Manpower and time are now of the essence.'

Another finger, another officer. 'Sallustius, the councillors of Ruspina tell me that sufficient grain for a force twice our size is stored in granaries on the island of Cercina. Take five of the largest ships and go there. Secure me that grain.'

'Vatinius? Take ten warships and supplies for a week. Head across the bay. I want the rest of the stray ships located and the disposition of the enemy's fleet noted.'

The man bowed his head, face bleak at the thought of another, even longer, stint at sea.

'Rufus and Sulpicius, take the fastest ships in the fleet and sail with all haste for Sardinia and Crete. I want reinforcements and supplies. Whatever they can raise in a few days.'

He turned to Galronus. 'Anything else?'

The Remi shrugged. He'd not have considered half of that, let alone anything else, and so Caesar gave a business-like nod. 'Good. Get to it, gentlemen. The rest of you pass the word among your men. We shall remain encamped at Leptis for tonight, and on the morrow we depart for Ruspina once more, which we can assume is closer to the enemy.'

The men of the Leptis ordo exchanged worried glances, and Caesar gave them a reassuring smile. 'Never fear, my good men. We shall not leave you defenceless against the potential wrath of Scipio. I will leave Quintus Saserna here with six cohorts to defend Leptis against any enemy action.' Turning to the younger Saserna, he fixed the untried young officer with a firm look. 'You will have six veteran cohorts. Keep Leptis secure, but make sure your men are respectful of the city and cause no harm or offence.'

Saserna saluted and waited patiently with the others for further orders. 'I presume you are encamped on the far side of town near the ships but a respectful distance from the town?' Caesar mused. Asprenas nodded. 'Good, then make sure the army knows that we move out at dawn. I want the camp broken before first light and everything loaded on the ships for our return to Ruspina. Have six cohorts assigned to this place first, though. They can move into position around the city tonight under Saserna's command.'

'Sir,' Asprenas said, 'the ships are poorly supplied with provisions and water.'

Caesar brushed it aside. 'Provisions are not currently an issue, since the journey is only two hours and the men can break their fast at Ruspina when we arrive. Returning and uniting the army is our prime concern. Water we need, though, and I understand from earlier reconnaissance that there are streams and water sources to be found just inland all along this coast. We have sufficient light left yet to load water. I suggest the ship crews get to it, seeking out sources.' He turned to Galronus. 'Have the ships anchor, but the cavalry can stay aboard. No point in disembarking and setting up camp for a single night. Have those ships load water too. It is in short enough supply at Ruspina, so it will be of value to return with excess.'

Galronus nodded and scurried back up the ramp and aboard the ship, crossing to the stern rail. He knew how his men would feel about spending the night on the ship, with their horses, since it hardly appealed to him either. Cramped, warm and pungent with the constant gentle swell of the sea. Still, there was some sense to the general's decision, for it would speed departure in the morning and minimised the risk to the cavalry in the meantime. Reaching the steering oar, he waved his arms wide, attracting the attention of someone on the next ship.

'Anchor to the west offshore,' he shouted. 'The men stay aboard for the return journey at first light, but send out boats to gather water.'

The man saluted and disappeared to pass the orders on to other ships. Galronus waited at the rail as the general's orders were disseminated among the fleet. Caesar would be busy for some time with the ordo of Leptis and planning with the other officers and could do without him. Galronus' only real reason for being here was as commander of the cavalry Caesar had brought and, since that force was now being ordered to remain on the ships and would not be required for anything, that meant that their commander was in a similar limbo.

Something was nagging at him, though, and he drummed his fingers irritably on the rail. Damn the Romans. They got under your skin and even changed the way you thought. Before Caesar came to Gaul – *Gaul* even was a Roman concept, as though there were such a unified thing until Caesar – the tribes of the Belgae would have laughed at how easy it was to overthink things. Warfare was a simple and direct business. Tribes argued and then mounted and drew swords and rode at one another howling with rage until one was beaten. But Galronus had been serving alongside Romans now for a decade, and he was starting to see strategy ahead of necessity. It was an odd realisation. And right now there was something wrong with the strategy.

He thought it through, but could see nothing wrong. Ruspina was still adequately defended and in no direct or immediate danger. There was no indication of trouble here and the ordo had done nothing to suggest they were anything but faithful allies. The army here was dug in and the fleet sizeable. Six cohorts should be adequate to defend Leptis against any anticipated assault, and anything big enough to ignore six cohorts would be too much for the army in general anyway. The cavalry were safe on the ships, if uncomfortable, and could get away at short notice. Nothing was amiss…

Yet he could not escape the feeling that *something* was wrong.

Turning, he waved back at that ship. It took a moment for someone to see his signals and pass the word to someone important. A Remi rider, bedecked as a decurion but with the tell-tale beard and braids, reached the rail. 'Sir?'

'Despite the orders I just gave, put one turma of cavalry ashore with their mounts and have them report to me.'

The man nodded and disappeared from the rail. In short order, among the many small boats being put ashore from the fleet, each with six or eight rowers and barrels and sacks, a few pinnaces were launched carrying riders and their mounts. Galronus still couldn't quite pin down what it was that was bothering him, but he'd feel a lot better about it with some tense, heavily armed Belgae around him. It was at times like this he missed Fronto. The other officers may occasionally rip him to pieces as a pessimist and a storm crow, but the simple fact was that Fronto's gut feelings had seen them weasel out of a potential disaster more times than he could count, and for all that Galronus right now knew that something was off, Fronto would already be running around and giving orders to avoid it.

Still chewing his lip and pondering what could be wrong, he waited as the turma of thirty-two riders and their commander were rowed to the shore, clambered into the water's edge, then gathered around him, one of the men from Caesar's ship walking his own horse towards him. They all mounted and sat astride their mounts patiently, expectantly. Eventually, the decurion cleared his throat.

'Sir…'

'Tch,' replied Galronus, waving the man to silence.

'Sir?'

'I don't know yet. Let me think.'

The man waited beside him for long tense moments, while all around them was activity. The general had now moved into Leptis with the ordo and several senior officers, sailors were heading to refill the water barrels from the wadis, the fleet was at anchor, and six cohorts were settling into position as a defence force for the allied city under Saserna. Nothing was going wrong. Behind him the riders, becoming bored, began to chat among themselves. The decurion snapped them into silence, and that quiet reigned again for a short while.

Galronus continued to scan his surroundings. The hair was standing proud on the back of his neck in anticipation of something he still couldn't quite identify. Inevitably, the riders began to murmur once more, and the decurion craned in his saddle to shush them again, but Galronus, brow knitting, turned and held up a hand to stop the man. Looking back at the riders, he tilted his head curiously. 'What did you just say?'

Three men replied simultaneously, three conflicting answers, and Galronus threw them an irritable look, then pointed at a man fiddling with a pendant of Taranis and his sacred wheel hanging at his throat. 'You. What did you say?'

The man frowned. 'Just a harmless complaint, sir. I said this place is like Aegyptus but without the heat, sir.'

Galronus felt something slip into place.

'But really…' the man began again, though this time it was Galronus who silenced him.

'Like Aegyptus. Damn it, but it is. *Far* too like Aegyptus.'

'Sir?' the Decurion said.

'Water gathering. Last time in Aegyptus it was trouble, and it's happening again.'

'I can't hear anything, sir?'

Neither could Galronus before, but he could just sort of feel it. Now, though, it was there to be heard. As he sat in silence for a moment, distant cries of panic and pain reached their straining ears.

'Ride.'

The Gallic cavalry put heel to flank and the entire turma burst into life, racing inland. Wadis were plainly identifiable all the way along the coast by the greenery that grew up around the water, the rest of the land so brown and parched. Unlike the summer months, in this season the wadis were running with fresh water all the way from the inland hills and mountains to the sea.

One such green channel ran directly beneath the walls of ancient Leptis, another less than two hundred paces away, both already teeming with sailors filling barrels and hide sacks with fresh water for their ships. But there were too many sailors and too many ships to fill them all from here and the more distant vessels anchored further along the coast had sought out peripheral wadis, of which there were several, for Galronus could remember passing at least half a dozen just on the approach to Leptis. The noise was coming from the west and a little inland and they raced for the source of the sound in traditional Gallic form, as a mass of individuals bonded by a common purpose rather than the ordered block that Roman riders seemed to feel necessary even for moving from one place to another.

As they rode, the many possibilities of what they could face passed through Galronus' imagination, and he wondered whether he'd been impetuous in ordering this charge. What if they emerged from one of the many olive groves through which they rode and found ten legions waiting under Scipio? He cursed himself. Then at least they'd know where the man was.

Damn it, but he'd been around Fronto far too long.

The source of the trouble was easy enough to identify as they cleared the latest grove of ordered olive trees to find the dotted figures of sailors racing back towards them, bellowing in panic. Some were bloodied and even as Galronus looked this way and that, two staggered up the bank of a narrow seasonal stream, crying out for help, one immediately falling face down on the ground, a narrow spear standing proud from his back. The second man only cried out briefly, for in a heartbeat riders began to pour over the crest, the first scything out with his sword and delivering a killing blow across the sailor's back as he raised his face and gave a strange ululating cry.

Galronus waved his men on, casting a professional eye over the enemy in the middle distance. These men were clearly natives, for they had the same colouring and general look as the civilians they had met so far at Hadrumetum, Ruspina and Leptis. They were, as far as he could see, dressed and equipped much the same as the riders Piso had sent after them. If they were of the same quality, they should present no real danger, depending, of course, on how many of them there were.

Behind him, the Gallic cavalry drew their swords and hefted their spears with a chorus of clonks and rasps, and half a dozen gods were invoked in bellowed cries, only one of them Roman. Galronus locked eyes with the lead rider, for both of them were at the front of their respective units. Was this the same group they had fought near Hadrumetum? If so then it meant that Piso had been sending men southeast beyond the sight of the Romans, circumventing them. Or perhaps they were native raiders not in service to Rome at all? Certainly there would be such a thing, this close to the deserts where the tribes beyond the republic could find easy access to rich Roman lands. But the chances of raiders deciding to attack anyone so close to a huge Roman camp were minimal., and to target men gathering supplies was a military objective, not a greedy civilian one.

No, these were Roman auxiliaries, and probably not Piso's riders after all. And that meant they had come from somewhere else. Scipio was said to have ten legions with him, but presumably there were auxilia too? What if this was the lead element of Scipio's army? Or at least scouts for them. Or perhaps they were just a stray lone unit who had stumbled across Caesar's army quite by accident.

Whatever the case, they had to be dealt with.

Galronus felt a tiny thrill of nerves as all along the wadi, white-clad riders crested the slope, whooping and ululating. There were a lot more than thirty of them, he thought with momentary concern. Probably twice as many, in fact, and they were not displaying the nervousness he had seen with Piso's riders, which they had galvanised into full-blown panic with a reckless, suicidal charge. This looked like trouble. Still, they were committed now, and whatever sailors remained alive here should be protected.

Amid the thundering chaos, a horn call echoed across the endless olive groves from somewhere close behind them, loud enough to hear, just, over the pounding of hooves. Galronus turned and peered with his sharp eyes over the heads of his men. A unit of regular Roman riders was angling in at a tangent to fall in alongside the Gallic riders. Galronus waved his men and they slowed just slightly to allow the Romans to catch up. As they closed, he recognised the insignia of Caesar's praetorians, and at their head, grinning like some insane monster, was Salvius Cursor.

'Thought you'd start without me, did you?' he bellowed breathlessly as they bore down on the white riders together.

'Shouldn't you be protecting the general?'

'He's in conference with politicians, he only wanted six men,' Salvius replied dismissively, and there was no time for anything further, for that moment they reached the enemy horsemen. Galronus saw the man in front of him edge his mount slightly left and grip, ready to swing low in the saddle. In response, the Remi waited until the last moment and jabbed his knees into his own mount's side, veering it sharply and suddenly to the right. The two beasts almost collided but, as the white-clad rider was already ducking to his right and sweeping his sword around in an attempt to score an unexpected low blow on Galronus, the Remi simply passed him by on the far side and delivered a powerful chop to the exposed ribs on the man's other side.

Unarmoured but for white linen, the blow was appalling, smashing ribs and pulping meat and organs within, a crippling death blow even if it took some long moments of agony to reach that conclusion. Galronus ignored the stricken man further. His riders were engaging the natives all the way along the wadi, and somehow Salvius had managed to get himself coated in blood merely from dealing with the second, spear-wielding rider. Swords rang out as they met swords, screams and hollers of fury, the din of battle, and among the riders hammering at one another the occasional sight of a terrified sailor trying not to be trampled or caught up in the melee as he fled for his life. More white riders were emerging from the wadi even as their fellows fought hard, and Galronus rode on for the next man, sword out to his right. He could see the man rising in his saddle, ready to sweep down with his sword, and so Galronus hunched low over his horse's back, pushing her head down out of danger. As the two riders met, the local's blade swept through the air above Galronus, but his own blade slammed into the man's thigh, cleaving it to the bone, and then he was past and onto the next man who was just cresting the bank of the wadi.

Just off to his left, Salvius had dealt a brutal blow to a rider, cutting his neck right down to the bone. Rather than leave the ruined rider and move on, though, the man made sure that his victim was dead in the saddle before seeking out another target. The next rider reached level ground, but his eyes widened as he saw the extent of the Gallic and Roman threat, the figures of his fellow Africans lying in the dirt and shuddering or lolling in the saddle with horrific wounds. A handful of Romans and Belgae were stricken too, but the battle had very much gone in their favour and the greater percentage of dead and dying were in white.

The man tried to turn his horse to retreat, but Galronus was on him, sword cleaving down into barely-protected flesh. The man screamed, and so did the horse, as the tip of the blade continued on through the blanket on the beast's back to rake across its hide. The man fell from his steed, the horse taking to panicked and agonised flight.

Growling with satisfaction, Galronus passed the last rider to reach the top of the slope. Dozens of sailors lay dead or groaning with spears jutting from them down in the gulley, the water of the seasonal stream running pink as it chuckled towards the sea. Here and there were other riders among them finishing off the surviving sailors in the stream. A brief scan confirmed that there appeared to be no infantry presence nearby. This was all the work of one unit of African cavalry and, as Galronus had hoped, they seemed to be alone and had come across the sailors by chance.

'Don't let them get away,' Salvius Cursor shouted, waving a sword.

'Too late,' Galronus replied, pointing.

The natives had realised that the fight was already weighing badly against them and were trying to disengage and fall back. Those men in the wadi who had been wandering from injured man to injured man sticking spears in their backs looked up now and turned swiftly, quickly melting away into the trees and undergrowth along the defile.

'What happens when they report what they've see to their commanders?'

Galronus shrugged. 'We don't know who their commanders are, but if they do then it can only be to our benefit.'

'What? How?'

The Remi nobleman smiled as he watched the last of the white-clad Africans disappearing among the greenery. They would never catch them anyway. These men knew the region well, were born to it, and would easily evade the Gauls and Romans. He turned to Salvius Cursor. 'If someone important learns of this, then with luck they will assume Leptis to be our muster position for the campaign, which gives us at least a *potential* advantage, since we'll actually be eight miles west of here at Ruspina by mid-morning tomorrow.'

Salvius gave him a noncommittal grunt. 'Let's hope they're not close enough to attack us tonight, then.'

Galronus watched the last figures melting away into the haze. 'I don't think they'll be back for a fight in a hurry.'

CHAPTER FIVE

Ruspina, 2nd January 46 BC

Fronto watched the flotilla of ships approaching Ruspina from the east and could picture the general's face. A mix of marvelling, bafflement and relief, he imagined, for there was no room for the general's ships to anchor off the coast at Ruspina. He watched as the fleet approached, many times the size of the one that had left, which confirmed the truth of the rumour. Caesar had found the fleet, or at least some of it, at Leptis. He leaned back a little and observed as the mass of ships closed on the headland and anchored as close as they could, Caesar's own ship at the head navigating between still vessels and anchoring close to the town, despite the lack of room.

Fronto sat astride Bucephalus, with Plancus beside him and a small guard of men at their backs, as the general and his horse, along with a few chosen officers, were ferried by boat from the main ship. Unloaded on the sand, they mounted and rode across to Fronto and Plancus. Fronto recognised with relief perhaps half of the staff officers they had not seen since the storm. Caesar's expression was carefully neutral now, but there was a curious shape to his brow, as though he were trying to hold in the excitement.

'Fronto,' Caesar said in mixed greeting and conversational opening, 'you have acquired ships. Sufficient ships, in fact, as to make anchorage for my fleet difficult.'

Fronto grinned at the general as he threw out an arm to draw the general's attention to the scene behind him. What had been a small camp, sufficient for a single legion, was now a sprawling affair more than twice the size. 'They arrived last night as darkness fell. They'd been blown very much off course in that storm and had found themselves on course for Utica. Reaching the peninsula on which Clupea sits, they had a confab and made a fortunate choice. Instead of continuing to Utica, they followed the coastline south, a few days behind the rest of us. Almost two legion's worth of men. It looks, miraculously, as though we lost less than a dozen ships in total to the storm, if Plancus' estimate of your fleet number is correct.'

'It's correct,' murmured the officer beside him.

The general leaned forward in his saddle to stroke the neck of his horse as he smiled for the first time. 'We have an army, gentlemen. Six legions and auxilia. We must still be very careful and circumspect, of course, as we are still heavily outnumbered, but now we can at least offer a threat to the enemy. With luck my missives will bear fruit and further manpower will arrive in due course. In the meantime, we must be wary, but with a greater degree of confidence, I feel.'

Plancus shifted in his saddle. 'How certain are we of our information? Despite all warnings, we have thus far seen only a city garrison and a relatively minor cavalry force. Perhaps we are the victim of rumour and disinformation and in truth Scipio lurks with only a small force in Cato's Utica?'

Caesar shook his head. 'Our intelligence is sound. Curio managed to leave a few agents in the province before he fell in that disastrous winter. Their reports have been sporadic and necessarily careful, but they generally agree in all major details. The overall force arrayed against us is perhaps twice the size of ours now, and will only increase if Juba of Numidia manages to come east and join them. And we cannot rely upon outmanoeuvring them, for Cato is moving the pieces on the board, and he is a master player. Scipio and Labienus are both tried and tested men, the former a proconsular commander and the latter a propraetorian general and both are in the field with forces ready for us. Scipio may suffer tendencies to incautious action, but Labienus is a career soldier and a talented tactician, enough to counter any failing in Scipio. Rest assured that both those men and their sizeable army are out there somewhere, and we are not yet strong enough to face them with confidence of victory.'

'We tarried too long in Aegyptus,' Fronto grumbled, and then only realised in the uncomfortable silence that followed that he'd spoken the thought out loud. He winced.

'Fronto?' Plancus prompted.

Caesar was giving him a hawk-like look, and Fronto tried hard to find a way to put his point across that did not land the blame squarely with Caesar and his dangerously manipulative Aegyptian harlot queen. The general had been quick to anger when the subject of his new son's clever mother and their time on the Nile arose.

'For all the importance of what was achieved during the time we spent in Aegyptus after Ptolemy's death, every day we spent there allowed Pompey's supporters to gather in Africa like flies on a horse turd, and they've used that time well, turning the province into a fortress against us. I would say the gods have to be with us just for us to have found support in two minor coastal towns. All the great cities will be arrayed and fortified against us. Had we moved last summer, we might have been able to put paid to Africa before it became such a fortress.'

Caesar's withering look remained, but his voice came out surprisingly levelly. 'How uncharacteristically diplomatic of you, Fronto. But I am aware of the opinions over our time in Aegyptus. Cassius retired ostensibly because he refused to face Romans once more, though I fear he maintains a personal grudge over my alliance with the Aegyptian queen.'

He sighed. 'The fact remains that Africa is now a tough nut to crack. As such, I intend to avoid a full scale battle until our forces are adequate to at least give us a fighting chance. Currently we can field six legions to their ten, perhaps three thousand auxiliaries against their six or seven, and less than a thousand horse against their ten thousand at least. Labienus commands cavalry well and he knows us and our tactics. Moreover, the core of his cavalry are our own men, trained and tested in Gaul. Our only hope is that their infantry let them down.'

'Sir?' Plancus frowned.

'There are few veteran legions among them.'

'Nor among ours yet,' Fronto reminded him.

'But even our fresh legions are drawn from good Italian, Illyrian and Gallic stock and formed and trained in the traditional manner as were the veterans we command. Scipio has been forced to rely upon the drafting of men from all over Africa, even into the desert tribes. His legions may be of sufficiently inferior quality to make a difference, though this is not supposition enough to commit to war. No, we shall fortify at Ruspina until we have sufficient numbers to move, and until we are better aware of enemy dispositions.'

He turned to the officers behind him and singled out Publius Saserna with a nod. 'As your brother holds Leptis for me, so you will take command of the Twenty Ninth Legion and garrison Ruspina town. They may complain, given that it will weigh heavily upon them in terms of accommodation and supply, but you may remind them of the enemy awaiting them inland and comfort them that they have been given a full legion for their defence such is their level of favour with me. Have the men gather all the supplies they need for extra fortification. Stockpile stone and lumber. If Scipio comes to Ruspina he will find a fastness of rock and steel.'

'And food, sir?' Saserna noted. 'We need more food. Shall we forage?'

Caesar shook his head. 'You will have to move too far from the city to find sufficient food, while quarries and untouched woodland lie close enough by. I have already sent out a small fleet to hunt down a known source of grain at Cercina, and we shall put out requests through our allies in these two towns. Gentlemen, we continue to play a waiting game. At least four more legions are expected at Lilybaeum, as well as any support sent from Sardinia and Crete.'

As long as they haven't mutinied again and abandoned us, Fronto thought darkly. If even the favoured Tenth could turn against them, nothing could be relied upon right now. Caesar nodded, drawing the impromptu meeting to a close. 'Let us return to my headquarters and go over matters in more detail, though I would appreciate the opportunity to refresh myself first.'

As the staff officers moved off in Caesar's wake, heading for the sprawling camp outside the town Fronto paused long enough to let two figures that had been lurking together behind the general catch up. Salvius Cursor bore a new fresh scar on his cheek, attesting to some recent conflict though he bore it with his usual lack of concern. The three men fell in together, walking their horses along at the rear of the command column.

'You met trouble?'

'Itinerant local cavalry,' Salvius said dismissively. 'Just unarmoured riders.'

'An ambush of opportunity,' Galronus added, 'against sailors collecting water for Caesar's ships. Hiding in the stream beds.'

'Sounds familiar,' said Fronto.

'Quite. They killed and injured quite a few but we made them pay for it and drove them off. It is possible that the enemy commanders are even now receiving reports from them that we are at Leptis Minor and in greater strength than in our previous encounter.'

'Then it won't take them long to pin us to Ruspina,' Fronto murmured. 'Caesar's waiting game may not succeed. If the enemy come against us in force, we may find ourselves besieged. I think we should give thanks to Fortuna that Scipio is the one pulling the strings around here, and not Cato.'

'I do not understand,' Galronus said. 'Cato is the better strategist and the more respected senator. Should he not have control of the army?'

'Be grateful he doesn't,' Salvius Cursor muttered. 'Our best advantage is that Scipio has the army and he is impetuous and sometimes foolhardy. Cato is far away and any strings he pulls are too long for the puppet to dance quickly.'

Fronto noted the blank look still on his friend's face. 'Cato is playing by the rules, fortunately. He's never been a consul, while Scipio has. Cato can only claim propraetorian powers, while Scipio is a proconsul. As such, senior command in the province naturally falls to Scipio, though he can legitimately accept Cato's strategic advice from Utica.'

'How you Romans ever achieved an empire is beyond me,' Galronus muttered. 'How you even got down from the Palatine without a millennium of administration and paperwork is a miracle.'

Fronto laughed. 'On this occasion it works in our favour, so don't knock it. Cato can only lay down general strategies from his council chamber way up north, and Labienus is comparatively junior in terms of senatorial authority, so we're facing Scipio as principle commander, and he might… just might… slip up and offer us an opportunity.'

'But for now we sit in Ruspina and wait.'

'We do, until we have either enough men to face the enemy…'

'Or we run out of supplies,' Salvius added darkly, nodding at the worryingly low grain store as they rode back through the camp.

* * *

4ᵗʰ January 46 BC

Fronto looked out along the ranks of legionaries. Caesar sat further along the line, plainly visible on his white horse with his red cloak, a living standard for the men. The general gestured to the gathered cohorts, arm coming out in an oratorical manner.

'Men of Rome, while Ruspina continues to strengthen with fortifications, and its garrison gather sufficient supplies for its ongoing defence, the time has come to concentrate on consolidating our food supplies.'

He noted the twitchiness of the men, and took a breath before beginning again in a calm and reassuring tone. 'I am certain that many of you have already heard the rumours.'

Fronto found that he was chewing his lip and deliberately stopped the nervous habit, irritably. The rumours had started yesterday morning. As the army had gone about its various tasks, a party of desert traders had arrived in town from the south, and with them had come tidings of legions and cavalry not more than two days from the coast. When pressed for details, the men had been vague and evasive, unable or unwilling to provide any further detail, other than that there were 'as many of them as grains of sand in the desert', which was clearly hyperbole and of little tactical use. It had taken only hours for this information to spread, and with it a heightened tension. Caesar had gathered his officers for a meeting and the situation had been laid out clearly.

If the force that approached from the south was the entire African army, then a pitched battle would likely end in disaster. Flight, on the other hand, would only result instead in a running battle that lost them any advantage of position and terrain. The only reasonable option was to remain, prepare for a siege and pray that sufficient reinforcements were on the way to make a difference. The problem with that option was one of supplies. There was only enough food to see the army through a couple more days, and though a good supply was theoretically on the way from the island of Cercina under the command of Sallustius, there was no sign of it as yet, and a *potential* store that could still be a week away was of little use.

'Whether the rumours of the desert traders prove to be true or not,' Caesar announced to the gathered legionaries, 'we find ourselves in short supply. As of now, until the grain arrives from Cercina, the army will be placed on half rations. And in order to maintain even this paltry level, we must rely upon forage to bolster our dwindling stores.'

Men were looking at one another nervously and with the dismay of soldiers facing rationing, and centurions along the line snapped their units back into silent attention. Caesar gestured out around himself. 'All coastal sources of food have been exhausted, partly due to the careful reaping of all possible supplies by the enemy before our arrival, and partly due to the inconvenient winter season. It is our considered opinion that good forage will remain to be had further inland, however. The forces of Cato and Scipio have been mobile across Africa and they must have gathered stores in towns and villages away from the dangers of the coast. It is these we now seek. I grant you that thirty cohorts is a large number of men for a foraging mission, but it has been deemed a sensible figure on reflection. We are moving into the unknown, into lands where the enemy are rumoured to be active, and will need to retrieve a huge weight in supplies without the adequate wagon train. Extensive manpower is the answer, though you are kitted for light travel.'

Fronto could see the nerves across the faces of the gathered legionaries, and apparently so could Caesar, for the general gave his men an easy smile. 'Units of mounted scouts will keep us apprised of any danger,' he gestured to Galronus and a few hundred horse gathered at the far side of the column. 'If Scipio and his cohorts appear, they will not be able to move any faster than us, and we should be able to retreat to Ruspina in good order before any action is committed.'

This put some of the fears to rest, though the tension level remained high. With a few more rousing words to the men and instructions issued to the tribunes and centurions the general gave the signal, and nine thousand men, split into thirty under-strength cohorts, moved out from the camp before Ruspina, marching steadily inland. Galronus geed his cavalry up and the horse split into scouting turmae of thirty-two men, ranging out ahead in a fan shape.

Fronto settled into a steady pace on Bucephalus, matching Caesar at the far side as he led his huge foraging force into the unknown. Helpful locals in Ruspina had explained that the towns and villages in this region stored grain for the winter in low chambers like dry cisterns, so they knew what to look for. Other supplies in the form of animals and fruit and vegetables should not be too hard to find in stores. The hope was that Scipio had been wise enough to gather supplies to keep an army going as it moved around, and it was these Caesar's men would seek. The cohorts were under strict instructions to take only excess and to leave sufficient to see the locals through the rest of the winter.

As they moved at a steady march, Fronto's eyes raked the lands ahead of them. This region was brown and scrubby green, reminiscent of the lands of southern Greece or of Hispania, given over to carefully irrigated fields and olive groves. Seasonal streams ran to the coast all the way along the coast, but between them the ground was dusty and hard even now, the parching summers robbing it of the ability to retain more than the slightest moisture. The one thing that struck Fronto, though, was the topography. The region was impressively flat. In a perfect world, that would mean excellent visibility and plenty of warning of trouble. Africa, sadly, appeared not to be the perfect world. Between the ever-present dust that hung over the horizon like a low fog, and the scrub brush and olive trees, it was no easier to see more than a quarter of a mile than it would be if hills stood in the way.

The large force crossed a pleasant narrow river with ease at an ancient fording point, the water chuckling past at shin-depth, clear and crisp. Within a short time they had passed out of sight of Ruspina and the salt pans and moved into true countryside. Fronto started to feel a little more comfortable with every passing moment. They paused perhaps a mile from the camp at a small village, the first such that they found. Some careful enquiry and negotiation led them to the village store, a low structure shaped like a half barrel sunk into the ground, with a thick door at one end. The locals did not look particularly pleased with losing supplies, but were mollified when it became clear that the army was taking only half the stored grain, especially when backed by Caesar's personal guarantee that their sacrifice in aid of the senate-appointed forces of Rome would not be forgotten.

Similar scenes played out twice more in other villages over the next half hour as they crossed another low river with a wide ford and, though the gathering of supplies was slow, the ease with which it was happening spread a wave of relief throughout the army. There would be other villages to pass through before they reached their first major destination. The town of Uzitta was purported to be a relatively minor one and without fortification or garrison, but maintained a weekly market and sat at a junction in roads. Thus it would likely hold a good supply of food and hopefully without any defenders. Uzitta lay a mere five miles inland from Ruspina, though the army was moving at less than two miles in an hour, due to the regular stops at villages and the need to move carefully and in formation.

Fronto estimated now that they'd come perhaps three miles so far, with a solid level of minor successes, and his gaze played across the land once more. He could see minor clouds of dust that marked their mounted scout units, which eased nerves for all of them. Then he realised that one of the clouds was growing. The scouts were coming back to the column. Indeed, now all the clouds were increasing in size as they closed on the cohorts and the two officers. A sense of troubled anticipation hit Fronto and he kicked Bucephalus' flanks and hurried across the front of the marching lines, heading for Caesar. The general had a similar look of tense expectation as the two men settled side by side at a steady walk, watching the scouts closing on them.

In a matter of heartbeats, Galronus was slowing, his men gathering behind him.

'Enemy force spotted, general.'

'Where?' Caesar asked quietly as he held up a hand in signal for the legions to come to a halt. 'How many and what dispositions?'

Galronus' shoulders bunched in a shrug. 'It's very hard to tell, sir, given the dust and the terrain. All I can say at this point is that the force is sizeable enough to be of concern and from the growing dust cloud they are closing on us. They are perhaps a mile away, not more than a mile and a half at most, though seemingly slow moving.'

Caesar looked at Fronto, who nodded. 'Let's have a look.'

The two men joined Galronus as he wheeled his mount and began to ride out forward once more, a turma of men at his back. Praetorian horsemen were with them before they had even pulled ahead of the cohorts, Salvius Cursor joining the three commanders from where he and his men had ridden at the periphery.

The four men and their accompanying horsemen rode fast, though not enough to exhaust the horses, to a rare low rise dotted with scrub and rocks and with a reasonable view of the plains. Fronto could see it even as they reined in. Whatever they were, they were a good sized force. Their immediate makeup was hard to determine with the low dust cloud and the distance, and all four men squinted into the south.

'I cannot make them out,' Caesar admitted. 'From the size of the cloud, I would put their numbers at similar to ours.'

Fronto nodded. 'I'd say so. Maybe two legions' worth. What and who they are I can't say. They seem to be in close formation, though, from the look of it.'

Caesar nodded. 'I concur. Galronus?'

The Remi nobleman was frowning. 'I'm not sure, general. It's too hard to see in the dust. We need to make a decision now though, sir, else we'll be out of time.'

Caesar mused for a moment, tapping the horn of his saddle. 'Their legions are almost certainly going to be weaker than ours, less disciplined, less well-trained – the *majority* of them, anyway. There is a good possibility that our force is superior to theirs in training and discipline, and we more or less match their numbers.'

'You're thinking of staying to fight?' Fronto murmured. It *was* tempting, he had to admit. It was a risk, but Caesar's logic was solid and the boost in morale they had experienced after Galronus ran off the African cavalry had changed the whole army's mood. Spirits were sinking once more at the prospect of a siege, and of protracted hunger, and if they could inflict another wound on the enemy, it might make all the difference. Fronto looked to Galronus. 'You have sharp eyes, the best among us.'

'I just cannot see, Fronto. The dust is too much. Had it rained in recent days the dust would be suppressed, but now, I cannot tell.'

Caesar turned to the Remi officer. 'Send riders back to the camp at their fastest pace. Summon all our archers and cavalry. It they move at full speed they can join us in time to put that force to flight.' He turned to Fronto. 'They're deploying in a wide line. Have the men don their helmets and fall back half a mile to the low ridge we passed and do the same ready to meet them. It is little more than a hummock, but it will give us a terrain advantage such as it is, and will buy sufficient time for the cavalry and auxilia to join us. Would that we had time to call the full army out, but the enemy will be on us before the legions can reach us. Only light auxilia and cavalry can move fast enough to bolster us in time.'

Fronto nodded. 'Your favoured formation, general?'

'A wide front, I think. They seem to be adopting the same, so let us meet them as equals.'

Another nod, and Fronto turned and rode back to distribute commands to the tribunes and centurions commanding the various cohorts. The army began to track back across the wide field in which they had come to rest, heading for a low lump in the land that it was being incredibly generous even to call a rise. As they moved, Fronto once again peered back off to the south, trying to determine the length of that line of dust. He looked again at the cohorts. They would have to create a wide line to meet the enemy and with the numbers they had, that meant very thin lines. There would be precious little support behind the front men. As he watched the legionaries reaching their position and lining up, ten deep, he began to feel doubt settle into him. Was this just *too* much of a risk?

Fronto passed between the ranks and sat behind the centre of the line astride his horse, watching as the general returned to the line. The mounted scouts under Galronus split into two groups and moved to the wings of the extended line, while Caesar and his praetorian riders joined Fronto to the rear of the line's centre. The general had a blank expression, but his knuckles were white as he continued to worry at the saddle horn, which had a frayed thread. Much like the man's nerves, Fronto suspected.

Half an hour passed in very tense silence, and Fronto could feel the nerves building all along the line. The cloud of dust gradually came into view and then grew at a slow but steady rate. It was possible that the enemy was adopting a stately pace to preserve their strength and freshness for battle, but Fronto was privately and silently forming the opinion that the enemy commander was drawing out his approach as much as possible to allow nerves among Caesar's men to blossom into fear and then into full-blown panic, which it might just do.

There was a sense of relief all around as a second cloud appeared behind them, and the light troops from the camp joined the cohorts on the rise, already looking exhausted from a high speed run across three miles to fall in with them. Roughly four hundred cavalry split into two groups and joined their compatriots at the wings. One hundred and fifty archers were ushered through the lines to form up at the front, ready to receive the enemy.

They were as set as they could be in the circumstances. On the face of it, the decision was acceptable. This was a reasonable tactical decision. So why was the back of his scalp itching as it sometimes did when he felt that something was inexplicably wrong?

Caesar motioned to two of his praetorian horsemen. 'Ride to the cavalry on the wings. Remind them that the enemy may well have horse of their own and they must take care not to be flanked.' The two riders raced off for the end of the line as Caesar pulled a little closer to Fronto. 'Their centre may be solid infantry, but we must assume that they have access to archers and cavalry.'

Fronto nodded, but his mind was really elsewhere, examining the field and unpicking whatever it was that was nagging at him. This was not right. Something was making him twitch. A rumble gave him the first clue as that dust cloud grew to immense proportions. 'Caesar, that's a cavalry force.'

Caesar frowned, shaking his head. 'They have infantry in the centre, of that I am sure.'

'If they have, they're moving too fast to be heavy infantry. That's not legions. It's not Scipio.' His eyes began to pick out details now, the enemy close enough to become visible despite the cloud of dust they threw up. A mismatched line, the enemy force was a strange one. Cavalry formed more than two thirds of the army, and while there were spear-wielding riders in white tunics or bronze shirts among them, there were also heavier cavalry in mail shirts and helmets with swords and shields. Gauls or Germans.

'That's Labienus,' Fronto said, his voice suddenly hoarse.

The enemy cavalry were interspersed with groups of light spearmen running at the same pace as the horses, and units of archers, pounding along with arrows already nocked to their bows. The entire group was far tighter packed than any sensible commander would keep cavalry, as tight as an infantry unit.

Fronto cursed. 'He's tricked us. He's approached as though they were an infantry force and lured us into staying to fight, but they're not. They're cavalry in the main and they're going to run damn rings around us. Labienus knows you too well, Caesar.'

The general was also cursing now, a most unusual thing to hear. It was a rare occasion that Caesar was tricked and trapped, but Labienus had served as his lieutenant all through those years in Gaul. He was a strategist himself, and he knew Caesar. The general looked this way and that, huffing. There was no chance of running now. Labienus' force was a light one, centred on cavalry, and would move much faster. Yet if the Caesarian army stood its ground it would be surrounded and cut down speedily.

'Stand your ground,' Caesar called to his men. 'Ready yourselves.'

Fronto watched as the enemy forces opened up. On their wings were Gauls, similar to those guarding Caesar's flank but in much larger numbers. They raced ahead now to engage Galronus' horse, preparing to flank and envelop the Caesarian army. Along the main line, the horse also pulled ahead ready to charge as the archers and African spear men ran on behind, ready. Fronto took a breath and drew his sword. Damn it, but they'd waded waist deep into the cess pit now.

CHAPTER SIX

Ruspina, 4th January 46 BC

The enemy line began to extend as they closed, Labienus opening up his forces to allow room for his light skirmishers, archers and cavalry all to deploy to the best of their ability. Galronus knew then what a mistake they had made in committing to battle, yet there would be no running from them now. They had to fight and, if not win, which seemed unlikely, then at least extricate themselves from this mess.

The Remi had seven turmae of cavalry on this wing, another seven at the far end of the long line. A little over two hundred riders on each flank. The cavalry coming at them from the end of Labienus' extended line numbered perhaps three times as many riders as Galronus' force, and he could hardly count on them being less effective, since they also were Gallic cavalry formerly of Caesar's forces in Gaul and every bit as tough and dangerous as those with Galronus. Caesar's orders had been to make sure they were not flanked, but Galronus could see no way to achieve such a thing facing three to one odds. He could hold them, but not indefinitely. It was only a matter of time. Watching the approaching riders carefully, he gave out his orders.

'Thin out the ranks. Make sure our lines are wider than theirs.'

The Allobroge nobleman serving as his second frowned in consternation. 'Sir…'

'I know. I know. Do it anyway.'

Ten, he thought. 'This won't be a spear action,' he announced.

Nine. 'This is a job for swords.'

Eight. 'Let's take a few out.'

Seven. 'Use your spear as a javelin.'

Six. 'Ready? Cast spears.'

Five. He watched as two hundred or so spears arced out inexpertly over his head and came down in a shower over the enemy cavalry.

Four. He watched several dozen fall to the hail and nodded in satisfaction. 'Draw swords.'

Three. 'Brace yourself.'

Two. Galronus hefted his own sword and threw his shield out forward to take the first blow.

One. He clenched his teeth.

The enemy cavalry ploughed into them like a battering ram, sending men reeling from their saddles, even knocking horses over with the force. Galronus' only advantage was that the initial charge used up the enemy's spears and they then had to draw their swords while Galronus and his men laid into them with their own ready blades. Still it was a tiny victory amid a huge disaster. The battle settled into a simple test of fortitude and luck as the two units hammered at one another, Labienus' cavalry still hugely outnumbering the Caesarian force. As Galronus swung his blade and shifted his steed as best he could in the press with his knees, he fought like a Belgae warrior, bellowing obscenities in his native tongue, desperately holding as long as he could, for he knew it would be a very short time before they were overcome by the enemy cavalry, and the only hope was that Caesar's genius would find them a way out of this mess before everyone fell.

* * *

Fronto watched the heavy cavalry on the wings advance ahead of the main line, making to envelop the Caesarian force and he was under no illusion what would happen. They were going to be surrounded very quickly unless they could somehow get out of this.

The enemy archers released their volley of arrows and in response Caesar's hundred and fifty Cretan bowmen let fly with their own attack, the two flights of shafts passing in the air, occasionally striking one another with a clatter and falling from the sky. Both groups of archers knew better than to be on the receiving end of such a volley, with their light armour and lack of shield, and even as Labienus' archers, their job done, dashed back between the rest of their fellows out of danger, so Caesar's archers hurried back through the ranks to the rear for safety.

The clouds of arrows came down simultaneously. The African riders and spear men were lightly armoured at best and with few shields among them and many of the arrows hit home and wounded. Most of the enemy shafts were caught in Caesarian shields or turned by helmets, though with there being so many more of them, the number of casualties was much the same.

As the arrow volleys petered out, centurions along the Caesarian ranks gave the order to brace. All along the line of Labienus' force riders and runners came side by side, keeping pace. Fronto found himself dithering. Against cavalry he would normally deploy his men in a shield wall of contra equitas formation, but these light, javelin wielding African horse were an unknown quantity, and when the infantry were thrown into the mix alongside them, contra equitas might do more harm than good.

A call went up somewhere in the mass of the enemy ranks and suddenly, only thirty paces from the Caesarian lines, the horse and foot of Labienus' army came to a sudden halt and all of them, mounted or not, cast a javelin. A panicked cry went up from the waiting legionaries, and shields clonked up together to form a wall against the cloud of shafts. Inevitably, many of the thrown missiles found a target despite the shields, and men all along the Caesarian lines fell, crying out.

'Pila,' bellowed Fronto urgently, and in response the legionaries began to cast their own pila. The call was picked up by the centurions along the line and in moments the heavy Roman shafts were thrumming through the air towards the Africans. It was of little value, for the deft and speedy men of Labienus' force were already dashing backwards out of range. A few pila found their mark, but the majority scraped to a halt in the dusty ground.

Someone cried out in triumph off to Fronto's right and in moments whole sections of the Caesarian force had begun to run, chasing the retreating javelin men. Fronto stared in shock as he turned to a cornicen nearby. 'Sound the *ad signum*, for the love of Jove.'

The cornicen began to blow the call, but it was too late. The impetuous centurion somewhere along the line who had taken the enemy withdrawal as a retreat had led his men forward. Even as the enemy retreated, suddenly their infantry halted again, turned, and hefted a second javelin like a hedge of points while the riders withdrew further. The chasing legionaries stumbled to a halt, realising their error, but it was too late for many of them. Even as the 'ad signum' cadence called them back to their standards and the legionaries scrambled to turn and run back for their own lines, the enemy javelineers jabbed out, taking a few legionaries by surprise. A second volley of javelins hurtled out from a second line unseen behind the first, peppering the Caesarian legionaries and decimating them. As the survivors began to race for their comrades, the African cavalry suddenly reappeared from whence they had retreated, now armed with fresh javelins. They raced past their infantry companions and after the running Caesarians.

Fronto watched in despair as half that force running back up the slope fell to a fresh volley. As no more than a third of the men who'd charged managed to step back into line and join their fellows, the enemy rearmed once more as the second wave of javelineers rushed forward. Fronto shook his head. They had no easy counter for this strange new tactic. They were going to die here unless they could get away, for there was no chance this could be turned into a victory.

'Caesar,' he called across to the general, 'we have to withdraw.'

'We will be cut down as we flee,' Caesar replied, voice wavering slightly, his usual confidence seemingly absent.

'We're being cut down while we stand,' Fronto countered angrily.

'Time. I need time to think.' The general turned and gave out fresh orders to his musicians and signifers. 'No further advances. No man moves more than four feet from his standard.'

As the call went out, Fronto moved over to the general. 'I'm sure it'll be a great comfort to them that they're dying so close to their eagle. We have to run.'

Caesar turned a look of uncertainty on him, which chilled Fronto, for it was not something he'd ever thought to see on the general in battle. '*Caesar!*'

He spun at a fresh sound of disaster to see the right flank shatter, the Roman horse broken under the sheer weight of the enemy cavalry. Almost instantly the same thing happened on the left. To the credit of Galronus' men they did not flee, but tried desperately to hold even as they were driven back and further back. Fronto waved to a tribune who was watching, ashen faced, nearby. 'Mount up and ride for the flanks. Tell them to pull out and regroup away from the fight before they're trapped with us.'

The tribune, grateful for something that took him away from the perilous centre, nodded and clambered onto his horse, racing for the left flank. Fronto watched him go, praying that the message would get through to Galronus and that the Remi would have the sense to follow the order. The cavalry were broken and battered and of no use now, and when the army were surrounded at least the legionaries could maintain a solid shield wall, while the cavalry would simply be cut down.

Having done all he could for the riders, Fronto turned back to the horror playing out in front of him. Labienus' army had settled into those tactics, his riders and runners all advancing, hurling javelins and then retreating to rearm a second line protecting them from pursuit. Each volley saw men die all along Caesar's line and all they could do was brace and take the hit each time, for they had already seen what happened when they tried to take the fight back to the enemy.

Unable to think of a solution, Fronto turned to the general. 'Caesar, do something!'

But Caesar seemed stunned by the simplicity of their impending defeat. Fronto's attention strayed at the sound of more calls going out among the enemy, and his spirits sank even further as he saw fresh waves of enemy infantry and African horse, just like the ones they faced here, having advanced from the enemy rear, hurtling around the flanks to envelop them. He watched in despair as the surviving Caesarian cavalry raced away to reform somewhere just out of reach. Labienus had planned his attack well, and his cavalry did not race after Galronus' men, content to drive them from the field and then join the forces encircling Caesar's army, which is what they proceeded to do.

Caesar turned, his drawn face pale, to see the fresh enemy forces falling in behind them.

'General,' Fronto shouted desperately, willing the old man to do something other than watch his army be crushed. Caesar turned and locked gazes with Fronto and in that moment something passed between them. In some indefinable way the general seemed to take strength from his old friend, and straightened. 'We will not be cut down yet.' He beckoned to the musicians and standard bearers. 'Give the order. Every second cohort turns about-face and moves to the rear of the next. We compact the lines to half the width, but double the depth and facing both ways, nobody with their back to the enemy.'

The musicians began to blow their unit calls and the signifers waved their standards as Caesar stepped his horse closer to Fronto.

'That won't win us the day, sir,' Fronto said.

'No, but it buys us valuable time to pull off something clever.' His voice dropped to a low level. 'The problem is that I have nothing. I cannot see a way to pull out of this. How's that mind of yours, Fronto? Any clever plans hatching?'

Fronto shook his head. 'Nothing leaps to mind. We can't advance as they cut us down when we do, but staying still is just taking its toll in attrition. The time to run was before we were surrounded,' he added with a hint of bitter recrimination.

'Think, then, for only you or I can save something of this day.'

Fronto wracked his brains for any idea as the Caesarian force redeployed even under attack, presenting a front to both sides, the ends of the lines having been turned to form an extended rectangle of shields. They were still being steadily picked off with a constant barrage of javelins, but at least they could hold for a while. The Caesarian archers were at the centre and of little use, the cavalry regrouped away from the field. The infantry could do nothing but hold.

He hardly noticed that the enemy assault had stopped until the reason became clear. As the last wave of javelin-hurling riders pulled back to rearm yet again, a figure emerged from the enemy lines and rode out into the dusty ground between the two armies. Fronto glared at the figure of Titus Labienus.

The man wore the same uniform he'd done in Gaul a decade earlier, with a general's crimson belt knotted about his middle. His plumed helmet gleamed and he wore a red cloak just like Caesar's, his own horse black as pitch. Fronto found himself gripping his Nemesis figurine on the thong about his neck and casting up prayers that something horrible happen to the man. Labienus had been as close a friend as Fronto had found in the general's staff, and the two had shared a mutual respect. To now face the man in battle, let alone be outwitted by him, left a truly sour taste in Fronto's mouth.

Labienus swept his helmet from his head and shook his hair free in the breeze as he turned, keeping himself just outside pilum range of the Caesarian force, and began to ride along the line.

'What gleaming, excellent recruits you've drawn to your despotic cause, Caesar,' the enemy commander spat viciously. 'And you men, freshly drawn from green fields in Italia, are you still enamoured with the glorious would-be king who pays you? Who has walked you into the mouth of Cerberus? Your master has made fools of you, and now he will make corpses of you. You have my sympathy.'

A sullen silence fell across the landscape. Fronto glanced at Caesar, and noted the vein bulging on the general's temple. Caesar was on the verge of explosion, and Fronto could quite understand, though a reaction to this childish tirade from the general would do more harm than good, and Fronto willed his commander to keep his mouth shut.

All along the Caesarian lines, men wavered. Fronto could imagine what was going through their minds, for every man here had to know they were trapped and outnumbered. If something didn't happen soon, morale might just snap entirely. There was even a very real possibility that men might just start to change sides and defect to Labienus. Fronto drew a deep breath to bellow something carefully disparaging, but before he could do so, a voice rang out from along the front lines.

'Up your arse, Labienus. I'm no raw recruit, but a veteran of the Fifth Alaudae. I was at Gergovia while you were poncing around in the north.'

The enemy commander paused, frowning, and turned to the man who'd addressed him from Caesar's lines.

'I don't see the standard of the Fifth here?'

'I'll give you a fucking standard,' bellowed the voice and Fronto watched, stunned, as a heavy pilum suddenly arced out from the line. His eyes widened further as the missile crossed a distance deemed safe from pila and plunged into the side of Labienus' gleaming black horse. The beast reared, screaming, and Labienus fought for control, forced to throw himself clear as the animal collapsed in order to avoid being crushed beneath it. Fronto marvelled as their enemy picked himself up from the dirt, snarling furiously, his armour scuffed, his general's knot undone and lost and his crimson cloak torn and dusty.

'There's your fucking standard,' laughed the legionary from the Fifth. 'Now piss off.'

All along the lines Caesar's men roared with derisive laughter as Labienus, his cheeks reddening, turned to limp away from the scene. Several other pila clattered into the dust behind him, though no other legionary seemed to be able to call upon such impressive strength, and none of them came near the humiliated general.

As he disappeared into the enemy ranks, Labienus raised and dropped his hand.

'Brace,' bellowed Fronto, as the action began once more, a fresh wave of African javelineers racing forward to cast their weapons in a fresh shower of death. The strange incident with the veteran had given the men the heart to remain and not to break and run, but now that the continual pressure of the enemy attack had resumed, still with no identifiable way out, spirits began to sink almost immediately.

'I'm out of ideas,' he said with a sigh, the general nodding his agreement.

'Might I cast a denarius into the pot,' asked a third voice, and the two men turned to see Salvius Cursor standing with a gleaming blade out. The praetorian guardsmen had been close to Caesar at all times at the rear, and had thus far avoided the fight, and Fronto could only imagine how much not being involved in the bloodshed must be getting at Salvius.

'You have an idea?' Caesar asked with curiosity, his voice almost bordering on disbelief. The former tribune had a number of useful qualities but tactical shrewdness was not one that either of the commanders would have readily named.

'Not as such,' admitted Salvius. 'More an observation.'

'Go on,' the general urged him.

'Well if we stay here we all die, yes?'

'That's about the long and the short of it,' Fronto agreed.

'Then why are we staying?'

'You saw what happened when our front line ran after them.'

'But at least they did something. Standing here and waiting to die seems a little stupid to me.'

Fronto and Caesar looked at one another, brows beetling. 'It's a persuasive argument,' the general noted. Fronto chewed his lip. 'So you say we charge them?' Fronto added.

'Better than standing still and waiting for a javelin.'

Again the two senior officers shared a look. 'It would certainly come as a surprise to them after all this. And if we hit them hard enough and fast enough we might break through.'

Caesar nodded. 'And we begin with a shower of arrows and pila to break their rhythm.'

Fronto turned to Salvius. 'Care to lead the charge, it being your moment of tactical genius?'

Salvius Cursor grinned a nasty grin and pushed his way forward into the ranks of the cohorts facing the way they had come, back towards Ruspina. The general's orders were swiftly relayed by mouth to avoid the enemy identifying the calls and anticipating their moves. Once every officer in every cohort was aware of the details, and word of such was returned to the commanders at the centre, Caesar looked at his fellow officer and nodded.

Fronto raised and lowered his hand. At the signal, the rear ranks of the cohorts passed their pila forward so that the front lines were ready, and after a count of fifteen Fronto repeated his gesture. Now it would all roll ahead without the need for further commands, each act triggering the next, every man knowing when to move.

At that second signal the rear three ranks, who had passed their pila forward just now, dropped to a crouch, huddling into their shields, clearing the view for the two centuries of archers, who rose in a line from the heart of the army, arrows nocked and strings tight ready, and released in a slithering volley.

Even as the archers shouldered their bows and the three rear ranks rose once more, Fronto heard Salvius and then half a heartbeat later the centurions along the front bellow their orders and more than a thousand pila rose to join the arrow cloud, though on a lower trajectory.

The enemy had become careless at the lack of Caesarian response and had gradually come closer and closer with each wave of attacks, and that was now their undoing. Fronto watched with immense satisfaction as near two thousand missiles in two distinct layers arced out from the army and ploughed into the African cavalry and infantry that were making their next sortie for thrown javelins. The effect was devastating, and men were pinned and impaled all along the enemy line.

They had no time for those men to recover, for the legions of Caesar were on the move already. Even as the missiles were released, the infantry were running, maintaining a tight line. On the far side, facing inland over the corpse of Labienus' horse, the cohorts there had launched their own volley of pila simultaneously, which had temporarily plunged the African javelineers into chaos as they tried to rally and pull back. It had bought them time.

As the lead cohorts under Salvius' bloodthirsty command plunged into the confused mass of Labienus' Africans, the rear ranks moved off at a run in pursuit. Caesar and the officers rode in their wake, surrounded by praetorians, with the archers and signallers and musicians all at a run. Behind them, in a carefully choreographed move, the remaining cohorts used the moments they had bought with their pila to turn and run off, forming the rear of the army now.

Fronto had no chance to take part in the conflict itself, trapped somewhere in the midst of the mass, but being on horseback he was able to see much of it. Salvius' unexpected and ferocious attack had achieved what he'd planned and punched deep into the lines of the lightly armed men surrounding them. At this range, no longer at the mercy of their javelins, the legionaries stabbed and hacked a swathe through the enemy, forging a blood-slicked path to freedom. There was a heart-stopping moment as the front ranks seemed to fan out a little, and Fronto wondered whether Salvius had made the unilateral decision to turn this carefully orchestrated flight into a full-on attack, but his fears seemed to be unfounded as the army pulled back into good order a moment later and continued to push through.

Here and there javelins arced out across the cohorts from the enemy they were passing through and more than once Fronto was forced to drive his horse out of the way of one of them, or lurch in the saddle to avoid being skewered. Then, finally, they were through. The front ranks burst free of the encircling Africans and they were out in the open with nothing between them and Ruspina.

Salvius had the nous not to stop once they were free of the enemy, and continued to move at speed. As the centre of the Caesarian force burst free of their enemies and passed into the open, Fronto spotted the remains of Galronus' horse angling in from a stand of trees nearby and making for the fleeing army. He pointed this out to Caesar and, with difficulty, they and a small squad of praetorian riders worked their way out of the mass and made to intercept the cavalry.

To Fronto's immense relief the figure of Galronus sat high in the saddle of the lead horse, and the Remi noble slowed as he reached the two commanders. Fronto had expected a look of relief and his blood chilled at the look of concern on his friend's face.

'What is it?'

'Enemy reinforcements,' Galronus said, pointing off to the north. 'Another thousand or more horse and several thousand infantry almost upon us. I don't know who they are but they're neither my countrymen nor Africans like these, though they're wearing bronze and riding local horses.'

'Did you see a flag?'

'Red, with a golden horse I think, though it was hard to be sure at such a distance.'

'Juba,' Caesar said irritably. 'He's supposed to be pinned down in the west with other troubles. We cannot afford to face Juba in addition to Cato's forces.'

Fronto shook his head. 'Juba does not go to war without his elephants, or so it's said. They may be Numidians, but there are only a few of them. On loan to Scipio, perhaps?'

'Whatever the case, we cannot afford to face them now.'

They were interrupted by the sound of fresh fighting, and all three officers rose in the saddle and turned to look back. The rear ranks of the retreating force were being harried by Labienus' men, for the enemy general had largely managed to pull his army back into order, and part of it was already pressing Caesar's retreating men in waves.

'We need to get back to the camp where we have ditches and ramparts and artillery,' Fronto said, urgently.

'These men will chase us all the way,' Galronus pointed out, 'and you will lose many soldiers over three miles of retreat. Also, those Numidians will be on us in the next half mile, which will increase their force by a large number.'

'Can we manage a mile and a half at double pace?' Fronto said, thoughtfully.

'It will tire the men, but minimise the damage from pursuit,' Caesar mused. 'It will push the men to the edge of their strength. Why?'

'Because about halfway back there was that river with a nice easy ford. It's very hard to be completely enclosed at a place like that. It we can get to the ford, we can have another go at them without having to watch our backs. Something we've seen twice so far is how readily these locals break at an unexpected and ferocious charge. Galronus did it at Hadrumetum and Salvius did it just now. If we can throw them into enough panic, we might be able to leave them behind and reach Ruspina safely.'

It was readily agreed as the only viable plan, and the orders were given a moment later. With a roar, the men of Caesar's cohorts began to run once more. How long they could keep up such a thing was the only worry, having already marched three miles and fought a desperate battle beforehand. Fronto and the officers rode at a steady pace with the men, the former occasionally dropping back to check on the rear. The army was continually under pressure from the enemy, but the attacks were now only coming from javelin-bearing riders, as the runners could not retreat and resupply with javelins fast enough to keep up.

The run went on. In truth it could not have lasted more than a quarter of an hour, but it felt like half a day to the retreating Caesarians. Fronto had rarely felt such relief as he did when word came back that they'd reached the river. As the lead elements crossed the ford the cohorts shifted slightly, so that the men of the Fifth, the army's most veteran legion, took the rear position alone. Fronto, determined this time to be part of it, was far from surprised when Salvius Cursor turned up next to him in the press.

The army had naturally slowed, passing into the bottle-neck, the rear coming under increasing pressure. The enemy's African cavalry raced back to the lines that followed on at some distance for a resupply of javelins while the Gallic riders continued to harry the ranks of legionaries, who were retreating backwards, presenting shields to the enemy as the army slowly crossed the river.

'Ready, men of the Fifth?' Fronto asked.

A roar greeted this, and he and Salvius smiled and took a deep breath. The orders had been disseminated among the men as they approached the crossing and every man knew what they had to do. At a blown whistle, the retreating Fifth stopped dead, allowing their compatriots to continue across, while they immediately reversed their direction, racing at the enemy in a tightly controlled charge, keeping their ranks as close as possible at such speed. The two officers remained mounted to one side but kept their horses' speed the same as the legionaries.

After a mile and a half of confident action for the enemy horse, continually chipping away at the retreating army, this sudden turnabout had the desired effect. The Gallic cavalry, wheeling for another charge suddenly instead found their prey running at them. While conflicting orders rang out among them, Fronto and Salvius and the Fifth hit them at speed, the legionaries charging in between the horses. Fronto and Salvius chopped and slashed this way and that, making sure to stay at the periphery, careful to avoid being mistaken for the enemy in the press, for the Fifth had adopted a horrible tactic of the Germanic tribes. Once among the cavalry they ignored the riders above and risked trampling as they ducked under the horses and ripped out their bellies with their swords. All across the enemy beasts cried out in agony, and riders yelled in panic as their steeds bucked or fell.

It was over in a matter of heartbeats, the survivors of Labienus' Gallic cavalry racing away back to the rest of their force, fleeing this nightmare attack and leaving behind scores of writhing animals and downed men. Fronto hauled Bucephalus to a halt and surveyed the damage. Among the fallen cavalry lay a hundred or so legionaries, which was appalling, but in truth small change when compared to the men they had lost back at the battlefield.

The African riders, on their way for another attack, were met instead by the fleeing Gauls and the panic infected the second unit, turning them and putting them similarly to flight. Fronto watched as the enemy horse disappeared into a dust cloud, fleeing to join the infantry. That was it. They'd bought enough time to retreat to Ruspina. They'd lost about a third of their foraging force, some three thousand men in a few short hours, but at least the rest would survive.

CHAPTER SEVEN

Ruspina, 8th January 46 BC

Fronto urged Bucephalus on from the camp's north gate, heading for the harbour. All around him work continued, turning Ruspina into a veritable fortress. The camp itself had been further fortified and was being augmented every hour, changing it from a rough temporary base into a stronghold capable of housing a dozen legions, should so many men become available. The ditch was deep and difficult, the approaches across it carefully covered with enfilade arcs by the artillery pieces mounted regularly along the defences, which were now of good timber and with regular towers and a wide fighting platform.

To strengthen the system overall, an extra ditch and rampart had been run from the fort to the shore, and in the other direction into the edge of the salt pans, effectively walling off the entire peninsula. Meanwhile, Saserna had been at work improving the defences of the town of Ruspina and carrying a similar extra rampart and ditch down to the sea, enclosing all the harbour facilities and protecting any landing sites from sea attack.

In just four days Ruspina had been fortified against attack, for Labienus had set up his camp close to the battlefield, less than three miles from Ruspina, and local rumour had it that other smaller rebel forces from across the region were flocking to his banner as a central rallying point against Caesar's invasion. Ruspina needed to be secure.

As he rode, he took in the scene to the north of the camp. A massive open-air workshop filled the parched ground, expert legionaries and local craftsmen on retainer working together to manufacture javelins, pila, arrows and scorpion bolts by the score. A little further on, he passed the training ground, where entirely new units loosed inexpert arrows or wildly cast javelins. Gaulish and Rhodian sailors and marines had been gathered into land units, forming light skirmishing infantry to bolster the legionaries and cavalry, for Caesar had learned a new trick from Labienus in a moment of bitter education. These units would be interspersed with Caesar's other forces so that should Labienus try the same strategy again, the Caesarian army could give as good as it got. Beyond the new units, Caesar's archers practiced, honing their skills. Cretans and Illyrians, Iturians and Syrians, all imagining Labienus' face on their targets. The next time the armies met, everyone was determined it would be a much more equal match and that it would end with Labienus lying stricken in the sand, rather than his horse.

On the bright side, supplies had started to come in by ship in small quantities, and at least the half-ration restriction had been lifted and there was sufficient food to keep the army going for a week or more. Past the town gate he rode, and towards the harbour where he could see the empty jetties waiting as most of the Caesarian fleet wallowed at anchor out to sea. As the report had indicated, coming to him at his tent from a breathless courier, the ships limping into port were not in the best of conditions.

Three fat-bottomed cargo vessels drifted listlessly between the harbour's moles and towards the waiting jetties. They sat low in the water, speaking eloquently of how well-loaded they were with supplies, and that should be an engaging and heart-warming sight, were it not for the difference between what had arrived and what had been expected. These vessels, which had set out for the granaries of Agrigentum in Sicilia four days ago, had been seven in number then, and with two warships for an escort. Three had returned, with a single trireme running alongside, and all four vessels showed signs of damage from both fire and artillery, the lead transport actually sporting a hastily-patched hole near the prow where a ram had managed a glancing blow.

Heart in his mouth, Fronto rode into the port and made for the small knot of mounted men where Caesar, his face grave, sat awaiting the ships' arrival. He joined the general and sat wordlessly as the battered ships put in at the jetties and the work of unloading the supplies began. The warship also put in and ran out its ramp, a small group of officers descending and marching over to the waiting general, their leader coming to a halt with a sharp salute.

'Caesar, it is with a heady combination of regret and relief that I can report to you the delivery of three ships of grain.'

The general looked at the tribune who had commanded the military escort and who winced as he finished speaking, and replied evenly. 'I take it we can safely assume that the other ships are not still on the way from Agrigentum?'

The tribune shifted uncomfortably. 'At first light today, half way across the bay, we were set upon by a small fleet of triremes. We had narrowly avoided engagement with a similar flotilla the day before, and I fear distant shapes we saw only an hour ago mark a third such group. It would appear that the rebel commanders have split their fleet into small hunting packs and are searching for our supply ships. We were hopelessly outnumbered this morning, and had we attempted to fight them all ships would have been lost. I was forced to make the unpleasant decision to flee here with as many ships as could escape their clutches.'

Caesar nodded, his expression unchanged. 'Fear not, tribune, you are to be commended for your choice. It could not have been easily made, I know, but it was the correct decision. Better we have three cargoes of grain secure here than seven at the bottom of the sea. Have your men fall out and once the unloading is complete, all your troops and sailors can take a full day of furlough to rest, and with a double wine ration. Following that the sailors will need to begin repairs on their vessels. Thank you, Tribune.'

The man saluted wearily and turned to distribute orders among his men, and Caesar leaned closer to Fronto in the saddle. 'I think we need to discuss matters. Find Plancus and meet me in the headquarters.'

Fronto nodded and turned, riding back the way he'd come. Plancus, he knew, would be in his own tent and fretting over plans, maps and lists. The man had been doing so in most of his free time since they'd landed in Africa, as if a solution to their defensive position would leap off a page and into his brain. Thus far it had failed to do so, and Caesar's invasion had turned into little more than an anticipated siege.

Back past the town, the training grounds and the open-air workshop he rode, entering the huge camp once again and making for the cluster of officers' accommodation at the centre. Plancus' tent was clearly occupied, one of Caesar's praetorians standing outside on guard. Fronto dismounted, tied Bucephalus to the rail nearby and waited while the guard announced him, and then entered as invited.

Plancus sat at his desk with a map of the region covered in small counters of coloured stone, each painted with numbers, a large pile of wax tablets to one side, scribbled parchments to the other.

'Fronto?'

'Lucius. Half a grain shipment just arrived, having been battered by Cato's fleets out in the bay. Caesar wants to see us.'

'Good,' Plancus said, rising wearily from his seat and scrubbing his hands through his thinning hair before knuckling tired eyes and stretching. 'Not that half the fleet was sunk, I mean. I've had the latest scouting reports in, so now is a good time to report.' Fronto nodded, accompanying his fellow officer out of the tent and deciding to leave

Bucephalus here for now, since he seemed content enough, and Caesar's tent was but a few paces away.

Small detachments of cavalry had spent the last four days in an almost constant round of patrols, roving everywhere they could, repeatedly coming as close as they dare to Labienus' camp, to glean the latest intelligence. With the scouts had gone native translators, for while they sought information from locals, a good source of critical intelligence, in the backwaters there were still stubborn communities who favoured ancient Punic or nomad languages over Latin. Often the scouting missions ended in a brief scuffle with some unit of Labienus' scouts or pickets and were forced to withdraw at speed. Every time Galronus returned to camp, Fronto heaved a sigh of relief, and the man was out there right now, somewhere close to the enemy forces.

The two officers strode a few tents across and reached the headquarters just as Caesar was dismounting, Salvius Cursor at his heel and riders falling into guard positions while others took away their horses for stabling. Caesar inclined his head in greeting at Plancus and slipped into his command tent, the two officers and the praetorian commander following him in.

Inside, the general sank into his campaign chair and gestured for the others to sit also.

'Such news of the attacks on our transports is grave,' he said with a sigh, ' though I suppose it was only a matter of time before enemy shipping started to make things inconvenient, and I sense Cato's decision making behind this. Scipio is not imaginative enough. He would keep his fleet together and strong and use it to defend the coast. Cato has created packs of sharks to hunt our wallowing heavy fish. I would dearly love to do something similar in response, but I can spare too few ships for that. All our transports and escorts are in constant use. Vatinius is out there somewhere with a small fleet and we can only hope he is making good account for himself. We shall simply have to combine our supply fleets to create fewer but larger ones, accompanied by a stronger military contingent, which will hopefully be adequate protection from these hunters.

Plancus scratched his neck in thought. 'I think there is a better solution, General. I've been perusing the maps, and it occurs to me that these enemy fleets cannot simply roam the sea with impunity. Like all sensible sailors, especially at this time of year, they need to stay close to the coast and to put in to shore repeatedly. Our best decision may be to station small fleets of warships at various critical positions along our supply routes. There are several points in particular where enemy ships will need to pass in order to intercept our transports. Take the escorts away from the cargo ships and bolster them to form attack patrols of our own, covering the most likely and critical of all places and we should be able to intercept the vast majority of their packs before they come anywhere near the fleets.'

Fronto looked at the man with a cocked eyebrow. Years ago in Gaul, as a fresh-faced young politician seeking military fame, Plancus had been a feeble tactician. Years of navigating the treacherous currents of Roman politics seemed to have sharpened his mind immeasurably. This notion alone was worth all those hours the man had spent in his tent, pensive, at his desk.

Caesar seemed to be of a similar mind, for he smiled for the first time that day. 'A capital idea, Lucius. Proactive and ingenious. See that it is done. This is your command.'

'Sir, we've also had the latest round of reports from the scouts and the news is, for the first time, a blessing as well as a curse.'

'Oh?'

'It now seems clear that the force of which we have been hearing rumours for two days, closing from the west, is that of Scipio. He makes to join with Labienus and form a sizeable army to field against us.'

'This is unfortunate,' the general responded, 'though far from unexpected. Indeed, I am somewhat grateful that it has taken this long for him to show up, and that he has granted us sufficient time to dig in at Ruspina.'

'As I said, though, sir, not all the tidings are bad. We have now had reports, corroborated by other sources, that the army Scipio brings consists of eight legions and some three thousand cavalry, a considerably smaller force than we feared.'

Caesar let out an explosive breath. 'Smaller by two legions and many auxilia. This is excellent news. I wonder whether initial reports were inflated or whether Scipio has been forced to leave some of his men in garrisons. Whatever the case, it works in our favour. Very well, we should have a few more days before there is any movement from the enemy. I am determined to continue consolidating our position. What news of the smithies?'

Fronto leaned forward in his chair. 'We've set up a separate compound near the water to the north of the camp. We have a dozen smithies up and running already and another half dozen in the works. We're concentrating at the moment on producing tips for arrows, bolts and javelins for the new units, and once the new ones are up we'll be on to creating sling bullets for the units of slingers that arrived yesterday.'

'Can they not just use stones?' Salvius put in.

'We looked into it, but the local stone is not suitable for shaping ammunition. It's soft and crumbly sandstone. For every stone that was shaped adequately for use five cracked and shattered. It will be more efficient to have them forged. That being said I still have patrols scouring all the beaches around the town and camp for good pebbles, so they will form part of the ammunition.'

'Unless they have fallen foul of more of Cato's hunting packs,' Caesar said, changing the subject, 'then we should receive six ships of good timber from Syracusae before the end of tomorrow. We have exhausted the poor supplies in this region, but with fresh supplies we can begin to build new artillery and siege weapons. By the time our army is strong enough to break "fortress Africa" I want adequate supplies and support to do so. If Scipio will oblige us by granting us adequate time, we can be ready for him. I have put the word out via traders to the local towns that I am willing to pay up to triple the going price for grain. Even without local supplies I am confident that greed will work in our favour.'

'Will Scipio wait for us to move, I wonder,' Fronto mused, 'or will he commit to a siege at Ruspina. He is unimaginative enough to do the former, which would give us the time we need, but he is also impulsive enough for the latter. Of course, I'm just thinking aloud, for we'll not know what he plans until he does it.'

The meeting was interrupted by a rap at the doorframe and Caesar looked up. 'Come.'

A soldier, sweating and out of breath, appeared in the doorway with a sharp salute. 'Sir, I beg to report a large force approaching from the southwest, sir.'

'Details man. Who are they?'

'Sir, it seems a little confused. We can see enemy standards among the unit, which is both cavalry and infantry and thousands strong, but one of our cavalry patrols seems to be at the front.'

Caesar frowned and cast a look about the other officers, who shrugged. 'Best go check it out,' Fronto said, pulling himself up from the chair. The rest followed suit as Caesar dismissed the messenger and adjusted the hang of his tunic, pteruges and cloak. 'Look your best gentlemen. I have no idea who this is, but let's make Rome proud regardless.'

The small group of officers emerged from the command tent and the praetorians were already mounted and waiting, holding Caesar's, Plancus', and Salvius' horses. Fronto walked over to Plancus' tent and pulled himself up into

Bucephalus' saddle, walking the mount to join the others as they angled away to the south gate of the camp. As they approached, they could see how the forces of legionaries had gathered there to observe the approaching force.

'Do we meet them at the gate?' Fronto muttered.

'A show of confidence,' Caesar replied. 'We meet them in the open.' Then to the guard centurion. 'Open the gate.'

They paused as the heavy timber leaves were drawn inwards and the dusty landscape of Africa awaited them without, and then, at Caesar's gesture, the group of four officers and a dozen praetorian riders walked their horses out of the protection of the ramparts. As they emerged into the open, Salvius Cursor made an unhappy grunting sound.

'Something wrong?' Fronto asked.

'It goes against everything I'm supposed to do. It's my job and that of my men to keep you safe, Caesar. How can we effectively do that if you put yourself in such danger?'

The general waved away his concerns. 'If our cavalry are leading the force, then I am hopeful that this is good news. I am also confident that if anything untoward should happen you and your men are competent enough to see us back to the safety of the camp.'

'Oh good,' grunted Salvius. 'Over-confidence. Always a winner.'

Fronto turned his attention to the approaching force. Now that they were coming closer the ever-present dust cloud no longer obscured the details. As the messenger had noted, a unit of Caesarian horse, bearing the Taurus emblem flag of the general, led the force, and Fronto was relieved to see at the head of that group of thirty-some riders the figure of Galronus sitting tall in the saddle. That clinched it for Fronto. If there were any danger, Galronus would not look so satisfied and confident.

Behind the scouts came a small group of officers, one bedecked in a general's uniform, the rest tribunes and prefects. Behind them were perhaps three cohorts of legionaries, then several of auxilia, both infantry and archers, with Gallic or German horsemen riding on the wings. All in all perhaps two and a half to three thousand men.

As they neared, Galronus gave them a cheeky half-wave, half-salute and his riders peeled off to either side, moving ahead and then coming to a halt alongside Caesar's party and turning to face the other new arrivals. Salvius Cursor looked happier at the increase in numbers, and cast a curious look at Galronus, who had joined the general and his officers. The column came to a halt and the unknown commander stepped his horse out ahead, alongside Galronus and facing Caesar, where he saluted. The general returned the gesture and waited expectantly.

'It is my honour to present to you, Proconsul, a force of three veteran legionary cohorts, six cohorts of varying long-service auxilia and riders of the Boii and the Bellovaci. All are ready to take the oath to you and to the republic, sir. I, Vibius Pacideius Secundus, and my officers are at your service.'

Caesar gave the man a warm smile. 'It is good to meet you, commander. Your illustrious name, and that of your brother, are well known to me. Had you been in Rome and not Africa, I would have sought you for my staff before we sailed, be assured of this.'

The man bowed his head at the compliment, and Caesar turned to Plancus. 'Find a place in the camp for our new friends, inform the camp prefect of their arrival, and then meet me once more at my tent.'

He then turned back to Pacideius. 'If you would be so kind as to join me in the command tent? I'm certain your story will be a most engaging one.'

Fronto fell in with the others as Caesar led the group back towards the camp while Plancus took the other officers and discussed accommodation requirements with the new arrivals.

Back into the camp and up to the cluster of command tents they rode in polite silence. Fronto could sense how urgently the general wanted to quiz the commander, but out in the open surrounded by the ears of all and sundry was no place to do so. They reached the command tent and gave over their reins to the praetorians, who led the horses away and fell into position on guard once more. Inside, Caesar motioned for all to be seated, and Fronto, Salvius and Galronus each took a place and waited patiently for Pacideius, who slipped into a central seat opposite the general.

'I have much to report, Proconsul.'

'Of that I am certain, but first I would appreciate it if you could enlighten us as to your motives for bringing this force and its officers to Ruspina?'

The officer nodded in a business-like fashion. 'As you can perhaps imagine, the strength of conviction among your opponents varies somewhat, and occasional frank discussions have led to a number of rifts. It has become increasingly clear to a number of us recently that while our seniors continue to claim the moral high ground of being good sons of the republic, the evidence is beginning to suggest otherwise. You are here with dictatorial powers granted by the legitimate senate, backed by an army manned and supplied in the republic and with a number of ex consuls and ex praetors on your staff.'

'Cato likes to occupy the moral high ground,' Caesar murmured, 'for it is the closest he will ever come to commanding in the field.'

'The upper echelons are a large factor in our decision, General,' Pacideius agreed. 'I was, and always have been, a client of Pompey's and when this war started, my brother and I naturally answered his call. And in truth if the great man still lived, I would still be beneath his standard. But I did not answer that call to run errands for Cato or command provincials for Scipio and Labienus. *Senatus Populusque*

Romanus is the oath we took, but we seem instead to be serving Cato and the people of Utica.'

Caesar nodded. 'Then be welcome to my staff. Loyal sons of Rome are more than welcome here and no stigma will be attached for your former affiliation. Pompey *was* a great man. He has been my son in law and a friend in times past.'

'The breaking point for me occurred four days ago,' Pacideius said, almost conversationally. 'On that brutal field out there,' he added, pointing back towards the tent door. 'I was at the rear of one wing, my brother at the other. There we were dressed like Roman officers of old, but all the men I was commanding were recently conscripted desert dwellers from the south and riders from southern Numidia. I don't think I'd be far wrong in suggesting that less than one man in ten I commanded had been born within the republic. And across the field the men we were facing were Romans. Legionaries. I think I'd had enough even then. I'm sick of serving in an army of ego-driven rebels and barbaroi. As far as I'm concerned our legitimacy ended with Pompey.'

'I have heard rumour that Scipio's army is far from legion quality,' Caesar said carefully.

'Not just Scipio, Proconsul. Ever since Curio was defeated using strange African tactics the commanders here have been becoming more and more influenced by native methods. Labienus has been waiting to try this tactic for some time. He will be crowing that it worked. Had Petreius arrived earlier, he may have taken over as senior commander, I think, but he was too late.'

Fronto leaned in. 'That reserve force that joined was commanded by Petreius?'

Pacideius nodded. 'He was one of many expected to arrive and bolster our forces. Unlucky for him, though. Your lunatic German charge at the ford turned the tide. Petreius himself was badly wounded. His horse was gutted beneath him and someone got a lucky blow in his side as he fell. The medicus says he'll live, but it was no light wound, and he may have to sit out the rest of the war.'

'Good,' replied Fronto with feeling, remembering the man from Hispania and the battle of Ilerda. A man who had been a thorn in their side during that campaign and who should never have been given clemency only to run back to his friends and rebel once more.

'He was one of the many wounded Labienus sent back to Hadrumetum for convalescence. Scipio is under the impression that your army consists largely of raw recruits freshly drafted, and that the veterans upon whom you can call are but one step from mutiny. He believes that a few hefty defeats in the field will demoralise your men sufficiently to break the entire army's will and leave you powerless.'

'He is shrewder than I gave him credit for,' Caesar admitted. 'We are in not quite such a poor situation as that, but it holds echoes of fact, for certain.'

'His grand plan, from what I understand, is to draft in sufficient poor auxiliaries and pseudo-legions to swamp you with men and exhaust you.'

Fronto cleared his throat again. 'We saw a standard of Juba of Numidia. Is he fielding his army too?'

Pacideius shook his head. 'Much as I'm sure he would like to, border troubles keep the king busy in his own kingdom, but he had agreements in place with Cato. He came briefly, and had quite an army, but took them with him and withdrew when fresh word of troubles at home reached him. At one point there were a hundred and twenty elephants with us, which I can tell you means a lot more men on dung duty than with just cavalry. He's left thirty of them with Scipio, and two small regiments as per his agreements.'

'A mere thirty elephants,' Fronto noted ironically. 'Best get some greased pigs ready.'

'They will only be fielded in a major battle. Too much effort for a minor skirmish,' Pacideius said dismissively.

Caesar steepled his fingers. 'Do you think they will besiege Ruspina or wait for an opportunity to fight us properly, in the open.'

'I doubt Scipio will wish to commit to a siege,' Pacideius replied. 'His army is populated by drafted natives and Gallic and Numidian cavalry with very few veterans from home. These men have their uses in the field but they have no experience or skill in siegecraft. I believe Scipio will think as Labienus does, that the only answer is to provoke you into meeting them in the field. Labienus believes that you can be brought out of Ruspina by steady starvation. It *is* a siege of sorts, in truth. The fleet prowls the sea searching for and sinking any ships carrying you supplies, while the army camps a few short miles away, cutting you off from forage.'

'It is a surprisingly sound tactic,' Caesar admitted, 'for if we cannot secure sufficient supplies we will need to leave our secure position to hunt for them.'

Plancus rubbed his chin. 'A centurion with the Twenty Ninth has been experimenting with seaweed, sir.'

Every pair of eyes, frowns hanging over them, turned to him.

'What?'

Plancus smiled weirdly. 'Just an interesting thing I heard. Apparently numerous of the local varieties are edible, and some are surprisingly nutritious. A local farmer told some of the men, and they've been cleaning it with fresh water, then drying it and adding it to meals to bulk them up. Apparently it's not bad.'

Caesar and Fronto shared a look, and the latter burst out laughing. 'Bless you Plancus for bringing much needed levity to a dark hour,' Caesar smiled at the man and then changed in a heartbeat, all business once more. 'Our supplies and fleet fail and falter, the men I sent to secure support do not return. I find it increasingly difficult to rely upon help coming from further afield. Plancus, I have a mission for you. Put your wits and your oratory to the test. Take a fast ship from the harbour and race for Lilybaeum. Find Postumus and Governor Alienus and tell them that time is up. I need whatever ships and men remain on Sicilia, and I need them now. I don't care how you do it, but I give you five days. That's two to get there, two to get back, and one to load every ship and secure every soldier on the island. Can you do this for me?'

Plancus nodded thoughtfully. 'With Neptune's will, yes, General. One fast ship should be able to escape any lurking hunters out there.'

'Very well,' Caesar said. 'There is much to do, and with the ever-present threat of Scipio hanging over us. Let us be about our tasks. Pacideius, I shall have appropriate quarters arranged for you close by.'

Fronto rose with the others and fell in beside Pacideius as they left the tent. 'Until then, my friend Galronus and I were planning on an hour or two's recovery with a little wine if you'd care to join us?'

The other officer smiled wearily. 'I fear I must find a bath first, but then I would be happy to join you.'

'There's a good public bath in the town, or if you're not fussy the soldiers have made a small lagoon bath down near the sea, but you'll get a little salty and have to sluice down with fresh water after.'

Pacideius chuckled . 'My brother advocates a sea swim, though I prefer good clean indoor water.'

Fronto frowned. 'Your brother did not come with you?'

The man's face darkened. 'We do not share beliefs entirely. He remains at Labienus' side, sadly. I am not looking forward to facing him on the field of battle.'

Fronto nodded soberly. 'Gods willing this season will see the war ended. I've had too many years now of fighting against men I've served alongside. Until later.'

'Until later.'

CHAPTER EIGHT

Ruspina, 14th January 46 BC

T he turma of cavalry emerged from the olive grove onto the bank of the narrow stream, one of the better viewpoints in the area, from where, on a good day, you could just see the low shape of Scipio's camp on the horizon. The thirty-two riders gathered in a knot at the top of the bank behind Galronus and looked across the low, wide stream bed with the shallow sparkling river running along merrily.

Low murmurs broke out among the men in his own language and Galronus blocked them out as he scanned the horizon. These were good men, his best men, for they were Remi like him, each and every one, half a dozen of them even from his home oppidum. He had taken to selecting the Remi from this ala as his favoured scouts, and they had begun to treat him as theirs.

'Can you see anything?'

The commander turned to find his deputy, Samaconius, sitting confidently just behind him, both hands gripping the reins on his saddle horns, shield on his left arm as if for battle. He shook his head. 'Not yet, but they're close.'

It had been a fairly standard outing so far. From the camp at Ruspina they had ridden a mile west towards Hadrumetum, encountering nothing more than locals and farmers, and had then turned inland. Two miles they had ridden into the dusty interior, using the landmarks that had been noted by Caesarian riders over recent days, and which had become geographical markers for patrols. Finally, they had turned east as the drizzle began and men grumbled about returning to camp, and passed across in front of the enemy lines at a distance of around a mile.

At the river they had intended to cross using a ford just a little downstream where the banks were gentle, and then head back to Ruspina in time for a rest and a bite to eat at noon, but as they'd approached the bank they had heard the tell-tale rumble of horses in the distance. Galronus had been in two minds. Very likely it was just another patrol, one of Labienus', on a similar mission to their own from the enemy camp. Gods knew how many times patrols had bumped into each other over these past few days, each one ending in a scuffle and a hasty withdrawal for one side or the other. It would perhaps be better not to suffer another of those endless skirmishes, but then to avoid contact would rather defy the very nature of their mission, for what if those horses turned out not to be a standard patrol, but instead the lead unit in an unexpected attack?

Thus they had moved on from the ford and followed the river inland in the direction of the noise. Every hundred heartbeats Galronus had held up his hand and stopped them all to listen, cocking his head and cupping a hand to his ear until he picked up the sound once again, when they would move on, tracking those horses.

Here, waiting by the river bank, he motioned his men to silence again and concentrated. The sound was louder now, but more gentle, more languid. The riders were close but had slowed from a run to a walk. There were several dozen of them from the sounds, which strongly suggested a turma, near enough identical to his own. They had to be enemy cavalry, for Galronus knew where the other two active Caesarian patrols were to be found at the moment, and neither of them should be near here. The only question was whether they were native African levies or Labienus' Gauls and Germans.

Even as he listened, the sound drummed to a halt. The enemy were pausing and listening just as Galronus had been. It was enough to raise a wry smile. They were clearly enemy scouts. Galronus held his hand up, motioning his men to stay quiet, and caught the grin on Samaconius' face. He nodded.

Slowly, as quietly as he could, he drew his blade, and a muted chorus of rasps behind him told him that his entire turma had done the same. If there was to be trouble, they would not be caught off-guard. The enemy horses were moving again now, the noise increasing rapidly as they closed. Finally a rider emerged from the trees on the far side of the river, others appearing behind him, the entire group reining in opposite. The leader of the newly-arrived horsemen folded his arms as he sat facing Galronus across twenty paces of river gulley. Gods, but their men looked like Galronus' own from here.

'Identify yourselves,' the rider shouted across the gap.

'We serve the proconsul, Gaius Julius Caesar,' Galronus called back.

'I guessed that,' snorted the other rider. 'But who *are* you?'

'Galronus of the Remi, commander of Caesar's cavalry. You?'

'Vecatus of the Nervii, third to Titus Labienus.'

Galronus' eyes narrowed. 'I suggest we turn and go our separate ways.'

The Nervian rider sat silent for a long moment, and then nodded, eyes narrowed.

'Sir, you can't just let them go,' called a man from behind Galronus.

'Bloody right,' agreed another, and in moments a gaggle of protesting voices arose behind Galronus. The Remi officer ignored them, watching his opposite number. In an almost laughable reflection, the Nervian riders behind Vecatus were shouting at their commander.

'Quiet,' Galronus snapped over his shoulder, the Remi grumbling swiftly into silence. Across the river, the Nervians were similarly silenced. 'The problem is,' he called out, 'that my men don't like Nervians. The Remi never did. Long before the legions came, your people were raiding our lands and taking slaves.'

'That's history,' the man snapped, 'and you Remi did exactly the same to us. At least we stuck to our roots when your precious proconsul came and didn't fall to our knees and worship him.'

Galronus felt his own anger rising now. 'And a lot of good that did you. Now we're all Roman, eh? And while we serve a general who's valued us since first we met, you ride in the name of a rebel you spent most of the first half decade of the war trying to kill. Try not to trip over your morals on the way down from your high horse, Vecatus.'

'Why you jumped up, mouthy little Remi shit.'

Galronus tested the edge of his sword with a thumb. 'I thought we were trying to avoid this?'

'Up yours, Remi.'

With a loud rasp, the enemy cavalry drew their own swords now, both units moving imperceptibly closer to the edge of the river bank, faces set in a grimace of anger, voices issuing low growls and hisses of hatred. Galronus sat still, measuring this. It did little good for either unit to throw themselves into a fight here. Both sides were evenly matched and the only true victor would be the scavengers who picked over the bodies.

Still, he thought, on the *other* side of the coin, Vecatus was a prick and so were his men.

'For Rome,' he suddenly shouted and, heeling the flanks of his mount, leapt down the side of the river bank, steeper here than at the fording place they'd intended to use, and ploughed into the shallow river, sword held aloft. Behind him, his men echoed to the call and charged, flooding over the edge and down into the river.

Almost instantly the Nervii did the same, even calling the same battle cry, racing into the water to meet them. Galronus let his men launch into combat, keeping his own gaze focused on Vecatus. The enemy commander had no intention of letting his men take down Galronus, and he steered his mount to get between one vicious looking bastard and the Remi leader.

The two commanders met mid-stream, horses whinnying and water splashed up like transparent crowns. Galronus threw his shield into the path of Vecatus' swinging sword and took the heavy blow on the boss with a dull clong, the blade bouncing, scraping and then skittering across the board until it swept free harmlessly into the air. In a heartbeat, the Remi's own sword was cutting down as he dropped his shield out of the way, though the Nervian commander instantly had his own shield up to take the hit, Galronus' Gallic long sword tearing a chunk from the board and then glancing off the boss with a ding, leaving a visible dent before scraping free into the air once more.

With that the two men were past one another, but neither made to engage any other rider, both turning their horses expertly with their knees and coming back for a second meeting. This time Galronus struck first, his blade swinging low, aiming for his opponent's thigh, and Vecatus only just managed to drop his shield into position in time to turn the blow, his own attack a high one that Galronus just recovered in time to deal with. His shield came up to stop the dropping blade, and with that the two men were turning their mounts again.

A third and a fourth meeting followed similar lines, swords rising and falling, scything out and reaching for contact, always meeting a shield and being turned away before striking home. Finally, the two men danced apart. Vecatus was heaving in deep breaths.

'You're good, Remi.'

'You're no slouch for a Nervian.'

'Shall we continue?'

Galronus straightened in the saddle and looked up into the faint mizzle that seemed to have settled in for the day. 'What say we retire for the noon meal and get out of this weather. We can pick this up again some time on the battlefield.'

Vecatus laughed. 'Yes. Why fight in the rain when we can wait for sun. See you around, Galronus of the Remi.'

'I'll be looking for you on the battlefield, Vecatus of the Nervii.'

With that both commanders bellowed the call to pull back and the two sides swiftly extricated themselves and retreated up the slope of the river banks. Separated by the wide gulley once more the two units sat opposite one another, each man's chest rising and falling as they dealt with the aftermath of strenuous effort.

The skirmish had not been costly. Seven bodies lay in the river, their mounts generally untouched and milling about on the edge of the scene. Galronus tried to identify his men among the dead and gave up in exasperation. It was impossible to tell his men from the Nervii of Vecatus. Only when he did a headcount would he know how many of those seven men were his.

'Line up and count off,' he said, and watched as the turma moved into ordered rows and began to sound off in their unit order. He waited patiently until the end and counted the missing. 'Three,' he told them. 'I'll call that a victory, then.'

He turned to the opposition across the river. 'Swords away while we retrieve the fallen?'

Vecatus nodded. 'No one should be left for the birds out here.'

As the two officers watched each other carefully, soldiers descended into the river on foot, gathering the men they knew, throwing them over the backs of the horses milling about and leading them up to the river bank. A hundred heartbeats later the entire turma was disappearing into the trees, making for the camp once more.

The absurdity of it continued to strike Galronus though, as they rode slowly back to Ruspina. Old enmities survived even the changing of the world. When he'd been a boy, moments like this had been commonplace, bands of Nervian riders and Remi horsemen meeting over a stream somewhere, hurling insults and fighting hard. Then Rome had come, the entire Belgic world had moved on as part of the republic and now here they were at the other end of the world in a gods-forsaken, dusty and unfamiliar land, fighting one another all over again, but on behalf of new masters.

* * *

Quintus Saserna stood on the tower beside the south gate of Leptis Minor and peered out across the scrub land. At least this morning's light rain had dampened the ground and suppressed the ever-present dust. 'Here they come again,' he said to the tribune who stood close by, waiting, pensive, with a signifer and a musician at the ready.

'Will they try something different this time, sir?'

Saserna bit his lip for a moment. In truth, he'd little more experience of this than the tribune, though common sense answered much. 'I doubt it. They're cavalry, hardly made for sieges. And their commander is too shrewd to keep throwing riders at us for no reason, which suggests that he has a strategy of which we are not aware and this is all part of it.'

His eyes picked out the command tent, back at the enemy camp, visible even at this range beyond the approaching force and at the heart of the ordered rows of tents. Two days ago, as this mass of cavalry had arrived and penned in the defenders of Leptis, one of his centurions, a veteran of Caesar's days in Gaul, had recognised the banner that flew beside the enemy commander. Saserna had been worried initially when he learned that Titus Labienus had come for Leptis. The man had a fearsome reputation, and his cavalry were veterans of that same decade-long war.

Yet they arrived and immediately hurled a baffling mounted attack on the city. Admittedly, they had succeeded in swiftly overcoming the port and seizing control of it, and had secured several outlying settlements, but the walls of Leptis held true. Saserna had used his time well in the preceding days, continually strengthening the defences of the town and mounting artillery everywhere he could, having his soldiers training with slings and bows, which would inevitably be of far greater use from the city walls than a sword.

Still, he'd expected more of a challenge, especially from someone like Labienus, yet the veteran commander spent the next two days throwing wave after wave of attacks. Admittedly none of them were truly strong or costly, and Labienus' force was hardly diminishing with the small number of losses he was suffering, but neither was he achieving anything, for his force contained no engineers nor any men with true knowledge of siegecraft. Admittedly they'd sealed off Leptis, but Saserna could not see what value that was to the man. They had adequate grain to keep them going for a protracted siege and sufficient sources of clean water. They did not need to rely on the port, though irritatingly they could not inform Caesar of the situation. What was Labienus gaining from all of this, though?

The only thing he could conclude was that something was happening that the enemy didn't want him to discover. Perhaps some allied town inland was beleaguered and needed help and they were being kept out of the way, or some new supply route had opened up and Labienus had rushed in with his army to block it. Whatever the case, Saserna was comfortable that unless fresh troops turned up to aid the enemy, the defenders of Leptis were cut off from the rest of the world but comfortable and secure and could remain so for months yet.

The horsemen were closing now, racing towards the city once more. Perhaps fifteen hundred of them approached at speed in a tight formation, the front ranks and both wings formed of the light African horsemen, each armed with a fine and sleek javelin, with the core and rear consisting of heavier, chain shirted Gauls. At the heart of the unit, between the light Africans and the heavy Gauls there was a small knot of standard bearers and musicians with a gleaming officer in a red cloak.

'Do you think that's Labienus?' he murmured to the tribune, who shrugged his answer.

Saserna looked across to the other tower, where that veteran centurion of the Gallic wars stood in command of a second ballista. 'Centurion, is that Labienus?'

The veteran turned and shouted back. 'I don't know him to look at, sir. Those are his standards, though.'

Saserna leaned close to the four legionaries manning the ballista, one of the more recent designs made to fire bolts rather than stones. 'You're good with that, I presume? Your centurion gave you the duty because you're the men for the job.'

'Yes, sir,' said the man at the rear, continually adjusting the angle of the machine to track the approach of the cavalry. 'Publius Popillius, sir, ten years on these buggers. Cut my teeth against the Belgae, those same bastards as is riding at us down there, sir.'

'I want you and your crew to prove to me you're the best,' Saserna smiled. 'I've a bronze torc for each of you and an amphora of Setinian wine for you all if you can kill that officer down there in the red cloak.'

The answering grins from the ballista crew were infectious, and smiles broke out across the defenders, their spirits high anyway in the face of such futile opposition. Saserna watched with fascination as the crew worked in perfect harmony to keep the loaded and taut weapon perfectly angled, shifting their focus from the front ranks of riders to the knot of officers and signallers at the centre.

Closer and closer they came, and as they reached a position some twenty paces from the wall and just outside the steep defensive ditch, the lead ranks hurled their light javelins and then peeled off sharply to left and right, circling round the flanks to retreat as the next group loosed their weapons and moved to follow suit. It may be largely futile, but it was beautifully choreographed.

The height of the walls, combined with the distance, made the throw a difficult one, and nine in every ten javelins hit the sandstone walls of Leptis and clattered away harmlessly, falling into the new ditch outside the ramparts. The odd one crested the walls, and of those in that solid volley only two met flesh, the defenders now very familiar with the tactic after two days of repeated assaults and most able to easily duck out of the way. None came close to the towers, which added an extra eight feet in height in comparison to the walls, and the ballista crew did not even flinch, continuing to sight as the enemy closed.

Another wave of javelins came, and then another, and finally Publius Popillius whispered 'now!'

With a simple click the monstrous machine was triggered. The great sinews wound and tightened over a hundred breaths snapped straight in a flash, swinging out the two flexible wooden arms and jettisoning the bolt, a deadly, iron-tipped shaft almost two feet long. As the machine loosed, Saserna couldn't help flinching. Anyone who spent time in the army

heard horrible tales about the artillery, of how every now and
then one of these would develop a weakness, and instead of
loosing a missile at the enemy would explode in every
direction, peppering anyone within range with foot-long
splinters and shards of twisted metal. Still, there had been no
need, for the great weapon just shuddered into stillness as
every pair of eyes on the gate towers watched the bolt's
flight.

The officer on the horse was concentrating on directing his
men and never saw his death coming. The blow of the bolt
was so powerful that it struck him between neck and heart,
punching through the decorative bronze cuirass, smashing
through his ribs and organs and even out of the rear of his
cuirass, low down and close to his backside. There the bolt
continued its deadly passage through the leather saddle and
into the back of the horse. The beast reared in agonised panic,
and Saserna was stunned that the officer managed to stay in
the saddle until he realised that the bolt was still in him,
pinning him to the wounded steed.

Chaos erupted down below as the horse screamed in panic
and bolted, the shaking, gurgling shape of the officer still
pinned to it and flopping this way and that with the animal's
movements as it broke free of the force and raced away across
the hard-packed ground, bearing its dying rider.

Hardly had the enemy the chance to recover when the rest
of the defenders, encouraged to great effect by this wondrous
display joined in. The musician who had been close enough to
the mounted officer to be sprayed with his blood, wild-eyed
and ghostly pale, raised a tuba to his lips to sound some
command or other and was immediately plucked from the
saddle by another ballista bolt and hurled to the ground,
where he died, writhing, horn still gripped in his hand.

Saserna turned to look in appreciation across at the other
gate tower, whence the second shot had come, and that

veteran centurion was grinning. 'My lot say they're as good as yours, sir!'

The commander laughed. 'Tell them I'll match the prize for them too.'

And now all along the walls of Leptis arrows, pila and sling stones were hurtling out at the mass of cavalry, making a shambles of their formation. One of the older-type, stone throwing ballistae on the next tower along completed the deadly triad of artillery shots as some prefect, who was trying to pull some sort of order out of this mess in the absence of his commander, suddenly exploded in a pink cloud and a shower of unspeakable fragments, parts of his upper torso slapping into riders nearby, head rolling away, and what was left of him after the impact of the sixty pound stone ball lolled this way and that in the saddle as the horse bolted in fear.

'That's given them something to think about,' Saserna said, wincing at the sight, his stomach turning over unpleasantly.

Down below, the cavalry of Labienus fled back from the walls of Leptis Minor in demoralised terror.

* * *

Caesar stood on the viewing platform of the camp's ramparts along with Fronto. Below them the advance pickets and the scouts, the work parties, the hunters and the foragers all flooded back into the camp at speed, obeying the call of the cornu which blared out the ad signum cadence repeatedly.

It had not taken long for such a drill to become a practiced and well-oiled manoeuver, given that Scipio had taken to leading his cohorts from their camp every morning, keeping them there in the vain hope of tempting Caesar to battle, and then leading them back in before sunset. Caesar's reaction each time had been to withdraw his men into the defences and prepare for an attack, which Scipio was clearly unwilling to undertake.

And so the strange stalemate had gone on. Scipio, never a man to let imagination ruin a tried and tested formula, continued with his routine. Then, this morning, things had changed. It was Fronto's private opinion that someone in Scipio's command with more nous than the senior officer had goaded the man into something new. The men on watch a mile from Scipio's camp had seen the army assemble outside as usual, but this morning they had not stopped, lined up and silently offered battle there as usual. *This* morning they marched determinedly towards Ruspina instead. The scouts had fallen back to inform Caesar and the order to pull all personnel inside had been issued once more.

The ramparts were full now, lined with legionaries, grim-faced and ready to take on the master of Africa's army. Artillery were interspersed all along the line, units of archers and slingers ready just behind the ramparts, prepared to loose massive clouds of missiles at the attacking force. Galronus had the cavalry massed outside the camp but behind the extra rampart that connected it to the sea, ready to issue forth from three different gates at a moment's notice when the command was given.

They were as prepared as they could be. The rampart was eighteen feet high, backed with a solid mound of dirt and topped with timber fortifications and wattle fences, with wide fighting platforms behind. A tower rose every fifty paces along the length, and each of those bore scorpions, catapults or ballistae. In front of the rampart ran a ditch eighteen feet wide and ten deep, and the twelve foot berm of flat, dusty ground that lay between ditch and rampart was planted all along with concealed sharpened stakes, waiting to impale, impede and break legs.

'Look at that,' Fronto murmured as the massed forces of Scipio came into view. As the last of the Caesarian army pulled inside the defences and the gates were closed and barred, the officers watched in fascination. It was not the vast mass of infantry that were gathering there, falling into position and widening, extending their lines, both infantry and auxiliary, that attracted their attention so much. Nor was it the huge units of archers or the mass of cavalry.

It was the shape of thirty elephants plodding slowly towards them with towers rising from their backs, archers sitting inside them, like mobile missile platforms, each capable of crushing a horse and rider underfoot. It was a sight to behold, and not a pleasant one. Even for a native with a national history of utilising the beasts in war, like King Juba, they were something of a random and dangerous element. For a Roman commander with no experience of fielding such creatures, like Scipio, they were a completely unknown quantity.

And while they could quite readily go horribly awry and ruin Scipio's attack, they could also work out perfectly and carve a battered and bloody swathe through Caesar's army. Worst of all, given their size, strength and weight, there was a distinct possibility that they might just charge through all these carefully-prepared defences as if they were a child's fort of chairs and blankets.

The enemy force came to a halt a thousand paces from the defences, out of range of even the strongest artillery, and there they lined up, the full might of Scipio's army on display. They currently outnumbered the Caesarian force by a margin of more than two to one.

'I wish I knew what he intended,' Fronto muttered. 'Scipio's such an unknown. On the one hand he's most likely to follow the rulebook like a good little Roman general, and that would make it easy to stand against and plan against, but on the other hand, we know that he also has a tendency to get annoyed or bored and simply throw the whole thing out of the window and run at us, screaming obscenities.'

Caesar frowned. 'I cannot fathom what he is up to. His cavalry are mostly centred on the left flank, which is idiotic, as he must know where our cavalry are. There's only one place they can reasonably sortie from, and yet he's put his horse on the other side. Also, I suspect Labienus is not here, for his horse look seriously diminished in numbers, which could mean that there is no one in his command of sufficient rank to dare oppose Scipio's tactical decisions.'

'If he's clever, he'll send the elephants in first. They've got to be the most expendable of his forces, and he's better sending them against us a long way from the rest of his troops in case they panic and turn round.'

Caesar tapped his lip. 'Unless he is worried about wasting precious forces from his ally Juba of Numidia. It may be that he doesn't want to risk losing Juba's elephants unless he has to. But I do not understand his array. His forces make no tactical sense like this, and he has seriously overextended his lines. It is as though he is doing this simply to show off.'

Fronto snorted. 'Maybe that's exactly what it is.'

Caesar drummed his fingers on the timber parapet. 'Do you know what this is, Fronto? This is Scipio doing exactly the same thing he's been doing for days. He's like a child who keeps calling us names and hoping for a reaction. Since he's had none, he's taken a step closer and thumbed his nose at us. He's not come to attack us, he's just offering battle in the open again, but a lot closer, hoping to tempt us from our defences.'

'Are you sure?'

Caesar gave Fronto a wide smile. 'I am, in fact, positive. So much so that I'm going to wander over to the harbour and see if there's any sign of our overdue ships and then I'm going to retire to my tent for a lie down. Have the cavalry stand down for now and just keep everyone on basic alert. Watch that fool out there and send me a runner if he does anything more exciting than scratch his backside.'

As Caesar disappeared from the ramparts, Fronto settled in to wait, Scipio's army finishing assembling in careful order facing the Caesarian defences but at a safe distance.

He watched.

And he watched.

At noon, a soldier brought him wine, water and some kind of goat's meat broth with good bread. In the middle of the afternoon, he received a plate of fruit. Then, as the sun finally started to slide towards the west, a buccina call went up among Scipio's army and the entire force turned and marched off into the dust. Fronto watched them leave with a slightly mystified smile. Caesar had been quite right, and Scipio had proven himself as unimaginative as ever. Fronto continued to smile to himself as he gave the order for the entire defensive circuit to stand down.

If Scipio would just keep doing this sort of thing, then Caesar would soon have more than sufficient manpower to take him on. Or, tomorrow, the man might try and muster his troops outside Caesar's tent and bare his arse cheeks at the general.

Fronto chuckled at the mental image all the way back to his tent.

CHAPTER NINE

Ruspina, 21ˢᵗ January 46 BC

Fronto threw on his cloak against the night cold and shuffled over to the door of his tent, edging it open. 'What is it?'

The man who'd knocked was one of Salvius Cursor's praetorians, which was an odd enough sight at Fronto's tent in the middle of the night to warrant interest, and standing behind the man was an on duty legionary. 'Sir, this man begged to report to the general, but Caesar is... temporarily indisposed.'

The tone the man used meant he might as well have been waggling his eyebrows meaningfully. Fronto frowned for only a moment, trying to work out what was going on, before it sank in. The general was still having occasional incidents of the falling sickness, though it remained a thing hidden from most of the army. Salvius and the praetorians, though, had been brought into the circle of the knowledgeable, for as his bodyguard they might be expected to deal with the issue from time to time. Caesar had probably still been working in the middle of the night as was his wont when the latest seizure struck. The timing was inconvenient, but Fronto was the second most senior officer in camp, and so the man had naturally come to him.

'Report,' he said to the soldiers, beckoning them inside, where he quickly kitted himself out properly as an officer while the legionary addressed him.

'Sir, we've two enemy deserters at the gate wishing to speak to the commander.'

Fronto paused in buckling on his cuirass, something most officers allowed their slave to deal with but that he had long since started doing himself in an almost automatic, mechanical process. 'I'm not sure that's worth waking a senior officer for. It's hardly new.'

And that was a fact. For seven days now, since the enemy had drawn up outside Caesar's camp only to retire at sunset, Scipio had returned to his earlier routine of displaying his troops outside his own camp hopefully, and each night now members of his force drifted across the three miles of scrubland between the two armies and arrived at Caesar's camp, requesting to be taken in. They'd had more than two hundred already in seven days. It would have been a relief to acquire such valuable extra manpower had not Plancus and his anticipated reinforcements now become long overdue. He'd been given five days, and ten had passed already. Caesar was becoming edgy and irritable at the lack of response to his many couriers and messages.

'Sir,' the soldier replied, 'these two claim to be officers, and important men with valuable information.'

Fronto frowned again. 'Where are they now?'

The praetorian answered. 'We have them close to the headquarters.'

'Bring them here instead.'

As the two soldiers ducked out, Fronto finished dressing appropriately, raked a comb quickly through his hair, knuckled the sleep from his eyes, and then sat by his table, shuffling a half-eaten meal out of view and replacing it with a stack of wax tablets and a map of the area for the look of things. Mere moments after he'd positioned himself carefully there came another knock. At his call, the pair of soldiers opened the door and escorted two men inside, coming to a halt behind them.

'You can go,' Fronto said, gesturing to his two soldiers.

'Sir?'

'They're not armed, are they?'

'No sir. We searched them and took their weapons.'

'Well I am, and I know what to do with the pointy end, so I'll be fine. Off you go.'

The soldiers, looking worried and slightly disapproving, left the tent and the door slapped shut behind them. Fronto looked the two men up and down by lamplight. They were not armoured, and each had a drab soldier's cloak over their arm, dripping with wet from the night's rain, but underneath that cloak which had seen them safely out of their camp and across the no-man's-land in between, they both wore tunics that marked them as narrow-striped junior tribunes. Fronto was immediately interested, for he had no doubt from the skin tone and the shape of their faces that both men were natives of this region. It seemed that Scipio really *had* made legions out of provincials.

'Who are you?'

One of the men looked to his friend, who nodded, and then replied 'I am Iarbas of the Gaetuli, now of the Sixth Legion under Scipio, and this is my companion Hastas of the Fourth, also a Gaetuli. You know of our people?'

Fronto nodded. 'A little. You fought with Marius against Sulla half a century ago.'

'We did, and many feel that as loyal sons of Marius, we should cleave to that same loyalty with his rightful successor, Caesar.'

'We've had a number of defectors recently, gentlemen. I concede that as tribunes you have to be noblemen of your tribe, and Scipio must value you to put you in such a position, but all of this could have waited.'

Iarbas shook his head. 'You do not understand. I know that many of our people are coming over to Caesar, and you will be pleased to know also that many Numidians serving in Scipio's ranks are also deserting and returning west to their own kingdom. But that is not the point. Scipio is concerned over Caesar's seeming inactivity. He is convinced that the general is up to something, for it is well known that Caesar is a man of action, and to sit behind defences and wait seems out of character. Scipio charged us with slipping in among the defectors and gathering information for him.'

Fronto leaned back in his seat. 'So you're spies who have decided to defect, instead.'

'In a nutshell. He expects us to return and report what defences you have put in place against his elephants, your dispositions and your plans. Instead, we seek a rightful place with the sons of Marius. We have much information on Scipio and his forces and timely warnings to deliver.'

Fronto sucked air in through his teeth like a cash-hungry tradesman. 'Then first tell me where Labienus is. His cavalry are absent from the forces gathered here and we have no information as to where he went.'

The two deserters shared a look, and Iarbas took a deep breath. 'Scipio dispatched him east some days ago. We have been receiving reports of numerous cities in the east declaring for Caesar. It seems that out there the locals are far enough from the rebel power centre in Utica to prefer the new strength in the land.'

'We've heard no such thing since Ruspina and Leptis declared for us.'

'Have you heard from Leptis recently, commander?' Iarbas asked pointedly.

'No. Not that we were expecting reports, but I admit there has been an absence of news. It had not struck me as odd before, but then Leptis is close. Perhaps there has been no news worthy of sending.'

'Leptis has been besieged by Labienus. He has kept the city busy and cut off to prevent information and supplies reaching you via coastal cities, and no ships could put into port there safely. And while he kept Leptis busy, his riders patrolled all around, preventing any envoys, troops or supplies from passing west towards this place. Labienus effectively cut off the east, just as Scipio has cut off the south and Considius in Hadrumetum the west.'

Fronto rubbed his neck. 'That is unsettling, especially with our reinforcements overdue and Cato's fleets patrolling the sea looking for our ships. The fleet is trying to finish the job, sealing off the north. I thought Scipio was being unimaginative, but if this is true, then it smacks more of Cato's careful planning.'

'But herein, commander, lies our warning and a great opportunity for you. You missed my point, you see. I spoke in the past tense. The siege of Leptis has been lifted. Labienus returned to the camp this very evening with his riders, having been brutally ousted by your garrison there. His own lieutenant was killed in the fighting, a relation of his, I understand, which has not improved his mood. Leptis Minor is now free, and with it the towns of the east that would declare for Caesar, along with no small quantity of supplies. But your window of opportunity closes.'

Fronto leaned forward now. 'Go on.'

'The city of Acylla sent envoys to you offering their support and their grain, though these men were picked up by Labienus' riders and never reached you. Scipio moves once more to seal off the east after the failure of Labienus' cavalry. Tomorrow morning Considius will depart Hadrumetum with a solid force of eight cohorts and a cavalry unit taken from Labienus. He will march on Acylla and seize it, garrisoning it against you. Acylla sits in a crucial position where the coast curves inwards. All shipping passes close to its walls and harbour. If you delay, you will lose Acylla and your position weakens. Move fast and you may secure it before Considius, which will grant you freedom to move in the east.'

Fronto looked at the two men. Gods, but he wished he was better at reading people. The two Gaetuli certainly *seemed* genuine, and it was true that their people had been drifting in as deserters recently, but this was too important to act on a guess. If Fronto moved on their information and it turned out to be falsehoods, they could march into a trap, and thereby weaken the force here. He fretted.

'I cannot dispatch a force without corroboration of any of this.'

'You do not have time to spare,' Iarbas noted.

'Considius marches in the morning, you say. He comes from Hadrumetum, which is near ten miles west of here. That gives us half a day of leeway. If our forces leave before noon tomorrow we should still be ahead of him. That gives us until midday tomorrow to find some way of corroborating your story.'

'Then I pray your gods send you messengers swiftly, else our subterfuges will have been worth nothing.'

Fronto nodded. 'Thank you for this. I truly hope to corroborate your intelligence, and that we can welcome you to the fold. For now, I will see to it that you are well looked after.' He rose and opened the door, gesturing to the two soldiers still outside. To the praetorian: 'Take these two men and see them to comfortable, secure accommodation for the night. They must be allowed to bathe if they wish and food provided. See to it that they are given fresh clothing too, of appropriate rank.' He then turned to the legionary. 'Run and find the legate Gaius Messius. Wake him on my authority. Tell him that we have fresh intelligence and that I am awaiting confirmation, but I want him ready to move with the Twenty Ninth Legion. If all goes according to plan, that legion will march east at speed for the city of Acylla late tomorrow morning.'

The two men left, escorting the deserters, and Fronto sagged back into his chair. This was a critical decision. He would have to run it by Caesar, but the general would not be in any shape to discuss it until the morning, which was cutting things a little fine. He had a full legion making ready to move at speed, and their current commander, Messius, was said to be a good man, though Fronto knew little of him yet. The big problem was one of trust. How could he know what was right?

* * *

22nd January 46 BC

Gaius Messius looked back at his legion and once again threw up a heartfelt message to Fortuna and Minerva, for the gods had answered both his prayers and those of Caesar and Fronto at first light. A new fleet had been reported out in the bay, coming from the west at dawn and bearing Caesar's banners. Before that had even arrived, though, a courier vessel hurtled into the harbour from the east, unloading a breathless visitor, who was shown to Caesar's tent.

It so happened that Fronto and Messius had both been in the general's tent apprising him of what had happened during the night and arranging plans for the potential urgent march when that man had arrived and been admitted to the three expectant officers.

'Report,' Caesar said.

'Sir,' the visitor saluted with a smile. He wore a tribune's uniform, though Fronto couldn't place the man. 'It is my pleasure to bear you tidings from the east. I was dispatched back here with advance warning from my commander, Sallustius Crispus.'

Caesar and Fronto looked at one another. It had been three weeks now since Sallustius had been sent with his fleet to hunt down supplies. 'Go on.'

'We arrived on Cercina with only a small military force as escort. Cercina was barely defended at all and what few troops there were, stationed at Scipio's orders, fled the island along with its commander, Gaius Decimus, in a fast

Liburnum, at the sight of our fleet arriving. We proceeded to secure an enormous grain store, far more than would fit on the ships we had, but fortunately there were many merchant vessels in port on the island and we negotiated fees with the traders and hired their ships. We left the people of Cercina with more than adequate supplies to see them through to the summer and still have abundant grain. We would have returned much sooner, but there have been storms in the sea down there which have ravaged the waters, and no trierarch was willing to risk the open water with wide-bottomed and heavily-laden merchant ships until the storms had fully passed. Now, however, the grain fleet is perhaps two days behind me.'

Caesar sat back in his seat with an explosive exhale. 'This is most wondrous news. And given the extreme likelihood that the fleet even now approaching the port bears veteran legions for our reinforcement, Scipio's position in Africa grows ever weaker. Thank you.'

'There is more, General. On my return I put in at Leptis Minor and have gathered dispatches for you.' He produced a leather wallet of reports and placed them on Caesar's desk. 'I cannot say what is in them, sir, but I know from my visit that the city holds strong despite having spent days under siege from the cavalry of Labienus who only departed after one of their officers was killed by a ballista bolt. This is still the talk of the population, sir. And gathered at Leptis are representatives from several towns, including Thysdrus, who have thrown in their lot with us to the east.'

Fronto had given a small smile at the near confirmation of last night's interrogation. 'Were there men from Acylla too?'

'It is not a name I heard, sir, but neither can I deny it.'

The dispatches confirmed much, and Messius reported that the Twenty Ninth was ready to move in light order as soon as the command was given. Fronto held off yet until he and Caesar were more confident – until the fleet arrived, almost an hour later. Plancus was contrite over the delays he'd suffered and landed the blame squarely with Governor Alienus on Sicilia. However, he had brought with him every man gathered on the island, which consisted of the Thirteenth and Fourteenth legions, eight hundred Gallic cavalry and more than a thousand archers and slingers who had mustered at Lilybaeum in response to Caesar's requests, sent there from Sardinia and Crete.

For Messius, though, the best news was not the arrival of the much anticipated veteran reinforcements, but the news Plancus had brought from this very morning as the fleet had made its way along the coast from the north-west. A sizeable army had been spotted marching east from Hadrumetum. When Fronto had asked if it matched the eight cohorts and cavalry support of which the two defectors had spoken, Plancus had thought for a moment, and concluded that it sounded about right. Fronto had all the confirmation he needed that the two men had been honest. Between the reports from the east and the west, the truth had been gleaned. And because of them, the Caesarian force knew precisely where Considius was headed with his force and for the first time this year they had the chance to be proactive and get ahead of Scipio's plans.

In response, the legion had departed Ruspina mid-morning. They had taken only two turmae of riders with them, for whatever Considius had planned, cavalry were largely useless in a siege, and whichever force reached Acylla first a siege was undoubtedly what would result. With the horsemen ranging both ahead and behind, the legion moved swiftly, equipped only for battle and without all their usual kit. Riders soon confirmed that Considius was behind them, moving as fast as he could, and despite the need to keep his men strong and ready for a fight, Messius coaxed his men into a slightly higher pace, sacrificing their comfort for a little extra speed.

According to reports and maps, Acylla was fifty miles from Ruspina. At a reasonable standard pace, a legion in light order would make that in two days. Messius had decided, in light of the pursuing force and the fact that this was nothing more than a race, that the legion could reasonably manage some thirty miles the first day and he was satisfied that they had achieved considerably more than that as light faded from the sky. For a moment, Messius had considered suggesting they march on through the night, but had relented, and when the scouts reported that Considius had also called a halt to his march, they set up camp for the night.

In light of the weariness of the legion, who had been pushed hard all day, Messius decided that there would be no time and effort spent on fortification. Watches of only a single hour in length were set up in order for every man to have as much rest as possible. Men ate cold rations from their pouches, having left all cooking supplies at Ruspina to allow for a lighter method of travel, and without the heavy leather tents, men rolled up in their cloaks on the hard ground. During the evening, Considius' cavalry came close to the Twenty Ninth, but wisely stopped short of actual engagement, turning round and heading back to their force without trouble.

The legion arose two hours before dawn and moved out immediately with no need to decamp. They had done so just in time, for early scouting patrols brought news that the army of Considius had arisen some time earlier and were already closing on their position.

The Twenty Ninth force-marched once more, heading almost directly south now. By dawn, it became clear that the race would be a close run thing. In rising unexpectedly half way through the night, Considius had closed much of the gap and his force was now all but nipping at the heels of the Twenty Ninth. More than once Messius considered stopping, turning, and trying to commit to battle. His cohorts outnumbered those of Considius, though being below-strength, there was likely little in it by way of manpower, and with the added danger of the cavalry he'd decided against it. Moreover, he was aware that the garrisoning of Acylla was the critical thing here, rather than any victory over Considius and if he paused for battle, Considius might just decide to split his force and send his cavalry out to take Acylla ahead of him. At the moment, that possibility did not seem to have occurred to the enemy commander, and Messius was content to leave it that way.

Two hours after dawn, the scouts reported that they were almost within reach of their destination and even as the dust cloud of Considius at their rear grew with a desperate push to the finish, Messius finally laid eyes on the distant walls of the city of Acylla. He called in his scout commander, a tall and gaunt Bellovaci noble.

'Ride ahead at speed and take all your men. Get into Acylla and tell them that a full legion of Caesar's men are on the way to garrison the town, but that Scipio's troops are also closing and that the town's defenders whoever they are need to prime their artillery and get ready to close the gate behind us.'

The Gaul nodded and rode off to gather his men, then broke into a gallop, all sixty-four riders making for the walls of Acylla. Messius turned in the saddle and looked back. Considius must have had the same idea, for his cavalry was now pulling ahead, racing for the town. There was a full ala of one hundred and twenty-eight men, by Messius' estimate.

As the enemy horse closed on their rear, the legion tensed and centurions started giving orders to prepare to repulse cavalry, but Messius sent back word to counter those orders. The cavalry were not coming for the legion. Not yet, anyway. Sure enough, as they closed, the rebel cavalry swung out wide to avoid contact with Messius and his legion. Their gaze was locked solely on Acylla and control of it.

Messius, his men now moving up to a slightly faster pace once more, sweating and panting with the exertion of the contest, watched as the two units of horse raced for Acylla's gate. The enemy cavalry was twice the size of his, but that mattered not if they got inside. He watched them close on the city and, with a flood of relief, saw his riders vanish inside only a few heartbeats ahead of the cavalry of Considius. The gates slammed shut behind the Caesarian horse, and Messius was pleased to see that word spread immediately through the city and the other gate he could see from here was closed a moment later. Acylla was sealed.

The Twenty Ninth ran on, and as they did so the rebel cavalry milled about outside the walls, seemingly uncertain of their orders now that they had failed to secure the city. Then, predictably, they turned and faced the approaching legion. The senior tribune of the Twenty Ninth looked across from his saddle to the legate.

'What now, sir?'

'Now,' Messius said, 'we need to get inside and join the horsemen. There's only a hundred or so cavalry, and four thousand of us'

'Four thousand tired and lightly armed, sir.'

Messius straightened in the saddle. 'Have the first century widen their ranks. I want them running with a width of half a century. Here's what we're going to do...'

The tribune nodded along as Messius explained, and then passed the instructions on to the signallers and musicians running alongside, sweating and groaning under the weight of their standards and instruments, an unfortunate burden that they couldn't leave behind with the unnecessary kit.

The rebel horse lined up three deep, forming a wide enough line to face the newly-extended front of the Twenty Ninth, and began to move into a trot. Messius held his breath. They would get to the city, he knew, but given what would inevitably follow, he needed to do this with as few losses as possible.

'One,' he called to the tribune, holding up a finger. As the second in command relayed the orders, the front century of the First Cohort pulled out ahead in two lines, gripping their pila. In three heartbeats the army moved to a charging pace though the front two lines, forty men wide, and had pulled out ahead so that there was a gap between them, and another between the second and third line.

The enemy cavalry also moved to a charge, their tired horses bearing down on Messius' force, their only hope now that they could break the Twenty Ninth and delay them long enough for Considius and his cohorts to catch up and engage them. If the rebels could beat the Twenty Ninth in the open, then the cavalry defending Acylla would be forced to capitulate extremely quickly.

Messius was not about to let that happen.

'Ready.'

The two forces raced towards one another, the cavalry forty horses wide and three deep, presenting a wider front than the forty infantry of the Twenty Ninth. The horsemen lowered their spears into position ready to break the legion, confident that the soldiers would have no time to change formation and fall into the contra equitas defence.

'Now,' Messius shouted as the two forces raced towards mutual annihilation. At the relayed command, the front two lines of legionaries, the most experienced and veteran men in the legion, pulled back their arms, pila angled carefully, and released at their centurion's whistle, immediately changing formation the moment the missiles were in the air.

The panic among the cavalry was palpable as a cloud of pila hurtled at them on a low trajectory and loosed too close for them to do anything to avoid. The width of the rebel lines made it hard to miss, and the majority of the pila found a target, striking either man or horse. Much of the front line of riders crumpled and collapsed at the barrage, the second and third lines forced to slow and bump into one another in an effort to avoid ploughing at speed into the stricken riders and horses in front.

Messius gave them no time to recover. Even as the missiles were heaved, the First Cohort was changing. The men who'd thrown the pila immediately melted away to the flanks, revealing that the rest of the cohort behind them had reformed into a wedge as they ran, a triangle of shields, braced with powerful shoulders, swords out ready, their pila passed to the men of the Second Cohort further back. The men from the front, now free of their pila, drew their swords as they dropped back and turned to form the barbs at the outer edge of the human arrowhead.

The wedge hit the chaotic and panicked horsemen at speed and with very much the same effect as a real arrowhead punching into flesh. The men of the cohort smashed aside the cavalry with their shields, strength and speed, most of the riders doing their level best to dance desperately out of their way. In moments they were through the rebel horse, having destroyed around a third of them, and racing for the gates of Acylla. Messius hurtled through them alongside the tribune, both men unusually involving themselves in the fighting. Since they were forced to pass through the ranks of the horse in the wake of the barbed wedge, both officers drew their swords and managed to land at least one blow in passing. As they moved on towards the city, behind them the commander of the cavalry ala was desperately trying to pull his force into order, but with little luck or effect, for his men were divided into two chaotic, milling groups by the legion charging through the middle. Moreover, the legionaries all had swords or pila in hand and each of them did what they could to wound any rider or horse that came within reach as they passed.

It was over surprisingly quickly. By the time Messius, now having pulled out to the head of the legion, approached the city gate, which now stood open and welcoming, the rear ranks of his legion had managed to pass through the ineffectual cavalry blockade and into open ground. Messius felt a wave of triumph and relief as he passed through the gate and into the city.

They had done it, and the defences of Acylla, even at first glance, would be adequate to hold Considius outside almost indefinitely as long as they could count on sufficient supplies. As he reined in just inside the gate to one side, he spotted the legion's primus pilus and waved him over.

'Sir?'

'Have the men distributed around the walls. I want every legionary up there, barring one century, who'll accompany me to the city ordo as we make their acquaintance. Then those men will need to start checking stores and supplies, but otherwise, every man holds those walls against Considius.'

The senior centurion saluted and began to disseminate instructions among his juniors.

Heaving in exhausted breaths, Messius turned to the tribune who'd accompanied him on that last charge. His eyes widened to see that the man's tunic at his left hip, below the cuirass, was soaked with blood.

'Tribune? You're wounded.'

The man gave him a dismissive smile. 'A parting gift from an angry cavalryman. It's not bad, sir. Just a flesh wound.'

Messius frowned. 'I hope so. We've no medicus with us. Find a capsarius and get him to look at it until we can find a proper physician in the town. Then, this afternoon, once you're stitched up and well, I'm shipping you out.'

'Sir? It's not bad.'

'It might not be life-threatening, but that's too much blood for a scratch. Anyway, I have need of you. I want a man I trust to take the fastest ship in port and sail for Ruspina to report our success to Caesar, and once we've spoken to the city council, you'll undoubtedly have plenty more to report too.'

Messius turned, sagging in the saddle, to see the last of the legion pulling into the city and the gates being shut and barred. Already centuries of men were filtering along the walls. The few artillery pieces in evidence were being manned, and the tired-looking cavalry were coming down one of the nearby streets, saluting with wide, beaming grins.

They had done it. They had beaten Considius in the race and secured critical Acylla for Caesar.

CHAPTER TEN

Ruspina, 24ᵗʰ January 46 BC

It had been two days since Messius and his legion had left for Acylla. Word had not yet arrived from the east of the result of his desperate run, though by now they had to have reached the important town. If all had gone well, by now the Twenty Ninth would be garrisoning Acylla and Considius railing over his failure. If they had succeeded a messenger would probably arrive in the next day by ship. If not, the battered legion would probably limp back to Ruspina a day or two later.

Still, Fronto mused, the Caesarian forces had been kept too busy to ponder on the fate of their sister legion out in the east. The next morning had seen the appearance of more than a cohort of deserters from Scipio's legions, members of the Gaetuli who had no wish to serve in the rebel army. To bolster their spirits, Caesar had now gathered all the Gaetuli at Ruspina into two cohorts together and put them under the command of their own nobles, swelling these units with pride.

The loss of further manpower seemed to do nothing to change the staid Scipio's tactics, and still that morning his entire army was lined up and paraded outside his camp, three miles from Caesar's lines. Not his entire army, Fronto reminded himself, for the incidents of clashes between foragers and rebel patrols had increased somewhat. In the absence of Considius, who was off at Acylla, Scipio had sent a secondary garrison to Hadrumetum in the west and, according to deserters, with instructions to harry any Caesarian troops that might come within six miles of the place. Given that Scipio's own army lay to the south, the only places left where troops from Ruspina could manage to find any resources at all was in the flat bowl of land that lay along the coast between there and Leptis, and now the cavalry of Labienus had taken to attacking these stray units with unpredictable strikes, much like a land-borne version of Cato's attack fleets.

Caesar had fretted throughout the next day, trying to decide how to resolve this situation without accepting Scipio's offer of a direct battle in the field. Even with the recently arrived veterans Caesar was uncomfortable with the odds, at least until the Ninth and Tenth arrived. *If* the Ninth and Tenth arrived, Fronto thought bitterly. It was at least a possibility that those units might mutiny once more as they had over the winter and decide not to come.

The decision had been made when Caesar, Fronto, Plancus and Galronus had ridden out with Salvius Cursor and his praetorians to check out an idea the general had formed while poring over the maps of the area. That bowl of flat land was important, for as well as the only meagre source of forage, it also contained the land route east to Leptis and beyond, and allowing Labienus to patrol it with impunity and attack when he felt like it was unacceptable.

Plancus had begun it, by pointing at the map and noting small squares in a rough line, inquiring as to their purpose. It appeared upon investigation that they represented small defensive towers that had been constructed over two centuries earlier, during the Third Sicilian War as part of Agathocles' attempt to secure Hadrumetum and the area. Scouts warned that they were little more than ruinous shells now, but Caesar had pointed out that with a little work they could be made to form a defensive ring around that much needed flat land, connecting Leptis to the salt flats beyond Caesar's camp and effectively fortifying the entire area.

Galronus had pointed out that such a line would advance Caesar's control to little more than a mile from Scipio's camp, and might provoke an unpleasant reaction, though both Caesar and Fronto had claimed that at least this might goad the man into attacking, and Caesar's defences were strong enough to give him an advantage in such a siege.

And so the officers had ridden out to examine the possibility. With just riders they had been swift and had moved off to Leptis, where it appeared that the ancient tower nearest there had already been largely reconstructed by Labienus when he'd launched his failed siege. From there the antiquated turrets were easy to spot in a line, each on the highest point in the area and roughly a mile apart. Some were in better condition than others, for some had been left to decay, while three of them had been partially maintained by local farmers for storage. At the last one, only a mile and a half from Caesar's camp, they realised that they had passed the place on the day of that gods-awful battle and that it actually overlooked the ford where they had held the enemy off at the last. From this hilltop tower they could see some detail in Caesar's camp and some in Scipio's, the ford being roughly halfway between the two.

'Scipio's not going to like us controlling this,' Fronto murmured. 'If you squint, from here you could watch him squatting in the latrine.'

Caesar turned a disapproving look on him, but nodded. 'Unpleasantly put, Marcus, but your point is noted. If we provoke *any* reaction from Scipio it will be here. Very well, strong work parties with armed escorts will move out to each of these towers and fortify them as redoubts. We will do so in order, from Leptis outwards, such that we should be able to consolidate much of the line before Scipio and Labienus realise what we are doing. By the time we get to the end here and Scipio reacts, we should have much of the system finished.'

The party had then ridden back to camp and the work had begun. In a matter of hours three crews were fortifying the ancient towers, and a line of watch posts was being manned from Leptis all the way back in an arc to the salt flats of Ruspina. The officers had moved with the vanguard of the construction, while garrison units had come up to occupy the fortlets as they were finished, all the work of but a few hours using stones from the surrounding area and good Sicilian timber brought from the camp. Behind this new line of towers, the cavalry moved in individual alae, all within contact distance and able to mass into larger forces at short notice, smaller units serving as scouts, all keeping the area under surveillance as work continued.

Now, early in the afternoon, Fronto and the others pulled out ahead of the work party at the penultimate tower, heading for the scout unit who had ranged ahead and who were waving at them. As the officers fell in with the tense-looking scouts, Fronto spotted immediately the problem across which they had come.

The tower by the ford was no longer empty. Even as Caesar's forces had worked from the Leptis end of the chain five or six miles to the east, Scipio had been at work. A small force of Numidians in white tunics and bronze helms commanded the hill from the ruined tower, a hastily assembled fence of sharpened stakes surrounding them and the crest.

'We were concerned about provoking Scipio, but it looks like he beat us to it,' Fronto grumbled. 'What now? Do we shift them?'

Caesar frowned and scratched his ear as he peered at the hill. 'It's a small force, but by the time we bring infantry out in sufficient numbers to deal with them, Scipio can do the same. It's as far to our camp as it is to his. Anything we do there, he can mirror it. We can field the cavalry immediately, but they're not really suited to winkling out defenders from fortifications on a hill.' He continued to scratch irritably. 'I do not wish to start something here that will lead us into a pitched battle, as we're not ready for such a thing yet. We need to finish these fortifications and consolidate until we are strong enough to guarantee victory.'

The general turned and looked back. The furthest turrets would be complete now and well-manned, and even the nearest ones would be there soon. 'We complete the line we have. As soon as the nearest turret is finished, I want all the work parties turned back the way we came and to run a solid line of fortifications from tower to tower right back to Leptis. Let's abandon the idea of isolated observation towers and instead keep the entire bowl fully protected. By late afternoon we should have the entire system complete barring this last tower at the impressive speed the men are moving. For now I want the cavalry massed in this area, keeping those Numidians on that hill and stopping any further advance.'

With that, Caesar and Plancus and the protective guards began to move back along the line in the direction of Leptis. Galronus called over two of his subordinates and instructed them to keep one ala moving about the line to protect the workers, and mass all other riders close to the enemy's redoubt on the hill, imposing control from the salt flats all the way to the current fortification work. Once the riders were moving, Fronto and Galronus walked their horses up to the near-complete turret a mile from the Numidians and there they waited.

It was little more than a quarter of an hour before they spotted the first movement. In the distance, the gates of Scipio's camp had opened, and cavalry flooded out, filling the plain.

'Hello,' Fronto said. 'Looks like something's up. He usually sends his best-looking infantry out first to line up.'

Galronus, nodding, sent one of the riders nearby to Caesar with warning, and the two men watched as the enemy cavalry moved into formation and started to advance. Behind them, infantry began to leave the camp.

'Is this it? Is Scipio attacking?'

Fronto shook his head at his friend's question. 'I don't think so. Our defector friends had been sent to identify defences against an assault by elephants. He's not subtle enough to have bluffed there, so that suggests heavily that he intends any initial attack to be led by Juba's elephants, yet there's no sign of them. I think this is Scipio being just as circumspect as Caesar. The general doesn't want to get pulled into a pitched battle, but Scipio will be nervous about approaching, for he is still ignorant of our defences and his spies keep defecting to us. He will be wary of walking into a trap.'

'So what happens?'

'Probably nothing, but I think we need to be ready to react or to finish this job with what we have.'

'Sorry?'

Fronto pointed at the next hill. 'If we want to complete the line, we need to take that hill. Caesar doesn't want to bring up his infantry as it might goad Scipio into doing the same, and that could take us into full scale battle. I think Scipio is trying to look threatening. He's trying to put Caesar off without committing. That's why his troops have taken an aggressive stance and moved that close. He wants to disrupt the fortifications. The only way we're going to be able to finish them without starting something big is to drive those Numidians from the hill without bringing up new troops. Is there any way your cavalry can do that?'

Galronus sucked in damp air as he peered at that hill. 'It's not a job for the regular cavalry, but I have an idea.'

'Go on?'

'I have two turmae of Oretani from Hispania. You know Spanish horsemen?'

'I know they have as fearsome a reputation as your lot.'

Galronus snorted. 'Maybe. But they're different. The Spanish specialise in hit-and-run tactics, guerrilla type warfare. Their riders don't do charges by nature and, much though this lot have been trained to, they still don't like it. They tend to ride into battle, then dismount and launch brutal assaults on foot. One of my officers has been tearing his hair out over them, as he can't get them to stay in the saddle. It strikes me that on this occasion they might be useful.'

Fronto grinned. 'Sounds good. I'll have a word with Caesar, you shuffle your men so that your Spaniards are closest to the Numidian pickets.'

Leaving Galronus to it, Fronto rode off to find Caesar, who sat only half a mile away, overseeing the works. So far fifty paces or so of the defences had been put in place, a ditch hacked and dug, and piled into a rampart behind. A full legion of men laboured with feverish speed to complete the works as fast as possible. The general turned at the sound of Fronto's approach.

'Marcus.'

'General, Galronus thinks he can dislodge those Numidians with a unit of dismounted Hispanics he has in the field. If we want to take that hill and complete the line, that might be our best option.'

Caesar frowned in thought, and then pointed back to the west. 'Come. Let us have another look.'

Returning to the vicinity of the enemy post, the two men joined Galronus who sat on the slope watching the enemy. 'What are the chances of this working?' the general asked.

The Remi noble gestured to a unit some sixty men strong waiting almost halfway between them and the enemy position. 'The numbers are roughly even, but the strength is in our favour. I have yet to see a unit of these Numidians that is truly committed to battle. On every occasion they have broken and fled early, while the Oretani are vicious bastards to a man. This isn't about numbers but terror.'

Caesar nodded. 'Two forces of Numidians face us under Scipio. One is a trained army that are dangerous and should not be underestimated, but they are here as support from King Juba, and we have not met them yet. The others are tribes folk that Scipio drafted into his legions, and who have been deserting back to their own peoples in droves. They are unlikely to stand for long. I concur with your estimate of the result. The question is what *they* will do in response.' He pointed off to the south, where Labienus' entire cavalry sat in lines less than a mile from the hill, a solid infantry force at attention between there and the camp behind them. 'We need to be prepared in case this triggers something bigger. It is something of a gamble.'

Galronus swept out a hand, indicating the mass of riders gathered on the plain inside the line of turrets. 'We are as prepared as they are, General. Labienus might be clever and his horse strong, but regardless, his record thus far is not a glowing one. He failed to trap us in battle, and then failed to take Leptis.'

'So his determination for a victory will be stronger than ever,' Caesar noted.

'But so will his frustration and tendency to act rashly. My riders now know this area better than they know their own features. I am confident.'

'If they commit their riders, they might also commit the rest of their forces.'

'We can always pull back,' Fronto noted.

'What?'

'Well all this is gaining us good defences over a wide area, but if Scipio decides to commit his entire army, we don't actually have to meet him in open battle. We can still withdraw to the camp as we've done every day and we won't really lose anything.'

Caesar nodded slowly. 'Very well. Let's see what we can achieve. Galronus, the field is yours.' Fronto grinned, but

Caesar turned to him. 'Not you, Marcus. This is a job for cavalry.'

Fronto watched, slightly irritably, as Galronus turned and rode off towards the Hispanic cavalry.

* * *

The Oretani were very much an unknown to Galronus. He had spent his youth and early adulthood riding with the Remi, and since the day Caesar and his legions came, they had continued to do so under the flag of Rome, acknowledging a few factors in Roman horsemanship that could be of use, and adapting their ways so that they gained the best of both styles. He had commanded Italians who were sticklers for rigid rules and tactics, various Gallic and Belgic tribes, who were of the same stock and attitude as he, and even Germans who, for all their vicious tactics, were of a similar fashion to the Belgae.

What he couldn't understand was the Hispanic peoples. Their horses were not kitted for battle, but were instead highly decorative, with rich bronze and gold accoutrements and colourful fabrics. They eschewed the Roman four-horn saddle that the Gallic and Germanic riders had readily adopted, instead choosing to ride only on animal pelts, usually of large killer cats. They held mysterious ceremonies in the camp to which no outsider was invited, yet they invited their horses. And despite all of this attention to the beasts who were at the centre of their culture, they actually climbed off them to fight, given the opportunity.

Still, right now he was grateful for their presence, and the unit moved quietly and unobtrusively amid the other cavalry, towards that hill, trying not to draw undue attention. As they approached the edge of the Caesarian forces, without the need for a command, the Spanish cavalry suddenly kicked their mounts into speed. As they rode at that hill, now no more than a quarter of a mile distant, Galronus watched them preparing. Their swords were still sheathed and their shields slung over their back on a carry strap. In their left hand they held the reins and in the right a strange and vicious looking spear, formed entirely of iron with no wooden haft, much narrower than normal spears and with a long, tapered, and wickedly barbed head.

As they neared the hill, the riders shuffled their hands along the reins until they gripped a large and heavy iron piton attached to the leather strap with a loop. This they held and used to continue steering the mounts as they reached the slope. Now there were shouts and noises coming from the Numidian defenders, but they were merely bracing against the attack, thinking themselves safe. After all, cavalry were of little danger to them, for horses could rarely be induced to charge a pointed defence, and the line of stakes around the Numidians provided points in every direction.

What happened next, then, came as a dreadful shock to the rebel defenders, for rather than charging the line, the Oretani riders reached a distance of some twenty paces or so from the enemy, gradually fanning out so that they covered two thirds of the hill's arc and leaving a third free facing Scipio for any cowards to flee through.

As they reached that point, each man performed the same manoeuvre. Galronus had seen them practice it from time to time and had heard of its use, but he'd not seen it in action, and was utterly impressed. His mount thundering to a sudden halt, each rider vaulted from the horse's back, a simple manoeuvre, with only a pelt and no saddle horns with which to contend. Landing lightly, the rider, still gripping the rein-weight, threw it down hard, where the heavy iron point slammed into the ground. The man stamped on the top of the loop, thereby instantly tethering the horse in that place as he ran on into battle. It all happened in a matter of two heartbeats. Sixty-four riders had become sixty-four infantry, their horses safely positioned for them to return to.

Each man then hefted their long spear, a unique weapon called a soliferrum, as they ran at that pointed hedge of stakes and the stunned Numidians behind it. By comparison, Galronus, who belonged to a horse culture too and considered himself an expert rider, was slow and clumsy in his approach. Halting with the others, he simply let go of the reins and trusted to his mount, Cynric, to stay put. Heaving himself out from between the saddle horns he slipped from the animal and pulled his shield from his own back and drew his sword. By the time he was running into battle, the slightly crazed Spaniards had almost won it.

Each rider leapt at the stake fence and stopped just short of impaling himself. There, he lanced out with the spear. Many caught the confused and panicked defenders hard in the upper body with the spear first time, and then, in a moment that made Galronus wince, they wrenched the spears back out. The barbed tips burst ribs open as they came out, causing unbelievable agony, and some of the men repeated the process with any defender still in reach, while others watched the Numidians backing away out of range and simply threw their soliferri with deadly accuracy, the sleek and light yet iron-hard weapon an easy missile with the strength and flexibility of a spear and the weight and form of a javelin.

This done, the Oretani set about pulling the fence apart to get to the Numidians, while those who had cast their spears drew their swords and unslung the shields from their backs ready for a closer melee. As the Numidians fled in panic to the far side, unpicking their own fence in order to get away and run for their army, the Oretani overran many, hacking them down brutally or casting their spears at the retreating backs. It was over in moments, and Galronus found with surprise that he'd not even bloodied his blade. As the seven Numidians who had survived the encounter fled at speed across the plain back to Scipio's camp, the Spaniards retrieved what spears could be saved and then began to use their heavy blades to hack the heads from the fallen for grizzly trophies.

Breathing heavily, Galronus climbed around the ruined tower to the peak, peering away towards Scipio's camp and the fleeing Numidians, and there he stopped, his pulse suddenly beginning to pound. The enemy commanders had seen the clash at the hilltop, clearly, for the rebel force was moving. Even as the Remi noble watched, the entire cavalry wing on Scipio's right flank began to charge towards the hill. They appeared to be a mixture of white-clad Numidians and chain shirted Gauls.

Squinting, Galronus peered into the distant ranks, knowing he should run, but sure he'd momentarily spotted something. There it was. He saw it again. Deep within the ranks of that ala of riders: the standard of Titus Labienus.

The Remi looked about. There was a possibility here. The plain to the west was open barring stands of trees and the river running through. To the east…

He smiled, and turned. There was a chance. Hurrying back around the peak, he gestured to the Spanish horsemen. 'Get back to the rest and tell the officers that Scipio's cavalry is coming.' As the Oretani riders charged for their mounts, expertly hooking the pitons from the ground with their feet, vaulting up onto the horses' backs and pulling up the reins in order to turn swiftly and ride, Galronus reached his own horse and pulled himself expertly up into the saddle.

Even as he rode back towards his ranks, he was gesturing at his second in command who sat, tense, watching the events unfold. Pulling out to the side of the returning Spaniards, he became more visible, and his second spotted him. Galronus employed only two hand signals, for he and his riders had developed visible codes that could be read during the deafening thunder of cavalry charges. Two signals that were given and read in a heartbeat, and as Galronus veered off to the right, so Samaconius, his deputy, rode at a tangent to meet him, two entire alae of Remi, Allobroge and Aedui cavalry following on.

Galronus turned as he rode, and confirmed his opinion. The terrain would be both a curse and a blessing. Because of the olive groves no one back here could see the approaching rebel horse under Labienus' banner, which meant that no one had any idea of what was coming. But it also meant that Labienus could not see what happened here.

The commander and his alae met in a small clearing beside a farm track, where an ancient shrine stood next to a pond. 'Sir?' Samaconius asked.

'Labienus charges the hill. I've sent word, so the rest of Caesar's cavalry will be riding to meet them there.'

'And us, sir?'

'We are going to see if we can put an end to Labienus for good. Follow me.'

Putting heels to flank, the Remi officer led his men along the farm track in the lee of the olive trees. He had to pray that his estimates were right, but then he was fairly confident of them. They rode in relative silence for a short time until finally, with some relief, what Galronus had seen from the hill now came into view: a large country estate. The place consisted of a huge two-storey villa with three wings, numerous outhouses and sheds, and the tips of high bushes and carefully-shaped trees spoke of a delicate garden, though all of this was largely obscured behind high walls with a tower at each corner. It seemed landowners here worried about bandits and raids, and jealously guarded what was theirs. The villa wall would hide the entire force of two alae until they were well past the hill.

He turned and used gestures to explain his plan, which was repeated back through the lines until more than two hundred riders knew what to do. If Galronus had timed it right, Labienus and his own horse would be just about at the hill now. The Remi nobleman gave the signal, and the entire force burst into a canter and then a gallop, rounding the corner of the villa and then emerging from the far side.

Galronus grinned with satisfaction at the sight that greeted him. The enemy horse had passed by and were now engaging Caesar's cavalry around the watchtower hill. Scipio had still held his infantry back, which either meant that he was uncertain about committing as yet to a major push, or possibly that this attack had been Labienus' own decision, independent of his commander. Labienus and Galronus had passed one another, the olive groves and the huge villa estate keeping them hidden from each other until the last moment.

Now, Galronus was looking at the rear of Labienus' cavalry. Best of all, the enemy were so intent on revenging themselves for what had happened at the hill, and weighing into the Caesarian cavalry, that they were paying no attention to what was happening behind them. Galronus' riders hurtled across the plain towards the rear of Labienus' army, and the Remi laughed aloud as a desperate warning call went up at the camp some distance away, for Scipio's infantry had seen what the cavalry had not.

For a moment, Galronus marvelled at what seemed like a finished deal. The enemy had no idea of the danger they were in. Then, suddenly, a Numidian rider turned and his eyes went wide. In a heartbeat others were turning, horns were blowing, and officers were bellowing commands. Galronus locked his eyes on the standards that betrayed Labienus' personal location, and he raced for that marker.

The enemy were reforming now, conflicting commands ringing out, and several things began to happen. Firstly, utter panic broke out among the Numidians, who formed the bulk of the rear units and who were in the most danger. Secondly, Labienus and his officers immediately called a retreat. Thirdly, some Gallic officer confused the issue by sending out a call for his riders to press home the attack. The result was that the plain suddenly exploded into confusion, the

Numidians turning and racing for home while the Gauls and Germans continued to push forward into the Caesarian ranks.

Galronus' cavalry hit the scattering white-clad Numidians like a trireme's ram against a rotten barge, sending fragments out everywhere, killing and maiming with hardly any resistance, their enemy more desperate to flee than fight. As Galronus found himself engaged with one of them, who fought mostly to parry and escape, he lost sight of the standard he was pursuing. Cursing, he ended the Numidian with a hard slash across the lower back, and rode on, trying to reacquire his target.

When he spotted Labienus again, he knew his attempt had failed. In the confusion, the commander had slipped in among the bulk of the fleeing Numidians and even now he was racing at speed back across the plains towards the camp, where Scipio's infantry were already beginning to pile back through the gates to safety. For a heartbeat the Remi considered giving chase, but common sense quickly won him over. If he managed to catch up with Labienus it would be right outside their camp and Galronus would die needlessly in a hail of artillery.

No, the commander had escaped once more.

Turning, Galronus clenched his teeth. He may have failed to pin down Labienus, but an entire ala of Gauls and Germans had been left fighting for their lives. Whatever happened now, it was a victory for Caesar. They'd taken the hill from the pickets there, run off the Numidians, and now Labienus' prized Gallic cavalry would be cut down to a man by the massively superior numbers of Caesar's riders. And Galronus knew there would be no survivors, not because he was vicious and would order needless deaths, but because now it would become tribe fighting tribe, as it always had been, and pride would make them all fight to the last.

CHAPTER ELEVEN

Near Ruspina, 25th January 46 BC

Fronto replayed the logic put forth in the command briefing even as he gave the order to march and the legions fell into a mile-eating pace. There was nothing wrong with the general's logic *per se*, yet something indefinable about it still seemed wrong to him. The basic premise had been the need to press Scipio into doing something stupid, and the man had a solid track record of doing just that, after all, yet somehow Fronto felt that this was a plan marching into nowhere.

It was not supply issues that had driven the general to the decision to push matters after so long being reactive, nor was it enemy pressure, nor even news of fresh trouble back home. It was the ennui the legions experienced when doing little more than waiting and the frustration of the officers. The legions' reason for existence was to fight, and watching the enemy across three miles of dust for protracted periods was doing little for morale. In essence, the men were becoming bored, and bored legions became restive and troublesome. Already there were needless fights breaking out, and the relationship between the veteran Fifth and the new Gaetuli cohorts, who were still swelling with daily desertions, was abrasive to say the least. The legions had needed a focus for their anger.

And the officers were no better. Of course, most of them were relatively new to Caesar's staff and that level of trust that had always existed between the general and his lieutenants was not yet there. The men questioned everything. Why was a grand strategy not being formed? Why were all officers not included in tactical decisions? Was the general losing his touch? Fronto had tentatively suggested to the general that he needed to do something decisive, which involved all his officers and men to bind them back to the cause.

Caesar maintained, and rightly so, that he had no intention of meeting the enemy in the open field until he could be confident of victory, and this seemed to be a matter of waiting for the four veteran legions from the early days of Gaul. The Seventh, Eighth, Ninth and Tenth legions were the heart of Caesar's army and each had been honed into killing machines over the previous thirteen years. In their absence, a decisive action that brought about a pitch battle in open ground was unacceptable.

The result was Caesar's risky plan to goad Scipio into blind attack. The enemy commander had sat in his camp day after day, not willing to tackle Caesar's defences, offering battle in the open instead, yet given that Scipio had already sent spies to determine what defences would face elephants, clearly the notion of an assault continued to nag at him. If Caesar's army could push him far enough, then it was possible that the fortifications of Ruspina could balance their strength and even out the chances of victory. The question then had been 'what could draw Scipio out?'

Scouts had been dispatched to examine in more detail Scipio's disposition with a view to nipping at him sufficiently to make him react. His supply chain seemed to be excellent, foodstuff and equipment coming in that was more than adequate for his huge army. Moreover it was well-organised, coming from the west and the towns heavily under rebel control, but also from the east where, though the towns were more liable to waver in their support, the greater stores of grain were to be found. Water was abundant in the form of the seasonal river that ran past the enemy camp. In summer it would be of little use but at this time of the year it flowed freely. There was no defensive position of high value that could realistically be taken from him to pull him into a fight. Committing to take any town under his control would also draw out Caesar's army and result in precisely the mass open battle he was trying to avoid. Whatever happened they had to be close enough to both camps to withdraw behind their defences and bring Scipio to them. It was a fine balancing act, threatening the man but in a position to draw him back to Ruspina.

It had seemed to be an impossible decision until Caesar had begun to place markers on the map, where gradually one position had been revealed as a nexus of everything. Just half a mile from Scipio's camp lay the town of Uzitta, not large enough to be of great strategic value, without walls, towers or a garrison, but large enough to control the crossing of the river next to which it lay. Half of Scipio's supplies, coming from the east, had to cross the river at Uzitta to reach his camp. Furthermore it seemed that it was at Uzitta that water was drawn for the army, upstream of the houses where a good ford lay. Further inland, the flow broke up into the many small streams that fed the river, while further north towards the sea, water gathering was risky due to the proximity of Caesar's new line of defences. Uzitta was close to Scipio's camp, and at the heart of his supplies.

Caesar had his target. The army would march out as if to war, but rather than attacking Scipio's camp or meeting him in the open, they would threaten to hit Uzitta. There would be no hope of holding the place against Scipio's larger army, and destroying it would be of little value, but looking as though they were prepared to might just provoke the enemy into action.

So given all this, why were Fronto's senses nagging at him? Perhaps it was the fault of Plancus, who had met with he and Galronus for a drink after the meeting. Fronto had thought Plancus to be above the general mutterings and complaints of the officer corps, being Caesar's man from the old days, but it seemed he was wrong. The man had voiced concerns over Caesar's tactical decisions. He'd noted that the general seemed to be acting much more rashly than the last time the two had served together in Gaul. He simply could not understand why Caesar had dallied in Aegyptus with his mistress while the enemy consolidated their hold on Africa. He could not understand why the general had rushed through matters in Rome in time to launch an invasion in the middle of winter when he could only call on half his available troops, and precious few of his veterans. Plancus could not comprehend why the general had not decided upon his landing site and had a campaign plan worked out in advance, which would have nullified all the problems with lost ships and confusion. And while he could understand the need to lead the men into action before they became restive, for a trapped animal was prone to bite its keeper, he also pointed out that had Caesar simply waited until all his legions were ready, this situation could have been avoided altogether.

Fronto had argued against every point in favour of Caesar, and his responses had been reasonable and sensible, the very words the general himself had used, yet the more he defended the man, the more it became clear to him that he shouldn't *need* to. The Caesar who marched against Aduatuca would never have needed his strategy defending from concerned officers. Moreover, every mention of Aegyptus and that conniving queen made Fronto twitch. Cassius had abandoned the campaign entirely, citing his refusal to fight Romans in the field, but even Caesar privately believed the man's withdrawal was over the matter of Cleopatra.

The woman had involved herself in matters, and ever since then the general had struggled to keep up with events rather than marching confidently ahead. He hid it well from the masses, but the officers were beginning to see it. All through Gaul, Italia, Hispania and Illyria Caesar had planned, commanded and led. Even against Pompey, despite being outnumbered and outmanoeuvred, he had managed to turn the campaign around and grip the reins, moving with confidence from the disaster of Dyrrachium to the victory of Pharsalus.

Then he had reached Aegyptus, and in truth their only real reason for being there had been chasing down Pompey. With Pompey dead the general should simply have left the king and queen to their little conflict and moved on to Africa, chasing down the remaining enemy commanders in the aftermath of Pharsalus and annihilating them before they could recover.

Instead, he had become involved with the queen, supporting her over her idiot brother, bogged down in the internecine wars of that ancient land and everything had started to go wrong. They had been besieged and made to fight a desperate campaign in the delta that was purely the business of the queen and her brother and of no importance to Rome. Then, when it was over and things could still be salvaged, when Caesar could have moved on, gathering the armies he'd sent back to Italia and marching on Africa, he'd instead stayed with his new mistress while the enemy fortified here and while the legions in Italia became lax and restive and rebellious.

And because of all that, they were now fighting a hard war in Africa where a year earlier it would have been so much easier. Caesar was leaping into things without adequate preparation. Was he desperate to get all this over so that he could get back to the bed of his queen and their infant son? Fronto wondered in a bitter moment what the general's wife thought of all this, let alone the precocious great-nephew Octavian, who had been groomed for years now to take the place of a son.

The whole thing was something of a mess.

The only real positive was that word had come from the east that Acylla had been taken and held by Messius. A wounded tribune had arrived by ship to confidently state that the town was solidly defended and that there was no likelihood of the enemy taking it. Still, it was a single step forward in an otherwise stagnant campaign. Damn it.

Gritting his teeth, Fronto brought his attention back to the current situation, for they had now passed the tower where Galronus and his Spaniards had ousted the Numidians and the line of defences. Barring a single cohort left guarding the camp and the town, the entire Caesarian force moved purposefully forward towards Scipio and Labienus. Five legions, thousands of archers and light auxiliary infantry, and solid wings of cavalry, Gallic, Germanic, Hispanic and now also Gaetuli rode at walking pace on both wings. It would be a breath-taking sight, were it not for the fact that everyone knew how much larger Scipio's army was.

Each of senior staff led a legion, riding out front with a small group of signallers and standard bearers and the six tribunes of each unit. Galronus rode with the cavalry on the left wing and some wild-looking Allobroge noble on the right. Caesar rode at the front, at the centre of the line, along with his praetorian riders and Salvius Cursor. In an attempt to heal the growing rift between the veterans and the Gaetuli who had deserted from Scipio they had placed the two side by side near the centre, with Fronto commanding them both.

The army moved at a mile-eating pace, the standard Roman march, every man pensive, not knowing quite what to expect. They could arrive and find that Scipio refused to leave his camp, leaving them in control of a small town of little value. They could arrive, discover that Scipio was more proactive and prepared than expected and find themselves involved in a mass battle against a superior force. Or, in a perfect world, they could arrive, draw Scipio from his camp and then goad him into chasing them back to Ruspina where they might just be able to defeat him. Tension crackled across the entire army.

Finally they crossed a low hump in the ground and their target came into view. Fields of low stubble, barren for the winter, lay stretched out before them, uncomfortable for marching, and beyond them, Fronto could see the small sprawl of Uzitta nestled on the east bank of the river, not more than a mile from the site of that first disastrous battle, and only half a mile from the other focus of attention.

Scipio's camp lay clearly visible, larger by far than the town, and there was already activity there. Fronto fixed his squinting gaze on the distant mass, wishing he had Galronus' keener eyesight. Even he, though, could see enough to know what was happening. Scipio was reacting.

The army was pouring from the camp gateways.

Fronto peered into the haze, trying to judge their intentions. After all, Scipio repeatedly lined his men up outside the camp, trying to tempt Caesar and he could be doing just that once again. Fronto turned and glanced at the figure of the general on his horse just a hundred paces to the right, on the far side of the Gaetuli. Right now they appeared to be doing exactly what Scipio had wanted and marching to meet him in battle in the open. Sure enough, the enemy were not lining up outside the camp, but moving at speed, cohort by cohort, heading for Uzitta and the river. The scouts had reported that on the far side of Uzitta the river was shallow and easily crossable, and as those cohorts splashed into the water, crossing to be ready for battle, Caesar gave a silent order, relayed by the signifers, and the army slowed slightly. The last thing they wanted was to march into that very battle that Scipio anticipated. The trick was to slow enough to draw the entire army forth, and then to retreat once they were close enough to take the bait and follow.

Slowly, they closed on Uzitta and the army assembling there, and Fronto's gaze was drawn to the worryingly large shapes moving out of camp. Scipio meant business, for his elephants were deploying. The Caesarian army watched in nervous silence as they marched. The enemy were gathering at the far side of Uzitta, where they had crossed the river. The infantry were deployed in three lines, an immense force, the fourth line, at the front, formed by the mounted troops. A few elephants stood between cavalry alae along the line, the largest force of the massive beasts settled on the wings to either side of the small town.

Fronto frowned. The formation was strange, in the circumstances, for to march into battle the centre would have to navigate their way through the town, or the army would need to break that formation and skirt it. The enemy sat there, the last units falling into position, and as the Caesarian army closed on Uzitta, Caesar gave the signal to halt, messengers calling the officers to him.

Fronto rode across the army and reached the general, who waited for the rest to arrive, and then gestured at the scene before them. 'Gentlemen, your thoughts?'

Plancus huffed. 'He's inviting us to attack him again. He's not fallen for the bait, and invites us to mire ourselves down in the town.'

Fronto nodded. 'If he'd meant to attack us, he'd have deployed on *this* side of the town. He expects us to go for him, something only an idiot would do with the town between us.'

Galronus pointed ahead. 'There are indications that he's garrisoning Uzitta. I can see white figures there, moving about the buildings. Numidians, I expect. They would keep us busy while the main force moves to encircle us.'

'He *wants* us to march on Uzitta,' Caesar said with a sigh. 'Then he can bring his elephants and cavalry around our flanks and box us in. He has no intention of coming for us. Once again I can only wish that it were Labienus commanding there, for I doubt he would be lurking behind the town and crooking a finger at us. He would have deployed for battle now. Scipio, though, seems content to wait.'

'He knows he's strong enough to stand a good chance of victory,' Plancus muttered, 'so why delay now? He's been trying to tempt us into battle for days, so why, when we offer it, does he hide behind the town? Something has changed.'

Caesar nodded. 'I fear that like us he is waiting for something. He has more than adequate supplies, so it can only be troops. But Cato has few troops in Utica. We can assume there are at least two legions floating about somewhere in Africa, and probably new ones still being levied, but they would make little difference since he already outnumbers us. So who could be important enough to wait for? Cato will not come to command, and no one outranks Scipio.'

Fronto frowned, peering at those monstrous pachyderms once more. 'Juba.'

'What?' the other officers turned to him.

'He's got ample supplies and no legion would make a difference. The only person in this whole region who's important enough for Scipio to show deference is the king of Numidia. If Juba is coming, Scipio will hold off fighting long enough to allow his ally a chance at some of the glory. We know that Cato has agreements with Juba, and even Scipio will honour them.'

Caesar sat straight in the saddle. 'It is the only explanation that makes sense. Scipio moves to stop us taking Uzitta, which he has effectively done, but meanwhile he waits for his royal partner in crime. We are thwarted,' the general said irritably.

'So what do we do now?' Fronto grumbled.

'There is little we *can* do,' Caesar said, rubbing his neck. 'The hope was to goad him into attacking and following us back to Ruspina, and that seems extremely unlikely now. If we do anything here, we will be mired in the assault on the town and crushed by his strong flanking forces. We do what we can to taunt him, and if he does not take the bait, we have little choice but to retire to our own ramparts once more.'

Fronto turned and peered off into the distance, trying not to remember Plancus' words from the night before: '*If the general had waited until spring, he would have had all his veteran legions and more besides, and he could have simply selected his landing site and launched a proper invasion, instead of all this messing about.*'

Damn it, but it was looking more and more as though Plancus had hit the nail on the head.

* * *

Ruspina, Kalends of February 46 BC

'How can Scipio still not react? Labienus must be twitching and pulling in the traces, desperate to move,' Fronto grunted as he stood at the new line of fortifications.

Galronus simply shrugged as they looked along the line. Scouts had been sent far and wide after the failure at Uzitta, and it had taken only two days for them to confirm solid reports that the Numidian king had led his army out of his homeland and was perhaps two weeks away from Ruspina. The king's intervention was the talk of rebel towns in the west, and far from secret. If the reports were anything like accurate, then Juba brought three 'legions' of his best troops, several thousand cavalry, myriad light infantry, and another thirty elephants. In light of this news, Scipio's reasons for waiting were clear. Even if Caesar gained his four veteran legions, such a force as Juba brought would only make victory all the more certain for Scipio, and he would honour his ally in the process.

Knowing now that they had a limited time before the enemy force swelled immensely, and with the need to seem decisive and proactive, keeping the officers and men focused and busy, Caesar had settled upon the task of needling Scipio, goading him more and more. If they could only push him into attacking Ruspina they might be able to defeat him before reinforcements arrived.

Consequently their line of fortification through those hilltop towers had been extended, the ramparts now half a mile closer to Scipio's own camp. Indeed, from one of the new defensive positions, where the two officers now stood, they could see Uzitta itself and the mass of the enemy base close by. Still, even as Caesar's ramparts came closer and closer, Scipio made no move against them, lurking in his camp day by day, not even leading his army out to offer battle any more.

Of course, Fronto knew quite well why Scipio would not react. The man *had* to wait for Juba. And every day that passed made Caesar's army a little more edgy and ate away at their supplies with no achievement to show for their efforts but an ever extending line of fortifications. Scipio strengthened each day, while Caesar weakened.

Indeed, it had now become necessary to keep the Fifth and the Gaetuli truly separate. The veterans were suspicious of these men who were non-citizens yet had been drafted in as legionaries, and who had, so recently, served in the enemy force. The Gaetuli, on the other hand, held themselves as the veterans' equals, despite their origins, and refused to back down, resulting in frequent scuffles. Now, the Gaetuli were stationed at the Leptis end of the defences, the Fifth at the salt flats end. Fronto knew the men well enough to know that all this stupidity was merely a symptom of tension and ennui, and that as soon as they were called to battle, it would likely evaporate. Consequently, he continued to pray for movement.

The only movement they had seen had been encouraging, though not in respect of battle at Ruspina. The previous day, a large force had approached from the east and made for Scipio's camp, and it had taken little effort to identify them as

Considius' army. It seemed that Acylla was safe and that the rebel commander had abandoned his siege. The force had stopped for a while at the enemy camp and then moved off once more to take up their garrison position at Hadrumetum. Things then settled into routine once more, daily caravans under guard arriving to keep Scipio's men fresh and strong and well-fed.

Fronto looked up into the light mizzle that drifted down from the flat grey sky above, letting the cold mist settle refreshingly on his face. 'With luck we'll have a downpour and the cisterns will fill,' he said absently. 'It worries me drawing extra water from the river, given that Scipio's men probably piss in it upstream.'

'Hello, what's this?' Galronus said suddenly, squinting into the distance.

Fronto lowered his damp face once more and followed his friend's gaze, but could see nothing of particular interest. 'What's what?'

'Movement at the enemy gate.'

'Probably Scipio having a movement all over us,' Fronto grunted, as he focused. He could just make out movement of a sort but nothing more. 'Not a full advance, I presume?'

Galronus shook his head. 'A small group, some mounted. Officers there. And some sort of vehicle. Strange.'

'Let's take a closer look,' Fronto said, and the two men rode away from the new defences, a small party of Remi riders following on for protection, given that they were riding ever closer to the enemy camp. Here, where the river meandered sparkling towards Uzitta, the land was fairly open and the view good even in this chilly drizzle, and scouts had identified the various viewpoints in the surrounding terrain, some of which were already earmarked for the next set of defences should it be decided to move the lines forward once more.

No enemy pickets were to be seen, and Fronto felt confident in their safety as they rode to a low rise beside a farmer's shed, a hundred paces from the river bank and with a good view of the area. Coming to a halt and shivering in the cold grey air, the two men looked at the camp gate once more as the Remi riders gathered around them, eyes on their surroundings, ever watchful.

Fronto frowned into the grey, and realised what was happening with a sickening of the stomach.

'Gods, but what caused this?'

Galronus, face drawn into a look of angry contempt, took a deep breath. 'Is that what I think it is?'

Fronto nodded, watching the 'T'-shaped constructions being set in position along the front of the camp defences. Twelve of them in all. 'Crucifixions. What could possible drive the man to this?'

'Perhaps he is sick of the constant desertions?' Galronus hazarded. 'He might be making an example.'

'He's walking a dangerous path,' Fronto grunted. 'Crucifixion is for criminals and slaves. If it's the Gaetuli he's planning on torturing to death, then he's sending a deadly message to the men under his command.'

Galronus coughed. 'I don't think he needs to worry about that. I don't think that vehicle contains Gaetuli, Marcus.'

Fronto frowned and peered into the misty air. It took some effort, but it didn't take long for him to pick out enough detail to see what Galronus meant. His eyes widened and he whistled through his teeth. The vehicle was little more than a cage on wheels drawn by two oxen, and contained a dozen figures, whose nature Fronto would never have expected. 'He cannot seriously be thinking of doing that.'

'They're Romans,' stated Galronus.

'*Our* Romans,' Fronto added angrily.

'How can you tell?'

'Look at the mix of uniforms. I can see at least two centurions. One senior officer – a prefect I think. And among the others I can see a few blue tunics, but every one of them is a man of rank. There's a trierarch there I think.'

'Sailors,' Galronus frowned. 'They *could* be enemy ones,' he added, though doubtfully.

Fronto shook his head. 'I think the only explanation is that one of our missing triremes made it into enemy hands. Those are men who left Lilybaeum with us. They should be here as part of our army, but thanks to that damned storm they've spent weeks in enemy hands and ended up like this. Gods, but Scipio has become dark-souled if he can seriously crucify fellow Romans in front of us all. And they're *citizens*. If that *is* a prefect, then he's a nobleman and a member of the equestrian order. These men are supposed to be exempt from such punishments.'

'Is it a message, do you think?'

Fronto nodded. 'Given that it's being done in the open, out the front of his camp and in full view of the men working on our fortifications, I don't see how it can be anything else.'

As they watched, two figures emerged from the camp gate on horseback, both senior officers.

'Our two vultures,' Fronto said. 'Scipio and Labienus.'

'They're arguing,' the Remi noted.

'Yes. I'm guessing Labienus is against this. He might be our enemy, but he has a streak of humanity in him. I cannot see Labienus agreeing to such a thing. To be fair, though, I couldn't have seen Scipio doing so either. Whatever has happened it's incensed Scipio to the point where he'll order atrocities.'

They watched with rising anger and disbelief as the prefect, such as he clearly was, was led down from the cart-cage, his hands bound. He walked proudly with his head high, and as he passed in front of the two arguing men on horseback, he spat in the dust at their hooves. Scipio's soldiers roughly manhandled him over to one of the execution posts and heaved him down onto it, pushing his arms out along the horizontals of the T and holding them there while their friends bound the wrists tightly with harsh rope to the timbers.

The man had been remarkably noble until that moment, but now he began to kick and scream as the men pulled his legs together and bound them to the upright. As the man howled and begged, they dragged the entire apparatus across to a hole already hacked into the earth: a socket. The crucifix rose at a weirdly stately pace until it reached the vertical, when it dropped into the socket. Even at their distance, the two watchers could hear the scream, and Fronto could vividly imagine the sound of stretching sinews, tearing muscles and separating joints as the man settled into place, his body weight dragging him down and putting unbearable pressure on his limbs, the positioning making it hard to take more than a shallow breath. There would be no further screams. The man would simply not have enough oxygen to manage it.

Galronus and Fronto made themselves stay and watch the entire grisly process, a dozen iterations of agony as men were raised on their death frames to slowly sag into agony before a mixture of exposure, hunger and brave predators ended their suffering.

At the last, when the twelfth man was raised high, Scipio and his men returned to the camp. Fronto felt almost kindly disposed towards Labienus as he watched the man's reaction. His old friend waited until the senior officer had passed through the gate, and then walked his horse forward and snatched the staff from an optio's hand. Passing along the line, he swept out at each figure, smacking the heavy ash pole into their shins, breaking their legs. It would hasten their deaths. If the blood loss and pain didn't do it, at least they could no longer fight their predicament, pulling themselves up. Their inevitable pain would be foreshortened.

'We report this to Caesar?' Galronus asked, his voice betraying a sickened tone.

Fronto nodded. 'It has to be done. The old man isn't going to be any happier about this than I am.'

He turned back to camp and his gaze fell on the low line of strange purple and orange on the northeast horizon. A storm far out at sea. He hoped that was no portent of ill times to come, nor even of a change in the weather. All they needed now was torrential rain.

CHAPTER TWELVE

Ruspina, 17th February 46 BC

Fronto was startled from a very pleasant dream of family and that comfortable villa life which now seemed a lifetime ago. His eyes snapped blearily open as he tried to gauge both the time and what it was that had so disturbed him, all while suffering that momentary disorientation of post-dream waking. Then the noise insisted itself upon the world.

The incessant and very heavy drumming of rain on the tent roof.

Cursing, he turned over. There was not much he could do about it, not being a weather god. It had been a long time coming, but it was inevitable. After that dreadful event with the crucifixions, they'd seen the tell-tale storm cloud out to sea and Fronto had known it was coming for them. The officers had shouted him down, calling him pessimistic as always, and they had seemed to be borne out, for that storm drifted past a mile from land, peppering the surface of the sea with its drops before disappearing inland towards Uthina to the northwest. Following on in its wake the weather changed and storms became the norm. They seemed to breed in the east and pass across the sea just off Ruspina before hitting land further west. Crete, apparently, was known for birthing such tempests. For two weeks the storms had come close and yet blown past. It was about time one strayed closer.

He couldn't get back to sleep. Squeezing his eyes shut defiantly, he listened. It really had to be torrential out there, which made setting foot outside all the less enticing. He felt for the men, and knew that this was going to deepen the rift between units and cause further trouble. The army had advanced the fortifications a further quarter mile towards Scipio's camp in another futile attempt to draw him out, and in a simultaneous effort to bind the Gaetuli and the Italian veterans into brotherhood, the Fifth and the deserter units had been given the job, with Fronto commanding. Thus while the other legions and auxiliaries remained in the main camp near Ruspina, Fronto and his mismatched command occupied a temporary camp at the new defences, far closer to Scipio than to their own lines.

The problem was one of supplies, and not food in this case. When the various Gaetuli had defected, they had brought their clothes, armour and weapons, but had not been at liberty to carry anything else. The few spare tents the legions had carried had been donated, and with whatever leather could be swiftly acquired more had been made, but the men were coming to Caesar's standard faster than the tents could be found or created, and fully half the Gaetuli under Fronto's command were asleep under temporary shelters formed of cloaks held up with pila, or hastily woven reed screens, or suchlike.

Not much protection from a torrential rainstorm.

It had to be around midnight, he mused. He'd vaguely heard the second watch blown, through his dreams. Gods, but even as he listened he could hear it getting worse, sounding like a stampede of oxen thundering across open turf. He wondered how long his tent would last against it, and then guiltily thought of those Gaetuli in camp who would be in a far worse position.

The thunder faded, and Fronto heaved a sigh of relief, turning over.

Then it returned suddenly and with a vengeance. He sat bolt upright, his ears ringing at the fresh din on his tent roof. That could not possibly be normal rain. It sounded as though his tent was going to collapse. His eyes, now well trained to the dim interior, drifted up to the roof, and then widened in alarm. Between the taut seams, each panel of his tent sagged down bulbously beneath a heavy weight. If just one of those gave, the tent's interior would be soaked. Still, though, the noise was too much for even torrential rain. It sounded as though artillery ammunition was dropping on the leather.

Struggling upright, he hurried over to where his waxed, waterproof cloak hung and pulled it on over his rumpled tunic, hauling it round him and yanking the hood down to cover his forehead. Taking a deep breath, he lifted aside his heavy tent flap and took a step outside.

In a heartbeat, as his gaze took in the scene, he stepped back inside.

Something had smacked into his head so hard it had bruised, even through the thick leather of the hood. Looking down, he could see where the hailstones had bounced and rolled in through the tent door. They were the size of sling bullets!

That flashed image of the camp outside was still there in his retinas as the tent flap fell back into place. Men hurrying this way and that, holding shields above their heads to protect them from the painful hail, tents and temporary shelters alike collapsed in sorry heaps on the ground. Men bellowing in panic and pain. Shrieks. Even a legionary with blood running down his face amid the torrents of water, staggering this way and that in confusion.

Jove, but this was bad. Yet, he had to be out there, trying to sort it all out. Settling on a course of action, he shook his hood clear, gritted his teeth, and ducked out of his tent once more. Sure enough a small stack of armaments stood nearby, just where he thought he'd seen them. Running over to them even as the hail hammered at him, he grabbed the first defence he could, which turned out to be an oval shield from some auxiliary unit who's shield design seemed to include mostly wreaths and flora. In the blink of an eye he had the shield up over his head as the hail rattled off it, striking with such power that he could feel the heavy board being knocked this way and that.

Temporarily sheltered, he took in the scene once more, this time with deeper appreciation.

It was an unmitigated disaster.

He was standing on a slight rise which had been chosen for the camp's praetorium and officers' tents and it was the only thing that had saved them. The western side of the camp was ruined. The storm must have been raging inland for some time before coming northeast towards the sea, for the seasonal river, which was a reasonable flow by day, was now a raging sea that had risen above the banks and easily entered the camp. The western periphery was underwater, tents swept away by the flow, men struggling. He could see a couple of contubernia of legionaries desperately trying to rescue a cart of victuals which was even now on the river bank and about to slip into the deeper flow, where it would be carried away and scattered.

It was difficult to make out much in detail, for very few of the camp's fires and torches were still alight, most of them long since doused. A capsarius from the Fifth had set up a small aid station already, three wounded men clawing at him. Above him, the temporary shelter of a large leather flap held up by four pila sagged and leaned dangerously. Fronto shouted and started to run towards him, bellowing for men to help. Before he could reach the scene, four legionaries were there, two Gaetuli and two from the Fifth, and they each grasped a corner, lifting the pila and tilting the leather roof so that the weight of water and hail tipped to the side, easing the pressure.

Fronto heaved a sigh of relief, and even of hope at seeing men of the two different units working together under such circumstances. His hope and relief were torn from him, though, a second later. The black and purple boiling clouds above them seemed to open up for just a moment and the world was lit with a dazzling white flash.

Fronto blinked, both in temporary blindness and in utter shock, as the flash died away and a scene of absolute horror played out before him. The tips of those four pila were still wreathed in dancing electricity as the men holding them crumpled to the ground, dead and smoking. The leather roof fell on the medic and his charges and Fronto ran over, joined by an optio he didn't know, pulling the leather from the men and trying to ignore the burned shapes of the four legionaries.

Further lightning strikes lanced down here and there, and occasionally men screamed. Fronto knew how this would be taken later: an ill omen, the anger of the gods. But right now it was a matter of keeping control in the world of men. Their supplies had been almost entirely washed away, fully half the accommodation gone, and chaos reigned everywhere. Fronto spotted a tribune running towards him, similarly holding a borrowed shield over his head. Fronto waved at him.

'Get anyone wounded and all the medical staff into the headquarters tent. It's the largest one, and if there's an overflow, use mine. Then pull everyone who's devoted enough to still be on watch back into shelter. No one should be out on duty in this. Get everyone under cover, even if they have to stand packed-in, shoulder to shoulder.'

'Sir, we're trying to save the last of the supplies.'

'Screw the supplies. We'll request more when this is over. Get everyone to safety.'

As the tribune ran off, Fronto gestured to that optio who stood wide-eyed nearby, and between them they lifted the leather sheet and held it above the capsarius and the wounded and escorted them to the headquarters tent close to Fronto's. As the men gratefully dipped inside, Fronto was momentarily blinded by another flash of dazzling white light. A thought occurred to him and he grabbed the optio. 'Run around the camp quickly and make sure that all pila and spears are down on the ground. Nothing metal pointing upwards, and no one wears their helmet, despite the rain, alright?'

The optio saluted and ran off, removing his own helmet as Fronto dipped back into the tent doorway, out of the deluge but where he could still see the camp. It was awful, and when the storm passed there would be an immense task ahead in repairs and clearance. His gaze rose to the camp of the enemy little more than half a mile away. At least Scipio and Labienus had to be suffering the same conditions, though their men would at least all have proper tents.

His brow furrowed. It was hard to see little more than a dark smudge on the landscape beneath the heavy clouds, but something was different. He couldn't quite work it out, and it was very hard to make out any details.

The world was suddenly thrown into stark silver relief with another flash of lightning, and now Fronto saw it. A huge column snaking its way across the battered landscape towards Scipio's camp. Even in that brief flash, Fronto knew who it was. Legions' worth of infantry, light auxiliaries behind, and cavalry riding on the wings, but out front and leading the way: a force of elephants.

Juba of Numidia had arrived.

* * *

Fronto stood outside his tent on that shallow rise as all around him the work of clearing up went on in the watery, pale early morning light. The river's level had reduced once more, though it was still deep and fast, running just below the level of the bank, the landscape strewn with detritus that had been swept along. Fully half the camp had changed from being dry, dusty ground to being some kind of ankle deep sludge that was appalling to work in. The bodies of the dead, numbering eighteen, had been gathered together, some burned by lightning, others drowned, a few crushed under sinking carts and the like. There was simply not enough dry material to burn in a pyre, and so they were to be transported back to the main camp to be dealt with. The headquarters remained in use as the hospital. Still, things were gradually coming back into some semblance of order.

A blast from a cornu announced the arrival of the general. He'd come fast in response to Fronto's courier who had ridden out at first light, in the lee of the storm. Caesar, along with Plancus, Galronus and half a dozen other senior officers, came to a halt close to Fronto, their expressions grave.

'General.'

Caesar nodded at Fronto. 'You were hit badly. The main camp suffered, though nothing on this scale and our casualties were remarkably low. Where is this new force?'

Fronto pointed out to the west. Throughout the sleepless night as men battled the elements to keep some control over the camp, Fronto had stood on the hill and watched Juba and his army arrive. There was every element of which they'd heard, though the only part of the new arrivals that immediately combined with the settled force were the elephants. As Juba's thirty great beasts moved close, the other thirty emerged from Scipio's camp to join them. Then, Juba's army encamped separately from Scipio, though only a few hundred paces away. The royal party had ridden into Scipio's camp even in the terrible deluge and stayed there for the night.

This morning, as the light first arose, Fronto had been entirely unsurprised to see large-scale movement in each camp. Already the elephants were in position and the rest of the army was moving.

'Do they mean to attack?' Plancus murmured.

'It is quite possible now,' Caesar replied. 'They outnumber us by more than two to one, and those elephants are a potential disaster for us. Our current lines of fortification will hold against cavalry and even against besieging infantry for a time, though we will inevitably be pushed back to Ruspina. Still, we could hold if they attacked us within our defences, and be confident of a reasonable chance of success; more so than we would have in the open. The elephants are a worry, though. They very well might be able to simply batter their way through our lines and open up gaps for the rest of Scipio's forces to pour through behind them. I have studied my histories and I know of the dangers of elephants in the open and how to deal with them, but I have yet to hear tell of their strengths in a siege situation. They are an unknown quantity and I fear they nullify all our advantages. Our best hope, I fear, is to re-site our forces with a view to holding against the elephants.'

'And that would involve?' Fronto prodded, watching the enemy force assembling. They were gathering in much the same way as Scipio did regularly, offering battle close to his camp, but now with a vastly increased number.

Caesar pursed his lips, scanning the landscape. 'We need to move decisively, and we need to move fast. In our current position, I fear that Scipio could crush us, using elephants as his vanguard. If he hasn't realised this yet he soon will, especially with Labienus and Juba urging him on, and then our time will be up. We cannot abandon the coast, for further reinforcements will come and we need our port and beachhead, yet we need to advance now, while we still have the chance and while we can still be proactive.'

'*Advance*?' Plancus goggled.

'Almost to Uzitta,' Caesar nodded. 'From here, I can see a stretch of rough, broken ground with gulleys, then a large olive grove, and then a rise above the town of Uzitta, to the southeast, not from the direction of our previous advance.'

'I see it,' Fronto mused.

'Galronus,' the general turned in his saddle, 'why would Labienus not lead his cavalry out from their camp against that hill?'

The Remi officer squinted into the distance. 'Any cavalry attack would have to come from this side. There is a rough cliff facing the town. Not a tall one, and not vertical, but steep enough and high enough to make a cavalry attack impossible.'

Caesar nodded. 'The same, I think, can be applied to elephants. Scipio and Juba will not attack that place directly with their beasts as it would nullify his advantage.'

'It puts us at two disadvantages, though,' Fronto noted. 'We will have to move our focus away from Ruspina and the coast if we wish Scipio to concentrate on this place, which means we take our power away from the fortified landing spot for reinforcements, and though the cliff will face the enemy, he could still come around behind and attack from the safer side.'

Caesar nodded. 'Quite so, and we must therefore anticipate all problems. We must leave a cohort at Ruspina, another in our main camp, and appropriate garrisons all along our various defences, should we need to fall back in stages at any point. We must keep control of all territory we currently control and make sure that that hill, when we take it, is tied into the system. As soon as we fortify on it, the legions will start work swiftly on running two lines of ramparts back from the hill to here, effectively making that hill part of this fortification, just extended far forward. Once this is done, we position archers and sufficient artillery on those new defences to pick off elephants or cavalry if they attempt to come round behind us. They will have to cross the river either at Uzitta or upstream. Anywhere between there and the coast, the river is too hard to cross, especially after that storm.'

Fronto chewed his lip. 'That would put us spitting distance from the enemy. And I mean close enough that long range artillery might just be able to exchange blows. It's pushing them.'

'But it will push them into an attack that is not fronted by elephants,' Caesar replied.

'Scipio might be slow enough to react that he lets us take and hold the place,' Fronto retorted, 'but Labienus won't let us do it unopposed. We need to be prepared to fight for that hill.'

Caesar leaned back in his saddle. 'Yes. And we need to move fast. Scipio is simply parading again. His troops are lined up to provoke, but he'll lead them back inside once more. While he parades them, I will have the army move quietly and in separate cohorts up to our closest lines, behind this camp. We should be able to do that without being seen. Once our army is gathered here, we wait until Scipio is back in the camp and then we make for the hill and attempt to secure it before he can react adequately.'

Fronto nodded. 'It's possible. It's risky, but it's possible.'

* * *

Fronto rode steadily at the front of the Fifth as they reached the edge of that region of broken and gullied ground. Ahead he could see the densely-packed olive grove and rising behind it the hill that was their objective, itself home to small scattered stands of trees and areas of shrub growth. The men were moving at double time, for they had only half a mile to cover and needed to try and do so while they were still unopposed, and Fronto felt the tension rising as they came ever closer to the enemy camp.

As the legions, the Fifth in the van, scrambled down the unpleasant side of the nearest gulley, which had changed from choking dust to slippery mud thanks to the storm, Galronus and the cavalry appeared at the wings, ready to form an advance screen for the army now that they were in the open. Hurrying across the troublesome terrain, Bucephalus picking his way carefully, they clambered up the far side of the gulley and then crossed the next stretch, where small pits and dips honeycombed the ground and forced the legionaries to move this way and that, breaking up their lines to cross safely. Even the cavalry were forced to move slowly and carefully, lest they risk numerous lame animals to the scattered ankle-breakers.

For a seemingly interminable few moments they threaded their way across the difficult landscape, then reached the next gulley and slid and scrambled down it, crossing to rise once more. By now the cavalry were starting to move ahead, closing from the wings, and Galronus pulled his men in to create the screen in advance of the legions. A third gulley crossed, and finally the army rose to the edge of the olive grove with a sense of relief. The densely-packed trees would make it difficult to maintain formation, and would be troublesome for the riders, but it was still better than the open gulleys, and the cover would hopefully shelter them from enemy view for some time.

Fronto took a last look at that hill before they disappeared into the grove. It seemed a perfect analogy of their time in Africa so far. Another hill to climb. Since arriving, the whole thing had been a series of small climbs, none of which had afforded an apex, but merely a view of the next hill to climb. He could understand why they were forced to do all this, to play a defensive game, but it rankled all the same, and Fronto found himself longing for the days when they had marched across the grassy fields of northern Gaul, hunting down rebelling tribes and with a set goal and a solid plan. This messing around was starting to get to him. Indeed, the attitude across the whole army was souring, exacerbated by recent events which were mostly seen as signs of displeasure from the gods. After all, this place may bow to the lords of

Olympus, but it still clung weirdly and doggedly to the ancient and strange gods of the Carthaginians.

The Gallic horsemen began to disappear into the trees, fanning out as they went, and the legions slowed for a moment to give the cavalry time to enter before following. Then with just a gestured signal, they moved on into the trees, navigating their way between the ancient, gnarled boughs with difficulty, but moving ever on with purpose.

Fronto started at a cry of alarm from ahead, accompanied by a muffled clash, and cursed. This grove made it impossible to see further than perhaps two or three men and he had no idea what was happening ahead. Clearly they had stumbled across something unexpected. Snapping his head this way and that, he fretted. The rest of the senior officers were further back, beyond the Fifth, and this was his responsibility, but he couldn't see a thing and had no idea what was going on. He was effectively marching into the unknown completely blind.

His mind was made up by further sudden bursts of activity, shouting and alarm all scattered ahead and around. Turning, he waved to the legion's primus pilus a few paces away. 'Keep the men moving forward and be prepared for trouble. I'm going to see what's happening.'

As the senior centurion saluted, Fronto geed up Bucephalus and rode ahead, trying to avoid branches, hissing with irritation as foliage whipped at him. He fixed on the source of the loudest noises and lowered his face so that his gaze looked up ahead just below the brow of his helmet, saving him from painful twigs and leaves in the face.

The first sign of life he came across was a Gallic rider nursing a wounded left arm and riding slowly back his way. The man stopped at the sight of Fronto and tried to salute, failing with a whimper of pain.

'What's happening?'

The man glanced back over his shoulder. 'Not sure, sir. There's men all over this place. Riders mainly.' He nodded at his dripping arm. 'This was done by a German. Ubii, I reckon. They seem to be lurking all over the grove in small pockets, and they're fighting when we meet, but it doesn't look like a full force and they seem disorganised.'

Fronto narrowed his eyes. 'Labienus apparently has cavalry units out in a screen just like us. I bet they hadn't counted on bumping into us any more than we had on meeting them. But if it *is* a cavalry screen, that suggests there's infantry not far behind.'

He could hear the Fifth closing on them. What were they facing? He thought about it for a moment, and then shook his head. 'Whatever lies ahead there can't be many of them. We saw the bulk of Scipio's forces return to camp and we'd have noticed them coming back out. This is a small group of horse and foot Labienus has sent out to keep the approaches to their camp secure, I suspect. We press on ahead and take that hill. Go find a medic and get yourself seen to.'

The horseman nodded and set off, Fronto riding past him. A few moments later, he emerged into a small clear area, a farmer's track crossing the olive grove. Seven riders were busy battling hard a short way off to the left and Fronto momentarily considered involving himself, but realised with a frown that they were all Gallic cavalry, almost identical, and he had no idea which were those of Labienus and which of Caesar. He watched for a moment as the contest was won by an unidentifiable side, and he was only sure who had been bested when the remaining rider from one party turned and raced off into the trees ahead, yelling to his compatriots. It seemed Caesar's cavalry were coming off best in the woodland. Sure enough, as he moved ahead, wherever there was sufficient space, he saw similar contests playing out, always with the same results. Galronus' men were far more numerous here, and Labienus' scattered riders continually fell back.

By the time he emerged from the far edge of the olive grove the enemy cavalry, those few who had escaped unharmed anyway, were racing up and around that hill. Now, Fronto could see white figures up there, which suggested that the enemy had a small garrison of Numidians in control of the hill. Unexpectedly, another banner appeared from the woodland and raced towards the slope with a small group of riders, and Fronto's eyes narrowed.

Labienus.

The man himself had been with the cavalry among the trees.

'Labienus!' Fronto bellowed angrily, putting his heels to Bucephalus' flanks and racing towards that flag. His old friend shuddered to a halt along with a dozen riders, and Fronto suddenly realised how stupid he was being. He could hardly take on thirteen men alone, but the sheer opportunity of spotting Labienus in the field and in danger had been too tempting to resist. The enemy commander turned purposefully, his men gathering ready to take on this lone lunatic officer.

Fronto felt a surge of relief as a small group of allied cavalry burst from the trees close by and, taking in the scene in a heartbeat, raced forward to fall in with Fronto. As he crossed the open ground between the trees and the hill, the enemy beginning to waver, another small group burst free and ran to join him. In moments he had a force of riders roughly equal to that of Labienus.

He could end an old contest here, and it was a contest that had to end and could only do so at the point of a sword, as Labienus had made perfectly clear in meetings past. The loss of Labienus would remove an important commander and tactician from Scipio's staff and was worth the risk.

He felt the irritation rise as Labienus, realising now that he was in ever-increasing danger, wheeled with his riders, turning away from a potential fight with Fronto and racing away, past that hill, towards Uzitta, the river crossing, and the camp of Scipio beyond.

Fronto and his riders gave chase for a short distance, but the futility of it soon slowed them. They could not outpace the enemy commander and the longer they pursued, the closer they came to the enemy lines and to real danger. With the deepest of regret, Fronto let Labienus flee the field once more. Turning, he watched the Caesarian cavalry emerging en masse from the woods and hurtling up the slope of the hill.

The white-clad figures of the Numidian garrison broke and fled at the sight, long before the first ranks of the Fifth cleared the olive grove, and from the ranks of the horsemen Fronto saw Galronus emerge at the crest. Geeing his horse once more, Fronto rode up the hill, past the Gallic horse, to fall in next to his friend at the summit, where the Remi commander was looking ahead.

'Let's hope Caesar knows what he's doing,' Fronto muttered, looking down the steep scree slope ahead, beyond which lay Uzitta and the river, Scipio's camp on the far side and the landscape dotted with fleeing rebels both on foot and on horseback. Amid them, Fronto could still see Labienus' standard.

'The general was right about one thing,' the Remi said. 'No rider would attack that slope, and though I've never seen an elephant up close, unless they can climb or fly, neither will they.' He turned to look back across the olive grove and the muddy gulleys. Beyond, they could see the camp that had been ravaged by the storm and the ramparts of Caesar's defences. 'Now we just need to make sure we're not flanked and attacked from behind up that slope.'

Already the legions were emerging and separating, moving into positions. The Fifth were making for the hill directly, which they would man and fortify, while the other four legions split into two groups to fortify lines on either side that would stretch back all the way they had just come, attaching this hill to the fortifications back there and enclosing this newly-won battle ground.

They had taken the hill. Another one to climb, only to reveal the next hill.

How long would Scipio let them hold it, he wondered?

CHAPTER THIRTEEN

Uzitta, 18th February 46 BC

Galronus sat on the lower slope of the hill near the town of Uzitta, just below the scree escarpment that had been their choice of defensive positions against cavalry and elephants, and he grumbled irritably.

Samaconius, next to him, looked over, a question in his eyes as the pair shook the drizzle from their hair and shoulders. Samaconius still wore a very traditional beard, which had become thoroughly waterlogged, some vindication to Galronus' mind of his decision years ago to adopt the clean-shaven face of Rome, clinging still to his braided hair.

'Just the command decisions,' the Remi commander grunted in reply to the unasked question.

'It has always been said that Caesar is a genius on campaign,' the deputy said, his voice level. 'I have served since Uxellodunum and, while I've seen setbacks and troubles, he's yet to lose a war.'

Galronus frowned. 'You may be witness to that change soon, I fear.' He chided himself. He'd been around Fronto too long. He was turning into the same pessimistic storm crow. 'I have faith in the general,' he said with a sigh, 'but his strategy appears more erratic and hasty with every passing month. I remember Plancus from Gaul, before you and your riders joined us, my friend. He was the tactical dunce, new to command, and Caesar and Fronto corrected his every intended blunder. Now I watch them in briefings and it is *Plancus* who adjusts *Caesar's* strategy. Such a sight does little for the confidence.'

'You think Caesar's decision here is wrong?'

'Don't you?'

The two men looked about them. All around the slope between here and the edge of Uzitta the Gallic, German and Spanish horsemen of the Caesarian army sat in their units, watching for the next enemy foray, while the infantry were at work all the way back from here to the camp half a mile away. The dual fortifications that would link this place to the extant line of forts and ramparts already stretched two thirds of the way, the bulk of the army now half a mile back there, working hard to complete the line that would effectively create one great fortress with its closest edge on the ridge, overlooking Uzitta and the enemy camp.

The only problem was the gaps. So far the new defences had been flared at the eastern end so that they reached out like arms to envelop the town, not connecting with the fortifications on the hill. A gap of five hundred paces sat to each side of the hill before the new ramparts and the enemy were determined to push at them.

Caesar's logic had been twofold. The gaps allowed the workforce and the new hill camp access to the water of the river, which saved them a three mile journey back to Ruspina for water or braving the river downstream where Scipio's scouts probed constantly, looking for foragers to butcher. More importantly, Scipio had clamped down on his desertions. Those few native defectors who made it to Caesar's lines had tales to tell of draconian measures in place against any who would desert, and the number of men changing sides had died down drastically. But more of a deterrent to those men was the fact that Scipio had riders and light skirmishers out all across the ground between his camp and the Caesarian fortifications, and any man caught crossing them joined Caesar's unfortunate sailors on a cross outside the enemy camp. In response, Caesar had decided to leave welcoming gaps in his lines at Uzitta, as long as possible to allow enemy defectors a much safer way to reach the Caesarian lines.

It had worked to an extent. The number of arrivals had risen again slightly, though to Galronus' mind not enough to warrant the danger the gaps presented, for Labienus was not allowing them a rest. One minor officer who'd come over late the day before had explained that Scipio was unwilling to commit to battle in full, knowing that the elephants would be of little use, having to make their way through Uzitta and then having to make their way around the edge of the hills. Elephants were only of predictable use in the field if you could point them at an enemy and let them go. And to commit to a battle that might decide the fate of the republic denying his ally King Juba the chance to play his part and share in the glory would not be a politically sensible move. Thus Scipio continued to sit in his camp, instead sending out officers, emissaries and bribes in an attempt to consolidate his hold on rebel towns in the region and to turn those who'd gone over to Caesar back away. Caesar had been confident that those towns he had garrisoned could hold out and would stay loyal, and so the two armies glowered at one another as Caesar moved his works ever closer. If no one made an overt move soon, the ramparts would be so close they could drop rocks on Scipio's tent.

But Labienus, it seemed, was less content to sit and wait. Whether with Scipio's blessing or not, he had started launching raids almost immediately. Groups of Gallic riders, backed by a few light skirmishing infantry, had issued from the enemy camp, crossing the river and moving through Uzitta to attack any workers in the area, to kill water gathering parties and to test the new defences and the small garrison on the hill, presumably with a view to taking it back before the gaps in the lines closed and the entire area became fortified against them.

The first such skirmish had almost been a disaster, so unprepared for it was Caesar's army. Labienus' horsemen had flooded through Uzitta with insufficient time for the defenders to do much more than brace themselves on the hill. They had shown tremendous mettle and held off Labienus' horse until Galronus and his riders had come to their rescue and driven the rebels back into Uzitta and away. Since then, the hill had been garrisoned with archers and auxiliary infantry, the legions fully engaged in finishing the twin lines of ramparts, and Galronus and the cavalry had been placed at the vanguard below the hill to protect against repeats.

And protect they had. Rarely had two hours passed without a fresh attack, always new, always inventive and keeping Galronus very much on his toes. There was no pattern to Labienus' attacks and, given his previous near-disasters, the man no longer rode into the fray with his men. Sometimes they formed a wedge of riders and tried to break one flank or the other, driving Galronus to gather his full force in one position to repel them. Sometimes they split into two forces and circled the hill to both sides, forcing Galronus to split his men. Sometimes the light infantry came first and javelins were thrown in clouds, driving the Caesarian horse back and allowing Labienus the chance to bring his own riders very close. Every time a new tactic, and now, after a full day of such pushes, Galronus was tired, and so were his men. After all, Labienus had more cavalry at his disposal and could afford to rest half his riders every time, while Galronus and his men had been in action now for more than a day and a night with little more than forty winks snatched here and there as time allowed, and usually without leaving the saddle.

He could only hope that when the legions had completed their new lines of ramparts they came forward and blocked off the gaps that welcomed Uzitta and deserters, for he was not sure how much longer his riders would remain an effective force without rest.

Once again, Caesar's strategy was costing him dearly.

'Can you hear something sir?' Samaconius murmured.

Galronus stopped huffing loudly and cupped a hand to his ear. 'Yes, though I'm not sure what.'

His gaze rose above Uzitta. The afternoon was wearing on now and dark would soon fall. He was not keen on the idea of another night of fighting these interminable skirmishes, and already the light was in decline. Worse still, the horizon seemed to have become blurred, some strange illusion making it hard to make anything out in the distance, like a heat haze, though in the cold and damp. Sure enough, though, he could see horsemen pouring from the gates of the enemy camp. Labienus was coming again. Galronus looked at his own force which was gathered in alae all across the front of the hill, ready to move into whatever formation was needed in response. The sound that had drawn their attention was not the extremely familiar rumble of distant cavalry, though. It was something different, more muffled, more subtle, less identifiable.

'I think Labienus has a new surprise for us.'

Samaconius pursed his lips. 'We wait?'

'We wait.' They had to. Until the horsemen crossed the river, he wouldn't know whether they planned to force one of the flanks, or split to both, or push for the hill at the centre. He looked at his exhausted riders and nodded to the signaller behind him. The horn honked out a first call, warning the men to stand to, that the enemy were coming. The next call would order the units into formation, once Galronus knew what that formation had to be.

Behind them one of the support units was arriving with two more carts of shields, spears and armour to replace lost and damaged ones and to keep the cavalry lines strong. Galronus motioned for them to leave the vehicles and retreat speedily.

'Here they come,' Samaconius said, pointing.

The riders, a thousand strong, came racing across the shallow waters to the east of the town and there split. Galronus held out for only a moment, to be sure of their focus. Behind them light auxiliary spearmen were coming. He held his breath, but the attack was clear now, for the enemy had split into two wings, the one to Galronus' left moving slower and heading for the edge of the gap close to the outer fortification, the right moving at speed to move around and take the opposite flank.

'Give the signal,' he called, and the musician behind him blew the call for the cavalry to split and respond on both wings. A single ala remained at the centre in reserve. Galronus lifted his reins, ready to ride, but Samaconius gestured to him. 'Sit this one out, sir. We've cycled the alae in reserve and every man here has missed at least one engagement, but you've been in them all. You need a break.'

'You too,' Galronus noted.

His deputy grinned. 'Then I'll sit still if you do.'

The two men remained in place and watched the latest skirmish unfolding. The enemy cavalry, four alae strong on each wing, raced for the gap where, if they could circumvent Galronus' men, they would be able to swing round behind them and come at the hill from the rear where the slope would allow riders to attack and where the defences were weaker.

The Caesarian force had split into units of a similar size in response and were moving to block the advance, which they would do, though for how much longer the tired riders could be expected to do so, Galronus was not sure.

The riders now being clear of the river and Uzitta, battle was joined, and the enemy infantry, light and fast, were even now crossing ready to commit in support. An unexpected movement suddenly caught Galronus' attention, and his gaze snapped to the town. The source of that unidentifiable sound suddenly became apparent as scores of light infantry poured from the houses of Uzitta, bearing between them siege ladders, ropes and grapples, and racing for the hill at the centre.

Galronus cursed. Damn it, but this time the cavalry attack had been little more than a diversion. Sure enough, as those siege troops ran for the escarpment and the fortified hill at the centre, so the enemy infantry crossing the river flooded towards the centre behind them, ready to join a concerted push for the hill. Gods, but Labienus had thrown wave after wave of ineffectual skirmishes against them only to lull them into a false sense of security in order to achieve just this. Galronus had committed his tired troops to the wings where they were even now beginning to get bogged down. Now thousands of infantry, well rested and prepared for an assault, were racing for the centre, where only a hundred riders stood between them and the defences. Admittedly a few hundred auxiliaries manned the ramparts on the hill, but their numbers were dwarfed by the enemy force.

'This is a full scale attack to retake the hill,' Galronus said, his head turning this way and that to take it all in. His gaze fell on the town before him and, with a sinking feeling, he saw the floods of infantry pouring from Scipio's camp like a sea of gleaming insects beyond it. It really *was* a full scale assault. Scipio and Labienus had fooled them into complacency and now they would pay the price.

He turned to the musician behind him. 'Do you know infantry calls as well as ours?'

The musician nodded. 'We try and learn them all, sir, so we can identify what other units are doing.'

'Samaconius, take him and any other musician you can find and ride all the way back to the camp half a mile back, sounding the call to bring every man here. If the legions don't hurry, we'll lose the hill.'

The two men turned and rode away. As Galronus watched what was happening, he waved over a decurion from the reserves on the slope below him. 'Ride for those infantry near the town. Smash any ladder and kill any rope man. Let's try and slow their assault until the rest get here.'

Moments later, the reserves were riding out to intercept the leading enemy infantry. Galronus almost set off in their wake – after all, every rider could count here – but in the end, common sense overtook the urge to become involved. With the extreme danger they were currently under, he was needed in a position where he could see what was happening, and issue commands as needed. Looking about, he spotted a distant musician and waved the man over. He would need to be able to make his orders known across the field.

He cast up a quick prayer to Taranis that they could hold until sufficient relief arrived.

Time passed one nervous heartbeat at a time. His reserve ala ploughed into the force carrying the ladders and ropes and did all they could, though men inevitably slipped past, the fresh infantry that had crossed the river running in to support them. The flanks were being hard pressed. The numbers might be similar, but Galronus' men were exhausted and they were giving ground at a slow but inevitable pace. Despite that, the Remi nobleman fumed as he gave the order for two alae from each flank to pull back to the centre. That would put left and right in danger of breaking at a moment's notice, but the centre was largely undefended, and the hill could not fall after all they'd done to take it.

The call went out and riders peeled away from the conflicts on the wings, racing back in front of the hill to form up there and face the infantry, who were already closing on the slope. Damn it, but they should have been more prepared for this. His view was becoming somewhat restricted and, needing a better scope of events, Galronus turned and, gesturing for his musician to follow, rode up the slope to the base of the scree escarpment and then around the northern side. Making for a gate in the new hill defences, Galronus entered the fortifications and moved to the top. The crest, which had been covered in scrub and dotted with trees when they first approached, was now bare, allowing an excellent view in every direction, for the timber and scrub had all been employed in the creation of the defences.

His stomach turned over as he looked out across the field of battle. The enemy numbers were increasing. As well as the cavalry committed against his men on the flanks, a horde of white-clad riders was now coming to threaten the centre, while it would appear that all Scipio's light infantry had been sent out, only the legions and the elephants remaining in their camps.

He turned. Caesar's legions were on the way. It came as something of a relief, though he was not sure whether they would be in time. The five legions had split into two armies, each approaching on the flank, along the line of the new fortifications they had been creating. Squinting, he could see that each was led at a charging pace by an commander and a bunch of tribunes. Caesar was clear on the left flank with his red cloak and white horse, and Galronus was relieved to see the other unit led by Fronto.

Would the cavalry be able to hold long enough?

Calls began to go up among the approaching legions and Galronus wondered what commands needed to be issued when they were already running into battle in a straight line. Plus, as part of the works all the way back, the olive grove had been cleared on the flanks and the gulleys and pitfalls smoothed over and filled in, so that the approach was a relatively easy and safe one.

He realised with a start what he was hearing. The calls sounded odd because they were being issued through Roman horns, but they were not Roman melodies. He remembered those tunes all too well, blaring out from a carnyx as the Remi rode into battle with their neighbouring tribes in the days before Caesar and the legions came. They were songs of battle from the world before Rome. Hymns of blood and steel to Toutanis and to Taranis. They were…

They were a declaration of intent. They announced to anyone who knew the old ways that the army that came for them came to fight to the death. There would be no stopping, no quarter given. This assault was to the end. The musicians had to be taking their lead from the two Gallic riders Galronus had sent back. A slow smile spread across his face as he realised what was happening. Caesar and Fronto knew they might not get there in time, but their voices would.

Turning, Galronus looked down to the left and right. The flank attacks were faltering. He could almost feel the shock and fear among the enemy's Gallic and Germanic riders down there. This was the last thing they'd expect to hear and it shook them to the core. It was having less effect on the light infantry and the Numidian riders racing to join in, but to the Gauls, Belgae and Germans that had been almost pushing through the wings, it was a message of impending death. Moreover, Galronus could see his own Gallic, Belgic and German riders gaining heart from the sound, finding new reserves of energy and will, fighting back all the harder.

Even as he watched, Galronus could hear something new atop the cadences of war. Chanting had begun. It had started slow and quiet, only a few voices taking part, few knowing the words. That there were men in Caesars' legions who knew the ancient war chants of the Belgae spoke of the origin of many of his legionaries, and the words were not hard to mimic. Soon the rest of the approaching legions were joining in as best they could, chanting songs of intent to maim and butcher and invoking bloody gods in the process.

Galronus looked to the prefect in charge of the hill's defences. 'Get the braziers lit. The light is fading, so let's light up the hill for them.'

The man grinned and issued the orders. In moments braziers sprang to life all around the summit of the hill, and the units of archers based here dipped their arrows into pitch buckets and then the flames, waiting for them to burst into golden life and then nocking them and selecting a target from the myriad shapes approaching.

'Let's make them think they're fighting lions,' Galronus said. 'Give them a roar with every shot.'

Moments later the prefect, content that the enemy had reached a good distance, gave the order and several hundred arrows loosed in a shallow arc from the town-ward edge of the defences, accompanied by a roar that raised the hairs even on the back of Galronus' neck.

As the roar died away, there came from behind the hill a massive rhythmic crash as twenty thousand sword smacked into the rims of twenty thousand shields three times, and then the war melody and the chant of tribes seeking blood arose afresh.

Labienus' Gallic cavalry on the wings broke. The threat that came with the calls and tunes and chants had cut through the nerve strings of every man who knew what they meant and the fear had finally overtaken them. Galronus laughed, a wild, raw laugh that carried all the battle lust of his ancestors. 'The hill is yours, prefect. I'm going to take some heads.'

Leaving a confused and worried-looking officer issuing commands around the hill's defences, Galronus rode away, out of the gate and around the slope, back towards his original position, noting as he went the approach of the legions under the general and his friend. With the enemy faltering now, the legions would arrive in time to stop the light infantry taking the hill, and the cavalry attack was already being dealt with.

As the Remi emerged before the hill, he took it all in. The infantry were mired down with his alae of defenders, while both flanks had broken, the enemy riders racing back towards their own lines. There was still danger, though, for the war calls that had terrified Labienus' Gallic riders had meant nothing to the Numidian cavalry, and those white-clad horsemen were still coming, other auxiliary infantry in their wake. His men were making to pursue the Gallic riders, howling their victory, and Galronus chewed his lip, looking up. They dared not get too close to the camps, but then all they needed to do was break the attack with sufficient force that the enemy would stop their continual probes for a while. He frowned. That blurry horizon had grown, moved closer. Now he could still see the enemy camps but they were less distinct. Men were racing back into safety, and those soldiers that had only just issued from the gates to join the attack were already turning and running back inside.

He gestured to the nearest musician. 'Form the alae on me.'

The calls rang out and all across that small battlefield between the hill and the town, the Caesarian riders broke off their pursuit and wheeled around, making for Galronus. Squinting into the distance, he could see small units of commanders, on the far side of the river but in the open before the camps. One he could identify readily, for he'd seen Labienus' banners before. The other could only be Juba, King of Numidia. For just a moment, he wondered whether there was any hope of catching them, but the light was rapidly dwindling now, they were too close to Juba's camp, and that strange blurring was increasing. All they had to do was send the rest packing.

As the riders gathered around him, Galronus pointed at the white-clad horsemen, who had slowed now, aware that their Gallic allies had fled and that they were now charging the Caesarian army almost alone, barring a few units of light auxilia that were already in trouble.

Galronus pointed at the Numidian riders. 'We know they break like a samian bowl on a marble floor. Let's put the wind up them.'

With a roar, the tired cavalry found a last burst of energy and kicked their mounts, racing away across the open ground towards the white riders. The Numidians exploded in panic as the Gauls rode at them, bellowing and howling, and turned to flee, all too slow. In heartbeats Galronus and his riders were among them, the Remi commander in the fore, sword rising and falling mercilessly alongside those of his men. The Numidians were able horsemen, but they were largely unarmoured, only one in five sporting a shirt of bronze scales while most wore a simple linen tunic, their shields small and light, most heads bare. By contrast, the Gallic cavalry busy hacking a swathe through them sported helmets of both Roman and Gallic designs, chain shirts, oval shields with iron bosses, and they had forgone their spears for their long, Gallic swords.

The result was utter carnage, and Galronus was surprised when he realised they had reached the river in their violent pursuit. The Numidians were fleeing across the water now, and the rest of the attacking force who had not already broken and fled was trying to cross without coming too close to Galronus and his riders.

The Caesarian cavalry plunged into the water, racing after their prey, still killing as they went, and Galronus, aware that command here was his, and victory or disaster both rested upon his shoulders, beckoned to the musician. 'Call them back.'

A cavalry prefect nearby hauled his horse to a stop and turned a surprised look on his commander.

'Sir?'

'Don't chase them to the camps. We'll put ourselves in too much danger.'

'Sir, the enemy commanders are still in the open. We can take them.'

Galronus shook his head as the musician blared out the order to disengage. 'We've tried it before. They'll lead us into artillery range and then slaughter us. And can you hear that? Taste it in the wind?'

The prefect frowned, turning to face the northwest. The drizzle had stopped at some point unnoticed in the struggle, but the wind had picked up and it was coming from the west, beyond the enemy camps. And it carried with it a taste of parched and barren dust.

'What is it?' the prefect asked in a worried tone.

'Never seen one before, but I hear they have dust storms here, bad ones that choke cattle and bury farmland. I'd love to kick Labienus' arse a few miles further, but I rather think we need to get everyone into shelter.'

The man nodded, his growing fear clear on his face. Galronus looked across the river. A local scout had told him about these storms, and one thing he'd been adamant about was that you wanted to be undercover when they happened. They were half a mile from the camp that had almost been washed away days ago, which had now been extended to house the entire force as required, the accommodation had been set up, and the hill held sufficient shelter for a garrison of a thousand.

The camp of the Numidian king was no longer visible, that strange, speckled blur having overtaken it. The storm was coming, and coming fast, and the enemy troops were now fleeing into Scipio's camp, trying to get undercover before the storm overtook them all. Galronus gestured over his shoulder.

'Back to camp, fast.'

As the exhausted riders made one last effort, this time to save themselves from the oncoming storm, Galronus heaved a sigh of relief. Labienus had almost done for them this time. They'd have lost the hill, and then their control of all the lands in front of their defences, at which point their lines would have been pushed back to that earlier position, which was easy prey for an elephant assault.

Now they had saved it. They had won another victory despite being caught with their tunic up. How long, he wondered privately, could they keep pulling their backsides out of the fire before Caesar's strategic hiccups lost the war for them?

CHAPTER FOURTEEN

Ruspina, 28th February 46 BC

Fronto hauled himself up into Bucephalus' saddle and walked the proud animal away from his tent, where the legionary who'd brought him returned to his work. Caesar, Plancus, Galronus and the small collection of staff officers were gathered at the general's tent. One new addition was Amasan, commander of Caesar's Gaetuli, which now numbered six cohorts. Following the mass defection after the dust storm ten days earlier, there were sufficient numbers of the natives to form almost a full legion, and the arrival of a man who, according to intelligence, was the brother of the Gaetuli king, made the choice of commander obvious. Caesar had thus far treated the man in an odd and careful manner, somewhere between trusted lieutenant and favoured ally, and he was clearly part of the staff.

There was no denying the Gaetuli's value, for every man that crossed the open ground to strengthen Caesar's force weakened that of Scipio, and they had thus far shown a uniform loyalty that bordered on pathological hatred of the rebel forces.

As the officers rode through the original camp near Ruspina, where now only four cohorts remained on guard, he contemplated the recent battle for the hill, and its aftermath. On the surface it appeared that nothing had changed, and yet a little musing brought clues to the truth. Scipio and Labienus remained encamped in place, sending out their tendrils of control to try and secure the towns of eastern Africa, while Juba and his army remained in their own camp nearby.

Caesar's forces sat on the hill and within the new defences that had now been sealed at the Uzitta end, and would be difficult for Scipio to assail. For ten days nothing had moved. But *that* was the giveaway. *Nothing* had moved. Labienus had ended his cavalry forays against Caesar's men, and Scipio had stopped leading his men out before the camp and offering battle.

What the inscrutable bastards were up to was anyone's guess, and any strategy there was kept among the commanders and certainly kept well away from any of the native recruits who Scipio could clearly no longer trust. Intelligence concerning enemy intentions had dried up entirely.

The flood of men that had run to Caesar on the day following the battle at the hill had come, by their own admission, partially out of loyalty to long-dead Marius and to their companions who had already defected, partially because they were more than a little disenchanted with the way they were now being treated by Scipio and his officers, and partially through loyalty to Prince Amasan, who had watched the astounding turnaround at the hill, when by rights the rebel forces should have easily overcome the Caesarian defenders, and had decided that the gods were with Caesar. Two entire cohorts of Gaetuli had left the enemy camp the next morning under command of Amasan, as the dust settled and things returned to normal. They marched proudly through the gaps in the lines even as legionaries moved in to close and fortify them, their defection draining significant strength from Scipio's Fourth and Sixth legions.

Now they were encamped forward with the main force, close to their former camp and the enemy commanders. Fronto had returned to the old camp near the town of Ruspina with the other officers, principally to oversee a reorganisation of the entire defensive system and supply routes within it. This morning's planning meeting had been postponed, however, when news of the fleet had been brought by grinning, excitable soldiers to each officer's tent.

Scores of ships, they had said, largely heavily military triremes, though accompanied by fat-bodied and heavily-laden transports, all bearing the Taurus emblem of Caesar. Now the officers rode, pensive and silent, accompanied by Salvius Cursor and a contubernium of his praetorians, through the camp, past the abandoned training grounds, and down towards Ruspina's harbour. The place was a hub of mercantilism these days, few warships in evidence as most were busy in one role or another around the coast of Africa, while supply ships came and went on a daily basis.

Now, as the small party of officers arrived at the place, those ships were closing on the harbour. Fronto felt a swell of contentment to see the vexillum of the Tenth legion snapping in the sea breeze atop one of the lead ships, and almost as much at the sight of the pennant of the Ninth on another vessel. Two of the most veteran of Caesar's legions and with both of which Fronto had long standing connections, stretching back two decades and more.

As the riders came to a halt and watched the ships manoeuvring, Fronto caught sight of Caesar's face and pulled his horse closer so that they could speak in low tones without too many ears wagging.

'You don't look as pleased as I'd have expected.'

Caesar's expression did not change, radiating haughty disapproval. 'I am pleased to see the arrival of two legions that have ever formed the backbone of my army, Marcus, though given what we have been through I am interested to hear the commanders' explanations as to why it has taken two months for them to put in an appearance. Had they put things in order and marched in good time, they could have been here at worst half a month after us. Sixty days of delay speaks less of accidents and troubles and more of deliberate decisions.'

Fronto nodded uncertainly. His elation at their arrival should perhaps be tempered by dismay at why it had taken them so long, but then, given the mutinies of the previous winter, he'd not been certain they would come at all, so he remained pleased. They watched patiently as the fleet largely anchored in the waters just outside the port, while seven ships made their way inside, searching out jetties and drifting carefully to a halt, sailors calling to one another, throwing out lines and tying them, ramps being run out down onto the timbers.

Fronto frowned as he looked at those ships. Five of them carried men of the two legions, lined up on deck and at attention, ready to disembark. The sixth seemed to contain a few officers, horses and lesser ranks, from eagle-bearers to clerks. The seventh, though, displayed just one man in uniform, standing at the prow, wearing the broad-striped tunic of a senior tribune. The man, straight and tall with a lofty expression, turned and strode to the ramp as it was run out, where he waited until one of the sailors brought his horse up. As he pulled himself up into the saddle, Fronto frowned to see a motley collection of drudges in grey tunics appear, leading pack animals and carrying bags and chests, all overseen by an oily-looking swarthy fellow with a curled black beard.

The tribune walked his horse slowly down the planks and onto the jetty, then along that until he came to a halt a dozen paces from the waiting officers, where he gave a bored salute as his slaves unloaded his seemingly endless collection of luggage behind him.

'Gaius Avienus, General, senior tribune commanding the Tenth Equestris,' he announced as though speaking to an equal. Fronto glanced across at Caesar, whose expression had not changed, though his eyes had taken on a flinty look.

'Where is your legate, Tribune?' Caesar asked, evenly.

'Your lieutenant in Rome, Marcus Antonius, has removed the legates from command of the Tenth and the Ninth on your authority, General, citing their ongoing support of mutinous behaviour. As such, it has fallen to the senior tribunes to lead the legions from Italia.'

'It must have taken Antonius some time to come to this decision, I presume.'

The tribune frowned. 'No, General. The removal of the commanders occurred in the new year.'

'Then presumably, with their troublesome influence removed, you set forth from Campania on your knees and decided to swim half the way from Neapolis?'

The tribune's frown deepened in apparent confusion. 'General?'

'Even in bad winter weather, it takes no more than eight days by ship from Neapolis to here. If you marched the legion to Lilybaeum, crossing at Rheggium, and then took ship from Sicilia, I can allow that it might take up to fourteen days. It has been fifty-seven days since the new year. Perhaps you would like to explain your unfortunate delay while your ultimate commander, mandated by the senate as dictator to crush the rebellion across the republic, fights for his life in the dust of Africa for want of his veteran legions.'

The man recoiled as if struck. 'General, there were many concerns to be dealt with and much organisation required. We...'

'Silence,' Caesar snapped. 'Perhaps it took you too long to commandeer enough vessels to transport your family's estate here at my expense?'

'General, I...'

'The ships gathering at Lilybaeum were for the transport of troops and supplies, not a leisure cruise for halfwit nobles.'

The tribune shuffled back another step, his face going pale. Before he could speak, Caesar's head snapped around. 'And that goes for all of you. Don't think I cannot see the luxury in which my tribunes have wallowed on their crossing. True sons of the republic put the good of the state first and their comfort and convenience last. *I* crossed from Lilybaeum, as these men around me, among the soldiers of the legions and with crates of supplies. My entire entourage in camp consists of one body slave and one secretary. Avienus here alone has brought a gaggle of slaves of more than a score in number.'

Fronto saw the junior tribunes, who had disembarked from the second ship, stop in their tracks, panic showing on their faces. On the far side, two centurions had disembarked from one of the other ships, a small crowd of standard bearers and musicians at attention behind them. As they marched closer to the commanders, coming to a halt and saluting, Fronto was relieved and heartened to see the tall, blond figure of Atenos, the Tenth's primus pilus alongside his counterpart from the Ninth.

Gaius Avienus had begun to recover himself the moment the General's ire shifted from him, and he now stepped forward again, confidence returning, opening his mouth.

'I..'

'Quiet,' snapped Caesar, holding up a warning finger as he turned to the centurions. They stood impassive and professional, with the insignia of their legions at their shoulders. Atenos flashed him a momentary look of recognition, yet kept his face carefully emotionless.

'Tell me,' the general said to the two men, 'of your time in Campania since my visit.'

Both men had the decency to look uncomfortable now. The legions had, after all, mutinied against him, and no man could claim complete innocence in the affair, for all that some men were more culpable than others.

'Sir?'

'Your commanders and your men. The mutiny had been over long before I departed for Sicilia in December. I had hoped to see the Ninth and the Tenth at Lilybaeum before we left for Africa, and yet it has been two months, most of which the legions seem to have spent without their troublesome legates courtesy of my friend Antonius in Rome. Tell me of the nature of the delay, and the culprits of the same.'

Without flinching, both centurions remained straight, their gazes locked on some point in the middle distance. They had been placed in an uncomfortable position, for they had sworn loyalty to their legion and its commander, and speaking ill of their officers would go against their nature, yet this was their most senior commander, the dictator of Rome, and his authority superseded all others, barring perhaps a full vote of the senate. Finally, Atenos cleared his throat.

'Regrettably, General, the time the legions spent in Campania was neither honourable nor just. Many of the legionaries, veterans of Pharsalus and more, continued to feel that they had been treated unfairly, and the simmering resentment remained even after the mutiny failed. The removal of the legates, while it ended any attempt at organised resistance, simply opened up command to a squabbling collection of juniors.'

The centurion managed not to look at any of the tribunes he had thusly described, but Fronto almost laughed at the expressions of outrage, dismay and anger that crossed the faces of all.

'When the men demanded something be done in restitution, the more underhanded and less noble of the men decided to take matters into their own hands, plundering towns and estates in Campania as though they were nothing more than countryside bandits.'

'I see,' Caesar said in a quiet and dangerous tone.

The primus pilus of the Ninth now took over. 'The tribunes in command of the legions, who should have put a stop to such matters, variously turned a blind eye to the wanton thievery, and in some cases made sure to profit by it.'

'And these tribunes are they?' Caesar said, gesturing at Avienus and the other new arrivals.

'Some of them, sir, though in their defence these men are far from the worst. The senior tribune of the Ninth, who is not present, is said to have put to the sword the family of a senator on their estate near Capua in order to adorn his own villa with a collection of stolen works of art.'

'This criminal has been removed?' Caesar asked.

The centurion nodded. 'Over the past month, with the support of the Master of Horse, Marcus Antonius, we have removed the tribunes who were directly responsible for criminal acts, and all officers and men of the legions who took part willingly in such crimes have been summarily dismissed without pay or pension. One who seems to have been involved in the stirring up of the legions, a man by the name of Julius Pontius Artemas, appears to have vanished and, despite his name repeatedly turning up, there seems to be no record of him anywhere, so he has thus far escaped punishment. The officers have been delivered to Rome to be dealt with through judicial channels. Sadly, therefore, we must report that the two legions we bring to you number only two thirds of their official manpower.'

Caesar nodded respectfully. 'I am more content with seven thousand honest citizens than ten thousand criminals. You have acted truly and correctly.'

He turned to the tribunes. 'I am known for my lenience and forbearance which, in return, I always assume makes those with whom I am at odds curb their wanton and irresponsible behaviour. When, therefore, I encounter those who are incapable or unwilling to curb such impulses, I must set my customary lenience aside and act in accordance with military custom, the better to show the value of restraint to others.'

Now he singled out the senior tribune. 'Your conduct speaks for itself, Tribune. I am well aware of the gens Aviena, for some of your uncles and cousins have served with me during my time in Gaul. They were stout hearted and proud men of an extremely rural and even impoverished background. If I am not mistaken your family hails from the countryside of Latium, a village close to Ostia. Your relations who have served with me were legionaries and centurions, and one prefect, mostly plebeians, with just that last one rising to the equestrian class.'

His eyes hardened. 'I have no issue with such a family's origins. Rome's Palatine Hill was once farmed by humble families, and the republic's greatest victories were won by men who fought hard and then returned to the plough. You, Gaius Avienus, are the first of your gens I have met to have risen within the senatorial order, part of my reorganisation and rebuilding of the senate following Cato and Pompey's flight. What I *do* know is that when I had your family so honoured, they were still poor and proud, not rich and indolent. Yet here you arrive in Africa, having effectively *stolen* one of my military vessels for your personal use, bringing a train of fawning slaves your uncles could not afford, and belongings that would have made even *Crassus* blush. Your actions condemn you, man, for such wealth in a poor family does not suddenly happen without improprieties. I hereby denounce you as committing acts of plunder in the towns and estates of Campania and, while I can prove neither these allegations nor the suspicion that haunts me that I saw your face among the ringleaders of the mutiny, it is entirely my decision who serves in my army.'

The tribune's face had now drained of all colour and he had started to tremble, eyes darting this way and that, looking in vain for an ally. Caesar simply snorted unpleasantly. 'You are of no use to me, nor to the state, Gaius Avienus, and I hereby discharge you with ignominy from my army. Leave my sight immediately and be gone from Africa before the sun sets, lest I decide to punish you directly.'

Still shaking, white and wide-eyed, Avienus turned to the oily-bearded head slave behind him, raising a finger towards the vessel they had just left, but Caesar shook his head. 'No, Avienus, you will not order your goods returned to the ship. That trireme is mine, for the use of my forces and the advancement of the republic's campaign in Africa. Take your precious goods and toadies and find a local merchant who will take you home... and pray that I have forgotten your name when this is over and I return to Rome.'

A shuffling noise from one side caught their attention in the strained silence that followed, and Fronto shook his head at the stupidity of whichever tribune had scuffed his feet and drawn the attention of the general, whose wicked gaze now snapped in their direction.

'None of *you* have fared any better. Tribunes all, each of whom owes this, their first appointment on the cursus Honorum, to me. Perhaps you were not in your position when the mutiny first occurred, though I know for a fact that at least *one* of you was, but you represented the command of the legions at a time when they ran amok, breaking laws and committing crimes, when it was your sole and solemn duty to prevent precisely that. As such, in allowing theft, murder and rapine, you have failed as military men before ever you came near a war.'

Some Roman nobles – many in fact – retained a nomenclator to follow them around, subtly reminding them of pertinent people's names and salient facts about them to ease social acquaintance. Fronto had never been bothered, preferring instead to look faintly confused and to occasionally insult people by forgetting who they were, than rely on a secondary memory. Caesar had never needed such. His memory for names and places was unparalleled, in Fronto's opinion, so it came as no surprise to him when Caesar called these unknown new arrivals by name.

'Aulus Fonteius,' he announced, loud enough for his voice to echo off the port buildings, 'mutinous tribune and disloyal citizen, you are hereby dismissed from my army.' The young officer's face fell. The loss of this position would mean an end to his entire public career within its very first year, a disgrace that would likely cling to him for the rest of his days. His path looked bleak now and, given Caesar's popularity in Rome, he would be something of a pariah among the city's better classes. The others were clearly to fare no better, though.

'Titus Salienus, Marcus Tiro, and Gaius Clusius, you all attained your ranks not by merit but by favour. That favour is now withdrawn, for you have been neither brave in war, nor loyal and competent in peace. Whether or not you were involved in mutinous behaviour, you failed to uphold the respect and discipline that your rank demands. On this count alone I deem you unworthy to hold such a position. The three of you are all dismissed. I bid you join Avienus and Fonteius in departing this place. I want all five of you out to sea and on the way home before sunset.'

The four men stared in shock, and since they made no immediate attempt to move, Caesar turned to his praetorian commander. 'Salvius, gather your men here and see that these former officers leave. If the sun sets and a single one of them remains with a foot on African soil you have my permission to lop it off.'

Salvius Cursor gave an unpleasant grin and waved his riders forward. Fronto shivered. He'd known Salvius for three years now, and had absolutely no doubt that the man would follow those orders to the letter, whether or not Caesar had meant them merely as a threat.

But the point to focus on here was not the failure of greedy officers, rather than the arrival of much anticipated veterans. With the Ninth and Tenth here, fortunes might just change. Watching the tribunes stump disconsolately off, he wondered idly whether Caesar might grant him command of one of the legions? He was old and decrepit, with a trick knee and a tendency to wheeze when climbing, but his sword arm was still strong, and his mind sharp, and he'd commanded both legions before, one in Hispania, the other in Gaul. He grinned. He had a nice jar of Falernian in his tent he'd been saving for a get together. Perhaps Caesar might see fit to reassigning legates in return for a magnificent tipple.

* * *

Uzitta, 1ˢᵗ March 46 BC

Fronto sat on the hill and watched the newcomers arriving. With no gaps in the defensive lines near the town now, the defectors had crossed the river higher upstream, beyond Uzitta and come down the eastern bank to Caesar's lines. Their intentions were clear, for they rode slowly and with their weapons sheathed and shields slung on their mounts. Four wings of cavalry, each perhaps twice the size of a Roman Ala, each led by an officer, accompanied by his attendants and slaves. Not the panicky Numidian cavalry that Galronus kept terrifying but a better force, stronger and armoured in bronze, bearing sharp spears and colourful shields.

Gaetuli. Surely this had to represent the last of their number in Scipio's army, given the sheer scale of desertions over recent weeks. A thousand Gaetuli horse, approaching Caesar's lines, each led by a tribal nobleman. Fronto wondered how Galronus felt about acquiring a new unit of that size of whose skills and abilities he remained in the dark. He turned to see the other new forces moving into temporary camp in the gap between the twin fortifications behind the hill. Five legions were now gathered within spitting distance of Scipio's camp, and they were all legions to be reckoned with.

The Fifth were here as usual, the veterans who had been with Caesar since they left Lilybaeum, but they were joined now by the feared Ninth and Tenth, each of which had been given an entirely new senior officer staff from the men who'd been serving here since December, and who had proved themselves. Moreover, early that afternoon, the Twenty Ninth, who had raced to the defence of Acylla, had marched back into camp looking pleased with themselves. Messius had consolidated that vital coastal city once the siege had been lifted, had even brought several other local small townships into the fold, and had decided that an entire legion was unnecessary to hold the region now. He had kept a single cohort as garrison and sent the rest of the legion back to Caesar.

Now the Twenty Ninth, along with the Twenty-Eighth, had joined the three veteran units at the hill. The standards and vexilla of all five legions were gleaming and flapping openly on the hill in full sight of Scipio. Three legions who had conquered Gaul, and whose reputation would make most enemies sweat, and two others, one of which had seen off Scipio's forces at Acylla and the other who had denied him Leptis. It was a threat and a provocation at once, for their names and numbers would be spreading fear and uncertainty throughout the enemy camp.

Caesar now had nine legions in Africa, including many veterans, and an extra almost-legion formed of the Gaetuli deserters from Scipio's army. His cavalry had grown overnight, too, with more strength and more variety in their makeup and capabilities. Barring the elephants, and Juba's royal force, the numbers were becoming much more even now, and Caesar's army had the lion's share of the experience. Every officer felt the change in the air, just like the longed-for break in the weather. For two months, since landing in Africa, they had played a careful and defensive game, knowing they were in danger at all times. Now, the tables had started to turn, and any engagement was no longer a foregone conclusion. Now, it was equally likely that any great battle could go Caesar's way as it was Scipio's.

This all explained a great deal about why the enemy commander was no longer parading his army in front of his camp and offering battle to Caesar, confident and cocky. Now, he would be trying to find a way to put the odds back in his favour. And there was a new energy in Caesar, too. He was not quite ready to launch a full assault, but that time was coming, and everyone could see it.

Fronto straightened in the saddle automatically at the sight of Caesar approaching, up the slope of the hill from the ranks of the newly-arrived legions, other officers at his back. The general had a rare look of genuine mirth on his face, and Fronto raised his eyebrows as the general settled in beside him, the other officers hanging around close by in a crowd, listening to Plancus muttering strategic options.

'Hills are funny?' Fronto said to the general.

Caesar chuckled. 'Hills are hills. *Salvius Cursor* is funny.'

'Really? I've known him for years now and if you asked me to throw a bucket of descriptions at him and see what stuck, I doubt that "funny" would do more than bounce off him.'

'The humour was not his intent, Fronto. A panicked soldier came running into camp first thing this morning, desperately demanding to see me. He and his tent mates had been tasked with seeking out any available ropes in the buildings at the port and they'd found the poor feeble Tribune Tiro, who I dismissed and threatened yesterday, hiding in the stores. It seemed that his fellow wretches had taken all available ships out of port that afternoon, and Tiro could find no way to leave bar swimming north for Sicilia, or braving enemy patrols as he ran for Hadrumetum's port, so he went into hiding for the night.'

'I think I can see where this is going.'

'Yes,' laughed Caesar. 'The first officer he found was Salvius Cursor, who was overseeing the arrival of new equipment for his men on an early ship. In a matter of heartbeats the soldiers were standing between Salvius Cursor and the terrified Tiro, the former with his sword out and fully intent on cutting off both of Tiro's feet and, if the messenger is to believed, "cutting off the arse he sat with too".'

Fronto laughed out loud. 'Gods, but I can actually picture the scene. What did you do?'

'I went down there personally. I gave Tiro one slave, a loaf of bread, and the mangiest donkey we could find in Ruspina and kicked him out along the northern shore, telling him to find a ship in Hadrumetum. Salvius was most put out.'

Again, Fronto laughed. 'I'll bet.'

'He stomped around angrily for half an hour, kicking stray dogs and shouting at soldiers until he felt better, but still he is irritable. If he does not cheer up soon, I may have to find a severed foot for him as a gift.'

Fronto turned to Caesar, saw the humour in his eyes, and the pair laughed again. As their guffaws trailed away and the two settled again, Fronto looked at the assembling legions and the banners and standards. 'If the space here was better, I would have brought the Thirteenth and Fourteenth too. They're both renowned veterans these days. Scipio might shiver even more at the sight of the legion who crossed the Rubicon with us.'

Caesar nodded. 'I felt the need to keep some of the veterans back in the city area, though the time is coming to move forward, I think.'

Fronto frowned. 'Caesar, if you move any closer to Scipio's lines, we're going to have to dig the latrine trench in his back garden.'

Caesar laughed again. 'Quite, but the enemy can still cross the river further inland, and I have been studying the maps. There is another hill, not unlike this one just to the south along the river. You can see it from here, see? I am considering attempting to fortify that crest and bring a full line of defences around the contours in an arc between them. It would create a horseshoe into which we can perhaps draw the enemy, under missile shot from all sides and largely proof against elephants.'

Fronto chewed his lip. 'It might be overextending ourselves, and I'm not at all sure how elephant proof it would be. What do you think might make them walk into such a trap, and are we now considering full engagement?'

Caesar rubbed his neck. 'In the best of worlds we would not commit until the Seventh and Eighth legions arrived. I had word this morning that they have reached Sicilia and are imminent. With their additional veteran numbers, our chances improve drastically. However, the chances of provoking a straight fight are slowly decreasing. Just as we hoped Scipio would attack our defences and we could rely upon their advantage, it now looks as though Scipio is adopting a similar tactic, and *we* cannot afford to assault *his* camp. He has been there long enough that the fortifications and defences, including artillery, will be impressive.'

He turned to look south. 'No, I think we still need to try and bring him to us, if possible, at least until the last of the legions arrive.'

'What do we do first, then?'

'I think a new fortified camp in the plain, where the centre of the horseshoe will be. We will build it and fill it with veterans in an attempt to provoke him. We'll then work on the second hill and bringing the arc of ramparts between the two.'

Fronto nodded slowly. 'I'm still not sure, Caesar. Why not build the hill's fort and the ramparts first, and then place the camp in the midst? It looks like overextending ourselves to me, but let's see what we can do. Scipio is impulsive, after all, if unimaginative.'

Caesar smiled. 'If Scipio lets us build, then we will attempt to snare him in our trap. If he takes offence at the camp on the plain and attacks it before we move on to the system, then we have pulled him into open battle, which we now know there is a possibility of winning. Either way, this seems like the correct decision.'

I hope so, Fronto murmured silently. *I hope so.*

CHAPTER FIFTEEN

Uzitta, 2nd March 46 BC

A horn began to blare out an urgent tone, and Fronto squinted into the grey air, trying to spot the source. The lookout sat astride his horse at one of the few rises that would form the curve of the fortified 'U', and in addition to the desperate honking, he was waving his arms madly and pointing west across the river which here consisted of three smaller tributary flows. Fronto, along with half the men present, looked up in that direction. It was hard to miss what he was indicating. Scipio's army was on the move, gleaming ranks pouring from the gates of the enemy camps, the massive shapes of elephants moving in lines among them.

Alarms went up all across the works in response, and Fronto cursed at the enemy's sudden move. Caesar had been right after all that building the camp would draw Scipio's attention. The problem now became one of organisation and logistics. If Scipio's forces were coming, then his strategy and deployment would already have been decided in advance and all he had to do was move into position. Caesar's army, on the other hand, was somewhat strung out, and would take precious time to deploy.

Fronto's gaze roved across the works from south to north, left to right. Off to the left stood the next hill at the other end of the 'U' that they'd planned to take and fortify, though as yet there was no force there, just a few scouts and lookouts like the man with the horn. Such figures also dotted the higher ground around the arc, overlooking the plain where the new camp was now almost ready, carefully sighted back

221

behind the marshy land near the river. Within it, five legions worked hard, the Thirteenth and Fourteenth, the Twenty Fifth and the Twenty Ninth, and the legion of Gaetuli defectors. The other five legions and the auxilia were off to the right, encamped on that hill close to Uzitta and within the ramparts behind it. The cavalry moved in wings around the plain, scattered.

Already those Caesarian legions off to the right were moving, emerging from their fortifications and marching out. Fronto could see the red-cloaked figure of Caesar on his white horse leading them, and quickly kicked Bucephalus into speed, thundering across the flat plain to meet the general.

As he passed the new camp all work there had now stopped, every legionary hurriedly lacing up armour and helmets, gathering up shields and pila, simply leaving shovels, plumb lines and dolabra wherever they lay as their centurions and optios hurried around blowing whistles and bellowing orders. As he rode, Fronto peered off towards the enemy, trying to identify their disposition. One force, separating from the rest and composed of white-clad Numidian infantry and other light and fast auxilia raced ahead. If they were not to be part of Scipio's main battle line then they had to be performing some secondary task, and the direction of their run suggested that very hill that Caesar's men had intended to occupy. There they could threaten a flanking action. On the far side, behind Caesar and the emerging legions, that flank would be anchored for both sides, for Scipio still had a garrison in Uzitta, while Caesar had strong auxilia in control of the hilltop camp.

What Scipio had planned in between he could not yet say, though the cavalry led the column, so they would likely be deployed at the south flank towards that untaken hill, and the elephants that lumbered forth in two units had thus far also been placed at the wings when deployed, so it seemed likely that would continue.

Caesar had moved ahead of his legions now and was making for the nearest high point, with a small cadre of officers, Salvius Cursor and his men. Fronto converged with the general on that rise and reined in beside him. 'Cavalry to the south, on the flank,' he said, 'elephants split on both flanks, and a small and fast infantry force heading up to the hill over there. Legions and infantry in the centre. That's what I can see.'

Caesar nodded. 'It also appears that Scipio's legions are moving separately from Juba's, so they will be deployed independently.' The general sucked in air and nibbled his lip in thought. 'The auxilia on that hill will easily oust our scouts and could then flank us, so our wing needs to be strong and reactive. The northern edge will be jammed up against our fortifications and the town, so there will be no attempt at flanking there.'

'I don't think this will come down to ingenious strategy,' Fronto muttered. 'This will be won by willpower and stamina alone. The first problem will be those elephants, and then the possibility of being flanked over there.'

Caesar pointed towards Uzitta. 'I am more confident still in the value of good strategy, Fronto. We can deploy and face Scipio, but we shall not make the first move. We offer battle, but do not give it. Let Scipio have that honour.'

'Why, General?' one of the staff murmured from behind. 'I thought we were strong enough now for battle. Why delay if we can force one?'

Caesar turned a frown on the man. 'A myriad of reasons occur to me. Firstly, the land separating us close to the river is marshy and whomsoever moves first will have the joy of becoming mired in the terrain. Secondly, we would prefer his elephants to move first rather than launching an assault against them, for if they are moving and we can spook them, then they could run riot within his own ranks rather than ours. And thirdly, if we move forward we invite the fast auxilia on the hill to close the flank behind us, while if *they* are forced to move first, we can react with a measured response. We are strong enough to win now, but not if we throw it all away. No, we offer battle and we hope that Scipio is feeling impulsive enough to take up the offer. That he is deploying so close to us is a hopeful sign.'

He turned back to Fronto. 'The right flank will be pinned by the town and the defences, and facing elephants and native auxilia. Have the Gaetuli cohorts take that flank, and pull a single cohort from the four oldest veteran legions in support. The Gaetuli are locals and make use of elephants themselves, so they will not be as fazed as some of the other units, and stand a better chance against the beasts.'

Fronto nodded as Prince Amasan saluted and rode off to gather his Gaetuli infantry. Caesar gazed off south. 'The left flank will be the main danger point. They face both elephants and Labienus' cavalry, and will also have to watch for a flanking move from those auxilia. Galronus, take the entire cavalry to that wing. Keep an eye out for that flanking move and keep Labienus contained. As for the elephants there, Plancus, take the Fifth and secure that flank in support of the cavalry. The Fifth have been in Africa longer than the other veterans and have seen more action recently, plus they have had time to become accustomed to the presence of elephants, which suggests that they will be less prone to panic.'

Plancus and Galronus saluted and rode off.

'So that leaves all the other legions to line up against theirs at the centre,' Fronto said, 'where, no matter the strategy, it will all come down to stamina and will.'

'Quite. We shall intersperse the newer legions with the veterans in pairs to keep the line strong. The Ninth and Tenth fight well together, so they can take the left, with two of the newer legions next in line, then the Thirteenth and Fourteenth, who are also used to working together, and then the remaining two.'

'And that's us deployed,' Fronto mused. 'Gods willing, we can settle this today.'

'One way or the other,' the general agreed.

* * *

Galronus sat at the very edge of the army, his mass of cavalry gathered on the wing with the Fifth in support, the capable Plancus in command. The lines of Caesar's army stretched over more than a mile from here back to the hilltop fortifications and Uzitta, more or less out of sight from here. Galronus could only concentrate on the flank, which was their responsibility. The enemy auxilia on the hill remained still and threatening off to the left, a solid and speedy force, ready to run around their flank when the fighting began.

If the fighting began.

The forces of Scipio had emerged from their camp only an hour after dawn, while Caesar's legions had only just started work, and by the end of the second hour they had been fully deployed in their battle lines. Caesar's army had reacted at speed and deployed in response, facing them, and there the two armies had stood for interminable hours, watching one another pensively, in a tedious stand-off.

At around noon, Galronus had sent a rider to Caesar, who commanded the field from the raised ground behind the army's central lines, requesting an update in orders. The rider had returned with the general's decision. He still would not launch the attack, for his reasons remained pertinent, but neither would he withdraw until the light began to fade, lest Scipio launch an attack as they moved. Caesar needed Scipio to commit and move first while there was still sufficient daylight for a clash, yet the enemy commander once more showed no sign of intent to commit, presumably eyeing that same marshy ground with distaste and unwilling to risk the first move.

And so Galronus had waited and watched with his tired riders, until the growls of hunger from empty bellies began to contend with the muttering and grumbling of bored and achy men. He watched the sun slide slowly from the apex into the west and now, with perhaps two or three hours of light left at most, finally there came a thunder of hooves as a messenger rode along the rear of the lines towards him. Galronus walked his horse out to the rear to meet the rider, looking across the lines of his men as he did so. They were a disparate group. Gauls, Belgae, Germans, Spaniards, and now Gaetuli natives. Passing the Fifth Legion, he fell in beside Plancus, whose own bored expression indicated how he too felt about this protracted stand-off.

The rider thundered to a halt and saluted the two officers.

'The general has made a decision?' Plancus asked.

The messenger nodded. 'He has, sir. It is Caesar's considered opinion that Scipio has no intention of launching the assault he threatens. The army is to stand down and return to its defences and encampments. The cavalry will split into units accompanying all infantry forces. The Fifth are to be part of the garrison of the new lowland camp, keeping a watch on that hill, for tomorrow the hill will need retaking.'

Plancus and Galronus shared a look 'And if Scipio decides that there's still time for a fight while we pull back?' the legate muttered. 'There is still two hours or so of daylight, and this could still be carnage.'

Galronus snorted. 'Scipio has lost his impulsiveness and his edge. For a month he did nothing but line his men up before his camp, and now he simply does the same once more, if a little closer. He will not commit to battle, even though he has the advantage, with control of the hill on the flank. If he has not attacked in eight hours of daylight, he will not do so now.'

'I hope you're right,' Plancus muttered, as all along the lines Caesar's musicians repeated the calls to stand down and withdraw. Plancus had the calls given for the Fifth, and the cohorts turned and began to march back towards the new camp close by. Galronus returned to his cavalry where Samaconius had ridden out from the edge of the crowd, waiting for him with an expression of disbelief.

'We're pulling back?'

Galronus nodded. 'No one is willing to commit to the first move. We've never been closer to a full battle, yet we are settling back into the camp again. I want the entire force split into four groups. One will base themselves back at the hilltop, one at the new lowland camp, one between those two locations, and the last I want out here on the flank at least until Scipio's entire force has gone home, watching those auxilia on the hill. There will be no battle today, but that flank remains a danger.'

Now the entire army was on the move. Scipio's force had not started to pull back yet, but neither had they made any aggressive move. With a sigh, Galronus gave the order, and the calls echoed out across the flat ground. Galronus and Samaconius remained in position at the wing, watching the enemy as the cavalry responded to the orders and began to separate into groups to withdraw.

'Wait,' the deputy commander said suddenly, his hand shooting up, pointing at the enemy. 'There's movement.'

Galronus followed the gesture with his gaze. The entire rebel army remained staunchly in position, but a sizeable unit of horsemen had broken from their lines and begun to move forward. He fidgeted as he watched them. They were native Africans, both Numidian and Gaetuli by the look of it. It seemed inconceivable that now, suddenly, the attack was coming, and especially led by a single native cavalry wing. Urgent horn blasts rang out among the enemy cavalry, trying to call them back.

Samaconius twitched. 'Sir, do we redeploy? Is this it?'

Galronus shook his head. 'No. They're not moving on the orders of Scipio or Labienus. The musicians are ordering them back into the lines. Those men are breaking orders. They're on their own.'

'They're not stopping,' the deputy noted, as that force of white-clad riders continued to surge forward.

Galronus glanced around, taking in the entire field. That flanking force on the hill was not moving, and Caesar's army continued to withdraw. 'They will not attack our lines. No one is stupid enough to take a few hundred riders and attack this entire cavalry force. That would be suicide. This is some native thing. I think they're goading and threatening our native contingent.'

Angry shouts suddenly rang forth from Galronus' own lines, and he realised what was happening with a chill. Damn it, but the goading had worked. Already there was movement in Galronus' own retreating lines. 'Have the order to withdraw blown again,' he called, angrily. 'Keep it going.'

'Too late,' Samaconius replied, pointing. Galronus ground his teeth at the sight of one of his own units now racing forward from his lines. The new Gaetuli cavalry who had defected from the enemy had responded to the goading of the opposition and were riding out, whooping and bellowing, to meet their countrymen, swords up and spears out ready.

'Keep sounding the damn horn,' Galronus bellowed as he kicked his horse into movement, racing after the foolish, impulsive Gaetuli. As he rode out to the front of the lines, he could see that a force of light, skirmishing auxiliaries from that same tribe had also advanced from the Caesarian lines a little further along and were converging with the reckless horsemen. They were doomed. Even with infantry support, the enemy Gaetuli and Numidians would outnumber them at least three to one.

Galronus heard other hoof beats behind him and turned to see that a Gaetuli officer, a musician and half a dozen riders had joined him. He beckoned to the musician even as they charged. 'Keep blowing the call for them to pull back. Don't stop.' And to the officer: 'can you call them back?'

The man shook his head. 'Insults have been issued. It will be very hard to make them walk away.'

'Do they all speak Latin?'

The officer shook his head.

'Then when we're in earshot, you shout loud in your own tongue and tell them that any rider who doesn't withdraw has betrayed his commander and will be dealt with accordingly.'

They would be too late to prevent trouble, and he could already see that, for the two forces had met now in the marshy area of low ground where the recent storms had seen the river break its bank and flood the low plain. The infantry were instantly in trouble, floundering in the murk, able to do little more than stagger and flail, precisely what Caesar had been avoiding in not making the first move. The cavalry were faring better, though they would still be butchered if they did not withdraw damn soon.

Galronus realised with a small sense of relief that although the two forces were engaged, they were struggling in the marshy conditions, and their blows were often going awry. There was still a chance to stop this developing into a large-scale disaster. With the musician still honking his call to withdraw and the Gaetuli commander bellowing threats in his own language, Galronus rode into the fray, drawing his sword and hefting his shield. He was armed not to kill the enemy, but simply to attempt to separate the forces As he reached the first man it occurred to him, and not for the first time in this stupid, complex war, that it was going to be extremely difficult to identify which of the riders were his and which the enemy.

Growling his anger, he rode in among them, using his sword to knock aside blows, parrying men and stopping them fighting even as he rode between sparring pairs, presenting a shield to the enemy even as he turned the blows of his own men.

'Back, damn you,' he bellowed as he drove them apart, the other riders that had come with him following suit, trying to force their own men back. Slowly, he was making a difference, and by the time he'd pushed his way out of the far side of the fight, the units had begun to draw apart. The Gaetuli officer was having an effect too, chastened riders flocking to his side, pulling back from the fight at the threat of severe punishments. By the time Galronus reached his side, the cavalry had separated. The light infantry were still struggling in the murk, but it appeared that, despite a few wounds to both men and horses, they had actually suffered few fatalities, a lone rider lying motionless in the muck, his equally lifeless horse nearby, and half a dozen light infantry scattered, half-submerged in twisted shapes.

'Back,' he bellowed again, pointing at their own lines, and the entire force began to withdraw. There were a few hair-raising moments as the enemy jeered and hurled insults, when Galronus feared that either the enemy might pursue them or that his own riders might break ranks and go for them again, but despite his fears the withdrawal continued and soon became an orderly affair. As he finally led the errant cavalry from the marshy ground and back to their own lines, he heaved a sigh of relief. Though he'd been ready for a battle today, that stupid and dangerous scuffle was not what he'd intended.

Damn it, but they needed to bring Scipio to battle and end this.

* * *

Near Leptis Minor, 3rd March 46 BC

'Are you sure?' Galronus said quietly to the scout.

The man shrugged. 'I can't say whether it's the same lot, sir, but they look the same, both Numidian and Gaetuli.'

The Remi commander allowed a slow and cruel smile to play across his face. 'A hundred, you say.'

'Or thereabouts, sir.'

Galronus looked back at the cavalry plodding along behind him. If the scout was right, and it was his *job* to be right, then it seemed that the gods had gifted Galronus revenge on a platter. After the previous day's long stand-off and brief, stupid clash, the two sides had withdrawn, Scipio's army returning to camp before dark. Though there had been no true battle, it rankled throughout Caesar's army that the only deaths that day had been theirs, courtesy of the Gaetuli's foolish ride, while Scipio's army had whooped all the way back to camp as though they had secured the most astounding victory, jeering the Caesarian lines.

Caesar had said little about the incident, though Galronus felt the man's disapproval just in the weight of his gaze during the debrief meeting that evening. All that had been said on the matter was that Caesar left it to the Remi to discipline his riders appropriately. Galronus had thought long and hard what to do with the two hundred or so Gaetuli who had broken ranks. It could not be anything too harsh, for though they had to be disciplined, he could hardly afford to drive them away, back to their old place in Scipio's ranks. In the end he had settled for posting them to the most tedious task the cavalry endured.

Each few days, a caravan of wagons left Ruspina and visited Leptis and the villages nearby to gather supplies, and without a doubt the most boring detail in the cavalry was convoy guard duty. Consequently, today, two hundred Gaetuli escorted the wagons, grumbling miserably. Galronus had taken personal command to be certain they stuck to their duty.

What they had not expected was to run across what appeared to be the same men from whom Galronus had been forced to separate them the day before. Of course, they probably were not the very same men, but they were Gaetuli and Numidian riders from Scipio's army, so they might as well be.

Kicking the horse's flanks, Galronus rode ahead with the scout as those wagons trundled on behind him, slowly making for Leptis. A small stand of palm trees on a low rise stood on the edge of a slope that led down to a shallow depression filled with well-tended fields and small but neat farm buildings.

Galronus felt his smile return as he and the scout reined in beneath the cover of the trees, hidden from view in the shade. Sure enough, the man had been spot on with his estimates. Around a hundred riders, and very clearly Gaetuli and Numidians. Labienus was getting bold sending small raiding parties this way. Since Caesar had fortified the area and there was a small garrison strung out among those ancient towers and the new defences in between, they'd not expected to see enemy soldiers in the area. Yet here were some of the enemy cavalry, close enough to those towers to throw stones at them. Very bold indeed.

The enemy riders were in disarray. Not more than half of them were in the saddle, the rest of their horses tied up to the farm's fences, while the riders ransacked the buildings. Galronus could see the farmer and his family, slaves and servants all penned up under guard. They were lucky to still be alive, and the chances were that that would change when the riders had picked over anything of value and decided to move on. A hundred enemy horse, unprepared for a fight. And on the other side of this rise, Galronus had two hundred cavalry who were still bitter about the previous day's events and would, he was sure, love nothing more than an opportunity to kick the living snot out of Labienus' men.

It was outside his remit, really. His duty was to escort the wagons there and back, and what he should do was to report this encounter to the nearest garrison commander in one of the towers and let them deal with it. But really, was he going to let that happen? To let an opportunity like this slip through his fingers? Besides, by the time the garrison reacted, the riders would probably be gone and the farmers dead.

He turned to the scout. 'Ride back to the caravan. Summon the men, quietly, and get them here without drawing attention.'

As the scout rode off, Galronus watched. The riders below may be natives of the region, and may be cavalry of the enemy, but their actions were more like those of common brigands. He could see men dragging bundles and bags from the buildings. Another chased around the farm yard and jammed his spear down again and again until he managed to pin a squealing pig, laughing out loud. Wasteful. Cruel, yes, but mostly wasteful, when there were armies to feed. Galronus watched the scene with distaste and growing anger as his horsemen closed in behind him. Once the scout gave him the nod that all were present, Galronus turned to the riders and spoke in a low tone.

'You want a chance to pay the enemy back for yesterday and to regain some honour? Look there.' He pointed down at the farm. 'We outnumber them two to one. Kill as many as you like, or take them prisoner if they surrender. All I ask is that you let just a few escape to carry the news back to Labienus. Are you with me?'

The riders gave a low murmur of glee, trying not to raise their voices and draw attention.

'Three units from here, each of two turmae. One, with me, will wait here, while the others curve around the sides of this hill. As soon as the flankers put in an appearance we'll charge for the farm and the enemy. The other two wings will encircle them, then once they're trapped we get to work.'

With a few gestures, he split his force and sent them off. As the rest of the riders sat quietly, drawing swords or hefting spears, Galronus watched the scene, praying the enemy would not kill the farmers before he could get there, and slowly counting. He'd reached eighteen when the first wing suddenly appeared around the edge of the hill to the right. Galronus bellowed and the men with him put heel to flank and raced from the trees, down the slope and towards the suddenly panicked enemy horsemen at the farm. Before the enemy had even registered the presence of this second attack, reeling from the appearance of the first wing, the third unit closed, riders passing the far edge of the hill, the three prongs of the trident lancing out at the enemy now.

As they descended the slope, Galronus noticed that he was slowing slightly, allowing his men to pull in ahead of him, and shook his head at the realisation. He'd been commanding large cavalry forces now for long enough that it was starting to seem natural to sit at the back and direct things like a Roman general. Well, he was *not* Roman. He was Remi, and had been weaned on border raids with the Suessiones, and right now he was going to bloody his blade. With a roar, he urged his horse on, racing out to join the leading ranks, and swiftly passing them.

Ahead, the enemy immediately went to pieces. With sixty-four riders circling in from each side to -contain them and another sixty-four pouring down the slope at them like a pack of wolves, there was no escape, and little time to prepare. Those riders who were already in their saddles reacted variously, some racing for whatever gap in the tightening snare they could identify, others ripping out swords or gripping spears and wheeling their mounts to face the attack. Those who had been gleefully looting and ravaging either leapt for their horses, their fun forgotten, or ran for the nearest building to hide.

It was going to be carnage. Galronus heard Caesar's Gaetuli all around him bellowing out phrases in wicked, gleeful voices and, though he could not comprehend their tongue, he was almost certain they were the very same deadly insults that the enemy had hurled on the battlefield, causing the trouble yesterday. Today was about revenge, pure and simple. With no hope of mimicking their calls, Galronus simply bellowed out blistering insults about the riders' parentage in his own language, grinning like a lunatic as he closed on the farm.

He was the first to leap a fence and race across a lush paddock now empty of animals. Half a dozen men had managed to pull themselves together into a defensive huddle in the centre of the farm, and Galronus did not slow. He took the next fence at a leap and came down onto the hard-packed dusty ground with just enough room to slew sharply to his left and avoid riding directly onto the spear tip of the nearest man. As the desperate and terrified rider attempted to bring the spear round to bear in the continually shrinking space, Galronus leaned to the side, used his knees to guide his horse back closer and then, his sword held low, swept it up with gritted teeth and every ounce of strength he could muster.

The blade smashed into the man's spear arm just above the elbow, and though it didn't quite sever it, the blow smashed the bone so thoroughly that the arm flopped and sagged, misshapen and stretched as the spear fell away and the man stared at his own arm in horror, so shocked that the pain had yet to kick in. Galronus dragged his mount to a halt, and as his opponent finally began to let out a blood-curdling howl, the Remi swung his sword again, this time backhanded, and caught the man in the back, breaking his spine.

The rider sagged and collapsed in his saddle, sprinting to life's finish-line now. Galronus turned to find the next man, but there wasn't one. The other five who'd gathered here were already dead or fighting for their lives against Galronus' howling riders. All around the farm, the same scene was playing out. The enemy had been caught totally unprepared and those few who'd attempted to fight back had been swarmed and cut down. At least a score of them were now standing in the centre, arms held high in surrender. Others were now emerging from houses, looking petrified. One of them never made it to the centre where his friends were, for the farmer appeared from somewhere, roaring, and put a pitchfork through his back.

Galronus looked about him. 'Did any escape?'

One of his men pointed off to the south. 'Three of them, I think, sir.'

'Perfect,' Galronus grinned. 'With luck the news will rattle them and perhaps even push them into doing something stupid. Gather the prisoners and we'll rope them up in the wagons for the journey.'

He leaned back in the saddle and smiled to himself as the grateful farmer hurried over, babbling his gratitude. Some days it was good to be alive.

CHAPTER SIXTEEN

Off the coast of Africa, 7th March 46 BC

Quintus Aquila stood at the prow of his lead ship, pensive, eyes scanning the rugged coastline ahead. He tried not to feel bitter about the division of the fleet, though the numbers still worried him. A fast trader had arrived at Ruspina two days earlier and had carried the welcome news that the Seventh and Eighth legions had mustered at Lilybaeum and were preparing to sail. Indeed, they were probably already at sea by the time the news had arrived.

With the rebel fleet at large somewhere in the vicinity, Caesar had ordered immediate precautions to protect the arriving veterans from enemy attack. Almost all the available ships had been pressed into service. Lucius Cispius had been sent east along the coast past Leptis to Thapsus and Acylla to patrol and keep channels open for the transports, while Aquila had been sent west for the same purpose. It had not escaped Aquila's notice, though, that Cispius was to patrol the seas around the towns that had declared for Caesar, with good available harbours and ready supplies, while Aquila had been given the west, where not a single allied town lay, and where the next settlement along from the camp would be dreaded and well-garrisoned Hadrumetum.

Worse was Caesar's division of the vessels. Cispius would acquire a secondary role, shipping supplies back to Ruspina as part of his patrols, and so he had been given twenty-seven ships, while Aquila, who would not have to ferry supplies, had been given thirteen. He had wondered more than once what he'd done to piss Caesar off so much that the general sent Cispius into calm seas with twice as many ships as Aquila, who was bound for enemy waters with half as many.

Damn it, but even the *gods* were against Aquila today. Though the morning had been faintly damp and leaden, boiling clouds had filled the sky, it had been calm, yet hardly had the squadrons put to sea when the winds arose and, like Caesar, Zephyrus weighed against Aquila. He'd watched in irritation as the wind filled Cispius' sails, driving him east along the coast with ease, while Aquila's ships turned west and immediately slowed almost to a standstill, struggling to make headway. Now, with the sun rising to its zenith, or at least presumed to be doing so somewhere behind that boiling mass in the sky, the wind had brought him a storm. The west wind was supposed to be gentle, Aquila grumbled to himself, as he watched the storm crossing the flat land, driven east from the mountains where it had been birthed. It was going to be a nasty one. He frowned.

'Sir,' called the trierarch, 'we're going to come to grief in that.'

Aquila nodded. He knew as much. There was no hope of moving on towards Hadrumetum with that coming, but they'd only come six miles from Ruspina so far. If he now turned around and sailed the flotilla back, he could imagine Caesar's reaction. Any favour Aquila might currently enjoy – ha! – would vanish entirely then. The only hope was to ride out the storm and move on when it had passed. His eyes scanned the coast once more.

'There. Where the river flows, there's a small cove. We can fit thirteen ships there at anchor and the worst of the storm will pass us by. Send the orders. We anchor there.'

The trierarch saluted, and Aquila looked at the place. Perhaps at least one god was watching out for him. Any more than thirteen ships and he'd probably not fit in there. Maybe things were starting to look up, after all.

* * *

Thapsus, 8th March 46 BC

Lucius Cispius stood on the dock and stretched. They had arrived at their destination towards sunset the previous day, after an uneventful and swift voyage with a favourable following wind. The gods had been good, above and beyond Caesar's support, for though a horrible storm had blown up from the west just after departure and the strong wind had carried it in their wake, it had then angled slightly off to the north, missing Cispius' fleet by the narrowest of margins and raging off to sea close by as they all put gratefully in at Leptis.

The harbour was small by military standards, and half-occupied by native merchants and fishermen, and only three jetties had been made available. Consequently, Cispius had set the fleet at anchor in the waters outside the port, both wide and low transports and military warships, and had organised a rota for the fleet. The transports would come in two at a time to load the goods, and the rest would sit out in the water. Similarly, four of his warships would prowl the sea in the area as scouts, watching for the new legions or for enemy movement, while the rest remained at anchor.

They would be here for a few days, at least until the new legions had arrived and the supplies were fully loaded, and so he had allowed each ship's complement to enjoy shore leave, with skeleton crews left aboard and two warships out there as protection. Protection from what, he couldn't imagine, for they were in safe, Caesarian waters here.

The first watch on board had just changed, and the sun still hung low over the eastern horizon, slowly rising and bringing with it the promise of the first warm and comfortable day since they had arrived in Africa.

The first indication that anything was wrong was a honking of a horn on board one of the ships, out at the periphery and distant enough that it took precious moments for Cispius to become aware of it. Then the call was picked up by other ships, and gradually it grew to a blare of alarm that made it loud and clear to the port and the beaches beside Leptis.

Cispius stared in horror. A huge fleet bearing rebel colours had hoved into view from the northeast. Either his four patrol vessels had somehow completely missed them or, more likely, now sat at the bottom of the sea, unable to return with a warning. With virtually no wind the enemy were unfettered, and their rowers worked hard, every vessel, half a hundred warships or more, slicing through the water like racehorses, making for the anchored and defenceless fleet. Cispius panicked, trying to decide what to do. The ships' crews were scattered all over the place, some encamped on the beach, grilling local meat, laughing and drinking wine, while others were somewhere in the city enjoying themselves, yet more were unarmed and in just tunics and boots, working to load the transports with supplies. Precious few men remained aboard the ships. Indeed, Cispius could see just how many ships were critically undermanned, for only six of his vessels had reacted and started moving, most of them lacking sufficient manpower. His two warships were now heading out to meet that fleet, which was brave of them but ultimately suicidal, given the odds.

Even as he rattled out orders and men all along the shore boarded small boats and began to row and sweat and curse their way out to the ships, Cispius knew he was in trouble. The enemy would probably not enter the port, for that was in range of the artillery on the city walls, and they would start to lose vessels rapidly if they did so, but anything outside the port was also out of range and easy prey.

Where had they come from? They were heading east and so must have passed straight by Ruspina on the way here. The next place to the west large enough to accommodate such a fleet was Hadrumetum. He felt momentarily for Aquila, whose fleet must have been annihilated by this lot on the way. But his pity was not bottomless, and he needed most of it for himself right now.

As the ships of his fleet began to move the moment sufficient manpower climbed aboard, it became a race to save as many as possible. The two warships on guard lasted a matter of heartbeats before they were boarded and overcome. The transports, both laden and empty, were swiftly surrounded by the rest of the fleet and struck with flasks of pitch, and then with fire arrows that soon had them bursting into flame. The fires raged across the transports, becoming an inferno as sparks leapt from dry hull to dry hull. Cispius watched in shock as fully half the supplies from the port burned and then settled down onto the sea bed amid the skeletons of ships.

This was a disaster.

* * *

Aquila urged his ship on. They had waited all day in that cove as the storm battered the coast and passed them by, his thirteen ships remaining blessedly untouched. As the storm finally whipped off into the distance and the sea calmed, the night air had held some kind of unidentifiable post-tempest apprehension, but it was only when a lookout called out a subdued warning that he understood what the source of that tension was.

Under cover of darkness, in the wake of that storm and making use of the remaining westerly, a massive fleet had departed Hadrumetum and sailed straight past Aquila and his flotilla in the cove, entirely unaware of their presence. The relieved officer had waited until the enemy had passed and the first strains of morning light began to show, and then ordered his fleet back out to sea.

He'd been careful. He'd made sure that they were far enough back to not be obvious for any lookout aboard the rebel fleet. Aquila's ship ranged out ahead, shadowing the enemy, keeping them in view, the rest of his ships coming on a quarter of a mile behind. He watched now, as they closed on the headland at Ruspina, for the enemy fleet had clearly not made Caesar's city their goal, and sailed on brazenly past the Caesarian fortress. Aquila knew now, as they followed, that the enemy was making for Cispius and his flotilla. They had clearly set out to hunt Caesar's twin fleets, and Aquila now changed his mind about the favour of gods, since the rebels had undoubtedly been looking for him and yet had sailed straight past. Now Cispius would be their prey and, even with his bigger fleet, he would still face odds of two to one.

As he moved close to the port, Aquila could see Caesar's banners fluttering on the end of the mole, where a small party of horsemen had gathered. With consummate ease, the trierarch slowed and turned his ship so that the vessel closed on that great stone barrier and drew up alongside it, where Aquila could see the general and his officers gathered, tense and fidgety.

'General, the storm kept us from Hadrumetum, though I think the gods had a hand in that now.'

Caesar waved at him. 'Thank Jove, Aquila. I had thought your fleet lost.'

'Fortunately not, General, though given the number of enemy ships out there it could easily still happen. I fear Cispius is in danger at Leptis.'

The general nodded. 'Sail to his relief. There are six ships in port. Take them with you. Between your vessels and the ones already under Cispius' command we will have sufficient to face the enemy. I and my officers will ride for Leptis and will attempt to move the fleet out to meet them. With luck we can catch the rebels from two sides and crush them.'

Aquila saluted. He hoped so, though a lot of that depended on how prepared Cispius was, for the enemy would already be attacking him when Aquila arrived. Even as his own fleet caught up with the lead vessel, the six warships in port were now moving out to join him. Nineteen vessels. Not much against that enemy fleet, which was now already out of sight ahead and moving fast. He would have to pray that Cispius could hold until relief arrived.

He settled into the prow as they raced on, his fleet moving openly and close together. Now it was about speed and efficiency, not subtlety and caution. As they passed the endless stretches of coastline in the wake of the enemy, he gave all the preparatory orders he could. Archers were ready, artillery loaded, everything made straight for battle. It did not take long to pick up the scent of the enemy he had lost during that brief dally at Ruspina. As they bore down on Leptis, just six miles' sail from the headland of Ruspina, a journey that took less than an hour at this speed, his eyes took in the dreadful sight ahead.

Cispius had been caught with his tunic up, oblivious to danger and thinking himself in safe waters. His fleet had been largely anchored at sea and there much of it remained, sending columns of smoke into the sky as the bones of vessels settled into the shallow coastal waters. The enemy had clearly attacked swiftly. They could not have arrived much more than a quarter of an hour before Aquila, or *half* an hour at the most, and already it was over and the enemy fleet was leaving. Fifty vessels or so had turned their back on Leptis and Cispius and had readied to head home.

Which put Aquila and his nineteen ships in the way.

The commander squinted into the good morning light, heart thumping, trying to identify what was going on at the city beyond. What was left of Cispius' fleet was crowded into the port for safety, within reach of the artillery on the city walls. At least the man had had the sense to pull his remaining ships into a safe place, for he'd have stood no chance in a straight fight. His gaze roved from the city back along the rugged brown shoreline, and it did not take long for him to spot a small cloud of dust just a few hundred paces from the place. That could only be men on horses racing along the coast, which meant Caesar.

'Commander,' the trierarch called, 'we can't take a force that size.'

Aquila nodded. 'Help is coming. All we need to do is try and stop them leaving. Have the fleet deploy one hull-width apart and then move in concert directly at the enemy.'

'Sir?'

'We're going to slip between his ships and withdraw our oars at the last moment. Any enemy vessel that doesn't do the same in time… well, you know what will happen.'

The trierarch shuddered at the thought. 'And what happens if they change course and try to ram us head on, sir?'

'That would put each engagement in the hands of the gods. I don't think an enemy commander would risk it. But most importantly, though they're in a belligerent frame of mind right now, I suspect that will change at any moment and flight will become their priority.'

'Sir?'

Aquila pointed off towards the port below the city. The dust cloud had now dissipated, for the riders had reached the dock. Already those warships that had sought shelter within the enclosed calm waters were turning and putting out to sea. A sleek cutter left a dock and immediately moved to battle speed, passing the warships and leading them out. Though Aquila could not make out any individual figure aboard, he felt certain that he knew who commanded that ship. Caesar had reached Leptis, jumped from his horse bellowing orders at Cispius, and immediately boarded the fastest ship he could spot, leading the attack in person.

They said, albeit in subdued whispers, that the general had lost his spark these days, since the Aegyptian witch had got her claws into him. Aquila could see no such thing in the man even now racing to overtake the rebel fleet. Seventeen Caesarian vessels were pouring from the mouth of the port and fanning out, moving to attack speed and racing after the enemy. Along with Aquila's fleet, that would make thirty-six. Still only perhaps two thirds the number of the enemy, but there was more to consider now than numbers.

The Caesarian fleet might be smaller, but they were angry and on the offensive, and they were in two groups, able to move fast and attack from more than one side. No naval commander wanted to be caught between two fleets. Sure enough, the rebel vessels were more concerned with a speedy departure than a fight. The fleet had begun to fan out, hoping to run wide around Aquila's ships, though clearly not all would be able to do so. The trierarch continued to shout orders to his signaller, who relayed them to the other ships, and with every tiny course adjustment the enemy made, Aquila's fleet adjusted to compensate, remaining on course directly for the centre of the enemy. Those vessels now ahead had no option but to run the Caesarian blockade, for they could not slow in time, and their flanking allies gave them insufficient room to turn.

Aquila squinted past them into the distance. He could only just see beyond the fleet bearing down on him, but Caesar and Cispius now had the other flotilla out in open waters and were moving at ramming speed in the wake of the rebel ships. Panic was visible among the enemy vessels who could not avoid the collision. Aquila vowed two things as his score of ships bore down on a fleet more than twice his size, yet who were terrified and desperately trying to escape. He would set up an altar to Neptune and to Victory at Leptis when this was over, and he would see his trierarch decorated, for even at this late stage, the enemy were trying to turn their vessels to bring their rams to bear, but with the lack of space they had little chance and every tiny move on their part was both anticipated and dealt with by the trierarch.

At the last moment the entire Caesarian fleet drew in their oars in a swift and practiced manner. The enemy tried to do the same, though through a combination of panicked disorder and lack of time, the manoeuver was something of a shambles, and as the two fleets met, Aquila could hear a multitude of oars being torn to shreds, along with the screams of men who were being pulverised by the heavy oak beams as they were slammed back into their rowers, crushing ribcages and legs in the process.

Aquila moved from prow to stern, watching with sickened satisfaction as the ships to either side of his were battered, many of the oars not fully withdrawn in time. As he reached the stern rail, where his excellent trierarch stood beside the pilot and the steering oar, he watched the result of his charge. The enemy ships were drifting one way or the other, slowing as their momentum dissipated, some slewing wildly, two colliding in the disorganised panic.

With a swift order given and relayed, Aquila's fleet turned in perfect unison, each vessel cutting sharply through the water as they carved a graceful arc to bring themselves back facing the way they had come, following up behind the fleeing rebels. The Cispian fleet from Leptis now fell in alongside them. As Caesar bellowed his gratitude and congratulations from that fast cutter, Aquila took in the situation. Fifty-five vessels, he thought, had faced them and now just thirty-five or so had managed to pick up full speed and were sailing away back to Hadrumetum, out of reach. Of the remaining twenty, many were already picking up speed and making to follow, and unless Neptune himself intervened, most would escape. Many of those that escaped would be damaged and humiliated, though.

'Caesar,' he called across to the next ship, 'what now?'

'We harry them back to their lair,' the general laughed. 'But I want two of those ships.'

'Sir?'

'The trireme that lags is laden. It contains something heavy to bring it so low, and I want that ship and its cargo. And I want that quinquireme.'

He pointed at the huge vessel, the largest in the enemy fleet, and Aquila immediately realised why. The monstrous ship was still flying the Taurus banner of Caesar's fleet. It had been captured just now at Leptis and was being taken back to Hadrumetum as a prize.

The two Caesarian fleets separated once more, concentrating on those two ships. To their credit the rest of the enemy swiftly recovered and even those running on insufficient oars began to move with the speed of the petrified prey, racing away from Caesar's hunters. Those two ships, though, were beginning to lag behind. The laden trireme was too heavy to outrun them, and the quinquireme, while it should be able to do so, was not. Perhaps it was simply that its size and weight made it slow to pick up pace, or perhaps there was another reason, but whatever the case, it was now falling behind and the enemy were unwilling to slow in order to save it. The rebels were sacrificing those two for the ability to escape.

Caesar's fleet raced for the laden trireme, and Aquila set his sights on the quinquireme. With swift orders given, his trierarch brought the ship round so that it was following on the great vessel, gaining swiftly and off slightly to starboard, ready to come alongside. Another of his ships did the same on the far side, and the two Caesarian vessels raced forth, coming up beside the quinquireme. As they met, both their vessels and the enemy drew in their oars to prevent a repeat of what had last occurred, and the three vessels gradually slowed.

The sailors on the Caesarian ships threw out grapples as the corvus boarding plank was swung across and dropped, the teeth at the far end biting down into the quinquireme's deck, anchoring the two vessels together and immediately proving a boarding ramp. Men hurtled up and across it, swords out and grim expressions of war plastered across their features.

There would not be much of a fight, though, and Aquila could see that straight away. The Caesarian ship had been captured with a skeleton crew aboard, and the rebels had put a prize crew in command to sail her home, but the moment the battle had begun to go Caesar's way, the ship's captive crew had begun to fight back, attempting to retake their own vessel. *That* had been why it had slowed and lagged behind.

Aquila watched as, within moments of his men boarding the quinquireme, the enemy dropped their weapons and surrendered. Off to the right, he could see Caesar's ships surrounding that heavy trireme and boarding it. The rest of the rebels were away and fleeing to safety, but the Caesarians had managed at least to bloody the rebels' noses for what they had done. The losses to Caesar's fleet had been more serious than any gain, but this could have been so much worse.

* * *

Dawn, 9th March 46 BC

Aquila peered ahead, once more at the prow of his ship. The enemy would not come out and fight – of that he felt certain – now that the odds were so heavily against them, but Caesar was determined to revenge himself for Leptis.

They had enjoyed a relatively leisurely cruise back to Ruspina. They had all known that they could not catch the rest of the rebel fleet in time, so there was no reason to push the crews, and instead they were allowed to rest a little while the enemy fled back to safety at Hadrumetum. In their few shouted exchanges, it had become clear to Aquila that the general was irritated with their inability to catch the rebels, but as they had rounded the headland back to their home harbour, everything had changed.

The port was too full for them to put in, for just over forty triremes sat at the jetties, waited in the harbour, or remained anchored out to sea in preparation, all bearing the Taurus flags of Caesar alongside the banners of the Seventh and Eighth Legions. The reinforcements from Sicilia had arrived, and not only did that mean that the army could now comfortably face Scipio in battle with a reasonable chance of success, it also meant that the fleet available at Ruspina had grown to around eighty, compared with the fifty or so that had sailed from Hadrumetum.

Caesar had been all action immediately. Leptis would be avenged. They had waited a few hours for the two legions to disembark, for there was no race to be run now, though Caesar had twitched with the delay. By the time the fleet had gathered in full, the newly-arrived legions encamping at Ruspina, the light was already beginning to fade. They had raced west with what sunlight remained, and had anchored close to shore for the night.

This morning the light had been encouraging, as golden filaments threaded through a high, blue and white sky. The day was going to be a warm one, and even before the sun had put in an appearance as a golden arc on the eastern horizon, the fleet was on the move again.

Now, Hadrumetum hoved into sight, and Aquila heaved a satisfied sigh of relief. He'd half expected a horrible trap to await them, but instead the sight that greeted him was a welcome one. The city's harbour was full of a combination of native merchants and fishermen, and what rebel warships could fit inside. A number of low transports sat anchored out in the water, along with a few more triremes. All along the shoreline before the city, though, sat beached vessels – the damaged ones from the previous day's conflict, drawn up onto the beach for repairs.

Aquila glanced across to the quinquireme, now made Caesar's flagship, and in moments the signal was given. At the prow of every ship, and at several points along their rails, braziers burst into life, fuelled with pitch and ignited by sailors with tapers. Artillerists carefully manhandled pots of pitch into on-board catapults and flaming missiles into the great bolt throwers, while archers nocked fire arrows.

The fleet ploughed through the waves, separating, each making for the best targets. Triremes swept along parallel to the shore and, as they did so, flaming shots arced out like burning rain to fall upon the seasoned timbers of those beached ships. Each stricken hull bloomed into an orange inferno within moments of their passage. Other ships in Caesar's fleet angled out into the open waters outside the harbour and performed the same brutal action against the transports and warships anchored there.

The Caesarian force utterly brutalised the rebel fleet, more than revenging themselves for what had happened at Leptis, the damage here far more critical and all-consuming. Cries and blared horns of alarm rang out from the walls of Hadrumetum at this shock attack, so unexpected, though there was nothing they could do. Just as had happened to Cispius at Leptis, the rebel crews were ashore, their ships undefended, the only vessels safe being those within the harbour.

Aquila watched as the ships in the port began to move, yet not one of them dared the arms of the harbour and the journey into the open sea, and he could hardly blame them. The bottom arc of the sun was not yet clear of the horizon and already every hull outside the protective moles of the harbour was done for. The sea was a mass of burning hulks slowly subsiding beneath the waves, and in between them, Caesar's ships prowled like hungry predators.

From the rail, Aquila observed as his ship joined those circling like sharks. For an hour the fleet threaded their threatening way among the charring and sinking remnants of more than half the rebel ships at Hadrumetum, and throughout it all, the enemy ships lurked safely within the harbour, glaring in impotent fury at the aggressor. The walls of the city were lined with miserable faces watching their fleet burn.

It was not until the last of the anchored vessels had disappeared beneath the waves and the hulks along the beach had begun to collapse in on themselves that Caesar gave the order to withdraw, now confident that the enemy had no intention of coming out to meet them in combat.

As the fleet gathered and turned their back on Hadrumetum with a few last parting shots, Aquila scanned the result of their actions. The sea all around the city was a blackened mess of wreckage and charred timbers, and the beach was little more than a naval graveyard, skeletons of hulls blackening and collapsing.

All in all a good day's work, considering it was still just a little after dawn. By noon they would be back at Ruspina, celebrating and welcoming the last two veteran legions Caesar expected. The tables had begun to turn for real, now. After months of playing the dangerous, defensive game, Caesar had the advantage on both land and sea, and Scipio would have to look to his defences.

CHAPTER SEVENTEEN

Ruspina, 12th March 46 BC

ow H in Hades do you know they're *your* Gaetuli?'
Fronto said, frowning at Galronus.
'My riders are told to hang a bull pendant
from their bridles for identification.'

'Perhaps the enemy have realised this?'

Galronus shook his head. 'Only those men I send to
infiltrate use the method. It won't be seen in bulk or on the
field of battle. It's good. These men are mine.'

They watched the three riders being checked over by the
duty centurion and his men and waited patiently. Once the
centurion was satisfied that nothing was amiss, the men were
released and led their mounts into the camp and towards the
two waiting officers, where they stopped and saluted
Galronus.

'You have intelligence for me?' the Remi officer said.

'Yes sir. Important, too.'

'Come on, then.'

The officers led the three cavalrymen through the camp
and towards the headquarters tent at its heart. As they
approached, Fronto saw one of the praetorians duck inside,
carrying warning to the occupant, and so it came as no
surprise when they were admitted to find the general standing
behind his table, fully armoured and alert, hands clasped
behind his back in a business-like manner.

'Gentlemen,' Caesar greeted them.

'General,' Galronus said, saluting, 'these men are riders
from my Gaetuli cavalry and, along with a dozen of their

countrymen, they have been mixing once more with their former allies in the enemy camp, gathering information for us.'

Caesar smiled and Fronto realised that, though he'd had no idea the cavalry spies were being used, clearly the general had. 'You have news?'

The riders looked to Galronus, who nodded, and so one of them stepped a pace forward and saluted Caesar. 'Sir, there are enemy spies within this camp and, though we have been unable so far to identify them, they have reported our fresh foraging missions to the enemy commanders.'

Fronto grunted irritably. They had all naturally assumed that the enemy would have spies in their camp, just the same as Caesar had in Scipio's, and knowledge of the fresh forage missions would inevitably leak out, though this had been quicker than they had expected.

In the wake of the loss of half a fleet of supplies outside Leptis Minor's harbour, new plans had been hatched to make up the lost supplies and keep the army fed. As they had known from the start, local towns and villages kept their grain in underground stores, largely hidden from view, and the Caesarian army had taken from only a few of them, such missions cut short by the arrival of Scipio's army and the near disastrous battle. Moreover, in the east, where the towns were allied to Caesar's forces, foragers had needed to be careful, taking only as much as left sufficient for the populace, and now, as winter ended and spring hoved into view, those stores were already shrunken and lacking.

Thus had been born a daring new plan. It seemed certain, with Labienus, Juba and Scipio all encamped close together a stone's throw from Caesar's lines, and with Caesar's army being stopped up in his fortifications, that the enemy were entirely concentrated here and were not patrolling land they considered theirs. Consequently, the previous day the Twenty Fifth and Twenty-Sixth Legions had moved in light kit away from Ruspina, well behind the fortified lines and out of sight of the enemy, crossing into open ground a few miles to the southeast, and had skirted around the outside of the enemy camps to a distance of some ten miles, finding stores that had been hoarded as reserves for the enemy force. Two or three such trips would make up the missing supplies, and last night the officers had celebrated their success.

That the enemy had become aware of this audacious escapade was hardly surprising.

Caesar kept his level gaze on the spies. 'What does Scipio intend to do? Will he gather in his supplies? Protect them with garrisons?'

The Gaetuli rider shook his head. 'The rebel camp has more than adequate supplies to see them through at least the next month, so those stores are superfluous. The general will not devote men to protecting or gathering them and put his position at risk by losing those troops in case of sudden attack from our lines at Ruspina. It is the cavalry commander who plans to move.'

'Not surprising,' Caesar agreed. 'Scipio has been solid and increasingly defensive since our first encounter. He seems unwilling to commit to battle now that we have a sizeable force. Labienus, on the other hand, is proactive and shrewd. He knows we need those supplies. What has he planned?'

'Sir, the commander has this morning taken two of Scipio's legions, some light Numidian auxilia of Juba's and a large number of horse to the ford over the river your foragers crossed yesterday, some seven miles from here. There he lays an ambush for your foragers, knowing they must pass that way if they wish to repeat their success.'

'Thank you, gentlemen,' the general addressed the three riders. 'Take yourselves off to the stores and draw an extra ration of wine with my compliments. Fall out and enjoy some well-deserved rest.'

Once the three men had gone, Caesar waited for a pause of twenty heartbeats to be sure they were out of earshot and then slumped into his seat. 'You trust these men?'

Galronus shrugged. 'Insofar as we can trust any of the enemy deserters. There is always the possibility that they are double agents, or even playing both sides. However, these were among the men who almost cost us dearly near Uzitta when the enemy riled them into an attack, and who fell upon that same enemy at the farm near Leptis. It would truly appear that they have no love of Scipio's army.'

'Then on balance we must trust this information. Labienus moves to ambush our foragers with two legions, light auxilia and cavalry. Several options present themselves.'

Fronto nodded. 'But we all know which is the most advantageous.'

'As long as those men are *not* double agents.'

'But as you said, Caesar, on balance we're forced to trust them. Labienus thinks to ambush us, but with foreknowledge we can turn this around and give him a thrashing. And who knows, we might even be able to catch the slippery bastard this time.'

'We must appear to be falling for the trick,' Caesar said, tapping his lip. 'For the best results the same two legions should move with their minimal cavalry escort on the same clear route as though nothing were amiss.'

'Bait,' Galronus nodded.

'Quite. And while the bait moves openly, a second force will move in the shadows to outflank them. While the Twenty Fifth and Twenty-Sixth leave by the main gate and march ahead, I will lead the Fifth, Seventh and Ninth from the rear gate, lightly armed for speedy travel, as well as several alae of cavalry. This force will move a great deal faster.'

The general reached up and pulled a leather thong loose, unrolling a map down the wall of his command tent. After a little searching he found the location of which the three riders had spoken. 'Seven miles, or thereabouts. For a force moving at standard speed, slowed by ox carts, that would mean a journey of perhaps three hours. This river is but one of the tributaries of the same that flows past Uzitta, and we know those to be crossable. This ford is only used specifically because it is an easy route for vehicles. Horse and fast infantry could readily cross in other locations. The second force should be able to move a further mile out from the foraging route, keeping them far from enemy eyes and could be expected to cover twice the distance in that time.'

Fronto nodded. 'Sounds feasible. We did similar with expedited marches in Belgae lands.' He cast an oddly apologetic look at Galronus, who shrugged. His tribe, the Remi, had been allies to Caesar from the beginning.

'This second force, then, can move into position early near the ford and be ready to pounce when the enemy moves,' Caesar decided. 'With five legions and appropriate support we can outnumber them by more than two to one, and with the added element of surprise, the battle should be a foregone conclusion.'

'And you intend to lead the second ambushing force, General?'

Caesar nodded. 'Galronus will take the cavalry contingent and I shall command the infantry. You, Fronto, shall lead the foragers who walk into the trap. Deploy the moment the ruse becomes clear.'

Fronto smiled. 'With luck I'll be able to meet Labienus face to face.'

* * *

The journey had passed with interminable slowness and every half hour Fronto had been forced to speak to the legions quietly through their officers, telling them to stop looking and sounding so fidgety and nervous, for they were supposed to be unaware of danger, and who knew when they were passing within sight of Labienus' forward scouts. After decades of commanding armies in the field, Fronto still chafed at marching speeds set by the slow ox-wagons at the rear, and his gaze kept straying up to the sun in an attempt to mark the passage of time. It had to have been around three hours by now.

His relief was palpable when one of his outriders returned, pointing ahead. The ford was in sight. Fronto peered ahead, trying to identify where the enemy lay. Like many water courses in this dry and dusty province, the narrow, shallow river had carved a gully through the grey land, and the road they followed descended twice the height of a man to the ford, rising once more at the far side.

There were stands of trees here and there and olive groves, but not dense enough or sizeable enough to conceal an ambushing force. They had to therefore be hiding in the many gulleys and ravines caused by the various tributaries. He turned to the primus pilus behind him. 'They're in the gulleys. They have to be. Pass the word.'

'Could they hide cavalry in them, sir?'

'No, but the legions and the auxiliaries can. The cavalry must be held back. Perhaps behind that treeline in the distance.'

'Or that one?' the centurion added, pointing off to their left.

'No. They'd have had to move to intercept us by now. That treeline, though, will shelter our own men, of that I'm certain.'

Galronus and his riders had to be there, unless there had been some delay and the second force wasn't here at all. But that sort of disaster didn't bear thinking about. They were here, somewhere. They all were, friend and foe alike.

'We're marching into the frying pan now. Have the men ready.'

Tense, ready for action, the two legions under Fronto's command marched down the long, gentle incline towards the ford, which was wide enough to present no obstacle for the foraging force.

The attack came with no warning, and had Fronto and his men been truly caught off-guard, the result could have been dreadful. White-clad Numidian light infantry suddenly appeared all around them, cresting the gulley tops armed with javelins and slings and bows and a rain of missiles began almost instantly. Thankfully, Fronto and his men were well-prepared, and the entire column immediately halted and dropped into testudo formation, the shields coming out and up to form a roofed shell all around them. Fronto, on his horse and an open target, turned and raced back along the line with the tribunes, out of range of the missiles, where he found a raised spot to look out across the field.

He hated playing a defensive game, his men pinned and occasionally howling as a missile managed to penetrate the shell of shields and wound or kill. Still, there was little he could do yet. Now it relied on the second army.

Stones, arrows and javelins rattled and clonked off shields and clanged off helmets and armour all around the front few cohorts of the pinned force. The horrendous din of so many missiles was deafening enough that he had to concentrate to hear anything else but the whirr, clack and thrum, a cacophony that was already preying on the men's nerves. As yet, only a thousand or so enemy auxilia had committed. They had to be keeping Fronto's force contained while the legions and the cavalry moved into position.

He felt a wash of relief suddenly at a new sound. A roar of panic arose among those men hurling missiles from atop the gulleys, as horsemen appeared as if from nowhere, having themselves used those very same ravines to approach the ambush unseen from that treeline off to the east.

Galronus' riders burst from a multitude of ravine mouths, racing up the sides and coming up behind the light auxiliaries. Fronto watched in grim satisfaction as those men busy battering his legions with missiles were suddenly attacked from the rear, many cut down in an instant. At the ford, a second force of white-clad light infantry suddenly poured out into the road in front of the foraging legions, running as fast as they could, whooping Gallic cavalry driving them on, riding them down and slamming spears into their backs. The enemy ambushers, driven from their hiding places, were racing along the road now and, the tirade of deadly missiles having petered out with the men above dealing with their own problems, Fronto bellowed the order to re-form and to charge.

The men of the Twenty Fifth, with a roar of sheer fury, dropped their shields back into position and immediately began to run at the panicked enemy ambushers who suddenly discovered they had nowhere left to go, riders driving them on behind and a wall of steel shirts and gleaming blades thundering along the road towards them ahead. Those who could scrambled up the sides of the slope and up onto higher ground, only to meet more of Galronus' riders there.

Fronto smiled grimly as his legions ploughed into the lightly armed and armoured men ahead, pulverising and maiming with impunity. The enemy ambush had failed dismally, and already they were paying the price. What would Labienus do? Would he abandon his light troops and cut his losses? As the battle raged near the ford, Fronto, accompanied by his musicians and signallers, rode up the slope to the highest ground to be found, where he could get a good view of the entire field.

Galronus' attack had been brutally effective. Fully half the enemy's light infantry already lay scattered in the dust, accompanied by remarkably few riders. A new noise drew Fronto's attention and he looked up, past the fight. Enemy cavalry had flooded from that distant treeline and were now racing to become involved. Moreover, two legions of Scipio's were emerging from the next row of gulleys and marching forward. Labienus could still be relatively confident. He had already lost more than half a thousand light infantry, but what would really count were the legions and the horse, and they were roughly evenly matched, his two heavy infantry units marching to meet Fronto's, his cavalry slightly outnumbering those of Galronus.

Of course, he did not know about Caesar.

Fronto watched the battle raging. His legions had obliterated the remaining panicked light auxilia and were marching across their broken corpses towards Scipio's legionaries, expressions set in a grimace of determination. Months of playing a defensive game or watching Scipio's armies lining up, trying to tempt them into battle, had clawed at the Caesarian army's nerves, and every man was determined to give the enemy a thrashing.

Labienus' cavalry came racing for those of Galronus, and Fronto watched carefully. As the enemy horse charged across the grey and dusty landscape, Galronus, sitting on a similarly high point and with a commanding view of the field, began to give out orders with gestures alone. His riders gathered once more into units, pulling back from the fight, their immediate enemy beaten. The remains of the rebel light infantry fled in panic, racing back to the south and away from Galronus' riders.

Fronto smiled grimly, aware precisely of what Galronus was doing. His horse withdrew level with the foraging legions, who were now close to the ford, on this side of the narrow river. Fronto could see no sign of further men, but they were there somewhere, and he knew it. On Labienus' riders came, content that they could still win this fight, even if the ambush had somehow gone wrong, with an unexpected cavalry force aiding Caesar's foraging legions.

Galronus remained still, his men falling into ordered lines, Labienus' cavalry coming ever closer. As the enemy horse closed on the river, finally, the Remi noble gave a wave and a horn blew. Like a tide of steel, three veteran legions suddenly emerged from the river gulley, into which they had slipped, unnoticed by Labienus and his riders during the main clash. Like a wave, they crested the gulley, well-armoured and bristling with weapons, veterans and with death in mind. As they reached the top of the gulley on the far side of the river, between Galronus' cavalry and those of Labienus, the legions pushed pila out between their shields to form a veritable hedge of sharpened points, the second and third rows joining in, angling their own pila between those in front. Thus arrayed, they began to stomp slowly but inexorably forward, chanting an age-old prayer to Mars as they did so, twelve thousand footsteps in time thumping rhythmically on the packed earth.

Labienus' cavalry panicked in an instant. A few units continued to charge, though most drew their steeds to a halt. Calls to withdraw rang out, and all was chaos in the enemy ranks. Caesar suddenly emerged from a gulley on his white horse, red cloak fluttering and, while the enemy were clearly withdrawing, Labienus and his officers having now decided the engagement had been lost, Caesar was not quite ready to let it all go. Those enemy riders who had come on regardless, or who had been slow to come to a stop and not immediately turned and ridden away, suffered for their delay, for with a single command, Caesar had his legions break their steady pace and surge forward, overrunning the desperate riders. Those unfortunates of Labienus' horse who could not withdraw in time were cut down in short order and the veteran legions marched on over their remains, approaching the withdrawing cavalry at speed. Galronus had given his horse the order to move once more and they were coming up behind Caesar's legions in support, forming a formidable sight. In response, Fronto did precisely the same, his two legions now marching at double time towards their opponents.

The enemy legions had also received the order to withdraw, and were even now turning in near-panic, desperate to pull back before they became embroiled in a straight fight they could neither escape nor hope to win.

Caesar's army had the enemy on the run. They had killed, by Fronto's rough estimation, between a thousand and fifteen hundred men across the various enemy forces. Not a war-ending engagement, but one that would further gnaw at Scipio and his men and which could only bolster the pride and confidence of the army at Ruspina.

As the legions stomped forward, seeking a position in line with the rest of Caesar's advancing force, Fronto rode off to his left, converging with where the general had stepped his horse back to meet up with Galronus. The three men sat on a high point as the enemy continued to pull back, trying to gather in a good order but finding it impossible to do so under the constant pressure of Caesar's pursuing force.

'It's a shame we couldn't have done that on this side of the river,' Fronto noted. 'Now they can flee back to their camp. On *this* side we'd have trapped a number of them.'

Caesar nodded. 'Unfortunate, but unavoidable. We must take what we can from the situation the gods give us, though, and be more than satisfied with what we have achieved here. Without the warning of those Gaetuli we would today have lost the majority of two legions. Instead, we have turned an enemy ambush into a humiliating and costly defeat for them. Moreover, listening to the din of the enemy missiles, I am beginning to form an idea.'

'So what do we do from here?'

The general gave him a smile. 'We press our advantage. I take the three legions, along with our Remi friend here and his cavalry, and we harry the enemy right back to their camp, not allowing them space to breathe until they reach missile range of their own ramparts. And while we do so, you continue on with the other two legions and take as many supplies as you can from the various stores right under their noses. I will be extremely surprised if they rally to any kind of further action today, so I believe you can take your time and be thorough. Once we have seen the enemy off properly, we will meet with your force to provide an escort back to Ruspina. With luck and care we can replenish our lost supplies today and have humiliated the enemy into the bargain.'

* * *

Fronto wearily shook himself out of his cuirass, letting it drop to the tent floor with a dull thud. He'd get someone to polish it before morning. Right now he was too tired for such things and wanted only to collapse into a chair and relax. Unlacing his boots, he slipped out sore feet and wrinkled his toes to bring life back into them, hanging his sword up on the wall of the tent. He had a few moments before company arrived, and so spent his time washing away the grime of the day in the water bowl on the cupboard and vigorously towelling himself before changing into a clean tunic that did not show the myriad stains of dust and rust from a day of travel and activity.

Must be getting old, he told himself. He'd not once drawn his sword today, watching the whole thing from horseback, yet he was as tired and achy now as he'd been after fighting rabid Belgae warriors a decade ago in northern Gaul.

Rolling his head and surprised at the number of clicks that issued from his neck, he fished four glasses from the cupboard and brought down to the low table the jug of Falernian that some helpful and well-informed slave had left on the top along with a jar of water.

He poured himself a cup, cut to the appropriate proportions, and sat back, taking a sip and exhaling the exertions of the day. Everything had gone precisely as planned. He had found villages and depots guarded by small garrisons of rebel troops and had stripped them of supplies, the soldiers fleeing immediately at the sight of Fronto's two legions. It had not taken many such visits to pack the wagons he'd brought full ready for the return journey, replenishing more of what had been lost in that naval debacle.

They had barely reached that same ambush site at the river on their return when Caesar and the rest of the army converged upon them and escorted them back to Ruspina. The army had been in high spirits, for they had kept the enemy at a panicked run all the way, continually picking off the slowest of the units. The safest among the enemy had been the white-clad Numidian auxiliaries who had first launched the missile ambush and who had broken and fled at the start of the fight, for they had not stopped running after their panic, and had fled to the enemy camp in individual terrified groups, completely ignoring Labienus' calls to form up with the army.

Despite the success, a slight pall had been cast over the day when the victorious force had returned to camp and found that a new display had been created for them. Juba had apparently been more than a little miffed with his men, both for their flight and for their refusal to react to Labienus' commands. Consequently a little over a hundred white-clad natives had already been crucified outside the Numidian camp and hung there, moaning and howling in full sight of both armies for their failures.

Fronto tried not to think on that now, nor on the grand cost to the republic this seemingly endless war was creating. He was grateful for the distraction when there came a knock at the tent door and Galronus asked for permission to enter. Giving it, Fronto refilled his glass and watched as the other three arrived. The Remi was a common visitor, of course, and Salvius Cursor, despite their long history of mutual irritations, had become a regular confidante of Fronto's. The new face was as welcome as any, though. Atenos looked older, wearier and more lined than he had since Fronto had last spent any time with him, in the days of Pharsalus and trailing Pompey across the east. He had finally got rid of his braids and wore a neat, Roman haircut, though his stature and his colouring would label him Gallic or Germanic no matter how he changed his appearance.

Fronto gestured to the table, and the other three made appreciative noises and poured themselves drinks, sinking into the prepared chairs.

'Is this an impromptu celebration or do you have ulterior motives?' Salvius said, taking a sip of his wine. 'Not that I'm not grateful or glad to be here. My current role might be important and prestigious, but it is often also tedious and, when it isn't, that's because the general is doing something stupid that goes against my advice. Like today when he rode off to spring an ambush and conveniently never mentioned it to his bodyguard, who were unaware he'd even left the camp.'

Fronto laughed. 'He was in no danger. Not with three veteran legions protecting him.'

'Not if they can be *trusted*,' Salvius replied archly, with a strange look at Atenos. 'Remember that the Ninth were recently mutinous.'

'Well they acquitted themselves well today,' Fronto replied. 'Anyway, with apologies to the good centurion here,' a nod at Atenos, 'those mutinies are something I wanted to talk about. Without Caesar being present, specifically.'

'Oh?'

'Caesar's presence can be a little stifling when discussing subjects like this, but I wanted to speak to you Atenos. I know the basics of what happened with the Tenth, and I know without doubt that you were no part of it. How, then did it all happen, and *why* were you not involved.'

The big centurion sighed. 'The senior tribune carefully moved those of us who would have stood against him into a vexillation and sent us to Rome with instructions to encamp on the Campus Martius and stay there until we received further instructions. We were effectively shuffled out of the way. I knew they were in the wrong, but to defy a tribune would be unacceptable for a centurion. You know that. So we did as we were told.'

'So you sat helpless in Rome while the rest of the legion mutinied and then ravaged the rest of Campania.'

'More or less. Once Marcus Antonius became aware of our presence he took command of our group in Rome and used us to remove the senior officers and to reinstate control of the legions. We managed to have all those directly responsible brought in and left it to Antonius to deal with them. I doubt he was lenient on them. He was not best pleased.'

'Good,' Fronto said emphatically. 'And what about this character you said escaped?'

Atenos huffed irritably. 'Yes, Julius Pontius Artemas. He is an enigma, and one that still plagues me.'

'You have no idea who he is?'

Atenos shook his head. 'Before we were dismissed to Rome he turned up from somewhere and ended up with the senior tribune and the legate as though he'd known them for years. I had only the briefest experience of the man before I was ordered away, but from later investigation, it seems likely he was at least partially behind my removal and that of my fellow loyal officers. More than that, I think this Artemas was the man who stirred up most of the trouble, putting criminal ideas in peoples' heads. I would have liked to have nailed him down and interrogated him, but by the time we were back with the legions and putting things right, he had disappeared.'

'It's not a familiar name,' Fronto admitted. 'Anyone else heard of him?'

Galronus and Salvius Cursor both shook their heads.

'I'm not surprised,' Atenos said. 'I spoke to the Master of Horse, Antonius, on the matter and he did some investigating himself. He reported in the end that he had found records of four people of that name. One was a quaestor in Illyria and had been in that province the entire time, and the same goes for the one who had been teaching rhetoric in Athens. Neither of them could have been the one in Campania. The third Artemas was only ten years old, and the fourth so corpulent that Antonius claimed the man had needed to come through his office door sideways. I had seen Artemas, and neither of those fits the bill. The man is a ghost. He simply does not exist.'

Fronto frowned. 'When we have time back in Rome, I think we need to investigate this Artemas further. I don't think he was merely a troublemaker. His actions effectively kept the important veteran legions in Italia when we needed them here. If it weren't for Marcus Antonius and for you and your friends, we might even now have been at Scipio's mercy. I would not be at all surprised to find that the same man had been behind the delays of the Seventh and Eighth.'

The others nodded their agreement, and Fronto leaned back.

'Alright, there's little we can do about any of that right now, so let's talk about what's next. There'll be a command meeting in the morning and I expect there to be changes. I don't know about you, but I've known Caesar a lot of years and I can tell when he's got the bit between his teeth.'

'You mean he's planning something big?' Atenos murmured. 'I've only been here days, but all the talk is of how neither Caesar nor Scipio have the balls to push this thing. Quiet talk, of course, but the general they describe isn't the one I remember from Pharsalus, Ilerda or Alesia.'

Fronto sighed. Such talk among the officers he knew of, but to find that the ranks spoke the same was worrying. Such lack of confidence could breed further mutiny. 'Caesar's planning has been somewhat... reactive,' Fronto said carefully.

'Haphazard,' corrected Galronus, earning a warning glare from Salvius.

'Not at his best,' Fronto admitted. 'Africa has been a bit of a mess so far and I know where many place the blame. But remember that we were woefully unprepared when we crossed to Ilyria a few years ago, and Dyrrachium nearly did for us, but Caesar managed to turn it all around and give us Pharsalus. Nothing is lost when he really sets his mind to it. I mean, the man opposed the senate and marched across the Rubicon with just one legion and wrested control of the republic from Cato. Don't write him off yet. Anyway, there was something new about him today at the ford. I saw the old Caesar from Gaul make an appearance, full of energy and ideas. He's onto something, I swear it. Expect action soon, and change is in the wind.'

CHAPTER EIGHTEEN

Ruspina, 13th *March 46 BC*

'Caesar, think about this carefully,' Fronto said, despite the general's warning glare.

'I have pondered the problem and all its potential solutions through a sleepless night, Fronto, and to me this is the clear path.'

Fronto gritted his teeth. He'd expected change and he'd got it, though not in the way he'd expected. Caesar *had* had an idea, but Fronto didn't like it.

'Abandoning our position here opens all the cities that have declared for us to danger. It means we lose direct control of our good harbour, all our fortifications will lie unused, waiting for Scipio to take them and use them to besiege Ruspina and Leptis. Months of preparations against Scipio and his forces to simply throw away, and all this in favour of the unknown? It's madness, and those men who already think our campaign here to be driven by hasty decisions and panicked reactions will have their fears bolstered. The men will lose heart, and you know now how easily they mutiny. We've won small victories constantly and we are almost fully supplied again. Why throw that away?'

The general's lips tightened in anger.

'The problem has plagued me, Fronto. We have pushed and pushed, and Scipio will not commit to battle here. Yesterday we won a small victory, yes, but in effect the result was the enemy holing up in their camp once more. After three months of digging in at Ruspina, both our armies are encamped in secure and well-defended systems. We need to meet Scipio in open battle now that we have the numbers, but he is not willing to do so now that our forces are more or less equal and the outcome uncertain. Like us a month ago, Scipio has become over reliant upon his defences. We need to nullify the value of such fortification systems. We need to pull him away from his excellent camp.'

'I thought we were just as reliant upon our fortifications because of his elephants.' Fronto continued to grind his teeth. He didn't like this at all, and yet there was something here, and he could feel it. After months of playing it careful the general was suddenly ready to move and, even if that was the wrong decision, at least it *was* decisive. Caesar was up to something.

The general waved a dismissive hand. 'Elephants can be overcome, I now realise. As long as we remain here, both armies sit in their camps and nothing happens because Scipio can no longer afford to commit to open battle and we cannot guarantee success if we besiege him. The defections from the enemy have all but stopped, and now his army begins to strengthen once more as new recruits are brought in, while we can expect no further increase in numbers. In short, staying here gradually strengthens Scipio, and eventually he will be too strong again, putting us back in the position we were in two months ago when it was us forced to hide behind walls. We have a narrow window where the advantage is ours, but only if we can draw him out. I need to be back in Rome, and the legions need victory and payment thereafter. This has to end.'

'I have to admit, Caesar,' Plancus said, 'that I do not much like it. I don't think he will follow unless we threaten something important. March on Utica, perhaps? Threatening Cato's base and the centre of rebel power in Africa would force him to deal with us.'

Fronto nodded, but Caesar remained unmoved. 'We move east, into territory that supports us. The enemy will follow because no matter how reluctant Scipio is, Labienus will be burning for revenge and Juba will expect action. Sooner or later the Numidian king will be forced to abandon this and return to his own lands. He will want to press now, while they can, and you can safely wager that Cato is becoming impatient too. Orders to move against us will be coming from Utica. Scipio will be forced to move whether he likes it or not. It doesn't matter if we put Ruspina at risk, for the enemy will have to move their full force after us to be sure of having the numbers they need. I will have the fleet split and patrol all our coastal installations, and Ruspina can be garrisoned just as Acylla and Leptis. They will remain safe. We will pull down our defences and burn what remains to leave no works the enemy can use against our garrisons.'

'But why not Utica, as Plancus says?'

'Because, Fronto, to march on the enemy's heartland will take us into vast tracts of land under their control, where supplies will be difficult to obtain. Moving east makes our supply situation far easier to manage. Moreover, to move west we would need to remove the obstacle of Hadrumetum on the way. No, Fronto. Barring a garrison for Ruspina, the entire army decamps during the hours of darkness tonight and marches east.'

'At night?'

'I want us to be well on the way by dawn, buying us time to manoeuvre without Scipio harrying us. As we did at Dyrrachium, we move out unexpectedly and the enemy will have to struggle to follow us at speed.'

The general turned to the great map on the wall. 'We control every coastal town of import from here to Acylla, fifty miles southeast around the coast, barring important Thapsus, which remains staunchly allied to the rebel cause under the competent Vergilius. Those ports we do not garrison support us anyway and grant us access and supplies. Away from the coast not one inland town of significance within that arc

remains a supporter of Cato, barring unfortified villages and
small townships as yet unaware of the political landscape.
The east is ours. We draw Scipio there, where we can claim
all the advantages, and we pull him into battle. I still want the
enemy to launch the initial attack, but I believe we can needle
them into doing so. Around the towns of Tegea and Aggar the
map seems to suggest wide open spaces suitable for our
proposed action, and so we make for those towns, twenty
miles or so from here. If we can decamp speedily, beginning
work this evening, and move suddenly and at a good pace, we
can stay well ahead of the enemy and reach Aggar in one
day.'

'I follow your logic,' Fronto grumbled, 'but I don't think it
matters whether you're here or there or on Mount Olympus
itself, Scipio's not going to change. We thought he'd be
impulsive, but he seems to have lost that side of his nature in
favour of an over-cautious approach.'

'His lieutenants will push him if we needle them enough.
Plancus was thinking along the right lines with his plans for
Utica, but Utica is not feasible. However, we have a
secondary target to the east that will have almost as much
effect. Cato places a great deal of value upon Thapsus, which
remains his only coastal garrison in the entire east. Thapsus is
a traditional stop on the trade routes from east to west, and
accounts for a sizeable proportion of the rebels' income. This
is why it is as well defended as Hadrumetum, and why we
have thus far not added it to our list of coastal allies. Cato
cannot afford to lose Thapsus, and he will not allow Scipio to
ignore any move against it. Threatening Thapsus will have
more effect even than threatening far off Utica.'

'I feel there must be a better solution,' Fronto murmured,
though with much less conviction, now. The general had
something planned, and this was just the start of it.

Caesar turned, eyes gleaming with dangerous intelligence,
and slapped both palms down on the table. 'The decision is

made, Fronto. The army decamps under cover of darkness and marches east.'

* * *

14th March 46 BC

Fronto rode at the head of the army with Caesar and the other officers. Behind them, the indigo sky of early dawn was already filled with distant swirls of smoke as everything no longer needed by the army burned amid the slighted ramparts of the camp that had been their home for months.

Ruspina faded into the distance, its walls heavily garrisoned, the only presence of Caesar's grand army that remained there. Out to sea, the fleet had separated into two groups, one under Cispius bound for Hadrumetum to blockade it against Scipio receiving fresh supplies by sea, the other under Aquila, making for Thapsus to begin putting pressure upon that place, stopping vital trade reaching the port and helping to push Scipio into battle.

Fronto chewed his lip in irritation. The general was up to something. No one else seemed to have noticed, but Fronto had seen it often enough to identify the signs. There was logic enough to the new strategy that it seemed to everyone as if Caesar had merely made yet another of the erratic tactical decisions for which he was becoming known. Fronto was of a different opinion.

He had argued against leaving Ruspina, and yes, there was the possibility of drawing out Scipio, but there was something else afoot too. The problem was that Caesar was keeping it all very close to his chest and had intimated nothing of what was to happen. And what was all that about 'elephants can be overcome?' Until now their entire fortified strategy had been built around defending against elephants, given the danger they posed. Now, though, he seemed quite blasé over the whole issue. What had changed to make him confident about facing those great beasts in the field after weeks of planning defensive strategies around them.

On the bright side, the general was full of purpose, which was somewhat infectious, and a new energy filled the army as they moved with conviction, grateful not to be lurking in garrisons. As they moved at a swift campaign pace, the scouts brought tidings that the enemy, surprised by Caesar's sudden departure, had broken camp at dawn and began to assemble for the march, all three forces coming together, Scipio, Labienus and Juba. At least that much Caesar had anticipated correctly. It seemed that the enemy commanders were intent on following them, and would be sufficiently far behind to allow Caesar room to manoeuvre.

The army snaked on through the warm spring morning, making almost directly southeast, further and further from the coast, which itself meandered in a much more easterly direction, turning south at Thapsus. According to the maps they had studied, the road they moved along connected Ruspina and Uzitta with important Acylla, via various small towns on the way. Caesar's strategy called for pulling Scipio to the east and to ground where they could be brought to battle, threatening Thapsus by mere proximity. They could not afford to actually invest Thapsus with siege lines, for then the Caesarian army would be caught between the pursuing army and the town's garrison, but around the town of Aggar, they were near enough to make that threat felt while still claiming open ground.

Galronus and his cavalry roved all about, acting as scouts and vanguard, keeping the flanks protected, and coming along at some distance behind, maintaining a watch on the enemy, who moved to follow. Sometime in the early afternoon they passed a small town by the name of Zeta, where a road marched off towards the coast and all-important Thapsus. At Zeta, while the army continued on their march, the general took his praetorians off to study the place from a safe distance, for the banners of Utica and Cato were hoisted at their approach, something they had not seen since Hadrumetum. Whatever the general saw there, he re-joined the column with a thoughtful and calculating expression. Pressing Salvius Cursor for information, Fronto learned nothing further of use, for Salvius remained equally in the dark, uncertain what Caesar had seen that had so interested him beyond those flags.

The small township of Tegea passed by on their right in the mid-afternoon and, as the sun began to slide towards the horizon, the settlement of Aggar appeared ahead and Caesar called a halt. The camp they pitched that night was large, big enough to shelter the entire army, and in low, open ground, with easy terrain lying to the west, granting them ample opportunity to issue from the defences and meet Scipio, should he move against them straight away.

Despite their proximity to Thapsus, and the naval blockade that must have already begun that afternoon, Scipio appeared to continue with his reluctance to commit. The enemy, pursuing them doggedly, yet at a distance, made camp in a hilly area around the town of Tegea, some six miles from Caesar, and there the two armies settled in for the night.

The following morning Caesar set out, leading two legions in person and returning towards the day's end with ample forage including wheat, barley, oil, wine and figs, but most important of all, bearing a look of calculating satisfaction. Fronto pressed Salvius for details once again, though this time the man was more forthcoming. The foraging army had covered much local ground, coming close enough to the enemy position to discover that they had split the army once again into three camps, and then hovering on the edge of the town of Zeta once more, observing the place while the legions gathered crops. There, Salvius had seen a small group of officers and men in rich clothes arrive from the direction of

Scipio's camp and enter the town of Zeta, though he could identify none of them.

Word arrived on the second day at Aggar that Thapsus was now fully blockaded by Aquila, and similar news must have reached Scipio by this time, yet the enemy commander remained in his hill camp, lurking there, inactive and not threatening Caesar. Fronto wondered how long the men would take this weird inactivity before they began to complain, though such idleness was not apparently destined to be their fate. He was standing at the gate of the camp, looking out into the middle distance, as though he could see Scipio's camp from here, when a messenger fell in beside him, saluting.

'Sir, the general has called all senior officers to the parade ground.'

Fronto, frowning, nodded and followed the messenger. He was interested to note as he moved through the huge camp and headed for the north gate, outside which a huge flat area had been cleared for practice and musters, that not only could he see other officers converging on the gate, often accompanied by a legionary messenger, but also a number of the centurions.

As he reached the gate, he climbed the steps to the wall walk above it, where the senior officers had gathered, while the centurions were being guided outside onto the large practice and parade ground. Fronto reached the parapet and stared, eyes wide. Wagons were arriving at the camp from the direction of Acylla and the coast, some score or more of them, accompanied by a small escort of soldiers. But it was not the caravan of vehicles that had Fronto staring in astonishment. That was what followed on behind: four elephants.

'I'm not sure fielding four of the beasts is going to give us an edge,' Fronto said, brow raised quizzically. Caesar gave him a sly smile.

'Are we all here?' the general asked, and at a general murmur of acknowledgement, he leaned over the parapet, addressing all present, both on the gate top and below it. 'I have assembled all my senior officers, along with the primus pilus and the senior training officer of each legion and auxiliary unit. We have learned to our cost this year the value of unexpected and unanticipated tactics. We suffered badly in our first major engagement due to a manoeuvre that Labienus had developed and for which we were woefully unprepared, and our men continue to fear the elephants the enemy fields. I intend to change all of this. In these vehicles travel some of the best lanistae and gladiators within two days' sail of Africa. I have brought them all here at no small cost to create a new training regime for the men.'

The centurions said nothing, though their general concern and disapproval could be felt in the air. Caesar smiled. 'This is no reflection upon the standard of training, nor the quality of the men. My legions are the best in the republic and I cannot imagine a way in which they could improve their skills with centuries of legionary tactics. What I intend now is to augment standard training and to provide the enemy, when we meet them in the field, with the unexpected. Each man will be training individually. When Scipio comes, he will find facing him an army that he can neither understand nor counter.'

This seemed to go some way to mollifying the centurions, and the general leaned down to the messengers below. 'Have the wagons move around to the east gate and unload within. Three of the elephants should go with them. The other, I want kept here.'

As the messages were distributed and the orders carried out, Fronto watched with interest. The elephants were not the youngest or best examples. They were not war elephants, he presumed, but all Caesar could lay his hands on. Still, they were huge and impressive, nonetheless. As the ground cleared, one elephant remained, held in place by a dozen slaves clinging to ropes, though as yet it seemed passive and disinclined to move.

Fronto's interest was further piqued as a unit of Cretan archers appeared from within the camp, following another of Caesar's runners, issuing through the gate and falling into position in a block of near three hundred men on the parade ground, some two hundred paces from the elephant.

'Good,' Caesar said, as silence fell once more. 'I have studied all accounts of action against these creatures, and also accounts of their physiology and strengths and weaknesses. I am led by my studies to a solid conclusion, which I am confident enough to put to the test before you all.'

He turned to the prefect of the archers. 'Have your best man step a pace forward from the unit.'

Commands were issued and one bowman stepped out from the unit, waiting patiently and professionally, though even from the gate top, Fronto could see the man's gaze twitching nervously towards the elephant two hundred paces away.

'The elephant's weakest spots, naturally are its eyes and mouth, when loosing directly at them,' Caesar said loudly. 'You may be a good archer, though at such a range, which is that we would expect in battle, the probability of such a wound is tiny. As such, we cannot count on removing the enemy elephants by targeting their weak spots. If you would do me the honour,' the general said, gesturing to the archer, 'loose a few arrows at your target. Try for a kill.'

The officers watched, fascinated, as the bowman nocked, lifted, sighted, and loosed. Fronto couldn't blame the man, the way as soon as the arrow was in the air, he took an involuntary step back, as though ready to run. Indeed, it was probably a very sensible reaction, for the arrow thudded into the beast's forehead, not more than a foot from its eye. The elephant bellowed its rage, and took a step forward, the slaves desperately holding onto the ropes, trying to anchor it in place. Half a dozen more men rushed forward and helped hold the ropes as the nervous archer nocked and loosed a second shot, which struck the beast in the trunk, bouncing off. Again, the enraged beast tried to move forward, only anchored in place by the men at the ropes.

'Thank you,' Caesar called to the archer, gesturing for him to stand down and rejoin his unit. A few minutes passed as the elephant calmed and settled, the threat now seemingly gone. 'You see, Caesar said, 'the likelihood of a kill is small, and missiles do little more than enrage them. The chances are that attempting to bring them down with arrows will simply result in their charging our lines. Thus, clearly, direct assault is no use. However, please observe.'

He gestured to the unit's commander. 'If you would be so kind, Prefect, as to continue the demonstration.'

The officer saluted and turned to his men. The entire unit turned slightly, nocking arrows and moving into wider spaced lines to issue a volley without harming their own. Once they were primed and in position, the officer gave the command to draw and, after a pause of three heartbeats, to loose.

Fronto watched in confusion as three hundred missiles thrummed forth, all aimed for the ground close behind the elephant and off to its left side. Not one missile was aimed at the beast, and yet at the horrendous sound of hundreds of arrows humming past it, the animal bellowed in panic. With far more strength and ease than when it had taken an angry step forward, the elephant swung to its left, away from the cloud of arrows, and began to run, dragging along the slaves, still clinging to the ropes. Fronto winced as one of the poor men disappeared with a crunch under the beast's massive foot, and most of the slaves let go. The elephant, still deep in the throes of panic, fled the ground, racing off into the parched ground.

Caesar turned to the assembled officers and centurions. 'At Zama the blasting of horns put fear into some of such beasts when Hannibal fielded eighty of them, and twenty such were turned at Beneventum by squealing pigs. Iron tips may not pierce the hide of these beasts, but they are prey to panic at loud and unexpected noises. See how this beast fled at a few hundred arrows and picture if you can, the effect of many thousand such missiles.'

'Scipio's beasts are trained war elephants,' Plancus noted. 'I would presume they have become used to such noises.'

'It is not so easy to overcome the nature of a creature,' Caesar smiled. 'Screaming and the blowing of horns are noises as often encountered in battle as missile clouds, but they had an effect on the war elephants of Hannibal and Pyrrhus. We shall turn his beasts into their own lines with the shock of the greatest volley of missiles we can unleash.'

He turned back to the other officers. 'The legions will learn to fight, as a lanista might call it, dirty. They will learn base tricks, unusual moves and new ways to employ weapons. When we are ready for Scipio, we will terrify his elephants and confound his legions. The cavalry, regardless of their origin, will learn each other's tactics. The Spaniards can teach the Africans the value of dismounted combat and how to move from one form to the other at speed. The Africans can teach the Gauls in casting light javelins effectively from horseback, and the Gauls can teach the Spaniards the use of a longsword in such engagements. Adaptability and flexibility. We will overcome Scipio by being better prepared than he. To that end, also, the remaining three elephants will be kept in the camp, and will be daily and constantly moved about, among the various units. Half the fear the men feel of such creatures is born of unfamiliarity. We will remove that. By the time this comes to a fight, and I feel we will need to push Scipio yet, our army will have no fear of elephants but, by Jove, we will teach the enemy to fear us.'

There was a rousing cheer in response to this, and Caesar continued to praise his men for a while before leaving them to their work. As the general dismounted the wall walk and began to stroll back to his tent, alongside several of his officers and followed by his praetorians, Fronto fell in beside him.

'I knew you had some trick in mind. This is no hopeful pulling of Scipio into the field. You have a plan for every step of the way now, do you not?'

Caesar smiled. 'In fact, it was the failed ambush at the ford that set me thinking. I observed both the effect of surprise and unexpected tactics and terrain on the men, and I experienced for myself the horror of a mass volley of missiles in terms of sound alone. We shall continue to press the enemy and push them into making a move, and every day that Scipio falters, we train and prepare.'

'So what's next?'

'Next,' Caesar gave a sly smile, 'we give them yet another push. You and I, and three legions, are going to perform a swift march, circumventing the enemy camps, and take the town of Zeta, garrisoned by two of Scipio's raw forage legions, behind them.'

Fronto blinked. 'That is insane, sir. We could never hold it on the far side of the enemy camps. They will do their best to destroy us there.'

'I did not say we would try to hold it, Fronto, merely to take it. Zeta has two important targets for us. It constitutes one of the main supply sources for Scipio's camps, and the place is currently the residence of one Publius Atrius, presumably here as Cato's attaché and liaising with the enemy commanders.'

Fronto frowned. 'I don't know Atrius. Is he a military man?'

'Far from it. He is a shrewd politician and a member of the equestrian order, but he is one of Cato's most trusted allies in Utica, where he is a member of the city council, forming much of the bridge between the rebel leadership and the

African administration. And perhaps more importantly, he is a childhood, and lifetime, close friend of Scipio's. We take Zeta and we can capture Atrius, poison Scipio's best water supply and burn half his grain store. It matters not that we cannot hold it, for the damage will have been done, and we will have given Scipio yet another reason to launch his attack.'

Fronto found that he was grinning. It was slightly foolhardy, very dangerous, and yet ingenious and daring. Just the sort of plan Caesar had come up with in the days of Gaul.

'When do we leave?'

CHAPTER NINETEEN

Zeta, 16th March 46 BC

T he army had departed the camp at the fourth watch, while the sky maintained the inky purple of night and dawn was yet but a whisper on the breeze. The three legions had moved in light formation, accompanied by a regiment of cavalry, carrying only their weapons and armour and leaving behind their other kit. They had moved at speed across the African landscape, carefully skirting any area where Scipio's scouts or pickets might be lurking.

Under cover of night they had travelled north, crossing a shallow stream and then following it on the far bank as it grew with tributaries to become a solid flow. Still some time before dawn they reached the mouth of the river where it opened out onto a strange landscape made all the weirder by the bright moonlight. They had reached the great salt lake that lay inland, close to Thapsus, and the powdery white shores rippled off in the silvery light into strangely green-white water. It was odd to think that the city they were threatening, which Aquila and his fleet had cut off, was just on the other side of that lake, and yet that was not their destination tonight.

In the darkness they followed the shore of the lake for two miles and then began to move inland at the urging of the scouts. They had passed by Scipio's camp at some distance and without incident, and moved west towards Zeta.

With Caesar's intuitive timing, the sun began to warm and lighten the sky as they approached their goal, and as the world turned blue and brown once more, Zeta came into view. The town was not fortified as such, lacking walls and towers, but had been planned with a view to protection from the nomadic bandits that plagued the border regions, all the houses that formed the edge of the town presenting a blank wall to the world, their windows turned inwards towards the heart of the town with just a few narrow apertures showing outside, providing positions for archers. Only five roads let into this outer shell. The town lay quiet and unmoving in the dawn sunlight, and Fronto huffed as the army drew to a halt and prepared. Galronus, commanding the cavalry, rode across to join Caesar, Fronto, and Oppius who together commanded the three legions.

'No sign of defences,' the Remi noted. 'No sign of life, in fact.'

'Where are Scipio's legions?' Oppius mused with a note of concern.

Caesar smiled. 'They are foraging legions, here specifically to gather supplies for Scipio's army. One of the very reasons we are here is because Zeta is the store house for almost half of Scipio's supplies. Two legions are based here, but by necessity they will spend most of their time moving about the area and bringing supplies in. Note the low rise of defences off to the south? This has been a legion's camp, and they have not slighted the ramparts so they intend to reuse it. Likely they will return here before sundown.'

'They will have left a garrison, though,' Oppius said.

'Perhaps, but it cannot be large if it is based within the small town.'

Oppius frowned. 'I hope you're right, General. The very nature of that place would make it an evil proposition if properly defended. A single cohort could hold that place for weeks unless catapults and full siege techniques were employed.'

'Scipio has no reason to fear for Zeta. He cannot believe we would make a play for it.'

'Let's hope you're right,' Fronto muttered, eyeing the blank, tan-coloured façade of the town's outer walls.

Caesar straightened in his saddle. 'Galronus, deploy the cavalry around the town. You cannot be of great use in taking the place itself, but I do not want anyone of consequence escaping. Oppius, split the Ninth and take them in through the two roads to the northwest. Fronto, the same with the Tenth to the south, and I shall lead the Fifth in from the east, which looks to be the warehouse district. Secure the surrenders of anyone you can, and put down any opposition. Try to preserve the goodwill of the residents if possible. Remember that our principle targets are Publius Atrius and his court and the storehouses and granaries.'

At a further signal, the three men returned to their legions. Caesar sat patiently as Oppius led the Ninth off and round to the right, while Fronto went left, the three legions forming a trident that would pierce Zeta's heart.

Fronto and the Tenth moved at a jog around the edge of Zeta and as they neared the camp where a legion had recently been based right outside the urban limit, he gestured to Atenos to take half the legion and move to the next inroad. The primus pilus nodded and moved off, taking half the cohorts.

As Fronto and his men passed across the ramparts of the temporary camp, it became apparent that Caesar had been quite correct. Cook-fire pits had been left in situ ready for reuse, and the latrines remained in use and uncovered. The legion expected to return to this place very shortly. It felt at once strange and familiar to be leading these men. The Tenth had been his legion throughout all those years in Gaul and some of these men would have been with him at places like Aduatuca and Darioritum, yet with the exception of Atenos, the officers and men he knew had now all gone, and those who had taken their places had recently mutinied. How far could he trust his old legion?

Striding across the temporarily abandoned camp he brushed such doubts from his mind. The mutineers and criminals had been dealt with. This was the Tenth Equestris of Caesar once more, and he could not afford to harbour doubts about them as he led them into battle. Still, as he and the first century of the second cohort neared that roadway in between the high, blank facades of Zeta, and his eyes flicked back and forth between the various small apertures he could see, nothing seemed to be happening. No arrows thrummed from the holes, and no rabid rebel legionaries swept from the doorways to oppose them.

They moved into the street, the perfect place for a blockade or ambush, and still there was no sign of Scipio's army. It seemed that they had timed their attack well, and both the legions based here were busy foraging in the area. As they moved, still at a jog, along the street, the only life he saw was the frightened eyes of Zeta's inhabitants as they cowered in their houses, peering out through windows and doors at this army silently invading their town.

The legions were not here for destruction, and made no move on any of the buildings they passed. It was a gamble, a risk, for there was always the possibility that the garrison here had known of the approach of Caesar's legions and had moved into the town's buildings to play a gods-awful urban defence just as the protectors of Pharos Island had done the previous year. Still, that did not seem to be the case, as they moved deeper into the town and found no sign of defences or defenders.

This road led with just a few gentle doglegs into the very centre of Zeta, much as the others probably did, and Fronto and his men ignored the narrower side streets marching off from this more major thoroughfare and jogged on to the heart of the place where their main objective lay. Any senior officers or civil administrators would be found at the centre, or in the camps around the town's edge.

The forum came into view, an open space at the end of the street, and Fronto set his eyes on the buildings opposite. Two relatively minor temples stood glowering over the open square, and next to them lay a public building of brick but with gleaming marble columns, the banners of Utica and of Cato's rebel forces hanging limp in the breeze. Fronto grinned. They were first here.

As the men of the Tenth emerged from the street and into the forum he grunted in irritation to see Oppius appear from another roadway with his cohorts. As the other officer paused to take in his situation, Fronto took advantage and waved his men on, racing for that building. Clearly it represented the political and military heart of Zeta, and if this friend of Scipio's was to be found in the town, surely it would be here.

The men of the Tenth swarmed across the open square at the heart of Zeta, swords bared and ready for a fight, yet silent other than the clack and clatter of hobnails on paving and the thunk and shush of armour and shields. They were halfway across the forum when a cry of alarm suddenly rang out from the building, and legionaries started to pour from the doorway.

Fronto clenched his teeth, trying hard to stay up with the leading men of his force. His legs ached after long runs these days, but he was damned if he was going to let these youngsters have all the fun.

The soldiers issuing from the government building were legionaries, kitted out with the same shield designs and tunics Fronto had seen fielded against them several times throughout this campaign, but these men had not been expecting danger as was made plain by the state of them. As they piled out to meet this threat, half of them were still jamming helmets on heads, some were running with boots unlaced and others with armour unfastened. One was still wearing a short linen sleeping tunic instead of his standard issue one. At this time of day they should all be prepared for anything, though very likely this was a supposed cushy assignment. While the bulk of their legions were out gathering supplies in the wild, these men had been granted a night in the comforts of the town centre, and this sudden attack had bewildered them all.

The men of the Tenth, aware now that all need for secrecy had passed, let out a roar of pure battle lust and ploughed into the disorganised ranks of the garrison even as they tried to form a shield wall. Fronto forwent the need for tactical calls, allowing his men the freedom to attack at will. After all, there could not be more than a century of men in the building, and he had near two thousand men with him.

As they clashed, he picked out a man with a transverse crest bellowing orders, standing behind the lines. His lip wrinkled into a sneer. Any centurion who led from the rear deserved anything that came to him. Leaving the legionaries to his men, Fronto ducked sideways past an inexpert lunge, leaving that man to come to grief. The would-be attacker died moments later, the boss of a shield smashed into his face and, as his sword fell away and his hand came up to defend his broken, bloody, screaming face, a sword was jammed into his side beneath the arm, robbing him of life. Fronto ignored it all, using his free hand to push the unfortunate dying legionary aside and launching himself at the centurion behind.

The man was clearly no veteran, and Fronto wondered for a moment whether this was the quality of officers to be expected in Scipio's army of local conscripts. The centurion hesitated for a moment, something Fronto had rarely seen in men of his rank. An officer in his position could not afford to hesitate, even for a moment, and this was his undoing. As the man struggled to decide on his course of action, Fronto's sword came across in a backhanded swing. It was not meant to kill, neither a stab nor a slash, for the man was coated in bronze scales, leather pteruges and iron helm, and sporting a round shield. Instead, Fronto's gladius came in rear-end-first, the pommel smashing into the bowl of the man's helmet around halfway between the crest and his temple.

The blow was solid enough to fold the metal into a deep dent, jerking the helmet to one side so that it obscured the vision from one eye and cut the man's chin even as it probably cracked the bone of his skull. The centurion gave a simple gasp and collapsed like a falling building, smashing to the ground, unconscious even before he landed.

It was over then, just like that. The two dozen or so defenders who remained upright pulled back from the fray, hands raised in surrender, faces pale with shock. With a fierce grin, Fronto set his most senior centurion to dealing with prisoners and waved the next century to follow him, stepping over the centurion's shivering form and pushing into the darkened doorway.

As they moved into the atrium of the grand structure, dribs and drabs of the garrison appeared from doorways, arms up, faces bleak. Each time, men from Fronto's cohorts peeled off to grab those defenders and haul them outside with their fellows.

One of the garrison emerged from a doorway ahead, and Fronto identified his role from the giveaway signs. Ink-stained fingers, squinty eyes and a form that suggested it had been some time since manual labour had been forced upon him. A clerk or secretary. Fronto grabbed the man by the shoulder. 'Where is your master?'

The soldier, eyes wide and sweat beading his brow, jerked a nervous thumb over his shoulder at the doorway from which he'd emerged. Fronto thrust the man into the waiting arms of more of his legionaries, and stepped through that doorway, a centurion and a dozen soldiers following him. Two more reedy clerks lurked inside, arms raised, and a figure in a pristine white toga stood behind a desk opposite, bearing a haughty expression that he had no right to bear under the circumstances.

'Publius Atrius?' Fronto barked.

The man's eyes narrowed. 'No, Gaius Minucius Reginus. I head the ordo of Zeta. We are loyal Roman citizens and you have no right to...'

Fronto cut him off with a wave of the hand. 'When you side with rebels against the republic's dictator, chosen by the senate, you forfeit all right to indignation. Minucius Reginus, you are hereby charged with inciting and supporting rebellion against the republic of Rome. Take him away.'

As the man continued to bluster protests, Fronto's men rushed around the desk, grabbed him and bundled him out, his white toga unravelling as he was pushed along, trailing along the floor and coming off as it was trodden on, leaving him in just a rich tunic. Fronto looked to the other secretaries, who were staring in horror.

'Atrius?'

'Still abed, sir,' one of them said.

'Show me.'

As the clerk hurried off, Fronto and half a dozen men followed. The whole complex was now filled with soldiers from the Tenth, searching rooms and accepting surrenders, and Fronto and his men moved through the chaos with purpose, heading for the chamber of the man they sought. The clerk stopped in a corridor, pointing at a door. 'There.'

Fronto nodded to his men and two of them took the miserable soldier and marched him back along the corridor. Fronto didn't bother to knock, simply pushing open the door unannounced. The light in here was dim, the shutters still closed, and Fronto let his eyes adjust for a moment, picking out the shape of a man in a creased sleeping tunic standing on the far side of a rich bed. He held up a short and light sword, defensively, eyes on the intruder, but Fronto knew in an instant that this man had neither the stomach nor the training for a fight. The sword tip wavered as the man struggled to keep it aloft, even held in both hands.

'The way I see it, Publius Atrius, you have two choices. If you're confident enough in your god-like abilities with that thing, you can attempt to kill somewhere in the region of eight thousand men and claim victory at Zeta, or die in the attempt of course, or you can place the pommel against the bedstead and throw yourself onto it in the honourable manner of a losing general. But I think we all know that you don't have the conviction for either of them, do you?'

Atrius, his face drawn and waxy with fear, tried to speak in the powerful tone of an orator, though what came out did so cracked and in squeaks.

'Do you know who I am?'

'I've been addressing you by name, Atrius.'

'I am a member of the corporation of Utica, a leading citizen of Africa and an advisor to the governor.'

'The governor is in his position in defiance of the senate, Utica is the power centre of a rebellion against the republic, and I'm sure you're aware that your only value to us is your closeness to the enemy's supreme commander in the field.'

'Scipio? I hardly know the man.'

'That's a lie,' Fronto grinned. 'As you are a civilian and a nobleman, I am minded to give you excellent treatment, and I'm sure you know the general to be magnanimous, by reputation at least. But if you don't drop that cheese knife and surrender yourself to our care, I might permit myself to give you a good punch in the face and knock that smarmy shit out of you before we go. What's it to be?'

Face falling, the man let go of his sword and raised his hands. Fronto grinned. 'Good boy.' Then to his men, 'take him out with the others.'

With the feeling of a job well done, Fronto strode from the room and through the rapidly settling building, out to the square. Oppius seemed to have located and secured the barracks for the rest of the garrison, for several centuries of slovenly legionaries were now lined up, disarmed as prisoners, and Caesar was even now moving into the square with his cohorts at his back, marching along a third group of prisoners.

'Another garrison, General?' Fronto asked.

'Just the guards from the granaries and stores,' Caesar replied. 'Zeta is a veritable cornucopia. Scipio will be most put out. Have you had success?'

'Oh yes,' Fronto smiled, gesturing over his shoulder to where Atrius was being marched out into the sunlight in his rumpled bedclothes. 'Scipio is going to be *most* put out.'

Caesar chuckled, and Oppius straightened. 'What's next, sir?'

The general rolled his shoulders. 'We are still somewhat at risk here. As soon as Scipio finds out about this, or his forage legions return, we could find the full weight of the enemy on us. I fear we must leave.'

'What of the supplies?' Oppius asked, frowning.

'We will have to take what we can and burn the rest.'

The other officer shook his head. 'Let me hold Zeta, General.'

Caesar's brow creased. 'Pardon?'

Oppius smiled darkly. 'A single cohort of good men, not the refuse Scipio put here, could hold Zeta for weeks. Give me a cohort and I'll hold the place for you.'

'You'd be behind his lines. Scipio could lay siege to the place.'

'Let him, but I don't think he will. If you return to camp with the army, he will be forced to concentrate on you and on Thapsus, which you threaten. If he does come for us, we can still burn the stores, but in the meantime I can begin shipping them back towards Leptis. Surely it would be better to make use of the supplies ourselves than to just burn them? And losing Zeta to us will be another thorn in Scipio's side. It is worth a cohort, General.'

Caesar nodded slowly. 'It is a risky proposition, Oppius. You are sure?'

The man nodded staunchly, and the general sighed. 'Very well. Keep two cohorts and do what you can, but do not get yourself and your men killed needlessly. If Scipio turns his full strength against you, burn the stores, pull out however you can and retreat to safe territory.'

* * *

Four hours later

It had been a gamble, Fronto admitted to himself as he started to bellow orders and centurions dashed this way and that, blowing whistles. If they had not sacrificed safety for speed, they could have returned to camp the way they'd come, skirting a wide arc and following the shore of the salt lake. In the event, Caesar had plumped for a more direct line of return, trimming an hour from the journey, but bringing them within two miles of Scipio's camp in the process.

The reasoning had been sound. Scipio could not have expected them to come from that direction, after all, and by the time he had sent forth men to intercept them they should already be out of reach on the way back to camp. What they had not counted upon was Labienus having his forces already out in the landscape waiting for them. How he had known they would be out there, or whether this was simply an awful accident, Fronto could not say. What he *could* say was that he had not expected the mass of cavalry and light auxilia who poured unexpectedly from behind a range of hills as they passed and fell on Caesar's rear-guard. Galronus and his men had already borne the brunt of it, fighting a brutal action to hold them there while the column reorganised to deal with the unexpected threat.

Already two score of horses and men lay in the wake of the retreating column as the legions fell into defensive positions and made to press the enemy, allowing the cavalry to pull away and move back. Fronto watched the fight, content this time to let the men handle the pointy end of the job. Labienus' cavalry and auxiliaries were employing that same tactic they had used in the first battle, when they had trapped the Caesarian army. Their riders and auxilia were uniformly African and were adept at throwing javelins. Horsemen and infantry alike were moving at the same speed, hurling their weapons and quickly retreating out of range.

Atenos and the Tenth fell in on the left flank now, along with the other legions, forming a barrier between the attackers and the cavalry. Fronto watched his old friend with pride as the legions gave an almighty bellow and held their ground in the face of the next charge. The moment the enemy screeched to a halt to cast their missiles, though, every centurion had his men running, not allowing the Numidians sufficient time to turn their mounts and pull back. The legions surged forth like a tide of steel and overran many of the horsemen, pursuing the rest and bellowing with rage even as the ranks that followed plunged their blades into those riders and auxiliaries who had been overcome. It was a brutal charge, and rather than falling back ready for another go as usual, this time the Numidians carried on retreating.

Satisfied that the attack had been beaten off, the commanders pulled the legions back into order and began to march once more, Galronus sending another rear-guard of cavalry to keep watch for the enemy in case they tried something new. As the column began to move once more, Galronus rode ahead to join the other officers.

'I wonder at their tactics,' the Remi said.

'Oh? It seems very much Labienus' standard now.'

Galronus shook his head. 'On the face of it perhaps, but I lost more than forty horses in that attack and only six riders.

The rest are now moving, unaccustomed to the march, on foot. Such a distribution of deaths can only mean that the enemy are specifically targeting the horses. Why is that?'

Fronto shrugged. 'Maybe they want to slow us?'

'Quite right,' Caesar said, turning to them. 'The day wears on. We tarried too long in Zeta after securing the place, assuming we would be able to march swiftly back to camp by sundown. If Labienus can slow us sufficiently, he can press us to make camp in the wilds. The men have only had marching rations to sustain them today and have been on the move since halfway through the night without rest or respite. If we are forced to camp here, close to the enemy, the men will continue to become fatigued, for we will need to be on our guard, and they will go hungry without the meal they are all looking forward to back in camp. Furthermore we can hardly continue to march into the night with exhausted men in an area we do not know sufficiently and where the enemy could have soldiers behind any hill. Labienus is shrewd. He is not pressing us to a full attack. He wants us to stop and camp.'

Sure enough, barely had the general finished speaking before a call of alarm went up from the rear. The officers pulled out to the side of the column and looked back. Riders and light infantry in white tunics and with a few shirts of bronze here and there were once more coming at the cavalry in waves, javelins whirring out into the air, pinning men and beasts. The officers did not have to give the order this time, for the centurions began deploying their cohorts, moving to the rear to cover the horse as they fell back.

'This is bloody ridiculous,' Fronto grumbled. 'Alright it's been almost half an hour since the first attack, but we spent so long deploying the legions, pulling back the cavalry, collecting the wounded, replacing the rear-guard and falling the legions into file, they've only actually moved a few hundred paces since the first attack.'

Caesar nodded. 'Labienus is no idiot. He is effectively slowing us to a crawl. If we do nothing, Scipio will have time to bring his entire army down on us before we can return to camp.'

Galronus pointed at the reorganisation of the rear once again, where his men were having their mounts killed right beneath them. 'If we don't do something, my cavalry are going to be nothing more than dismounted infantry within the hour.'

'True,' Caesar agreed, straightening. 'A cavalry rear-guard is not an effective choice in this situation. Have all your riders pull ahead. They will form the van for the rest of the journey.'

Fronto sucked on his lip. 'That does mean that the rear legionaries are going to be the next target of the enemy.'

'We shall put at the rear all our best arms. The moment the enemy come close we shall stop for moments, raise shields and cast pila at them. Pila are in limited supply, but only the rear ranks need them. We shall have all the weapons continually passed back so that the rear lines are permanently armed for the fight.'

Fronto nodded and had the orders distributed among the men. Once Atenos and his counterparts had charged again and scattered the enemy into the hills, they fell in. Galronus and his horse moved ahead, out of danger from the enemy, and with a little investigation the best men with pila in all three legions were chosen and formed a cohort of their own at the rear. The army began to move once more, their pace slow but steady, for the rear needed to keep in tight formation even on the march.

Fronto, Caesar and Galronus rode out to the side and watched as the column moved on. They had gone less than a thousand paces before the enemy came again. Fronto watched, tense, as the column halted and the ranks prepared. The rear line stopped first, the next taking an extra two paces and stopping, then the third following suit and then the rest of the column halting. Now adequately spaced for missiles, the rear ranks hefted their pila into positions. As the enemy cavalry and lightly-equipped auxiliaries charged at them with a uniform pace, the legions waited, patient and professional. Just as the enemy were closing and about to come to a halt for their volley, whistles called out their shrill command across the rear and several hundred pila rose in a cloud.

The men casting them had been chosen not for their accuracy, for this was not a job for close targeting, but for their strength. They needed good range, and the centurions had chosen well. The cloud of heavy spears, weighted with iron, plummeted into the enemy ranks just as they prepared to loose their own volley. The answering cloud of light javelins was paltry by comparison, for many of the enemy front line had been obliterated by the hail of pila. The chaos and panic as the enemy tried to scramble in flight was impressive, yet just in case they managed to rally for a second wave, pila were already being passed back to rearm those men.

After a safe pause, the centurions back there blew the all clear signal and the army began to march again. Though their pace was steady, they managed to eat a lot more ground a lot faster this time, for there was no pause to reorganise the column in the aftermath, and those few legionaries who had fallen foul of the javelins were either helped forward or picked up onto the horses of the cavalry for transport back to camp. The army was on the move again almost immediately.

'If they keep coming, it's going to be a slow job,' Fronto noted.

'But a secure one,' the general countered. 'We lose fewer men and horses, and we continue to move. With luck and the gods on our side, we will make camp by sundown.'

* * *

Fronto had rarely been more pleased to see a campaign camp than he was that evening. As the force moved in through the west gate, led by the tired cavalry, a number of riders on foot, the officers reined in to one side, rubbing sweat-soaked necks and foreheads and heaving in sighs of relief. Labienus had been dogged in his pursuit of the retreating column, sending in fresh waves to attack repeatedly, despite the losses he incurred, continually attempting to slow the Caesarian column. At least seven or eight more times they had stopped and fought the enemy off, the light increasingly failing and the men constantly suffering the ever-deeper effects of fatigue and hunger.

The worst moment had been when they emerged from olive groves to their chosen site at Aggar and should have laid eyes upon their camp, only to see instead a barren, wreckage-strewn wasteland where the camp had been. Then pickets had approached and guided them to an entirely new camp half a mile from the original, set on a raised area of ground above a low bluff.

It was only when they were in sight of this camp that finally the enemy pulled back and returned to their own lines. Thanks to Caesar's reorganisation of the column, casualties had been surprisingly light, but the going had still been tough and slow, and every man was glad to be back, where they could bathe and eat. Plancus strode towards them through the chaos of the returning army.

'You might want to explain,' Fronto grunted.

Plancus shrugged. 'I made a tactical decision, as the senior officer present. Scipio sent archers up to the high ground in your absence and managed to land arrows within our ramparts. I sent a foray out to drive them off, and they scattered, pursued halfway back to their own lines, but I decided that, since it had happened once, such a thing could happen again, so I moved our camp to high ground. I trust that meets with your approval.'

Fronto simply grunted again, though Caesar nodded. 'Thank you Lucius. Had I been here, I would have made the very same decision myself. All in all, despite setbacks and surprises, it has been a good day.'

'Your mission went well then, General?'

Caesar smiled. 'Oppius commands at Zeta, we have fought the enemy off repeatedly, and if you will follow me to the headquarters I shall introduce you to a special guest.' He turned a sly smile on Fronto. 'And while we do that, Marcus can find us some of his better wine.'

Yet again, Fronto's reply was little more than a grunt.

CHAPTER TWENTY

Aggar, 22nd March 46 BC

Scipio was not going to be drawn out without a special effort, and that much was becoming clear. Caesar had labelled him unimaginative even early on, and everything seemed to be bearing out that impression. The senior officer in Africa had offered battle constantly from the moment he had arrived near Ruspina, confident of victory and knowing Caesar to have far inferior numbers. As time had gone by though, Caesar's force had become ever stronger, while Scipio's had weakened with desertions. The closer things became, the less sure the man could be of winning, and there had come a point where Scipio had decided that the odds were now stacked too heavily against him and had stopped offering battle.

Instead, he now lurked in his camp on a daily basis, clearly hoping that Caesar would become impatient and attack him there, where his defences would once more give him the edge. Thus the stalemate continued. And the man was persistent in his approach. Caesar had threatened his most important port in the east, Thapsus, investing it with a naval blockade and moving the army close enough to endanger it. Then they had taken Zeta, his main store, which was still held by the brave and obstinate Oppius behind the enemy's camps, and still Scipio failed to react. They had taken captive one of the more important politicians among the enemy's forces in Utica, a childhood friend of Scipio's no less, and *still* he sat in his camp. How far would they have to push the man before he lashed out?

Caesar was under the impression that Cato would sooner or later send word from Utica, urging action, and he believed that King Juba would be similarly pushing for a battle, for the troubles back home would eventually call the Numidian monarch back there. Even Labienus seemed to be reacting as far as he was permitted, yet Scipio continued to lurk.

Two days after they had returned from Zeta, Caesar, exasperated that Scipio remained inactive, finally attempted to bring the man out directly. He had marshalled all his forces and led them out, deploying them dangerously close to the enemy camps. A slope formed a low ridge before the enemy camps and there Caesar had paraded Gaius Minucius Reginus, Publius Atrius and the captives from Zeta along with the entire captured garrison up and down in front of Scipio's army. They could hear the anger and frustration among the enemy troops across the open ground in between at the sight of the captives, yet still no one emerged to accept the challenge and as the sun had slid towards the horizon, Caesar led his forces back to camp.

Yesterday had been the celebration of Tubilustrium, and the army's horns, standards and weapons had been blessed and purified, marking the official start of the campaigning season. It was somewhat redundant, really, given that they were in their third month of the campaign already, but the gods had to be appeased, after all. There had been strange speculation in the camp that Scipio had been reluctant to fight because it was as yet not the official season for war, and the growing hope was that now the ceremony was out of the way the enemy commander might decide to do something decisive. The senior officers were not of such an opinion, of course, but any hope and optimism among the army was to be valued, and so in response to the Tubilustrium and the sense of anticipation, Caesar had settled upon another push. Sooner or later, they would push in a sore spot and Scipio would lash out, or perhaps Labienus and Afranius would decide they had

had enough of their commander and push him aside, taking up the challenge themselves.

There had been discussion late into the evening after the ceremony, attempting to decide upon a target that might trigger something with Scipio. The result was an assault on Sarsura. The scouts had identified this small town to the south-west of Scipio's camp, behind enemy lines much as Zeta was, as the next most important enemy storehouse after the one they had already secured. With Zeta's capture, Scipio had lost a significant portion of his supplies, and of what remained, much of the grain had been stored at Sarsura with a protective garrison of Numidians. How long could Scipio bear losing his supplies before he did something about it?

Thus this morning, while the army was still positive and optimistic in the wake of the ceremony, Caesar had led the bulk of his army out of camp and begun the audacious march on Sarsura, coming close to Scipio's camp on the way, teasing them. Plancus had been left in command of the small garrison back at Aggar, while the army would take Sarsura and hopefully push Scipio into action. And if not, then they would take a more circuitous route home and examine the one remaining rebel stronghold in the east, Thysdrus, some way to the south.

Fronto had fretted about coming so close to the enemy camp on the journey, given what had happened on the way back from Zeta. Despite Scipio's reluctance to act, Labienus was not so restrained and would undoubtedly attempt to do something similar to his previous assaults. Caesar had been confident that this time they would have the best of any such engagement. His retraining of the troops and employment of new methods would see them safe. Certainly, the cavalry ranged ahead this time, seeking out ambushes and scouting the route, forming the van rather than coming along at the imperilled rear. The rear-guard was now formed of veteran legionaries, and the kit of each unit in the army was somewhat unorthodox, too. Men from all across the legions of every rank had speculated as to why they were equipped as they were, but as usual the general kept his plans largely to himself. Of each legion, nine cohorts marched sweating, bearing heavy burdens. Every man carried either cooking equipment or quern stones, or pieces of campaign furniture in addition to their own weapons and armour. The remaining cohort moved in light kit, even their shields being borne by their fellows, while they moved freely and with little fatigue.

The various local traders and hangers-on who had established themselves close to the Aggar camp followed on at a distance in their wagons, seeing this move as a potential establishment of a new camp, and the officers generally assumed that Caesar had allowed them to remain so close so that the wagons could be employed in transporting supplies from Sarsura.

Five miles they had marched since sunrise, and a quarter of an hour ago the scouts had come close to the three enemy camps on the low ridge near Tegea. This was the dangerous moment, and they all knew it. Scouts kept watch on the place as the army closed, while their fellows searched out every hill and dip for hidden troops. Sure enough, as the Caesarian forces came within a mile of the enemy, while Scipio and Juba's camps remained sealed and motionless, the gates of Labienus' camp opened and his force of cavalry and light Numidian infantry poured forth. Whether the man was disobeying orders and taking it upon himself to harry Caesar or perhaps had been given permission to do so in an attempt to draw Caesar in, they could not say, but all the officers had been prepared for this eventuality after the Zeta offensive, so the appearance of that force came as a surprise to no one.

The enemy poured across the landscape on a course to intercept Caesar's column at the rear, Labienus' favoured tactic. Fronto watched the general, waiting for the orders to be given, and when nothing seemed to be happening, he rode over to the general.

'Caesar, are we going to halt the column?'

The general gave him a sly smile. 'Unnecessary, Fronto. It is all arranged. The appropriate officers have their orders and simply await the signal.'

'Your staff would find these campaigns more straightforward if you occasionally told them what was going on.'

Caesar simply smiled again and, turning, peered off at the approaching enemy force. They were moving at a reasonable speed, the light and fast infantry keeping pace well with the horsemen. The wagons of Caesar's camp followers had stopped, falling back to stay out of danger, and the rear of the heavily-burdened column was consequently open to attack. The enemy were coming close now. Caesar hummed a quiet melody as he watched, and finally gave a hand signal to his musician, who promptly blew a refrain with which Fronto was unfamiliar.

'Come. Let us study the effects of new strategies upon our enemy,' Caesar smiled, riding out along the side of the column towards the rear and up to a low rise with the best available view. As he and Fronto, accompanied by Salvius Cursor and a dozen praetorian riders, settled in the saddle on the crest, Fronto watched events unfold with surprise.

At the signal the majority of the army, burdened with half the accoutrements of permanent camp, continued to slog onwards, while one cohort from each legion, fresh and unencumbered, retrieved their shields from their fellows and then fell out of the column, forming up to make a new legion and then moving to intercept the enemy. To Labienus' credit he neither faltered, nor panicked. His force did not retreat, nor did they scatter, instead refocusing on this new unit that had poured out of the column to face them.

'I can see the benefit,' Fronto muttered. 'They've marched unburdened and so they're fresh for the fight, but I can't see how this will come as any surprise for the enemy. It's not really a new tactic.'

Caesar gave him an infuriatingly enigmatic smile and then simply turned back to watch. Fronto followed suit, his brow creasing as he tried to identify what was going to happen. When it did, he *was* totally unprepared for it. The enemy raced at the legion, ready to utilise their tried and tested tactic of waves of javelins, and sure enough the legion formed a protective shell of shields, in ordered lines, taking the shower of missiles with minimal casualties. What happened then, though, was straight out of the blue.

Instead of maintaining their shieldwall and waiting for the next attack, or forming up for a charge as they had done before, the fresh and new legion broke apart like a Gallic army. Abandoning all unit cohesion, the entire force began to run at the enemy as the riders turned to retreat and rearm, every legionary bellowing his own battle cry, invoking his own gods, every man running for battle as though he were alone, like the Gauls when their nobles and warriors attempted to turn every battle into a personal duel.

Labienus' force was utterly thrown. In moments the howling legionaries were among them, and even from a distance Fronto could see what was happening and was thoroughly impressed. The men had been training for almost a week now, using Caesar's new schedule, learning methods from the best gladiator trainers available for a hundred miles in every direction, and their new training showed. Having completely eschewed traditional Roman legionary tactics, every man fell in among the enemy like a murderous gladiator. Moving among the panicked force, they butchered and maimed. The legions were taught to aim primarily for the three kill zones: neck, armpit and groin, and to seek out weak points in armour and defences. These men were doing just that, but on top of their longstanding training, they were also being horribly inventive. Fronto saw men hamstringing their enemy, dropping to ground level and slicing through Achilles tendons, hacking feet off, using shields as giant chisels, raised overhead and slammed forth so that their bronze edges smashed into faces.

It was slaughter, and truly gruesome to watch. The fight had been going for less than forty heartbeats before the enemy were broken, fleeing in terror back towards the safety of their camps. It was not over yet, though. Legionaries rarely pursued a fleeing force, for that could easily bring fresh disaster, their officers calling them back to formation to prevent just that. Not here, though. As the enemy fled, so the legionaries went with them, still murdering on the move.

Worse still for Labienus, his reserves, sitting halfway between the fight and his camp, were as uncertain as to what was happening as the commanders were, and remained in position, ready to rearm the waves of Numidians, too late to retreat in time. Fronto shook his head in disbelief as the savage, bellowing monsters that were supposedly disciplined legionaries tore now into the ordered lines of reserves, repeating their unabashed and very individual form of slaughter.

It was only when the entirety of Labienus' force was on the run that Caesar finally waved his hand and his signaller blew a new cadence. It took another twenty heartbeats for the men to disengage and withdraw, returning to the column, where they fell back into their own legions once more, laughing and shouting comments to one another as their mates took their shields for them again.

In short order the column was moving again. Fronto had not had the chance to do a casualty check, but the force returning to the column had not diminished a great deal in numbers, and so the Caesarian fallen had clearly been few, while the landscape of their clash was strewn with rebel casualties. And the worst thing was that they were not all dead. Indeed, probably less than half lay still, while most writhed in agony, clutching stumps or maimed limbs, broken faces or missing feet, each man permanently disabled and removed from the war entirely, but each would live to spread horror among the rest of the army.

'That was horrible,' Fronto muttered, as the officers rode back to rejoin the column.

Salvius Cursor shrugged. 'War is not all wine and cakes, Fronto. Nasty things happen.'

Fronto shot a black look at the man. 'I appreciate the value of what just happened, but you should always bear in mind that our enemies out here are also Romans, and leaving them disabled and doomed for the scavengers is not an honourable way to prosecute a war. If Labienus has any sense of justice left, he'll have the ones who can't be saved put out of their misery, burned and buried before they can come to further grief.'

But that was clearly not in Labienus' plans, for his bruised and shattered force had been called back to their standards and were now moving west along the hills near their camp, keeping pace with Caesar's army, parallel but out of reach.

The morning wore on, Caesar's army moving further and further from the enemy camps, yet with Labienus and his men shadowing them all the way. As the sun rose to its apex, finally Sarsura came into view. The place was smaller even than Zeta had been, nestled on the bank of a stream that had already dried up for the warm season. Not only had Sarsura no protective wall, but it was small enough and insignificant enough that it had not even presented a protective façade to the outside as Zeta had. Little more than an overgrown village, the place was clearly on a crossroads of trade routes, for its market place was far larger than was called for by its size, and one side of the place was dominated by granaries and warehouses.

'That is our target,' Caesar announced, 'and there is our opposition.'

His finger rose to point at an encampment just outside the small town. A low bank surrounded it, a fence of stakes atop, with just a single gate left in the defences. The occupants, already scrambling into formation at the sight of Caesar's army, were an infantry force of Numidians or other African levies, their tunics of plain, off-white linen, accompanied with shirts of bronze scales or helmets of the same metal, some with shields covered with the hides of exotic animals Fronto had only ever seen in the arena. A couple of centurions were visible from their transverse crests, and a senior officer stood before them, addressing them even as they fell into ranks.

'If they have any sense at all, they'll surrender straight away,' Fronto said. 'There can't be more than a thousand of them at most. We outnumber them about twenty to one.'

Caesar nodded, though his face was sombre, grave even. 'I do not think that will happen, though. That man will fight us to his last breath.'

'Why? Who is it?'

Caesar sighed. 'Publius Cornelius Crassus, Scipio's cousin. A lesser branch of the family, but the man has a reputation as fearsome as his ancestors for all his current minor standing. He will hold, for his reputation and for fear of disappointing his cousin.'

'Shit.'

'Quite. Very well, let us overrun the garrison. Deploy the men.'

Fronto turned and gestured to the signallers, and moments later calls rang out and standards dipped. Legions moved into position in an arc around Sarsura. Fronto glanced off towards the hills at the north, where Labienus and his force now sat, still shadowing them, still out of reach.

'It will be aggravating Labienus that he can't come to their aid.'

'Yet it is important that he is here,' Caesar replied. 'Witnesses must take word of all this back to Scipio if we are to goad him into action.'

Fronto sat at the edge of the field and watched as one of Caesar's riders raced out to the enemy defences and delivered the ultimatum and an offer of clemency if the town was surrendered. He watched as the officer down there took the proffered scroll case containing the terms, snapped it in half over his knee and cast the pieces down into the dust unread. The rider turned and rode back for his own lines, and moments later whistles blew all across the ranks.

The legions marched upon Sarsura as Cornelius deployed his men along the defences of his small camp, where they hefted spears and prepared to fight back. Fronto had to give them their due, for they were uniformly brave men. Not one of those defenders panicked and ran, each standing in place at the jagged fence of stakes, awaiting what could only be certain death. Moreover, Cornelius himself flung his plumed helmet away, grabbed a shield and ripped his sword from its sheath, clambering up onto the defences alongside his men.

The Caesarian legions closed on the place and paused at fifty paces to release a veritable cloud of pila. The shafts fell in their hundreds along the line, sealing the fate of Sarsura's garrison before the fight had properly begun, for fully half the defenders fell back, stricken, from the volley. As the defenders recovered as best they could, fanning out to fill the gaps in thinner lines, the legions drew their swords with a deafening rasp and marched forward.

Fronto watched as the Caesarian force simply swept over the enemy defences, barely pausing as they overcame the poor defenders and heaved the stakes aside even while spears were jabbed desperately out at them. By the time the defences were dismantled with a small but significant casualty list, the remaining hundred or so of the garrison had withdrawn to the centre of the camp where they had formed up in a circle, the unit's standard held at the centre, though its commander remained a staunch warrior in his own right. Publius Cornelius stood in the line with his men, blood running down the side of his cheek from some wound, shield now gone and left arm hanging useless and crimson by his side. Fronto was impressed. Sadly, the man would not survive the day. He mused on how different this entire war might have been had this lion of the battlefield been made senior commander in Africa while his cousin Scipio garrisoned Sarsura. Very likely the campaign would have been over in the winter and by now Caesar and Fronto and their officers would be back in Rome planning how to form a new army and try again.

He watched as the legions closed in on the circle. Still Cornelius made no move to surrender and whenever his men faltered, he bellowed war cries and cheered them on. Fronto shook his head sadly as the Caesarian force simply crushed the enemy garrison in moments, overrunning the rebels. The last he saw of Cornelius, the heroic bastard was rising above a centurion and hammering at him with his sword, only to be brought down by half a dozen angry legionaries and to disappear beneath a mass of hacking and stabbing swords.

It was over so quickly and Labienus, sitting just off to the north, watched it all with his force on the low hills. Fronto turned to the general. 'Will we burn the grain? I'd assumed we would transport it back in the wagons, but now they've been separated and left behind we can't really carry it all. I guess destruction is all there is, if we want to deprive Scipio of it. We can't really leave a garrison here as we did at Zeta, after all.'

Caesar turned to him with a weird smile. 'But Fronto, the men have fought two battles and marched many miles. It's noon, and they are hungry.'

Fronto frowned. 'That's why they've brought all that junk?'

Caesar's smile remained, and Fronto gave a strange dark chuckle. 'You never intended to load the wagons. You brought the legions to Sarsura for what… a picnic?'

'Imagine Scipio's face when Labienus reports it all to him.'

Now Fronto couldn't help but laugh out loud. 'This is so audacious it's… I don't know. A little crazy?'

'Let the men taste the fruits of their labour.'

Caesar issued orders to his waiting riders, who hurried off to the various units. Those light-armed men who'd massacred Labienus' force a few miles back were set to work gathering the enemy dead, stacking them and raising a low mound of rocks and dirt over them as a burial site, protecting the bodies of the brave men from the depredations of predators and scavengers. The body of Publius Cornelius was retrieved, hung over the back of a horse and led up to Labienus, delivered into his hands for return to the enemy camp. This may be war, but there were limits imposed by honour.

While all this went on, the rest of the army split into two groups. One unloaded all the gear they had brought from Aggar while the other moved into the warehouses and granaries of Sarsura, retrieving all of Scipio's supplies from them. The salted meats and preserved fruit were distributed among the men, and the sizeable grain stores were likewise split among each contubernia. The wine was divided, with a single jar given to each tent party, while the rest was emptied into the sand of a nearby gulley. Depriving Scipio of it was important, but it was also essential not to have the legions drunk on the stuff while still so far from home and in enemy territory.

Fronto and the other officers joined Caesar at a table that had been set up in the heart of the huge picnic, and there he sat with a cup of wine while work went on around him. Camp fires were started all across the open ground with wood and straw plundered from the stores, and while the fires began to burn, grain was ground into flour using the quern stones that each tent party had brought. Fronto was stunned at the industrial scale of the endeavour. So much flour was being ground that they could not possibly eat it all, and while bread was being baked in hundreds of fires, more was prepared. Indeed, there was so much grain available that the men cast the grainy stuff, their usual fare, out into the dirt, and made their bread only from the fine white flour that was usually reserved for the officers.

Labienus and his men remained some distance away on the low hills, watching this display of gluttony as each man in Caesar's army cooked and ate more meat than they would normally see in any three days, washed it down with two or three cups of wine, and filled up with fresh white fluffy bread.

When the meal was over, the legions continued to bake until Sarsura's entire grain store was gone, casting the bulk of the flour onto the ground and making bread only from the best white powder. When all was done and the legions still had far more bread than they could eat, each man packed a few loaves to take home, while others distributed the excess to the civilian populace of the small town, folk who were ecstatic at the gift from stores they had watched guarded jealously for weeks.

Three hours after the fight there was nothing left. The supplies of Sarsura had been used or disposed of, reducing Scipio's goods yet further. As the legions hauled themselves to their feet and prepared to move out, finally Labienus and his men left their position, departing towards their own camp, bearing news and a new corpse that together were going to infuriate Scipio.

Safe from the danger of attack, Caesar decided that they would continue with their secondary objective, and the army marched at a leisurely pace southeast until the city of Thysdrus came into view. The sun was sinking by then, and the Caesarian army made camp for the night on the plains near the city.

With the rise of the sun the next morning the officers and the scouts examined Thysdrus. The place was the largest city in the east of Africa and the most important between Hadrumetum and the cities of neighbouring Cyrenaica, and it continued to declare for the rebels. For some time Caesar and his men considered the pros and cons of taking the city, before finally deciding against it.

Thysdrus would be an easy enough prospect, for it had no walls and its garrison was small, consisting of one or two thousand men at most, though still the problems were myriad. Taking it would be easy enough, but holding it would be evil. With no walls, any garrison they left would have to be sizeable enough to deter attack, and that would deplete the army at Aggar. Moreover, now the winter was over and the seasonal streams drying up, Thysdrus, like other cities in the region, would be relying on its single aqueduct and small cisterns for water, which might not stretch to adequately supplying a sizeable garrison. Most of all, the city, for all its size and grandeur, was not important in campaign terms. Apart from being held for the rebels it was insignificant, tactically. In short, the cost of taking and garrisoning the place far outstripped its value.

Consigning Thysdrus to the scrap heap, the officers gave the order to break camp and march back to Aggar. The twenty mile journey slipped by at speed, for the army was in buoyant spirits at their success, their audacious picnic, the decision not to launch into another fight for too little gain, and the easy, flat terrain they enjoyed on the return journey. The camp of Aggar came into sight as the sun began to sink, and Fronto sighed with relief. They had once again stuck a needle into Scipio's nerves. Two, in fact. Just as at Zeta, when they had taken Scipio's supplies from him and captured an old friend of his, this time, they had captured more supplies and killed the man's cousin. Surely to gods, Scipio would be spoiling for a fight now. Fronto could picture how Labienus would have spent the previous evening haranguing his commander.

He could feel battle in the air now, tingling like static. Something was coming. Something big.

CHAPTER TWENTY ONE

Aggar, 26th March 46 BC

'So we were just in time to help you end the war then, sir?' the cavalry prefect smiled.

Galronus harrumphed. 'The chances of getting Scipio to commit to battle are about the same as having lunch with your favourite god.'

'But surely if we offer battle, he'll take it up?'

Galronus just shook his head. It had been four days now since they had killed Scipio's cousin and made a merry picnic from the man's secondary supply base before their very eyes, and still the man lurked in his camp. Galronus, and the rest of the officers for that matter, were starting to wonder whether Cato had some other grand plan for Africa and had instructed Scipio to refrain from attack.

Caesar had been as irritable as the rest at this inability to force a fight. Now, unless inclement weather, poor terrain, fortifications or simple back luck intervened, the general's force was sufficient to be confident of at least a good chance of success, especially with these new arrivals.

They had come into camp late the previous day, having landed at Leptis and made their way from there. They constituted all the missing members of the force already at work in Africa, those who were on leave when the legions were deployed, those who were on separate assignment, some building an aqueduct in Venetia, and a considerable complement of men who had been on hospital sick lists. The force had gathered under the watchful eye of Antonius and then been sent to Sicilia to join the war. Their arrival had

315

been most welcome, some four thousand extra legionaries, a thousand archers and a little over four hundred cavalry.

Not that Galronus thought it would make a difference today. Still, Caesar was both hopeful and determined. He *would* bring Scipio to battle today. The general had sacrificed to the gods and an auspex had examined the entrails of a goat and pronounced that all the signs were good. He was even specific enough to say the enemy commander would fall. The troops, of course, were delighted with the signs, and songs were sung in the ranks as the army marched out of camp at Aggar, the entire force on the move, a fantastic sight, leaving only two cohorts in camp.

'The signs were good,' the prefect noted, nudging Galronus back from his mental wanderings.

'The only thing that goat's belly told you was that it hadn't eaten the night before it was killed. Scipio will not fight today, I think. I'm pretty sure that unless Labienus or Afranius step up and seize command you'll have to jam a spear point up Scipio's backside to get him to do anything other than sit down.'

'I hope you're wrong, sir.'

'I hope I'm wrong, too, and if we get the opportunity to start something, I have Caesar's blessing to do so.'

The small town of Tegea lay directly ahead now, another of those small frontier towns with few ways in but no true ramparts or defensive systems. Scipio's camp lay directly ahead, beyond Tegea and atop a low ridge, with Juba's camp off to the left and Labienus' to the right. Rebel banners would be hanging from Tegea's buildings, Galronus knew, though they couldn't see such detail yet. Tegea would be garrisoned by the enemy despite its proximity to their camps.

'They're coming,' the prefect said, gesturing excitedly up the slope. Galronus' gaze rose from the town to see that the gates of all three camps had opened and men were issuing forth. He frowned. After all this time, why was Scipio suddenly so eager? He looked this way and that, back down to the town, back up to the army. Down to the town. Up to the army. Down. Up. Then settled on the ridge in between.

'He's rushing to get the good terrain.'

'Sir?'

Unless we ride like the wind the enemy is going to control that ridge. We'd lose thousands attacking that slope. Now I understand why Scipio camped there and not closer to us.'

Even as he spoke, a force of cavalry began to emerge from Tegea through a rear access, racing up that slope and falling into place, abandoning the town in order to be certain of securing the high ground. The Caesarian army continued to march forward, and Galronus clenched his teeth. They might, just might, be able to get to that ridge and drive off the cavalry garrison, securing it for Caesar, but the general was delaying. He'd not given the order to speed up, nor that to halt and deploy. He would be busily weighing up the chances of securing the ridge, and Galronus could hardly blame the man, really. It *was* a gamble, and would most likely cost Caesar whatever force he sent.

In the end, as those horsemen deployed and the rebel army surged forward from the camps towards the ridge, it was Juba and Labienus who decided the matter. Before Caesar gave his command, his former lieutenant suddenly raced forth with his Gallic cavalry to support the men on the ridge, bursting out ahead of the rest of the army, while off to the far side, Juba's elephants were likewise driven ahead to reach that ridge. Scipio had positioned his forces to gain the advantage of terrain, and despite Caesar's unexpected arrival, the enemy was damn well not going to sacrifice his advantage.

The order blared out across the Caesarian lines a moment later and the entire force slowed, changing shape as the legions pulled forward to form into battle lines. The entire force deployed and at the appropriate signal, Galronus gestured for Samaconius to take half the cavalry to the left flank to face those elephants alongside the Fifth, their usual support, and the bulk of the army's missile troops. Galronus, meanwhile, remained on the right flank with the other half of the cavalry, close to the town of Tegea and facing those horsemen on the slope.

This was going to be another non-fight, unless Scipio could be forced to attack, which seemed unlikely. If the enemy commander sent his troops forward, they would advance down the slope to engage Caesar's legions on the lower ground, negating the advantage of the ridge. On the other hand, Caesar could not afford to attack *up* that ridge. The losses would be too heavy, and he could not employ his new tactic against the elephants, for the archers could hardly realistically loose a cloud of arrows up the slope without getting too close to the elephants for safety.

The ridge itself would force a stand-off today.

The Remi commander scanned the area, nipping his lip, deep in thought, taking in everything. He, along with every other commander in the field, had the same remit today: to start a fight. Caesar had been quite straight about that. If anyone saw the opportunity to push the enemy into action, they had to run it by Caesar, but they should most definitely do so.

His gaze reached the elephants at the far end of that immense line, little more than grey blobs rising above the swarm of ants that was legionaries at this distance. The ridge put the enemy perhaps fifty or sixty feet higher than the Caesarian army. The left flank was going to be immobile. Juba was not going to commit his elephants without the rest of the enemy force moving along with them, and Scipio was not going to abandon his high ground. And on this side of the fight, the archers couldn't do their job properly, so Caesar could not afford to commit against those beasts. The centre of the field afforded much the same situation. Caesar couldn't afford to charge that slope and put his men at such a disadvantage, while Scipio wouldn't rush down into the fight and lose his terrain.

That left this flank. The town of Tegea had been sited beside one of those seasonal streams, which was fed by narrow tributaries flowing down the slope that formed the battlefield, and the closer that stream and that slope got to Tegea, the less pronounced the gradient, such that it formed little more than a low rise behind the town. This flank was the weak spot. Here, Scipio's terrain advantage counted for little, and presented a lesser obstacle for the Caesarian force, particularly being primarily cavalry on this wing.

Squinting at the enemy, he tried to estimate their numbers. There was not a great deal in it between the two forces, he decided. He turned to the small knot of officers, standard bearers and musicians behind him, singling out a decurion. 'Ride for Caesar. Tell him that the cavalry are prepared to storm the slope on the right flank and push for action. Get his reply.'

The man saluted as he rode off and Galronus sat, clenching his teeth. It would be a hard fight. His men would have to ride up the slope, even if it was lower here, and the forces waiting were very similar to his own, largely made up of Gallic and Germanic cavalry that had ridden for Caesar a decade ago, but had followed Labienus to the enemy's banner. They would not simply break. They would have to be pushed hard, and they would be pushing back.

He became aware of a horseman edging his way through the crowd and turned his head. Bedecked in a senior officer's uniform, this was one of his divisional commanders, the officer who'd brought a sizeable number of these riders over from Labienus' camp, Vibius Pacideius. The man's expression was dark.

'Commander,' Pacideius said, reining in, 'I must request permission for reassignment to the far wing.' Galronus frowned, a question in his gaze, and the officer sagged a little.

'One of the banners atop that slope is that of my brother. I recognise that I have given my oath to Caesar, and I shall not shrink from my duty, but I have no wish to face my brother in combat.'

Galronus nodded slowly. 'Your presence will be missed, but I understand your problem. I suspect it will be one shared by others on the field today. Find Samaconius and report to him on the left flank.'

Pacideius saluted and rode off, and Galronus returned to studying the enemy lines until another thunder of hooves drew his attention and he turned to see his decurion returning. 'Sir, the general gives his compliments and approves of action on this flank. He will watch with interest and be prepared to support our push.'

Galronus nodded, rolling his shoulders and turning to address his officers. 'Very well. Scipio continues to shrink from a fight and place us in positions where we cannot afford to assault him, but he may have underestimated us this time. The slope here is low and the enemy a familiar one. You are all men of the tribes. I see Allobroges, Remi, Treveri, Menapi, Boii and many others. Our peoples were fighting one another long before Rome came, and those riders up the slope are just the same. This is just like the old days. Warbands contesting control of ancient lands. There is no need for a strategy. Units of auxilia and archers will support us, but the main crux of this fight is going to be warrior to warrior, horse to horse, and the army that proves stronger and more determined is going to win. That is us.'

The officers murmured a flat agreement with the statement.

'Good,' Galronus announced. 'Once the signal is given, we charge them. A full charge, giving everything your horses have to give, trying to punch a hole in their lines. If we can commit enough, we might force Scipio to doing the same and force the battle we've all been waiting for.'

The enemy were fully deployed now, all along the slope for more than a mile, and Caesar's men were similarly ready, both armies bristling, watching one another carefully across that slope. Galronus cast up a prayer to Toutatis and gestured to his musicians. A moment later the horns were blaring, standards waving, and the Caesarian horse began to ride. Galronus smiled at his cavalry as he kicked his own horse's flanks and fell in alongside them. Most of them were Belgae, Gauls or Germans, each gathered into units formed from their individual tribes, and most of his officers were also noblemen of the tribes rather than Roman imports. It showed. Those few actually Roman officers had fallen to the rear of their units where they could command and guide like a Roman general. The rest, men of the tribes, had fallen in with their riders, swords drawn and fierce expressions on display, ready to fight with their men like the old days.

The slope counted for little as the Caesarian cavalry pounded up the incline towards Labienus' horse. Galronus wondered for a moment whether the enemy commander was there with his riders. Taking down Labienus would be a true victory, for the man was without doubt the most dangerous and proactive of the enemy commanders, but he had come close to being captured or slain several times over the past few months, and seemed to have taken note, for recently he had kept himself back from immediate danger.

The enemy up the slope braced for the clash, clearly surprised at the Caesarian charge, but not panicked by it. Those men were, after all, also men of the tribes. The ground tore past beneath them, and the front lines of the Caesarian horse readied for the collision, spears lowering into place, shields up and facing the enemy. Galronus counted off the paces left, letting go of the reins, reliant now upon his knees for guidance and the solid Roman horned saddle for stability. His right hand came up, long sword ready, his shield held out in the left.

Fifteen.

Ten.

Five.

The two armies hit like a winter wave against a sea wall. What the Caesarians had lost to the terrain they gained in the momentum of their brutal charge. All along the line his men ploughed into the enemy, spear points lowered to a lethal level, swords out and ready to sweep, each man allowing just enough space between himself and his companions for a swung blade. Galronus angled his own steed between two men who he suspected were Nervii from their equipment, a fact that gave him immense personal satisfaction, for the men of that tribe had been a constant source of trouble in Galronus' youth, raiding Remi lands. He noted with interest that the enemy riders had each tied a length of blue-dyed linen around their upper sword arm. It seemed the enemy were as keen to identify friend or foe as Galronus' men were, who each had a red scarf around their neck and knotted at their throat. Good. That would make things easier.

His sword came round and bit into the thigh of one of the Nervii, and he wrenched it out immediately in an attempt to avoid it jamming and disarming him. The man screamed, his own blade dropping as his hand went to the maiming wound on his leg. At the same moment, the other Nervian thrust out with his blade, the tip thudding into Galronus' hastily raised shield and scraping across its painted surface, gouging a furrow through the boards. As the blade came free, it caught the chain sleeve of Galronus' shirt, knocking him back in the saddle, where only the four tight leather horns prevented him from being thrown from his mount's back.

Then he was in among the enemy and everything became a blur. Swords hammered and swept, spears lunged, the air was a din of clattering shields, the bellowing of men and horses and the clash of metal on metal. Galronus felt several blows caught on his shield and two turned by the chain shirt, both of which would have crippled but for the armour, and both of which would leave painful contusions.

In turn, the Remi nobleman slashed out with his sword and chopped down with wild abandon, secure in the knowledge that he was with the forefront of his army and unlikely to wound an ally in the press. As he fought, wounding and killing, he could feel the tide flowing with him. The momentum of their initial charge had naturally slowed as they piled in among the rebel cavalry, but it had not been entirely robbed away, and the enemy were very slowly, very slightly, but very clearly being pushed back. If this could be kept up, then the flank would eventually, inevitably give. Labienus would find his force being driven from the field, and Scipio would be forced to either commit fully to battle or withdraw entirely and allow Caesar to take the ridge, falling back to the camps.

A lance came from nowhere and caught Galronus a glancing blow on his helmet, scraping along the side of it with a nerve-tingling shriek and pushing the entire bowl painfully to one side. On instinct, knowing the opponent's location from the angle of the lance, Galronus threw out a lunge with his sword along the line of that wooden shaft. The man could not have his shield in the way so close to the spear shaft, and the blow was almost guaranteed. He was rewarded with a clink, a wheezing grunt and a solid feel of resistance as his sword point punched heavily into his opposition's chest armour, knocking the wind from him and causing a great deal of pain. Praying that no other enemy rider was coming for him right now, Galronus let go of his shield grip, letting the board hang loose on his arm by the strap alone as he reached up and yanked on the leather tie of his helmet's cheek pieces. They came undone instantly and he yanked the thing off with difficulty, noting the nasty groove along the side and feeling the long cut on his scalp as the cold sweat brought out the pain.

He shook his head, recovering his wits and only saw the sword coming for him just in time to throw up his own blade and block it. With a moment's struggle, he pulled the shield back up into his grip and turned to identify the worst threat. As he spotted that same man coming for him again, he went momentarily half blind as blood running from his hair now filled his left eye, and he blinked away the warm red, desperately throwing his shield into the way.

Their momentum had now ground to a halt and the fighting had intensified. Galronus, turning that latest blow, swung his own sword, only to have it knocked aside by his opponent's shield. Before he could react further, he was forced to lean right to avoid a flailing spear point, and the angle brought fresh difficulties, as now the blood flowing freely from his scalp ran into both eyes and he lost sight of everything for desperate moments as he blinked away the blood. Starting to feel the edge of panic, he brought up his sword arm up, using the short length of tunic that protruded from the chain sleeve to wipe his eyes. It did little good, for moments later they filled with blood again, leaving him just enough time to block another blow.

His time in the fight was done. He was constantly blinded and it was only a matter of time before he was killed while unable to see to defend himself. Grunting his irritation, he slowly backed his horse up, blinking constantly. His regret intensified as he suddenly realised an enemy officer was coming for him. The man's resemblance to Vibius Pacideius made his identity clear, for he had to be the man's brother, and that made him Labienus' second in command in the field. Short of killing Labienus himself, felling this man would be the most useful and satisfying act on the battlefield, but there was simply no way Galronus was going to able to do that, for even now fresh trickles of blood were filling his eyes.

As he blinked it all away again, his eyes almost as sore as his scalp, he saw Pacideius make his mistake. The officer had clearly seen Galronus and decided much the same, pushing through the press to get to him. In doing so, though, he put himself among too many Caesarian riders and, though he valiantly parried and blocked numerous blows, one of Galronus' men lunged out with a spear and caught Pacideius in the head. The Remi went blind again and, having pulled back far enough now to be out of danger, his own men fighting in front of him, he simply dropped the shield beneath the mass of horses and men and used his free hand to wipe the blood away.

Pacideius was reeling. The spear point had managed to find the gap between his cheek piece and the neck guard and had actually hit the man in the head. As the spear was pulled back out, red and gleaming, the officer lolled in the saddle. He was still alive, for he continued to grip his sword and yell, but as was clear from the blood now pouring out onto his shoulder beneath his helmet, he'd been wounded badly enough to at least see him from the field.

Tit for tat, thought Galronus as fresh blood poured into his eyes. Wincing at the necessity, he sheathed his sword, still bloody. That would take some cleaning soon before it dried and stuck in. But he had to do something about his head, and quickly. Knowing that he would soon have to seek out a medicus, for only stitches were going to solve this, he tore the scarf from his neck, opened it up into a bandana and wrapped it around his head, tying the front tight enough to cause discomfort on his forehead. He felt the flow down his face slow and then stop, and wiped his eyes properly, carefully.

His vision clear at last, he focused on the action from a new viewpoint at the rear of the fight. Pacideius had gone, pulling back through the enemy in much the same way as Galronus had. The advance had ground to a halt, and now, with the advantage of a good perspective, he could see the danger arising. Labienus had committed a reserve to the fight, and it was a good sized force. The reserves had moved in on both sides of the fight, the enemy legions pulling aside to allow room. If nothing was done to counter them, they would cover both flanks, envelop and trap Galronus' riders and crush them.

He glanced off to his left. The rest of the two armies remained motionless, facing one another across that slope, neither Caesar nor Scipio willing to commit to the attack. The general was supposed to be watching. Sure enough, something *was* happening in the Caesarian ranks. While the army was not advancing up the slope, a cohort or so of men was moving towards the right through their own ranks, heading in Galronus' direction.

Quickly, the Remi turned to find signallers and was grateful to find that they and the musicians had flocked to him the moment he had pulled back from the fight. 'Sound the advance for the support. Get those spear men to the right flank, and the archers with them. Hold those enemy cavalry back so that they don't flank us.'

While the musicians began to call out the cadences for the various auxilia, one of the prefects there frowned. 'Just the *right* flank, sir? They're coming on the left too.'

'The left is covered,' Galronus said and turned. That cohort of men had now broken free of the Caesarian lines and was hurtling forward to support Galronus' push, making for that flank where the enemy reserves were pressing to surround Caesar's cavalry. Galronus felt a fierce smile reach his lips. He really hoped that Labienus had a good view of all this wherever he was, for those men who were now charging in to support the cavalry were the same light cohorts that had brutalised the enemy cavalry a few days ago on the day of their infamous picnic. Sure enough, while they ran, they only held together in loose formation. Then, as they neared the enemy horse, swords and knives and a number of other odd weapons were torn from their belts and they bellowed a hundred different war cries and ploughed into the cavalry, each of them a lone warrior intent on slaughter.

Galronus watched the enemy advance falter then, the rebel riders still uncertain how to effectively counter these nightmare gladiator-like legionaries who held to no known tactic. Moreover, Galronus was sure there would be a strong current of fear running through them at facing these men, given what they had done on the way to their picnic.

The tide had turned again, and Galronus could see the slow advance of his forces up the slope once more. The enemy were being pushed back, albeit with great difficulty. Horns blew somewhere to the enemy's rear and Galronus cocked his head, listening. The enemy calls were still very similar to his own, unchanged despite being on two different sides, and he could recognise another call to advance. Some other unit, unseen at the rear, had been committed to the fight. Sure enough, by the count of twenty, the flow of the fight had changed once more and his own men were being forced back down the slope. At least they were maintaining a solid front to the enemy still, for the light legionary cohort and the auxilia and archers had managed to prevent the enemy from surrounding them, and so they maintained a line. They were being hard pressed, though.

A new sound cut through the din of battle, and Galronus turned to his left, trying to confirm what he thought he'd heard. Sure enough, as he'd assumed from the distant call, the other cavalry wing were on the move. Having been called from the far flank a mile along the line, they were even now racing at speed along the rear of the army to this end in support. Galronus smiled, and then blinked in irritation as once again blood trickled down into his eyes. He reached up to the scarf wrapped around his head and was slightly alarmed to find that it was warm and soggy. He must be losing more blood than he'd thought.

He looked around and spotted a small group of legionaries a few hundred paces away, watching the fight. 'Capsarius,' he called, and half a dozen legionary medics, identifiable from the leather bags slung across their shoulders, turned to face him. One came running immediately, but before he could arrive, Samaconius was there, out of breath, his horse sweating and snorting, as the other half of the Caesarian cavalry pounded past to join the fray.

'You're wounded, sir.'

'And you're observant,' grunted Galronus in reply, raising a snort of dark humour from his second in command. 'Take control. Push them from the field.'

'With pleasure, sir.'

And with that, Samaconius was gone, joining his riders as they piled into the fray on the edge of the battlefield, turning the tide once more with their added momentum and force, pushing the rebel cavalry slowly back up the hill.

'I need you down here,' came a voice, and Galronus looked down to see the capsarius looking up at him as he began to rummage in his satchel. Sighing, the Remi commander lifted himself from between the horns of his saddle and slid fairly gracelessly from his horse. He'd gone blind again and had to rub the blood from his eyes.

'Gods, you're a mess,' the medic noted as he tied a fresh linen wrap around Galronus' head above the eyebrows to hold back the flow while he removed the sodden scarf. 'I need you to sit so I can work, and bite down on your baldric, because this is going to hurt, I'm afraid.'

Galronus sank to the ground, grateful that he could still watch the action from this position. He made no move to do what he'd been told, and moments later the capsarius lifted his baldric off his chest and jammed it between his teeth. 'I don't joke,' the man said. 'By the third stitch you'll have bitten off your tongue if you don't keep that there.'

The Remi clenched his teeth on the leather with a look of disdain. It was just a wound. Just stitches. Then the capsarius started work, and Galronus realised just how right the man had been. This was the first time he'd had his scalp stitched, and it was agony. Every tug felt as though someone was pulling his whole skin up to the top of his head and pinning it there. The blood was no longer an issue, for his eyes were watering so much they washed the orbits for him.

In between agonising stitches and stifled whimpers, he watched the battle unfold before him. It was a joy and an irritation at the same time. The fresh reserves Caesar had committed had done the trick. The speed with which the Caesarians were advancing and the rebels being pushed back picked up slowly until it became clear where victory was going to lie. Caesar's army had won the struggle on the flank. But then the result revealed itself with all its frustration. As the flank broke and Labienus' men fell back fully now, so the withdrawal signal was given all along the enemy line.

Scipio's army was falling back to their camps. Most of the slope showed no sign of a fray as Caesar's men watched the enemy depart, but even as Samaconius had the calls put out to rein in his own men and prevent a dangerous and potentially costly pursuit of the retreating cavalry, Galronus could see the shapes of so many corpses on the gentle incline that this could be called nothing less than a battle. The bodies were of both horses and riders, some with red scarves and some with blue wraps, but the overwhelming result was clear, for the majority of the fallen bore blue and many of them were in the uniforms of officers.

Scipio had once again refused to fight a full battle, yet the Caesarian army would return to camp in high spirits, knowing that what fighting there had been, had been their own victory without doubt. The non-battle of Tegea had been won.

'Ouch,' he snapped, the leather strap falling from his mouth, and even as the medic told him not to be a baby and jammed what felt like a pilum through his scalp, Galronus narrowly avoided biting through his tongue. Hurriedly jamming the strap back in, he braced himself.

The fight was over. The war would go on.

CHAPTER TWENTY TWO

Aggar, 4th April 46 BC

The officers in Caesar's command tent sat in strained silence, all of them knowing full well the only possible answers.

'Well,' the general prompted, 'are there any surprising and ingenious suggestions?' Even Plancus, now become known as Caesar's 'idea man'. remained silent. 'So,' the general concluded at length, 'we are left with two options if we wish to finish this in short order.'

The men nodded their agreement, and the fact was that they *did* need to finish it. A week had passed since the clash in which Galronus had been injured, and still nothing happened. Following that engagement at Tegea, Scipio had shut his army up in his camp once more and, as the light began to fade, Caesar had been left with no real alternative but to abandon the hope of battle and return to his own camp. Since then they had sent out patrols and sealed off forage routes for the enemy, prodded, needled and tempted them and still Scipio refused to meet Caesar in good open ground.

And the men were restive. The legions were becoming troublesome, and with the mutinies of the previous winter still looming in memory, every officer knew that the legions were around two paydays away from abandoning the campaign. Unless something could be done, the army might begin to fall apart. Caesar had sent dispatches to Rome, addressing Marcus Antonius and seeking financial support to grant the troops a bonus, though any action would likely come too late to be of use. And they all knew the answer. The mutiny in Italia had been caused by the legions seeking their promised bonuses after Pharsalus, and the loot to be had from Scipio's army, and from the cities loyal to the rebels, would pay that long awaited bonus and more besides.

They needed to beat Scipio, and they needed to do it soon.

'Two options, then,' Caesar announced. 'Pros and cons of both, please. Firstly, we take the war to Scipio. We finally bite down against the pain and assault his camp.'

'He has had almost twenty days to fortify,' Plancus said. 'And from the reports we've received from spies, we know that he has been using them well. His defences have strengthened every day, for his army have rarely left the camp. Any assault on Scipio's position now is more siege than field battle. I would estimate casualties at somewhere around ten to fifteen percent from the fortifications alone.'

A sombre murmur agreed with this.

'His men must be growing troubled,' someone called. 'We know they're hungry. We've stolen or used up three quarters of his supplies, and every day we further constrict resupply.'

'He will have plenty of warning of our approach,' another officer chimed in. 'He will be free to release his elephants into the open to deal with us without risking the rest of his force, and this is before we even try the assault.'

'His camps are well positioned. We would have to bring all our siege equipment up those slopes. And then we need to invest three different camps, one for cavalry, one for the main force and one for Juba's Numidians. Each would have to be planned and equipped differently. It's a logistical nightmare.'

Plancus cut in across the top once more. 'In total, a fair estimate suggests losses of fully one quarter before we can consider the effects of a face to face engagement, and of course, our men would then be tired from the march to Tegea, from the approach on the slope, and from assaulting the camps. The odds do not look good, Caesar.'

The general nodded. 'A bleak appraisal, but not an unexpected one. After all, this is why we have not tried such an approach thus far. We need to fight in open ground, face to face on the flat, where the only factors are numbers, experience and tactics. Our other option, then. We stop posing vague threats to his last remaining stronghold in the east and instead we launch a full scale attack. We assault Thapsus.'

Fronto leaned forward. 'While I don't much like it, it's the only thing we haven't yet tried to draw him out. There has to be a breaking point for Scipio, and Thapsus stands out as the most likely. He can't afford to let it fall. Even if it didn't represent financial loss to their cause, Cato is watching from Utica. Scipio might have seniority, but Cato has the support and the reputation. He will not let Scipio lose Thapsus, and Scipio has to know that. If he let us take it, Cato would have him removed from command so fast his head would spin.'

'It does mean attacking a well-defended city, though,' someone pointed out. 'Thapsus has strong walls and a good garrison under a solid commander. It's no easy proposal.'

'We don't need to *take* Thapsus,' Fronto reminded him. 'We just need to start the process, and Scipio will come to us. He *has* to.'

The man flashed a look at Fronto. 'That will land us in danger too, though, since we'll be trapped. We'll have Thapsus on one side with its garrison and Scipio's army coming from the other. We could be crushed.'

'Alesia,' said the general suddenly, across the heads of all. 'Few here were with us at Alesia, but I know *some* of you were there. You remember our difficult situation?'

'Vercingetorix and his army on the hill. We fortified against him, ringing him in with siege works.'

Galronus laughed and then hissed at the pain the facial movement caused, pulling on the stitches in his scalp. 'Yes, but the Gallic reserve army was coming. A second set of works was formed to face outwards. We were free to concentrate on the hill fort, because the reserves did little to threaten us.'

'Quite,' Caesar added. 'This, then, is Alesia in reverse. We invest the town with siege works. It is on the coast, but Aquila's fleet is already in position, and will form the rest of the siege line. Once we have those works in place, the city is surrounded and it will take only a small force to keep them pinned down while we look to our other trouble. In this case, we are not bothering with Alesia, but concentrating on that reserve army. We turn all our attention outwards, to Scipio.'

Fronto rose from his seat and crossed to the map. 'Land approaches to Thapsus are difficult. The huge salt lake covers most of it. There's a corridor perhaps a mile and a half wide between the marshy land and the sea shore to the south of the city, and another around two miles wide to the north of the marsh beside the sea. Not too bad to defend, if we presume that Scipio cannot cross the salt marsh.'

Galronus shook his head and winced again. 'I've had my scouts probe the area several times. There's no feasible way to get an army across the marsh. Not even a cavalry force. It's a solid defence. The two approaches from the south and the northwest are the only access to Thapsus, except by sea.'

'And Thapsus itself is closest to the northern approach,' Plancus noted. 'If we are investing the city the bulk of our forces will by necessity be based in that area. If Scipio comes for us, we need him to come to the northern approach, where our forces will be strongest.'

'Then we need to garrison that southern approach and drive the enemy to the north,' Fronto muttered. 'And Scipio's going to want to take the most direct route. That southern approach could be hotly contested.'

Caesar gave Fronto a knowing smile. 'And that is why I will have my most successful veteran commander there to stop him.'

* * *

Thapsus, 5th April 46 BC

Fronto stood on the ramparts and peered off into the distance. His men were working at breakneck pace, yet still he worried that it would be too little. The army had broken camp at Aggar in the middle of the night and departed for Thapsus at the third watch. They had travelled as fast as any fully equipped army could hope to and, though that was still not fast enough for Fronto's liking, at least they had the element of surprise.

It would have taken precious hours for news of Caesar's departure to reach Scipio. Inevitably they would then have spent at least an hour arguing over their next course of action before settling upon it. Given at least two hours to break camp, and that was being extremely generous, then the very minimum count gave Caesar's army at least five hours' head start. More than likely news of their departure wouldn't have reached Scipio until dawn, and the arguments and preparation would carry them through to noon. If Scipio force-marched to meet them, then he could do so in perhaps three hours. By those estimates, Scipio's army could be here within the hour, or any time between then and sundown. Fronto doubted they would take longer than that.

Caesar had reached the land corridor formed by the salt lake and the east shoreline and there they had paused, leaving Fronto with three cohorts to form his defence while the rest moved on to Thapsus itself.

Three cohorts.

Fronto had rather acidly told Caesar that he might as well be given a box of sweet pastries and a sick mule and told to hold the pass of Thermopylae as try to hold this place with three cohorts. Caesar had been unmoved, simply telling

Fronto rather supportively that he had faith in his old warhorse, and that the rest of the forces needed to be further north, investing Thapsus itself.

And so while the general took his army to the rebel city to encircle it with ramparts and trenches, Fronto took command of the southern approach as the sun began to peek above the horizon. At least he'd been allowed to choose his cohorts. He'd taken the First Cohort from the Tenth, for he knew their commander well and they were his old trusted legion. He'd taken the Tenth Cohort from the Fifth Legion, because they were primarily formed of pioneers and engineers and had proved to be the best in the entire army at fortifying ground over the recent months. And finally he had taken a cohort from the Ninth that had been trained in those unconventional gladiator tactics, and who had been involved in the brutal fights both on the day of the infamous picnic and at Tegea. If he could only have three cohorts he was going to make them count. He'd been granted five hundred archers into the bargain with only a little argument.

'Brooding on the numbers, sir?' said a familiar voice, and he turned to see Atenos, helmet off and head lathered with sweat, leaning on a post.

'Difficult not to.'

'I find it's better not to worry, sir.'

Fronto snorted. 'That's Gauls for you. Galronus is the same. What will be will be, worrying won't change things, and so forth. But think about it... we have how many men?'

'Just shy of fifteen hundred, sir.'

'While Scipio can field more than fifty thousand foot alone, not to mention his horse and his elephants. So if we want to hold this spit of land, each man has to kill how many rebels?'

Atenos laughed. 'Was never that good at maths, sir.'

'The answer, Atenos, is that every man here will have to kill more than thirty men. And probably ten cavalry and an elephant into the bargain.'

'Have you heard of the Dionysus campaign back in in Pompey's days in Syria?'

Fronto shook his head. 'No, why?'

'I was serving with him then. We went hunting a bandit chief by the name of Dionysus in the Libanus mountains. He was a right bastard. We had four cohorts and managed to trap him in a valley in the mountains. Dionysus had around forty of his brigand army left with him and had maybe half a day to dig himself in before we got there.'

'And yet he heroically fought off your four cohorts with his stout two score of peasants?'

'Gods, no,' snorted Atenos. 'We rolled over them like a cartwheel over a lame rat. Butchered the lot of them and Dionysus was taken back to Antioch and crucified.'

'What was the point of this story, then, Atenos?'

'Bit of fun. And to point out that you might be all fatalistic, sir, but I'm a hard bastard, and I won't go down without a fight. Scipio can field whoever he likes but by sundown he'll be struggling to extricate my boot from his arse crack.'

Fronto laughed. 'Ah yes. Insane Gauls. That's what we need when we're facing forty to one odds.'

Atenos shrugged. 'Anyway, I came to tell you that the enemy have been sighted.'

Fronto felt his pulse suddenly pick up. 'You could have mentioned this before you started rambling on about the good old days. Where?'

'About a mile and a half south. They were setting up camp. Our scouts spotted them but their scouts spotted us at the same time and chased them halfway back.'

Fronto cursed. 'Damn it, but if he's setting up camp, then he has his eyes on this route. What time is it now?'

Atenos looked up. 'About two hours after noon.'

'A good four or five hours until sunset, then. I doubt Scipio's going to delay. Camp or no camp, he'll push here before dark. Alright, have the men keep working, but I want every man's full equipment within reach. We're going to be fighting any time now.'

Atenos saluted and went back to the construction.

Fronto mused over what he'd done, which was realistically all anyone *could* do. They'd built a camp large enough for three cohorts, which was easy enough. Compared with their usual fare, this was small and quick. Then, once the rampart and stake fence were in place, he'd begun work on the rest. They had set up their camp right at the edge of the salt marsh, where the water was still shallow, but the bed beneath was viscous and sucked at the boots. While his engineers had already dug a ditch across the front of the camp, they had carefully worked it so that it remained dry, the stinking salt water kept out by just a tiny causeway that could easily be broken to flood the ditch. He'd purloined more scorpions from the army than any cohort had a right to, and they were now set up all around the southern rampart, bristling and ready, loaded since dawn. Stooks of pila were visible at intervals all along the line.

Unfortunately, there was still the better part of a mile between the camp and the shore accessible by Scipio's men, but he was already working on that. The ditches the engineers were digging across there were thigh deep, narrow, and were being planted with sharpened stakes and covered with brush and dirt so as to be barely visible. The archers had been positioned in groups hidden by scrub or thickets behind those multiple leg-breaker ditches and, in a moment of good fortune for which Fronto was most grateful, two of Aquila's triremes happened along the coast on patrol as the work was underway and, after a brief conflab, had agreed to remain here, just offshore where they could act as untouchable and mobile platforms for missile troops and artillery. All in all those defences wouldn't hold for long, but they would cause havoc for the men attempting to pass them for a time.

Fronto stood, fretting and watching the southern horizon as the sun gradually passed from its high point and started to slide down into the west. It was late afternoon when he saw the tell-tale signs. A dust cloud to the south. Scipio was coming.

A last moment check of his command revealed that the intervening hours had been put to good use. A fresh field of 'lily' pits had been dug on the far side of the ditch, and the engineers had worked hard and fast to create a third and fourth leg-breaker ditch down to the sea. Now, as Fronto waved to his musician and the man blew the 'ad signum' order, all he could do was pray that he'd prepared enough and that the gods were with them. Gripping the twin figurines of Fortuna and Nemesis that hung around his neck, he sent up a series of heartfelt prayers, and then gave the last order to the engineers. That dam at the edge of the salt marsh was cut through and stinking water flowed along the ditch before the camp.

All along the defences, his men stood to. The soldiers of the Tenth and Fifth garrisoned the camp, also manning the many scorpions, and each man was now moving into position, either grabbing pila or testing the manoeuvrability of the artillery. The other cohort had been working on the ditches down to the sea until the last moment, and had then pulled back into hiding with the archers.

Atenos appeared from somewhere. 'All's ready, sir.'

'The Fifth know what to do?'

'The moment we look like being flanked, they pull back from the south rampart and help box us in. All is planned. Even the escape routes for the archers and legionaries out there behind the ditches. There's nothing more we can do but wait.'

Fronto nodded, watching that enemy force coming ever closer. One thing was certain: at least it was not Scipio's *full* army. There were few cavalry in evidence, and no elephants, thank the gods. This was an infantry foray sent to test the southern approach. Given the rough size of the approaching force, Fronto estimated their numbers at somewhere between one and two legions. So only odds of eight to one. It was a poor world, he mused, when eight to one odds were a relief.

'No heroics,' Fronto murmured. 'I want every life here preserved as long as possible. This is about wearing them down. We need to hold this place long enough for Scipio to decide it's not worth the effort and head north for the other approach.'

Atenos sighed. 'With respect, sir, I'm aware of all that.'

'I know. It just helps to say it out loud sometimes. Alright, let's get to it. Scipio's underestimated us. We can actually hold that lot off, unless they do something unexpected.'

As the enemy closed, Fronto could see that they were indeed formed of two legions, their vexilla rising to display standards with which he was not familiar. These were Scipio's local levy legions. They'd proved relatively effective, but were no veterans and couldn't have had much experience with the sort of thing they were about to face. Fronto gave a wicked grin. Scipio was actually moving at last. Attacking Thapsus had done it. The enemy commander was coming and intended battle. Well, Fronto was going to give him his first bloody nose at Thapsus.

The enemy split into two groups, one legion moving directly for the camp, the other spreading out to a wide front and making for the mile-wide gap. Fronto could see what was going on in their commanders' heads. The one near the shore thought they had the easy job. They would cross the open ground, looking for hidden units and then come round in a flanking action and seal in the camp, while the other legion attacked them directly, keeping them busy.

'Mark your ranges.'

The enemy were closing now. Scipio's legionaries hefted their pila ready to brace and cast them when they were close enough. Sure enough, the front three rows of men were the ones preparing, in a standard tactic trained to all legions. But these were relatively raw troops. Fronto judged the distance carefully. If he worked this right…

'Artillery, loose.'

All along the line of defences, the scorpions unleashed their deadly hail with thuds and clanks and clatters. A hundred iron-tipped bolts took to the air in a low arc, crossing the open ground and ploughing into the front ranks of the approaching enemy. Just as they'd been instructed, the artillerists had aimed in clusters, and instead of taking out a swathe of the front line, they had taken men from the first three lines in small groups all across the front. The result was that the enemy approach faltered. Men hurrying forward to fill one space was a quick job and did not interrupt an advance, but men having to filter forward three at a time and collect pila to fill the gaps was a slower and less organised affair. Their approach was slowed at a critical moment to half-pace, and already Fronto's artillerists were ratcheting back the machines and dropping a second bolt into place, tipping the engines very slightly to account for nearer targets. This time an engineer gave the command and, just as the enemy had recovered to full pace, the second volley struck them. The artillerists had maintained their initial targets, saving them precious time selecting a new one, and all along the enemy line small clusters of men were impaled and thrown back in exactly the same manner as before. The chaos the second strike caused in the legion was more pronounced this time, as men continued to hurry forward and fill the gaps. Crucially, they had not done so in time to be prepared for pila range.

As Scipio's legion reached a point where they should have been casting their weapons they were instead still rearranging, centurions bellowing their anger at the slovenly and disorganised behaviour of their men. Fronto smiled and nodded to a waiting signaller. All along the ramparts, his cohorts hurled their first pilum and then ducked down behind the defences to gather up a second before the first had even struck.

Fronto watched the front line of the enemy legion crumble under the cloud of pila, men struck through limbs, torsos and heads, shields torn apart and thrown back with mangled pila jammed through them. The enemy legion was still coming, but they were in chaos now. Some managed to cast their own missile, though most were injured, struggling, or rearming themselves.

At Atenos' order a second and then a third volley of pila arced out, further battering Scipio's legion even as they struggled on towards the camp defences. Fronto took the opportunity to glance to his left, past the end of the ramparts to where Scipio's other attacking legion had made for the open ground. Untouched by the missiles, they had moved faster and surged ahead, only to fall foul of the defences. Even a simple quick look told him that there was going to be no immediate danger posed by that legion. The front ranks had marched straight into the hidden ditch, impaling legs and feet, crippling themselves, shock shuddering through the ranks as the second line marched straight into the back of their fellows, piling up and creating chaos. As their advance slowed, those few who managed to get past the crippled front line simply marched into the second ditch and the same thing began all over again. At that very moment the units of archers to the rear emerged from their hiding places, protected by the shields of the legionaries with them, and began to loose clouds of arrows at will into the chaos at the ditches. Fronto could not see as far as the coast, but he could only imagine how the attackers were faring down there, where Aquila's ships were also peppering them with shots.

It was all going better than he could have hoped. Now he could not afford to pay heed to the open land and what was going on there. The camp needed his full attention.

The enemy were almost here. Missile shots had become a sporadic affair on both sides, those attackers who could still find and throw a pilum doing so whenever the opportunity arose, just as Fronto's men continued to cast pila and loose scorpion bolts into the force. The missiles stopped at Atenos' command as the enemy neared the defences. At that point the lead men, including an unfortunate centurion, marched into the lily pits, their feet dropping into the hidden holes filled with caltrops, accompanied by a fresh wave of screaming.

Some enterprising enemy centurion had finally done something bright, or so he thought, and had pulled his men from the ranks out to the west, attempting to flank the camp on that side. Fronto left them to it with a grin as they reached the edge of the salt marsh and began to sink first to the ankles in the gritty, stinking murk, and then to the knees. They would be lucky to slog a hundred paces forward by the time it was all over.

The men along the rampart grabbed a last pilum as the enemy legion reached the ditch, ripping their swords out now and roaring defiance. The attackers dropped into that reeking, murky ditch and struggled through it to try and clamber up the rampart, coming face to face with pilum points as the defenders leaned over their fence and jabbed down, using the long missiles as spears.

Fronto took one last long look at the attackers, weighing things up. Gods, but the enemy was a mess. They were disorganised, three centuries now wading through the unforgiving salt lake, the men of the other legion still scrambling across the ditches as they were constantly hit by a hail of arrows, leaving a seemingly endless swathe of corpses in their wake, and as yet unaware that those vicious, gladiator-trained butchers were waiting for them once their first nightmare had ended. And back at the rampart, the men facing him had thinned out drastically. The attacking force had been reduced by a third at least. Now it came down to just strength and morale.

Tearing his sword from its sheath, Fronto stepped up to the rampart. The legionary and the optio between whose shoulders he appeared turned in surprise. 'Sir, you should…' the optio began.

'Give *them* your attention,' Fronto interrupted, pointing his gladius at the enemy scrambling up towards them. In truth, he was a little weary and could probably have been persuaded to sit at the back and command from the saddle, but this fight was already too close for comfort. The enemy were a shambles, yet they'd reached the defences and still outnumbered the defenders.

Atenos gave the command a moment later, and those men still jabbing down with their pila gave a last violent thrust with them and then let go, drawing their swords, the enemy now too close for spears. Fronto braced himself, shifting his legs so that his bad knee was in the best position to avoid twisting or his foot slipping, and a moment later the enemy were upon them.

Fronto saw the man who posed the most danger, who was using the bottom rim of his shield as an aid to clambering up the bank, his eyes on the defenders and sword held up ready. Bracing himself, he waited until the man was almost at attacking distance, and then dropped his free hand to the fence of pointed sudis stakes atop the rampart. With just a jerk, he pushed the fence, allowing it to pivot. It was extremely heavy, but as it reached the point of balance, it smacked against the attacker's shield. His footing was sufficiently precarious that the blow sent him sliding back, taking two men with him as he fell into the brackish murk below.

Allowing the fence to rock back into position and cursing at the weight and his strained muscles, Fronto spotted another man almost at him and lashed out. His sword took the man in the shoulder, far from a killing blow but enough to send him falling back down again.

And so it went on. All along the defences, the veteran legionaries of the Fifth and the Tenth, victors in Gaul, Greece and Spain, hammered out at the attackers, struggling to hold them back, but doing so nonetheless. Fronto stabbed and hacked until his arm hurt, knowing that somewhere in the press he was taking minor flesh wounds. A slash to the arm, a cut above the knee, a winding and bruising blow to the chest. At one point he had cause to be very grateful to the optio beside him, who pushed aside a blow that had been aimed for his face before turning back to his own opponent.

The first hint that it was coming to an end was the distant call of a buccina giving a standard legion call to withdraw in an orderly fashion, with an additional flourish at the start to identify which unit the call was for. It all fell apart for the attackers in moments from there. The call was echoed by more honks along the lines, and Fronto knew from the source that this meant the second legion, who'd crossed the leg-breakers, was now on the run. Heartbeats later another set of similar calls was going up, and the men assaulting the camp were pulling back.

As the enemy disengaged and began to fall back across the field towards their camp more than a mile away Fronto, breathing heavily, rose to the highest point on the rampart to survey the situation.

They had held. Better still, they had held without losing any ground or conceding any rampart. The enemy had been driven off, and the ones who'd had the best of it had been those men facing Fronto and the camp ramparts. Off to the east, the other legion was fleeing in a much less orderly manner, that fierce cohort of rabid gladiator-legionaries harrying them as they ran, bringing down the slowest men like lions with a pack of deer. Perhaps the worst of all, those three centuries who'd been slogging onward through the salt marsh had turned at the signal and realised that they had at least half an hour of wading back the way they'd come before they could even begin to run to safety. Their legion left without them and Fronto, in a moment of clemency, ordered his men to let them go. Still, some of the scorpion crews took great delight in launching missiles perfectly angled to plop into the water right behind the labouring soldiers, accompanied by jeering laughter.

Finally, as those men limped up to dry ground and fled, Atenos joined Fronto once more.

'Do you think they'll come again?'

Fronto shrugged. 'Not tonight, for certain. I doubt they will at all, in fact. The state that lot will be in when they get back and the terrible tales they'll tell will put their commanders off a repeat performance. Still, we'll use the time we have to repair and replenish all those works. And in the morning we'll send the scouts out. If they're still there, we'll prepare for a second go. If not, I'll run a report to Caesar. Either way, I think we can be proud of what we did today. The last battle is coming, Atenos. It's coming, and let's hope today set a precedent.'

CHAPTER TWENTY THREE

Thapsus, 5ᵗʰ April 46 BC

S cipio's legions had not come again. Whether Fronto and the Tenth had provided a terrifying enough defence of the southern approach to scare them off for good, or perhaps that the enemy commander had made an alternative tactical decision, by the time the sun slid westwards it was clear that there would be no further attempt that day. To be certain of that, Fronto had sent scouts out to reconnoitre the enemy camps and sure enough only a few cohorts remained in them, glowering in the direction of the Tenth, the rest of Scipio's army having departed some time just before dark.

Leaving Atenos behind to command the camp against any attempt to launch a second attack by those cohorts, Fronto had ridden north to warn the general in person. Even now he remembered the expression on the primus pilus' face as he left, for Atenos had been entirely unimpressed with Fronto effectively setting him aside from any coming battle, and it *was* selfish, really. Caesar had put Fronto in command of that approach and, though clearly it was no longer in any danger, Caesar's orders stood, and a senior officer still needed to control that line. And Fronto was damned sure it wasn't going to be him. Poor Atenos. Ah well.

He had mounted Bucephalus and ridden north with a small escort in the evening light, racing along the eastern shore of the salt lagoon for the siege works of Thapsus, five miles distant. He'd been impressed as he reached the lines in the last glow of indigo light. Thapsus was as well contained already as Alesia had been all those years ago, with stake-lined ditches, ramparts, palisades, towers and camps for the besieging legions. Of course, the arc of defences around Thapsus was only a quarter as long as that which had surrounded Alesia, for most of the circumvallation was carried out by the fleet at sea, and it required only defences facing one way, not both, but still the speed and efficiency was impressive.

Fronto had found Caesar with the officers in his command tent, doling out tasks, and had been shown in by Salvius Cursor, who veritably nipped at his heels for information on Scipio's army and its location. The general had been stoically calm in his reaction. He had congratulated Fronto on his work preventing the armies from taking the southern approach and then calmly finished his briefing as Fronto waited expectantly. Clearly, in the general's opinion, Scipio would take much of the night moving his army around the long edge of the salt marsh, and it would be dawn at the earliest before the enemy could present any real threat, while the Caesarian force was already in position and could move to meet them swiftly.

Orders had been issued in the fourth watch of the night, and as the first strains of light began to show in the east, the army was already on the move. The works of Thapsus had been largely abandoned, sufficient forces left in place to make sure the garrison stayed shut up within its walls and made no attempt to attack Caesar's army from behind. Similarly, Aquila was sent west, departing in the dark with three quarters of his fleet, bearing orders to find Scipio's army and shadow it from behind. The enemy would be constrained by terrain, given the salt lake, and would have to be within sight of the sea, where Aquila might be able to add his naval strength to the struggle.

Fronto had taken command of the Tenth once more, and the army marched west in light order as dawn began to lighten the land. The day promised to be gently and comfortably warm and dry. As the army moved, Fronto rode with the officers at the fore, Galronus' cavalry scouting out ahead. They had barely begun to pass the edges of that great salt marsh when the scouts brought word. Scipio's army had encamped at the far end of the marshy area, and already his force was mustering before it.

As they gradually approached reports came back thick and fast with details, including the disposition of the troops gathering before the camps ready to face Caesar. One thing that was clear was that Scipio had finally committed to battle. For good or for ill, the end was coming now. As usual, Scipio had positioned his elephants and his cavalry on the wings, while his infantry force continued to fortify that great camp behind them, close enough that they could fall into lines and form the centre at the first sight of Caesar. Scipio may be prepared to fight, but the man was still being careful and creating a fall back position even as he waited for his opponent to arrive. Fronto wondered whether the man had learned something from the defence of the southern approach by the Tenth, though it mattered not. If Scipio would commit, then they would either win or lose this day and there would be no need for that camp in the following hours.

'We utilise today everything that we have learned in Africa, gentlemen,' Caesar said as he rode. 'All our retraining for new fighting styles, all our experience of their new tactics and of their unusual units. Everything we can employ to counter them. The less tried legions will take the centre, where they should be a match for Scipio's locally-levied legions, while the veterans will take the wings. I want the Tenth and Seventh on the right, close to the shore, and the Eighth and Ninth on the left, near the lake. They will each be supported by half the Fifth, by the cavalry and by all the missile units we have available. The native cavalry will move with the light infantry in the manner we learned from the enemy. The wings will be the danger point, I believe. The centre will be contested by roughly equal forces of heavy infantry and it will be on one flank or the other that this fight will be won or lost, so the veterans and their support need to be prepared for a hard fight. Are we all prepared?'

Fronto looked across to the commander of the Seventh, who rode close by. He had little experience of Rabirius Postumus. The man looked faintly rodent-like, with beady, inscrutable eyes and a constant twitch of the upper lip. He'd been absent for much of the war so far, sent back to Sicilia in the early days to secure reinforcements, and had only returned with the last of those troops, the injured and furloughed soldiers from the various legions. He was as yet untried in battle, as far as Fronto was concerned, and he seemingly had no military reputation from which an impression of his leadership could be gleaned. He was primarily a banker with an unsavoury history, a member of the equites who had been granted a command far beyond his rank's norm. And in the coming fight, he would be commanding the flank alongside Fronto, not a place he liked the idea of an inscrutable unknown.

Sucking on his teeth in thought, he rode closer to the man as they made for Scipio's position, determined to engage him in conversation and perhaps begin to gauge what kind of man he was.

'A good command,' he said.

'Mph?' muttered Postumus, glancing in his direction.

'The Seventh. They're a good legion. I've been watching them in action since we battered the Helvetii twelve years ago. An auspicious command. A proper veteran force.'

'As long as they do what they're told.'

Fronto lapsed into a frowning silence. That had told him nothing.

'Mind if I ask you something?' Postumus simply shrugged, so Fronto pressed on. 'As an equestrian, you've done well to secure such a legionary command. I know the general is a little unorthodox at times, but still it's unusual. I wondered what you'd done for the general to grant you such an important role?'

Postumus turned a look on him and even then Fronto couldn't tell what was going through the man's mind. The banker rolled his shoulders. 'I've not much experience, in truth, though I served as a tribune, so I know the basics. You'd have to ask the general why, but if you really want my opinion, I would say it's because I'm a man who gets things done.'

'Whether or not it's strictly legal?'

He regretted the words even before they were fully out. There was just something faintly infuriating about this little and taciturn man. Postumus frowned. 'If you're referring to the Gabinian affair, I might offer the suggestion that men who weren't there, who have little knowledge of the world of loans and debts, and have spent the last two decades in the simple business of sticking pointy things into Gauls, might just want to keep their uninformed opinions to themselves.'

It was delivered in such a calm, reasonable and even polite manner that such a stinging rebuke seemed somehow venomless. He paused for a moment, uncertain how to react, and finally grinned. 'I think we might get along after all, Rabirius Postumus.'

The man snorted and turned back to face the ground ahead.

It took only half an hour more, as the morning sun truly began to illuminate the grey-brown landscape, before they found their foe. Scipio's army was truly impressive. The man had arrayed his entire force before the camp now, covering almost the width of the approach, from salt lagoon to sea shore. Fronto stared at the enemy and turned to Caesar. The general was carefully keeping his expression flat and unreadable, but Fronto knew him well enough to know that inside, Caesar's mind was in tumult.

How it had happened, they could not say, but Scipio's army had grown. Fronto had seen that force arrayed time after time since they'd left Ruspina, but it had never been so vast. Even in their stand-off near Tegea, he'd considered the numbers to be more or less even. Scipio must have called in all those garrisons nearby, and the units he'd deployed on various duties, for there was no denying it; Caesar's army was outnumbered once more. The enemy infantry numbered perhaps a quarter or a third as much again as Caesar's, and the cavalry were now perhaps three to one in favour of the enemy.

'This is not a foregone conclusion,' announced Plancus, a few bodies off to the left.

Caesar rallied quickly, straightening in the saddle. 'Very well. We have proved time and again that any deficiency in numbers can be counterbalanced with a combination of spirit, experience and strategy. We will simply have to be a little more careful in how we prosecute the battle. We must still fight here, and that is clear. Gentlemen, you have your deployments, issue the orders.'

Fronto nodded to Postumus and the two men hurried off to their legions, waving over musicians and signifers, who took the orders and began to disseminate them. Galronus led half the cavalry down towards the beach where they would form the ultimate flank. Fronto would then take the outermost of the legions' positions with the Tenth, with Postumus and his Seventh just inside there, a force of African cavalry and light infantry between them and the less veteran legions that formed the centre of the line.

The archers and slingers were lined up behind the Tenth and Seventh, with the cohorts of the Fifth behind them in support. Fronto sat astride Bucephalus out the front of the legion, and he could see Galronus off to his right and Postumus to his left. Other mounted figures were visible further along, and the army settled into a tense silence as the two forces glared at one another across the open field. There they sat for some time, Fronto wondering when someone would decide to make a move. As he peered along the front of the lines towards the centre, he could see the figure of Caesar, resplendent in his red cloak on his white horse, riding up and down the lines of the more recently levied legions, addressing them. Presumably, he felt that the veterans could be relied upon without the encouragement of their general, but the less tried forces in the centre would need to hold against the storm of steel every bit as much as the veterans.

Finally, the red-cloaked figure returned to his own lines, accompanied by a cheering from the legions there. The army waited, their opposition in place, immobile, across that stretch of open, dusty ground. All was silence, or rather that weird not-silence of a tense force of soldiers waiting to move. The occasional shush of chain shirts, the clonk of wooden shields and ding of helmets and sword hilts. A cough. The sound of surreptitious scratching. A fart and the consequent sniggering. The sounds of someone relieving themselves without falling out of rank and the grumbling of the men beside him. Above, the sound of gulls screeching, and off to the north the slap and crash of waves on the beach.

Silence that wasn't silence.

Nothing moved.

Fronto peered across at the enemy. He could just make out the senior commanders at the centre, a small knot of men on horseback surrounded by standards and banners. Scipio would be there, and almost certainly King Juba and Labienus. Afranius would be there, and if he had survived the recent encounter, probably Pacideius. The list went on: Petreius, Piso, Considius...

None of them looked as though they were about to give the signal to move. Some of those men would need to be commanding on the wings and were not yet in position with their men. They were in conference, clearly, planning their attack. Fronto's head snapped round to look along his own lines. Still nothing was happening. Did Caesar not see what was happening over there? The enemy commanders were all in one place. A swift attack now could commit both armies to the fight before the enemy's senior officers were in position with their commands.

That opportunity slid away even as Fronto watched, for that knot of officers broke up, the small command force remaining at the centre, other figures moving into place along the line. Fronto once again cursed his eyesight, squinting into the distance. He couldn't be certain, but the rider that had returned to this wing of the enemy force looked very much like Labienus, a notion supported by the banners around him. Fronto clenched his teeth. That made this fight all the more important and personal.

Thirty elephants rose powerful and frightening directly across the field, their backs covered with heavy blankets and then a small fortified wooden box bristling with spears and belted securely into position. There would be archers and javelineers in there. Each of those beasts was capable of putting an army to flight and Labienus would be relying upon their shock power to break the Caesarian flank. Behind the elephants lurked a mass of native cavalry and light infantry, white and bronze showing between the great grey beasts. Labienus' Gallic horse sat on the very edge of the wing, close to the beach, opposite those of Galronus, where ancient tribal rivalries would outweigh the importance of Roman values once the fighting began.

Everything was ready, and yet nothing moved. They had already missed one opportunity, and Fronto could feel the tension rising all around him. The longer the men had to look across the field at an army larger than their own, headed by terrifying war elephants, the more the army's nerves would get to them. Such tension could only be endured for so long before an army's will began to crumble.

Would Scipio's men be feeling such tension? To a certain extent, yes, though they would not have quite so much reason to quake, for they had the numbers and the beasts of war on their side.

The sound of hooves drew his attention, and he turned to see Postumus trotting along the front of the legions, reining in as he came close enough to speak.

'I have seen battle but once, Fronto, on a much smaller scale than this. My experience suggests that such events are usually fast and tumultuous affairs, yet nothing happens here. Why do neither army make a move?'

Fronto had been pondering that very issue, but found that now he'd been asked the question directly, the answers fell into place. 'Scipio has been careful and defensive for months now. Even when he made a try for the southern approach past the lagoon, he tested the defences with two legions rather than committing his full army. After what we did to him there, he will be wondering what surprises we have in place for him here. He'll be wary of simply attacking, suspecting that we have tricks up our sleeve, which, given Caesar's history of command, is a very astute suspicion. So Scipio will not attack until he is certain that doing so is the correct decision.'

'And Caesar?'

'Caesar will not launch the attack because of the elephants. We need those beasts to be out ahead of their lines, which would require them to be moving. Then we can pull Caesar's little manoeuvre, drawing them into a trap, and if he is as clever as we all think he is, those elephants can be turned on their own side. If *we* have to attack *them*, they might just stay in place and we will have to improvise, which is dangerous. Neither commander is comfortable committing first. This is a stand-off, and it will only end when someone's will breaks. Whoever moves first puts themselves in the greater danger of losing. To my mind, though it looks bad, Caesar is doing the right thing. Our men are solid, and the commanders are loyal to Caesar as overall commander. The enemy, on the other hand, might be led by Scipio, but there are other senior commanders there who are used to heading battles themselves. Given enough time, one of them will snap and order the attack. It could be Petreius or Afranius, both of whom have such records, as do Piso. But I think it will be Labienus, and this flank will be where it begins. So I want to be ready.'

Postumus nodded slowly. 'And when they come, we follow the plan to the letter, yes? Even though it hinges entirely on a supposition that has not been tested.'

Fronto drummed his fingers on the saddle horn. 'The elephants will come first. Labienus will use them as a battering ram. As they come into missile range, the legions, which are in thin lines, simply hold tight and brace. As soon as they are close enough, the archers and slingers will loose a cloud into the enemy and, if Caesar is right, the elephants will panic and run. Then, the legions begin to move and we can engage the enemy without dealing with those beasts in a melee. That, at least, is the theory.'

The other legate straightened. 'I shall watch for your signals. It would be best for all if our legions acted in perfect concert and without the constant need for instruction from above.'

'Agreed. And don't forget to fall back the moment we move. The last thing you want is to be trapped out front when those elephants come.'

With a nod, Postumus turned and rode back along the line to his position with the Seventh. Fronto returned his attention to the enemy. A lot depended upon whether Caesar's plan for the elephants worked. If it didn't, if the great grey beasts paid no heed to the din, if Juba had trained them sufficiently to deal with such things, then there was every chance that this battle would begin with the Tenth and the Seventh being largely trodden into the ground by giant pachyderms, while

Labienus and his cavalry swept over the remnants, mopping up before flanking the newer legions and cutting them into small pieces.

No pressure.

Silence reigned once more. Fronto listened to it intently, his senses twanging, and even the roar and crash of the waves was starting to get on his nerves now. The tension continued to rise, and he could feel it emanating from the army all around and behind them. Things were building to an inevitable head now, and yet still no command came from the centre and the enemy remained still and in place, waiting.

Something was wrong. He could feel it, like a miscoloured thread slamming into place in a loom, ruining the weave. Without knowing what it was that was coming, though, he could do nothing about it. He fretted in the still silence.

'Come on, Caesar,' called an impatient voice back among the Tenth, earning a murmur of agreement from those men around him.

'Stow that shit, soldier,' snapped a centurion, and silence settled in once more.

What was it?

What?

Then it happened. Somewhere in the midst of the wing, impossible to tell whether it came from the Tenth or the Seventh, the sound of a horn blared out. Fronto felt the colour drain from his face. That was the call for an advance. In moments, other horns were echoing the call, and the entire legionary force of the Seventh and Tenth began to move.

Fronto turned in horror to see the men advancing.

'Halt! Stop!' His bellows were just loud enough to be heard above the thunder of marching feet, and the centurions nearby threw him surprised looks. 'That call was unauthorised,' he bellowed. 'Back into position!'

Centurions along the line began to turn, gesturing to their men to stop, while others, who were as yet unaware of Fronto's counter-orders, were still busily marching forward.

'Shit!'

He turned at a distant hollering to see Postumus racing towards him across the front of the marching legions, who were still surging forth. The man was waving desperately, and Fronto could quite understand why. Now, the Tenth and Seventh were a mess, perhaps a quarter of each legion being halted and turned back by their centurions while the rest marched on towards the enemy. If they didn't manage to pull it together soon, they would be in chaos and a prime target for the enemy.

He turned, dreading what he would see, and sure enough, the enemy had begun to move now in response. If Fronto could stop his legion and Postumus the same with the Seventh, then they could perhaps still be in position and carry out their planned manoeuvre without losing the battle. But still three quarters of the men were moving forward.

To his added horror, a fresh sound cut across the field as Galronus' signallers ordered the cavalry to advance to meet the Gauls of Labienus, unaware that this was all a horrible mistake. Damn it, but now the cavalry were moving, and other calls told him that the archers and the cohorts of the Fifth had heard the call and joined in, their own musicians ordering the advance.

This had all the makings of an almighty disaster.

There was no way to stop it now. The entire wing was moving, bar those few centuries belonging to men who had heard Fronto's desperate order. He had to rescue what he could from this cock-up. The first thing was to change his mind. There was no way of pulling them all back into position now and so instead he pushed Bucephalus into the mess, scattering soldiers out of the way as he made for those centuries busily trying to retreat through their own force.

'Cancel that,' he shouted to the centurions. 'Re-form the line and join in the advance. We're committed now.'

Here and there legionaries began to run forward again, trying to find their original place in the line, forming a solid front. Fronto shivered, wide-eyed, as he moved from unit to unit in the press, counteracting his own previous order and telling them all to join the advance. When this was over he was going to implement some very harsh enquiries, find the musician responsible for this disaster, and stick his horn so far up his rectum he'd fart tunes for the rest of his life.

In short order, he'd made his way among his men, them ducking this way and that out of the path of Bucephalus, sorting things out and turning men around again. Now, his legion was once more marching forward with purpose, and as rapidly as possible rebuilding the front lines. He found himself at the edge of his legion, next to the Seventh and towards the rear. Pausing for a moment as the men thundered past, he rose in his saddle to take stock of the situation.

Things were recovering. Postumus had clearly done much the same as Fronto, and perhaps with more efficiency, for the Seventh were already almost back in formation. He caught sight briefly of the commander now at the rear of his legion, in position, ready for the fight. The man was good, after all, for all his inexperience. Once again, Caesar's intuition in choosing the man for the job was paying off.

He could hear other calls to advance, coming from the centre of the field. This might not have been the plan, but Caesar had clearly realised there was nothing they could do to stop it now. They were committed, like it or not, and so the order had gone out for a general advance, each unit hurrying to fall in line with the wing that had started to move early.

The enemy were coming, headed by those unstoppable grey monsters.

Fronto chewed his lip, looking this way and that. The moment the enemy commander unleashed those beasts, the shit was truly going to rain down on them. What could be done to counter it? He turned to the units of archers and slingers, who had once more shouldered or belted their weapons and were stomping forward towards the fight.

Bollocks to it. The plan would have to work. They were all on the move, but he would still have to pull the same manoeuvre somehow while on the march. Tribunes were converging on him, the chaos resolved, seeking orders, and he waved at them all. 'Get word to every centurion in the Tenth, and someone tell Rabirius Postumus too, so that he can do the same. As soon as the front lines are sixty paces from the enemy they need to stop suddenly, without a general signal blown. I want this to be a complete surprise. The entire legion stops dead at sixty paces, and every man takes a knee instantly. Got that?'

The tribunes, frowning their confusion, nodded, and rode off to distribute the orders. The legions were already closing on the enemy force and timing would be tight. If this was going to work, everyone would have to move fast and with perfect precision. He turned to the commander of the nearest support unit, a five-hundred-strong force of slingers from Sardinia. The prefect saluted.

'At sixty paces, the legion is going to stop and drop. Your men need to be prepared. Have your weapons out and ammunition ready. The moment the men in front of you drop, I want a volley off at those elephants just as we'd planned, only on the move. We'll be closer than originally intended, and all moving towards one another, but if the legionaries have dropped to a knee, you can loose at a low arc and that should make things easier. Pass those instructions along to every unit of archers and slingers. I want the whole thing to happen simultaneously. Got it?'

The prefect saluted and sent an optio running off to the next commander. Fronto turned slowly. The Fifth needed to be warned, and the cavalry. He waved over two tribunes from the Fifth who were moving forward to find out what was happening. He would send them with warning.

This was it. Things had gone horribly wrong, and Caesar would be furious later, so someone was for the chop, but that was only important if they won. Right now, he had to pull off a ridiculous manoeuvre with a heartbeat's precision.

And if it worked, they could still win this.

CHAPTER TWENTY FOUR

Thapsus, 6th April 46 BC

F ronto fell in beside the Sardinian slingers and kept pace with them. Each man sheathed their blade, untied their sling from their belt, and drew a shot from a pouch, all as they walked and without taking their eyes from the ranks in front. Off to the right he could see a unit of Syrian archers nocking arrows and pulling back the strings of their bows while keeping the point low to prevent accidental shots and injuries.

He began to worry about the realistic chances of the manoeuvre they were about to pull off. After all, would the missiles make enough noise even to be heard over the general din of an army marching into battle. And if that noise alone couldn't scare elephants, what made the general think missile shots would? Yet his mind furnished him with a memory of that great, grey beast at the camp when Caesar had ordered a single unit to launch arrows near it, and the sheer panic it had created in the elephant in the training camp, and he remembered that failed ambush near Uzitta and the din of the missiles there. He'd heard arrows and slings launching in masses before but oddly, being primarily a legionary commander, he'd never endured the sound of an entire large army's missile contingent loosing at once from close quarters. There were, by Fronto's estimate, four thousand archers and two thousand slingers ready to loose.

Would it be enough?

They were close enough now that Fronto could pick out shouts and calls among the enemy. His gaze rose above the ranks of the Tenth to those thirty grey giants stomping inexorably towards them, and he shivered, picturing what they would do if they got among the legions at a charge.

Mentally, he counted off the paces as best he could from his relatively poor vantage point at the rear, and was surprised when he still had it between eighty and ninety paces at the moment the legion halted. No signal went out, blasted across the landscape. It all came from the most senior centurion. One shout from the front and the entire legion stopped dead and grounded their shields, dropping to one knee behind them as though taking cover. The very moment the entire legion sank to the ground, granting Fronto a good view at last, thousands of archers and slingers loosed their shots in perfect unison.

Fronto flinched despite himself. The sheer effect of this volley was the whole purpose of the plan, and yet he was not prepared for what happened. The light was almost extinguished by missiles as thousands of stones, lead shots and arrows whizzed and whipped and thrummed through the air in a low arc at the elephants. Every man in the Tenth ducked instinctively, cowering behind their shields.

The noise was horrifying. Fronto felt a moment of panic that he would be made deaf by this move, for in the wake of the missiles' passing all he could hear was a tremendous hissing sound. He shouted for the legion to rise, somewhat redundantly, since a centurion had apparently already done so, and the men were even now coming to their feet. He couldn't hear his own voice, just that deafening hiss.

He stared at the enemy. Those great grey monsters had been stomping inexorably towards them, driven on at a steady pace by the drivers seated on their necks, bearing down on the legionaries. Now, suddenly, those soldiers had stopped and dropped and with a noise like the world crashing in on itself six thousand missiles were flying through the air towards them.

The effect was impressive. Of those thirty giant beasts leading the attack, only two continued forward unperturbed, another faltering but driving on once more as its driver smacked at it repeatedly with a stick. The others, en masse, halted in panic. Some reared, the small wooden castle on their back nearing the vertical and tipping screaming archers and javelin throwers out to fall some distance to the dirt where they were ground under the great beasts' feet. Others did not rear but simply turned, wild-eyed, and ran for it. Those that reared were not far behind them, having thrown their drivers and burdens off, turning and running back the way they had come. All the beasts were peppered with shafts and cut and bleeding all over from endless sling shots.

Even as the archers and slingers stepped back and the legions rose, Fronto could not take his eyes from the carnage before him. Twenty-seven panicked elephants had turned into their own lines, and the light riders and infantry behind them simply did not have the space to get out of the way. Some were mercilessly trampled, ground to a paste under four tons of muscle and bone, others, particularly the riders, were swept out of the terrified beasts' path with a sweep of their powerful trunks or enormous tusks, horses and riders alike actually thrown through the air to land among other horsemen. The monsters were unstoppable in their panic, carving a swathe through the ranks of Scipio's army.

The enemy advance faltered as this disaster continued to play out, but Fronto turned his attention to the three beasts that were still coming. 'Again,' he bellowed into the air in the wake of the missile cloud, still unable to hear his own voice. Nothing happened. No one else nearby could hear him.

Riding over to the slingers, he motioned to loose again and pointed at the three elephants that were faltering, but yet to come to a stop or turn. Fronto continued to yell at the men as he pointed at the elephants, and gradually he began to hear his own voice over that deafening hiss.

Slingers and archers started to loose sporadically, now aiming for those three beasts and specifically for the heads and the drivers who sat just behind them. Some forward thinking centurions at the fore had bellowed out orders, and the front lines of the Tenth and the Seventh alike were now hefting pila and casting them at the approaching beasts, the heavy javelins joining the stones and arrows in pounding at the thick hides of the great beasts.

Fronto felt elation and relief as the first of the three elephants was stopped, an arrow plucking the driver from behind the head and throwing him back to the dusty ground, unseen. Without the man urging it on, the animal halted under a hail of stones and turned, running back into that path of chaos its companions had created.

In moments the second elephant had succumbed, its driver lolling about in his saddle, dead. The animal, covered in wounds, crashed to its knees close enough to the Caesarian lines for the vibration to knock men from their feet. Even as it reeled and tried to rise, legionaries roared and hurled fresh volleys of pila at it until it gave a great cry and fell to its side, shuddering. It took only heartbeats for the last elephant to break and flee, standing alone against legions who continually poured iron-tipped death at it. Fronto watched the enormous beast turn and run.

The enemy army was in chaos. A swathe had been barged through the native contingent, and Fronto could see Juba's royal flag, emblazoned with an elephant, waving sadly among the human wreckage. It was too much to hope that the king himself had been trampled, but the Numidian force had been largely obliterated by their own elephants, a small unit remaining squeezed between heavy infantry and Gallic cavalry, and a sizeable part of that cavalry had been injured or killed or simply had fled in panic as the elephants rumbled through the flesh and bone of their own army, crushing and demolishing in their desperation to be away from the field.

Fronto looked to the left and could see that the army was almost engaged, though he couldn't see far enough to know what was going on at the far flank. He would have to trust that the other officers along the line were handling the fight well. All Fronto could do was deal with his flank. The enemy were still coming, and he could see how the enemy commanders, faced with the loss of their elephants and much of Juba's contingent, had spread the legions to fill the gap, As they closed, the enemy legionaries extended their lines from the troops at the rear in an attempt to engage the Tenth and the Seventh. This could still be a hard fight. Fronto, his ears still hissing beneath the sounds of battle, gave the order, and the Tenth roared and surged forward into the enemy.

* * *

Lucius Munatius Plancus hissed in nervous frustration. Some fool way off to the right had given the signal to move, and the army had done just that. Caesar had been almost apoplectic with rage, given that their entire strategy was based upon the enemy making the first move. As the general had harangued the officers nearby, his face almost puce in colour, men had raced off to try and halt the advance. The moment it had become clear that it could no longer be stopped, the general, wide-eyed and breathing in gasps, had snarled the order for a general advance and had promptly wheeled his horse and made his way to the rear of the army.

Concerned at this uncharacteristically furious behaviour, Plancus, who had been serving as Caesar's second, followed the general, to find him riding at speed towards the medical section. Heart pounding, he'd caught up with the general as the man reined in close to the first hospital tent, and he'd stared in horror as Caesar tried to climb from the saddle but was shaking so vigorously that he couldn't quite manage it.

The man's eyes were dancing around wildly and his face twitching.

Plancus had bellowed for help and swiftly dismounted, rushing over to the general and helping him from the horse with great difficulty. The man was shaking uncontrollably and was trying to speak. It took precious moments as two capsarii rushed over to help, while word was passed inside to a medicus. The physician hurried out and straight to the general, producing a strip of leather from somewhere and jamming it between Caesar's chattering teeth. As Plancus had looked in horror back and forth between the general and the physician, the latter had turned to him.

'Do not be overly concerned. Though it is not widely spoken of, the general suffers from the Alexander sickness. He will work through it without harm now I am here and will be himself in a matter of hours.'

'This has happened before?'

The medicus had nodded. 'It comes and goes, but certain things can trigger these episodes. I am afraid, though, that Caesar will not return to the battle.'

With that the general was loaded onto a stretcher and two orderlies picked it up. As they started to take Caesar away to the tent, the general reached up a shaking hand to halt them, and waved Plancus over. The officer had hurried over, and Caesar had manoeuvred the leather strap in his teeth enough to speak around it with difficulty.

'Win... battle.'

Plancus had stared, but then nodded and saluted. He'd stood for a moment and watched the general disappear into the medical tent, followed by the orderlies and the medicus, and had then run over to his horse and pulled himself up into the saddle, horribly aware that he was now the senior officer in the field, and that overall command had fallen to him.

Everything had gone wrong, and it really needed Caesar to put it right, but that duty had fallen instead to Plancus. What to do? How to turn this around? He kicked his heels and rode over to the best vantage point he could find. The right flank was closest to fully engaging, for that was where this had started. He peered over that way. Despite the disaster being something to do with those legions, Fronto was commanding over there, and Plancus felt he could rely on Fronto to manage. Indeed, even as he watched, a cloud of missiles began to fly there, and Plancus could see the elephants stumble to a halt amid the mess. The right seemed to be safe, or at least as safe as one could hope for right now. The centre was about to meet the enemy, but there was nothing unexpected happening there. That would be a contest of endurance and spirit, for the legions would be more or less evenly matched, and the battle would be won or lost on the wings.

What remained as a worry then was the left flank. There, Plancus could see no cloud of missiles flying. Instead, the legions marched on to meet the force of half of Juba's elephants. That was now the danger point. The right looked as though it might be a place to secure victory, the centre would hold as long as it needed to, but the left was in extreme danger.

Putting heels to flanks, Plancus raced in that direction. The legions there were going to be obliterated, and there had not been the opportunity, thanks to the unexpected advance, for the archers and slingers to deploy and create their cloud of missiles as planned, though clearly somehow Fronto had managed to pull that off. Still, this flank had to be saved. He sucked on his teeth as he rode. Two legions facing the elephants directly, the Eighth and Ninth, with the missile troops behind them, and cohorts of the Fifth in support. Between them and the other legions were the native contingent of mixed horse and infantry, and on the very wing, next to the salt lagoon, Gallic and Germanic riders.

His brow creased. It seemed ironic that he was facing a Scipio and trying to think of a way to overcome elephants, when a century and a half ago, not too far from here, Scipio's most illustrious ancestor had similarly been forced to face elephants under Hannibal's command.

His frown deepened. Scipio at Zama. Was there still time to make that great general's tactics work? He would have to be quick, and the units would have to respond with similar alacrity, but slim chance was better than no chance. Breaking into a gallop, he raced to the flank, bellowing for the nearest Gaetuli to let him through. As they melted aside, he raced into the gap between them and the men of the Fifth. Spotting the senior tribune of the Fifth, he waved at the officer.

'Ready your men to meet elephants, as Scipio did at Zama. The other legions will open the gates for them.'

Hoping the man understood the reference and, indeed, knew his histories, Plancus rode on past the missile troops in their thousands until he spotted a couple of auxiliary prefects deep in conversation as they rode ahead of their units. The pair looked across as Plancus reached them and, starting to become breathless, the officer pointed at them. 'Speak to your peers. All missile troops fall back to the rear, behind the Fifth.'

Leaving them to pass on the message, and knowing that time was as tight as could be, Plancus ploughed on, looking for the commanders of the Eighth and Ninth. Fortunately, both men were sensible enough to be leading from the rear, and he spotted in moments the small knot of tribunes around Hirtius, commanding the Eighth. The realisation that it was Hirtius he would be speaking to was an immense relief. The man might be insufferably dry and officious at times, but he also knew his literature and his histories, and he would know well of Scipio at Zama.

Shouting to get the man's attention, his own gaze was drawn ahead. The elephants were almost upon them. He was out of time. As Hirtius turned, Plancus cupped his hands round his mouth. 'Open up your legions, Aulus. Let them through, like they did at Zama. Zama, you know?'

Hirtius gave him a confused frown, but in moments understanding dawned and he nodded vigorously and started giving out instructions to the tribunes, who in turn raced off shouting to the centurions. Plancus turned to see that a large space was opening up now, for the archers and slingers were falling back behind the Fifth. It had all happened in moments, and they were out of time, but as long as everyone understood what to do, this might still work. The roar of hundreds of men close by, accompanied by the wild trumpeting of elephants, told him that the attack had begun, and he suddenly realised that he was right at the heart of their trap. Kicking his horse urgently, he raced for the wing, where Gallic cavalry were watching with fascination as they continued to move forward in line with the infantry.

It was happening. Gods, but let this work, else the left flank would fold and the battle would be lost before it truly began. Reaching relative safety, Plancus found himself the best available spot to observe, hoping he would not need to continually give out further commands.

It seemed that Hirtius and his fellow legionary officers had just managed to get the orders out to their men in time, for that very moment the elephants hit the Caesarian line. The men of the Eighth and Ninth, instead of bracing themselves or attempting to fight, dropped away in pockets. Wherever an elephant reached the line, the men were falling back and to the sides, the great beasts, surprised, lumbering past and on through the Roman lines. Some of the drivers cheered in victory as their beasts were simply allowed to filter through the ranks of legionaries. Others desperately tried to get their animals to halt, fearing what was coming, but once the elephants were moving through, they moved as a herd, and none of them seemed inclined to stop, even as men drummed them with sticks in wild panic.

In moments, the entire force of thirty elephants was through the Caesarian lines and into an open space where the missile units had so recently been marching. It was then that the elephants' drivers and crews realised their horrible mistake. The front two lines of the legions closed up once more and met the enemy infantry head on as though in a normal fight and nothing unusual had happened, while the rear lines performed a neat about-face that had them facing the elephants, and with the Fifth, the Gaetuli and the Gauls, effectively boxing them in.

The elephants broke into disorganised chaos, for none of the drivers seemed to be working in concord now. Some were trying to move back, turning to retreat to some semblance of safety. Others were attempting to drive on through the Fifth and into the open ground behind the army entire. Still others dithered uncertainly in the open square, unsure what to do.

Plancus wondered if the men were waiting for his orders, so he rose in the saddle and bellowed 'take them down!'

The response was instant, confirming that his men had only been waiting for the order. A short volley of arrows arced up over the Fifth and came down among the elephants. Only a small attack, for the archers had to be wary of hitting their allies, but it triggered panic in some of the elephants, which only increased as the box suddenly closed in from every side. The beasts were swamped by cavalry and infantry, Gallic riders coming in from the left, Gaetuli horse and foot from the right, legionaries from ahead and behind, and all using the longest weapons available, Gallic spears, Roman pila and Gaetuli javelins, all stabbing mercilessly at the animals. Plancus watched as the tactic took effect, elephants crying out and disappearing to the ground amid the press.

It was going to work. They were going to overcome the elephants just as Fronto had done on the right flank. There were still problems occurring, and he could see how a few of the elephants were getting the better of the Caesarian forces, but the majority were simply panicking and being taken down by furious soldiers.

He winced as a gap in the press opened up to grant him a view of the action, and his eyes fell upon a grisly sight. A man in a russet tunic and mail shirt lay screaming on the ground, one of the great beast's feet pressing down on him, covering his entire torso and leaving only limbs protruding, where they thrashed in agony. The man's sword lay nearby next to a shield with the blazon of the Fifth, and his agony continued into death as the foot pressed down and the screaming first became muffled and then disappeared entirely.

Another man of the Fifth, bellowing with rage at his friend's gruesome demise, hurled himself at the great beast, bellowing oaths to Mars even as he hewed and hacked at the leathery skin just above the foot and the puddle of former legionary. His blows certainly drew blood, for the creature suddenly bellowed in pain and its head came down, eyes full of fury, the trunk wrapping around the man's body and lifting him from the ground. The legionary continued to bellow curses. His shield was trapped within the coil along with his body, yet his sword hand remained free and continued to rain blows upon the animal, now hacking and slashing at the meaty trunk.

Suddenly the creature could take no more of this madman causing it constant pain, and the trunk unfurled, the legionary, battered but intact, falling to the ground as the elephant thundered away in pain, looking for a way out. That window onto the fight closed a moment later as legionaries filled his view trying to finish off one of the creatures that was on its knees.

They had done it. The elephants were finished. Scipio's greatest weapon had been nullified, and all that remained now was to best a larger force in the field, something that all knew Caesar was capable of.

But Caesar wasn't commanding now, was he...

* * *

Galronus watched as the Tenth beside them met enemy units that had been expecting to be screened by elephants, but were now exposed and facing the most notoriously successful of Caesar's legions. His own riders had ridden straight into the Gallic horsemen of Labienus and, as to be expected, the battle immediately became a personal affair for them all as ancient tribal disagreements were once more played out, thinly veiled as a Roman quarrel.

Galronus himself had initially ridden with his men, but despite the importance of the fight, he had pulled back before the action. He'd taken a small guard, standard bearer and musician and pulled out from the battle to somewhere near the rear where he found a low rise as a vantage point, watching the fight from behind. He had discovered this morning that it was going to be some time, possibly even a month, as the medic had intimated, before he could join in any fighting. He'd tried six different helmets to find one that was acceptable, but each one hurt more than the last, all of them feeling as though they were made of lead, pressing down on his wounded head like a marble statue plinth. He'd opted in the end to wrap a scarf around his head and make do.

He would be no use in battle yet anyway. Whenever he turned his head too quickly or nodded sharply, he immediately felt nauseous, and the stitches in his scalp pulled painfully.

And so he sat here, watching.

At face value it had been a worrying fight, for the cavalry of Labienus outnumbered his, and were of much the same standard. The chances of victory were not that high. Then

Fronto had pulled his little archery manoeuvre and the elephants had turned and fled in panic, trampling and scattering a whole swathe of the force behind them. By the time Scipio's army had managed to pull itself together, the numbers of cavalry had become much more even, and Galronus had felt a whole lot better about it.

The only problem was that the enemy were men of the tribes, just like his. As long as they had any kind of support they were not going to break and flee. It was not in their nature. And so, the battle on this wing would go on and on until attrition wore down one side or the other sufficiently to end it.

Then he saw the opportunity. If he could separate the riders of Labienus from the rest of the army, he might be able to break their spirit. They had to be on their own, though, with no hope of support for that to happen. With a slow, fierce smile, he turned to the riders around him.

'Find Samaconius and Fronto, as fast as you can. Tell them to concentrate on the African cavalry. Tell Samaconius that once they break, he needs to put the fear of Taranis in Labienus' riders, and then they will break too, but the Africans need to go first.'

As the men raced off with the message, Galronus watched them. In the wake of the elephants' loss, the African riders had found a niche. They had only been fielded as support for the elephants, a unit to mop up the survivors in the great beasts' wake, and now that the elephants had gone, they were accidentally front line troops. Accordingly, their leader had managed to form them into a narrow unit, squeezed between the Gallic cavalry and the Numidian spear men facing Fronto's Tenth. With Galronus' men pressing the Gauls and Fronto hammering the spearmen, the riders were barely involved, managing to hold off one or two enemies here and there, and stay out of much of the fighting. With the loss of the elephants, they and the spearmen represented more or less the last of Juba's real force, and the loss of one of the army's three main commanders from the field could be critical to morale.

They were light skirmishing riders, intended for swift peripheral work, not for facing the armoured might of a legion or the powerful Gallic cavalry. Armed chiefly with a light spear-cum-javelin, dressed only in white tunics and with bare heads, few of them could even claim a shield.

Galronus watched, praying. If the battle were to be a contest of endurance it would run through the morning and the afternoon, and very possibly beyond the hours of daylight, and if that happened, no one could adequately predict the outcome. The only hope was to try and break them, just as Scipio had hoped to do with his elephants.

He saw the fighting change as word reached the two commanders, saw the pressure ease on the very flank as his riders concentrated part of their weight on the African riders. The Tenth were doing the same from the far side, and those light skirmishers with little protection, who had been cowering and staying out of the way were now the prime target for Caesar's best riders and his most powerful legion.

He could not see the actual fighting at the front, but there was a way to keep track of how things were going. At the rear of that force, he could see the standards of King Juba himself, whose riders they were. Galronus had been somewhat surprised that Juba remained locked in battle when his elephants had all been destroyed or driven from the field, yet there he sat, quite close to the banners of Labienus, who was commanding the horse on this wing.

He kept his eyes on those banners, waiting, praying, and willing the Africans to break.

It did not take long. The combined pressure of Fronto's legionaries and the Gallic and Germanic riders crushed the natives' spirit even as it crushed their force, and though Galronus did not know their calls, the sheer panic audible in the warbling horn blasts made their nature plain. They were in retreat. He saw the enemy flank start to collapse. The white shapes and banners were diminishing all the time now, both in numbers and position, butchered and driven back, the red of Fronto's Tenth moving in to fill the gap where they had been, pressing home a breach in the enemy lines, heaving their way between the spearmen and Labienus' cavalry.

'Now,' Galronus urged the gods. '*Now* is the time.'

He watched, breath held, as it changed once more. Juba's standards at the rear began to move, fleeing the field, pulling back from the rebel army. The Numidian king had allied himself to them through Cato's politicking, and had put his own country at risk in order to supply a sizeable contingent for Scipio. And what had been his reward? The almost complete obliteration of his force before Scipio took any real damage. Juba had had enough. The Numidians were leaving.

Now was the time. They had the critical advantage, the chance to break the flank entire.

CHAPTER TWENTY FIVE

Titus Labienus sat astride his mount and watched his peers fail. He had argued with Scipio until he was blue in the face, more than once, against the decision to rely upon the Numidian king's elephants. Such beasts were dangerous and unreliable. Yes, if their attack succeeded they could win the day for you, and their effect was clearly brutal, but they were just as likely to take fright and turn upon their own side in the press, which was precisely what they had done today.

Scipio was too busy trying to please everyone and finish this in a strong position. He took no chances. He wanted to please King Juba by granting him a solid part in any victory, and he wanted Cato to be satisfied so that the man supported him and caused no friction in the coming days, and most of all he wanted to be the hero who won the war and saved the republic. He wanted to beat Caesar without any real threat to his army, so that he could then wash over the republic like a tide, driving men like Marcus Antonius from their positions and reinstating the old order. It was an admirable goal. It was also foolish fantasy.

Labienus had served with Caesar for years, his faithful lieutenant, and he knew that their enemy was only going to be overcome with incredible effort, ingenious strategy and an extremely healthy dose of luck. Had he been in command, this would have been over months ago, but every time Labienus had espied an opportunity, and there had been a few, Scipio had failed to put adequate support his way, and it had come to naught each time. And now here he was consigned to playing the guard on the flank while Scipio and Juba lorded it at the centre as the overall commanders.

It had come as absolutely no surprise to him to see the elephants panic and turn on their own. Indeed, he had made sure that his cavalry were positioned out of danger as far as possible. As Scipio had revealed his plan for deployment of the forces, Labienus had managed to change things so that Juba and all his spearmen and African horsemen were put behind his elephants. Let Juba bear the brunt of his own failures. Consequently, when the great beasts turned and fled, the majority of the carnage was visited upon other natives, with only minor damage to Labienus' horse. Admittedly, that brought his force to more or less equality with those of Caesar, but he was confident he could secure victory anyway.

Then things had begun to fall apart even further. Labienus had watched with a sneer as Juba flew into a rage a hundred paces away, at the rear of his own units. The Numidian king had watched his elephants beaten and then turn and crush his own men. Indeed, the king had been forced to flee to one side to avoid being trampled by his own beasts, and his best royal banner now lay broken in the dust. He had taken out his frustrations on his senior officers, even slapping some of them across the face.

Then something had changed at the front. Labienus had not been able to see precisely what was happening, but clearly fresh pressure had come to bear on the last of Juba's forces. His spearmen were being slowly but inexorably pushed back, unable to hold against the heavy infantry of the Tenth and the Seventh, but now those Numidian riders were being driven back at speed. Juba was enraged. Labienus could see him, striking a slave with a stick in fury, and when one of his officers rode back from that beleaguered horse unit, apparently delivering fresh unwelcome news, the Numidian king tore a sword from the grip of one of his guards and impaled the unfortunate officer in his rage.

Moments later the calls to retreat rang out among Juba's forces. Labienus cast a withering look in the king's direction. He had made such a grand arrival and lorded it over most of the Roman commanders, treating only Scipio as an equal, he had made such a thing of his elephants and his royal legions, and Scipio had done everything he could to placate and accommodate the Numidian.

And now, when the critical moment had arrived, it had turned out that Juba's forces were worth next to nothing, breaking easily and causing untold damage to their allies. The horns were blowing across the Numidian forces and they were beginning to pull back. Labienus looked this way and that. The Tenth would be pushing into the gap, which he was fairly sure meant that Fronto was leading them, for the man was ever proactive and fierce. If Juba's army left, the cavalry would be cut off on the wing, surrounded by legionaries and the Gallic riders still loyal to Caesar. If that happened, it was all over. His riders were good, and they would hold as long as possible, but no unit could survive pinned on the periphery between heavy cavalry, heavy infantry and the sea. It would only be a matter of time. And if the Numidians left, their only hope was to spread out and attempt to hold the gap that was left and which the Tenth would be trying to exploit. That would only be possible if Scipio ordered his legions to spread wider too and help close the gap. But the best possible solution would be for his pointless majesty not to panic and pull out.

Waving to his second to keep control, he wheeled his horse and rode towards the Numidian royal party. Guards saw his approach and made to block his way, requiring him to beg an audience, and Labienus, lip wrinkling into a snarl, ignored them entirely and bore down on the group at speed. The two soldiers, surprised, had to dance their horses out of the way unless they wished to launch an attack on a senior Roman, which would be foolish in the circumstances, and Labienus was left with a clear path to the royal party. The scene that greeted him was not encouraging. Two officers and three couriers lay dead near the king, his favoured executioner still standing with a great and heavy dripping blade. Slaves and courtiers cowered in panic all around. Labienus reined in, scanning the scene with growing disgust before fixing the Numidian king with a forceful glare.

'Rescind your calls for retreat Juba,' he demanded.

The king, shocked at such a direct approach, sat wide-eyed as one of his lackeys snarled 'How dare you speak to his majesty thus?'

'Shut your fat painted face, eunuch. I am addressing the king, not you.' He turned back to Juba. 'I know your forces have been brutalised, and you must be feeling humbled and embarrassed by your failure, but it you hold now, you can turn this into something noble. You can help save the cause and stop Caesar's men overrunning the field.'

'We have lost,' the king replied in a cold, matter-of-fact tone.

'No. Your men have broken and failed you, but only you can pull them together and stop them panicking. They look to their master. As a battle this is far from lost, for we still outnumber the enemy, but the moment your flag leaves the field, the heart will fail the army, and *then* we will have lost. Stay and hold, and with my riders we can still recover this wing and defeat the enemy.'

Juba's face slid from haughty superiority to nervous uncertainty slowly as he looked this way and that. 'I should not have come. This is not my fight. Cato persuaded me, for he is like a snake with a hypnotic way, and I found myself agreeing with him. And even then, I would not have committed had Scipio not all but begged me for extra troops. My own kingdom is being constantly pressed by the king of Mauretania and that Roman dog Sittius. I need to be there. This was a mistake.'

Labienus rolled his eyes. 'Don't be blind, Juba. Bocchus of Mauretania is Caesar's ally, and Sittius is a mercenary in Caesar's pay. They only attack your kingdom to stop you helping *us*. Break that chain and hold with us. When we beat Caesar, his allies who threaten your throne will melt away. Do not be a fool. Fight the master, not the lackeys.'

'No,' snapped Juba. 'No, this was a mistake. I go.'

'If you leave, it will be the end for all of us, yourself included. Do not delude yourself. As soon as you go, the flank will crumble and the army will fail. Caesar will ride across us all to his victory, but for those of us who commanded here there will be no clemency. You will be hunted down across Africa like a dog and butchered, just like the rest of us. You can only make it through this well if you stand and we win.'

But Juba said nothing more, waving his men to the west and turned his back on Labienus. The Roman clenched his teeth against such stubborn idiocy and put his hand to his sword hilt, almost prepared to draw it and challenge the foolish king, though half a dozen of the royal guards closed in to a protective arc, their own hands on their blades. There was nothing he could do.

Turning, he saw the Numidians in full rout now, the spearmen and horsemen alike falling back more in panicked clumps than in units of orderly withdrawal. He could see the standards and the banners of the Tenth moving behind them, driving the fleeing Numidians on in their terror. Every moment saw it move more from military withdrawal to panicked flight.

His gaze flicked to the south, past the running feet and racing hooves of Juba's army. There was no movement from the many legions at the centre. Scipio's heavy infantry were strongly contesting the core against their Caesarian counterparts, and they could certainly hold, but they were making no attempt to re-form and to fill the gap left by the

Numidians. Perhaps Scipio thought Juba would recover, or perhaps that Labienus would take up the slack. Whatever the case, unless Scipio's legions started to move now to hold the line, it was all over.

He turned back to the riders of his own force. They were *his* men. Good men. In those first years in Gaul he had seen something in the Gallic character that Rome could use. He had bemoaned their near extinction in those years, and it was partly Caesar's brutal handling of a war that could have been achieved with more negotiation and less steel, had pride not been such a factor, that had driven him to turn away from the general. Caesar was determined to rule Rome. His every success was another nail in the crucifix of the republic. He would be another Juba. Another Mithridates. Another Ptolemy. And to stop that happening, Labienus had taken Caesar's prized Gallic cavalry away and thrown in his lot with the republicans. Now, too late, he was learning that their values were strong, but their leadership weak. Without Pompey to lead them, they were mere pups on the battlefield. Scipio might outrank him, but with a decade of service to Caesar, Labienus would out-soldier the man any day.

And that was how he knew they had lost. Scipio would be merrily pushing away at the centre. He, Afranius, Petreius, Piso and the rest would be entirely unaware of the impending collapse of their army. He was challenged in that supposition momentarily as a figure appeared, pushing his way between the fleeing Numidians. Petreius, with a small bodyguard, was wide-eyed.

'What is happening?'

'Juba runs. The flank crumbles. Scipio fails to react.'

'It is Scipio who sent me to sort this.'

'Then he is too late,' Labienus said flatly. 'A hundred heartbeats ago he needed to push his legions out and plug the gap. Now Caesar's Tenth and Seventh control it instead. You have a choice to make, Petreius. Will you ride back and endure defeat with Scipio at the centre or stay here with me and make a valiant last stand?'

Petreius stared at him. 'It is not over yet, Titus. I will chase down Juba and bring him back.'

'No you won't. Chase the coward-king if you like, but he will not return, and when you do Caesar's bull banner will flutter across this field.'

Petreius gave him another look of disbelief and turned, racing off after the departing king. Labienus gave him no further heed. Turning back to his own men, he became aware of new noises on this flank. His blood chilled. He had heard those before, at the hill near Uzitta. Roman horns and carnyxes alike blaring out battle songs of the Gallic tribes from long before Rome had come. And along with it, rhythmic chants of the gods. They were coming from Caesar's cavalry, but from the sound of the instruments used, they were coming from the Tenth as well.

He closed his eyes and shook his head, then opened them to the very sight he expected. His riders were unsettled. They were being contested as strongly as ever by the enemy cavalry at the front, but they were being pressed back from the side now, by the ranks of the Tenth. They were already being forced out into the surf, further and further from help, and every honk or chant or heave of the legions was robbing them further of their will to fight.

His precious Gallic horse, the men who had followed him all the way from Gaul for the cause, were breaking. He could not blame them. Abandoned by their allies, cut off from their legionary counterparts who had failed to send any support, they were now trapped against the sea and outnumbered two to one by men who were triumphant and full of spirit.

It was over.

He turned to his small knot of companions. 'Send word to every officer: do not sacrifice yourself for these fools. Take your men and ride for Hadrumetum and then north. We will make a stand at Utica, but if they stay here until Scipio decides all is lost, everyone will die.'

With bleak expressions, his men nodded and saluted, scattering to pass word. The job could have been done quicker with a single call from a musician, which would have been picked up and passed on, but that was not a good idea. The enemy would hear the call and press for every kill they could make while they could. Moreover, the call would be picked up by other units across the line, and Scipio would despise Labienus for undermining his command. Disseminated orders by word of mouth meant that many of his riders might manage to flee the field and regroup without being destroyed in ranks before they could pull back.

Labienus left them to it, face ashen, knowing that he had effectively ended the battle, but seeing no realistic alternative. They had to leave while they still could. Every moment they stayed now put more and more men in danger. They needed to withdraw and regroup and then fight a second battle with better command. With less Scipio.

Turning, he rode through the last of the fleeing Numidians, coming worryingly close to the banners of the advancing Tenth, and made for the small command group he could see on the hillside behind. In what felt like moments, he was along the lines and climbing that slope to where Scipio sat with a face like thunder.

'Labienus, what are you doing here? You should be consolidating your men and regaining the flank.'

'The flank is lost, Metellus Scipio, and with it the battle. Juba has fled, and the gap left is now filled by Caesar's veterans. My men are isolated and being driven into the sea. Juba's flight and your failure to counter the problem have left me with no alternative. My men are beginning their withdrawal as carefully as they can.'

Scipio glared at him. 'Withdraw? We still outnumber them, Titus. If your men withdraw, we will be flanked and the battle lost.'

Labienus gave his commander a narrow-eyed and angry look. 'You have already been flanked. The Tenth and the Seventh have driven the Numidians from the field and cut my riders off. I can no longer get back to them, and all I can hope is that enough get away to give us a force for next time.'

'There can be no next time,' Scipio spat. 'We have rolled the dice here, and here the game will be won or lost.'

'Then the game is lost, but I intend to play on. I am taking my sestertii from the table now and finding *another* game. Utica still has a garrison, and Cato has control there. The more men we get back to Utica, the better our chances of winning next time.'

'There *will be* no next time,' shouted Scipio, repeating himself.

'Then the cause is lost and you will not leave this field alive. For my part I shall report to Cato and prepare to fight on. What you do now is your own affair, but I implore you to save as many men as you can. Whatever happens to you, those of us brave enough and sensible enough to see that we are done here will need all the manpower we have at Utica.'

With that he turned his back on Scipio and the doomed army, and put his heels to his horse's flank, riding west.

* * *

Lucius Nonius Asprenas stood at the parapet of the works around Thapsus and cupped a hand to his ear.

'Something is definitely afoot. I can hear it. What about you, Centurion?'

Atenos frowned, listening hard. There was definitely the sound of large-scale movement in the town, though what precisely that meant he could not say. His gaze moved across the siege works and then back to the town. He shouldn't be here at all, officially.

He had commanded that camp to the south throughout the night and had sent out scouts at first light, who had scoured the land and reported back that both camps had now been entirely abandoned and that there was no sign of enemy forces in the area. Tracks led off only towards the north, around the far side of the lagoon, and that could only mean that whoever had commanded there through the night had eventually decided to join the rest of Scipio's army facing Caesar. Consequently, Atenos had deliberated only another hour, and had finally decided that commanding an untroubled beach was a waste of time. He was essentially disobeying Fronto's orders, but they were stupid orders, and he would argue the matter later. For now, he had brought his two cohorts to Thapsus and reported in at the siege works there, before he marched off to help with the fight.

Arriving little more than an hour ago, he had been informed that the battle had already been joined a few short miles to the west, but Asprenas, the man Caesar had left in command, had flatly refused to allow Atenos to march west to join them. When the centurion had, rather indignantly considering he was addressing a man of far superior rank, demanded an explanation, Asprenas had turned an equally forceful look back at him.

'Because whatever happens there will be decided by those already present and two more cohorts will make no difference. However, just as Fronto left you out of affairs with a small garrison, so I am here watching Thapsus with barely enough men to man the siege lines. You and your cohorts will make a huge difference here, compared to a small one there. I therefore commandeer you and your cohorts for the defence of the Thapsus lines. And if you think to defy that command, bear in mind that you have disobeyed your orders in coming here, and I might be tempted to support your decision if you help me, but by gods I'll see you stripped of that crest if you disobey me too.'

Atenos had been so impressed with the man he'd swiftly found himself saluting and sending his men out to join those of Asprenas.

When he had asked the man why he felt that he needed any more men than he already had, Asprenas had pointed towards the northern shore. 'See those men over there?'

'Yes?'

'Look like solid legionaries, don't they?'

'They do.'

'Good equipment is all. Half of them are camp slaves and sick-listers. At best they will have a good go at throwing a pilum or sticking the correct end of a gladius in the enemy, but they have no training and half of them have never held a sword in their lives.'

'And you have them manning the defences?'

'Caesar left me virtually no one. Even my body slave Dilius is out there and armed, and the sharpest thing he's ever held is a sponge. If I wanted these lines to look fully manned, I had to make it up as I went along.'

'I have to commend you,' Atenos muttered. 'They look good.'

'They have to,' Asprenas replied. 'Even with your men, the enemy garrison in there now outnumbers us five to one, and their commander Vergilius is a good man. If he suddenly decides he doesn't want to be besieged there is little I can do about it.'

Atenos had agreed and had spent the next hour or more helping to reorganise the forces, content that they would be able to keep the garrison of Thapsus sealed up tight. Now, though, he felt a chill at the sounds from the place. If that was not the garrison of Thapsus on the move, then the general populace had decided to have an impromptu festival.

'They must know that the battle has begun.'

Asprenas nodded. 'The withdrawal of most of the besieging force and the disappearance of the ships make that fairly clear.'

'And it's a large garrison.'

'Large enough, yes.'

'And we're less than an hour from the battlefield. Imagine what difference they would make if they came up behind Caesar's lines and launched a fresh assault.'

Asprenas winced.

'Exactly,' Atenos said. 'I think they're about to make a sortie.'

The commander tapped his chin. 'Where, though. Our siege works are good, and the remains of the fleet would stop any ships leaving, not that there are any.'

Atenos listened to the sounds. He'd thought them centred in the north of the city, and now he was sure that they'd moved further north yet. 'What about the shore?'

'What?'

'If they come out of the sea gate near the port, they could move along the shore line. Our defensive works only go as far as the water, but the fleet cannot get close enough in the shallow water to stop them. There is a clear passage between our lines and the ships through which a cohort or more could move if they were determined enough.'

Asprenas shook his head. 'They would be knee or even thigh deep. They'd have to wade past us, those who weren't on horses, anyway.'

'And yet anywhere else they need to climb ditches and ramparts and fences and the like, or swim out towards enemy triremes. When you think of that, does it seem any less likely.'

The commander peered that way. 'The sound is emanating from that side of the town, certainly. We cannot afford to let them past.'

Atenos turned to his signaller. 'Pull every third man all the way along the siege line and send them to the northern shore fortification. Have them all fully armed with pila, and if any of them have non-regulation darts or slings, bring them with them.'

The signaller saluted and ran off, grabbing friends to help, and the two officers looked at the city. 'That is what's happening. Can we hold them?'

'We have to.'

The two men began to move along the lines towards the shore, watching. The movement of men concentrating in the north was slow enough and sporadic enough that with luck it might go unnoticed in the city, and the officers found themselves at the northernmost fortifications swiftly, overlooking the water. They could see Aquila's triremes out to sea, kept too far out by the water depth to be of much use.

'Here they come,' Atenos said as a distant rumble and clatter announced the opening of a gate. Even as men poured forth from that doorway in full kit, the Caesarians could hear the shouting of the people of Thapsus, terrified and furious at the garrison that was now abandoning them to their fate. The legionaries hurtled along the edge of the port that had remained unused and empty for days now thanks to Aquila's blockade, and down the edge to the shore itself. The Caesarian fortifications marched out into the water to a depth of perhaps two feet, and the moment the emerging soldiers took in the defences, they adjusted their angle, heading for the shallow water to try and pass around the end of the siege works. There were hundreds of them, and Atenos knew that was only the start, for the garrison would number thousands. They had to turn the tide while it was still small, still the vanguard, else they could easily be swamped.

As they moved to the shore, his eyes on the enemy, Asprenas stumbled, swearing, and came to a halt. 'Damn it, there are rocks everywhere in this land.'

Atenos looked down, and when he looked back up he was grinning. 'The slaves and the camp followers, they cannot be relied upon to throw a pilum. It's a hard skill to master, and a novice will just land it sideways or arse-first. No point in wasting them. Anyone not trained in it, give them a rock. They're everywhere, and everyone has thrown rocks as a child.'

Asprenas joined in with his own smile. 'Quite right. See to it.'

Atenos gave the orders and as the two men made their way to the corner of the fort, the best observation post. It was almost laughable to watch, and Atenos had to keep reminding himself that this really was not a comedic moment, but represented a very real threat to the success of Caesar's army. And yet he couldn't help but smile at the sight of hundreds of legionaries slogging slowly through the surf at waist depth, moving at a veritable crawl and carrying their shields over their heads, upside down to contain their swords and all that metalwork they could not afford to bring into contact with salt water.

As the men began to appear at this corner, thickening the lines constantly, some veterans and gripping pila with narrowed eyes, others conscripted slaves holding rocks the size of their fist, Atenos looked to Asprenas. 'The honour is yours, sir.'

The commander nodded. 'No need for a volley here, men. Mark a target and hit him at your own pace. Good luck.'

In moments, pila and rocks were hurtling forth from the rampart into the slow moving and troubled members of the Thapsus garrison. Cries of pain, consternation and outrage rang out from the enemy as they struggled on along the beach, taking an endless pounding. All along the trudging line, men fell with every heartbeat, struck by pila or smashed with rocks, and soon bodies were floating in the water as much as they were wading through it, the surf turning a pretty shade of pink as it washed up to the beach.

As they came ever closer, so the barrage became ever thicker and, realising that they were losing a large number of men so easily, a centurion gave the order to move out of range. Moments later the line of wading solders were heading out into deeper water until it reached their bellies, then their chests, and finally their armpits. There, out of range of all but the best shots on the walls, they waded on, slower than ever, hardly moving at all.

Their folly became apparent a moment later. Though they were now safe from Asprenas and his soldiers, there was a distant thud, a strange whooshing sound, and one of the men disappeared in a spray of water and body parts as a ball of stone almost a foot across struck him, obliterating him in an instant.

The entire column stopped and turned in horror at the realisation that in avoiding the stones and spears of Asprenas, they had moved within range of Aquila's ships. A bolt loosed from on board passed right through another legionary, leaving a crimson stripe through the water as the man cried out and then disappeared beneath the surface only to reappear a moment later, face down and bobbing on the tide.

Men began to pull away, back inland, only to fall foul once more of stones and pila hurled from the defences. Soldiers continually fell, shouting, into the surf. It was a disaster, and some officer clearly realised as much, for moments later the recall blared out from the walls of Thapsus. The garrison turned and began to wade back towards the town. Even as they went they were continually pounded with stones, pila and missile shots from the ships. Atenos conservatively estimated the enemy dead a somewhere in the region of two hundred by the time they were finally out of range once more and retreating through the city's seaward gate. The beach was strewn with bodies, washing back and forth with the tide, the water pink, though the pigment faded with every few heartbeats as the sea diluted the blood of their victory.

Taking a deep breath, Asprenas turned to Atenos. 'Still think I was wrong to keep you here?'

The Gaul threw the commander a grin. 'I think we've done the general proud, sir. We may just have saved his arse here, and I can guarantee I've had more fun than Fronto.'

The commander laughed. 'Good. Agreed. Let us lift a cup of good wine in celebration and hope that things are going so well for Caesar.'

CHAPTER TWENTY SIX

G aius Astala raised his shield to take another powerful blow. The Caesarian legionaries facing them were unbridled in their hateful violence, and not for the first time Astala regretted having left his farm in the village of Urta and taking the offered place in Scipio's grand army of Africa. Eight months he had now been a legionary, granted citizenship on the authority of the famous Cato and thereby eligible for the legion. He had trained fast and distinguished himself early, being raised to the rank of optio in the service of a centurion from Thugga, and had been proud of it all.

Better still, he had been *confident*. To a man like Astala from rural Africa, Caesar was little more than a name, yet another Roman politician involving himself in local affairs, just like the men who purported to rule Africa. Then Caesar had come, as the great Scipio had said he would, and the man had been woefully unprepared, short of supplies and men, totally inferior to the force awaiting him.

Scipio had moved his army around time and again, skirmishing with Caesar but never engaging him, and Astala continued in confidence, certain that Scipio had the right of it and knew what he was doing, for he was reckoned the most important man in Africa. And finally, that great and important general had brought them to Thapsus with the intention of bringing Caesar to battle and destroying him once and for all.

Astala had been strong and ready. He had trained for this for months, and he knew every move the trainers had taught. He had a better edge than most, for years of farm work had made him strong and hearty, and he stood half a head above anyone else in the century. As they had charged the enemy, he had felt a curious mix of fear and fierce joy unlike anything he'd felt before, and realised now why soldiers continued to fight and serve despite the danger of the career. It was a heady thrill.

Then, over the ensuing half hour, that had all changed. The mix had slid in favour of fear, and finally the fierce joy was all but gone, for the fighting went on and on with incredible brutality, and though he had killed three men so far, or so he believed, he had taken three wounds for it, each not quite enough to put him out of the fight, but when combined they were beginning to sap both his strength and his will.

Then, a hundred heartbeats or so ago, rumour had filtered through the legions that Juba of Numidia had fled, taking his army with him. Astala had been as shaken by that as he had been after the episodes with the elephants, though any African farmer could tell a general how foolish it was to rely on the great beasts in a fight. Astala had continued to fight, continued to believe. Juba had only been an ally, brought in to bolster the general's numbers, after all. And of what value was the king of Numidia to the republic?

Then new word had come that the cavalry on the sea shore had broken. If reports were true, filtering down by word of mouth alone, the horse had been left cut off by Juba's flight and had fought on only long enough to get themselves free of the enemy before they too broke and ran. Astala was new to soldiering, and he was no strategist, but even to him that surely meant that Caesar's troops were now coming round the left side of the army, trapping them.

Astala continued to fight, taking another wound on his forearm and butchering another of the never-ending tide of enemy legionaries. Another hundred heartbeats of blocking with his shield and thrusting with his blade, and fresh murmuring arose to his right, a groan of dismay rippling through the army. Fresh disaster burned through the ranks on the wings of rumour. The left flank had broken, the cavalry there unwilling to remain and fight, apparently, when their brethren on the far wing had already withdrawn.

What were they going to do? Someone had said early on as they had marched at one another that Caesar had put his best legions on the wings. If the men Astala was fighting were not Caesar's best, he couldn't imagine how fierce *those* legions were, and now both ends of the army had crumbled and fled, so Caesar's best would be flanking them, trapping them.

He turned to find the centurion, but remembered seeing him fall not long ago. Damn it, but that put Astala in charge, and he had the distinct feeling that now was a bad time to be in command of a century in this army. No call had yet been given to withdraw, and so they fought on. Men were looking at him now, awaiting a command.

'Fight on,' he shouted to the men of his century. 'Fight on for Rome. For Africa. For Tanit and Jove.'

And they did, they fought hard, and redoubled their efforts even as every fresh rumour rippled through the legion. The Caesarians had surrounded them now and only a direct retreat was left open to them. All the cavalry had gone. The reserves had refused to commit and had abandoned the field. Every rumour made the future bleaker, until the most disastrous of all filtered through to him. One of the tribunes had decided that they were done for and had gone to find the general to seek his permission for an orderly withdrawal, only to discover that the great Scipio was gone.

At this, Astala had felt the first real pang of fear. Leaving his men to it, he struggled back through the lines of legionaries, becoming aware as he did so that he was not alone in this. Men were abandoning the fight and heaving their way through their own units all across the field in an attempt to flee. Did they think that was what Astala was doing? No, he was made of sterner stuff. He was going to disprove the latest rumour.

It took some time to heave his way through the army to the rear, and as he did so the scale of the disaster became apparent, for the rear lines were already in flight. Indeed, more and more men were running for the defences of the camp a few hundred paces behind them. His eyes fell upon a centurion, a grizzled and scarred man, clearly a veteran, who was grabbing men as they passed, turning them round and pointing them at the enemy, bellowing for them to stand and fight.

'Where is the general?' Astala bellowed to the man as he closed on him.

'Fuck knows,' was all the centurion replied, turning his back on this questioning optio. The officer grabbed at a legionary fleeing past him in panic and the soldier simply slammed his sword hilt into the centurion's face, shattering it. The centurion cried out in a gagging, muffled voice through his broken visage and fell, to be trampled underfoot by fleeing legionaries.

Astala stared.

And then he started to run too. What else was there to do? The army was breaking up now like a puddle of ice on a warm day. There was no point in trying to fight any more. First he ran to the most open space he could see, which lay to the left, but as he made his way into clearer land, he could see the bull banners of Caesar's legionaries that way, and beyond them a vast sea of cavalry, whooping as they came in to surround the routed army.

He turned and made for the camp. Running as fast as his legs could carry him, he leapt the ditch and scrabbled up the rampart, clambering over the fence of sudis stakes, ignoring the pain of the sharpened timbers as they dug into him. Men were flooding into the camp, and he had the momentary feeling that perhaps it was not over. They would hold the camp and make a defence of it, keeping Caesar's howling monsters at bay.

But that was not to be. There was no sign of any officer above the rank of centurion, and no standards or musicians or flags. Just running legionaries. Nobody was even bothering to try and pull things together. The battle was done and there was nothing else but flight and safety. Those men who were flooding into the camp only paused to grab a loaf of bread or a spare weapon, and they were off, running for the far gate, seeking any copse or gulley in which to hide while the battle ended in blood and defeat.

Astala could see the cavalry coming around that side now, trying to hem in those men fleeing through the camp, and so he changed tack and made for the camp's north gate, running across the flow of panicked humanity. Now, half the men he could see were clearly Caesar's, butchering with howling glee as they ran down the fleeing army. Astala, panic nipping at his heels, raced from that gate and off to the north, towards the shore.

As he neared the sea, seeking a safe way out, he realised there was no sanctuary to be found there. The shoreline was filled with triremes, each rammed with archers and artillery, and arrows and bolts and rocks hurtled from them in clouds, pulping and pinning fleeing soldiers. It was a disaster.

Something hit him in the back and he fell, pain wracking him. He hit the dusty ground hard and lay there, waiting for the killing blow. It never came. Men ran past his prone form, some in panic, others bellowing war cries. Twice, men actually trod on him as they passed, but realising that this was his only chance of survival, he remained still and let it happen. He was covered in blood and lying on the ground, to all intent and purpose just one more corpse among so many.

He lay there until the men ran past him and even then, as silence descended, he remained still. Finally, when all that he could hear were groans and cries and prayers and the gluttonous cawing of carrion feeders, he looked up.

The victorious enemy were a distance away now, hunting down more and more men. Other Caesarian soldiers were already moving among the fallen, killing those who still lived and looting the bodies. His safety was an illusion. Soon they would find him and kill him. He looked into the cold glassy eyes of the body to his left and realised that the man, for all he looked so much like Astala, was actually one of Caesar's. It was hard to tell, really, apart from the colour of the crest and scarf, and the shield, which bore Caesar's bull.

Realising that he now had a chance, he swiftly ripped off his helmet with the crest and pulled free the blue scarf that marked him out. Grasping the red scarf from the dead legionary, he pulled it loose and shook it before tying it around his own neck. He reached out and grasped the man's fallen shield and used it with a certain amount of pain to pull himself halfway up. Whatever had hit him in the back had been stopped by his chain shirt, but by Tanit it hurt anyway, and every muscle screamed as he pulled himself up.

Suddenly, hands were around his arms and on his shoulders, helping him up. Two legionaries in Caesar's colours were looking at him with concern. 'Are you alright mate?'

'I'm... I'm fine,' he replied, keeping his voice low, trying to mask the worst of his clearly African accent. The men helped steady him, and once he was straightened on his feet they slapped him lightly on the shoulder in a comradely manner and then ran on, bellowing to one another. Astala turned slowly. A capsarius was approaching, fishing in his leather bag.

'Don't move, I'm coming,' the medic said.

Astala nodded with a sigh. On balance, things could be a lot worse.

* * *

Caesar sat up sharply, raising a disapproving 'tsk' from the medicus, who stood a few paces away stitching a shoulder. The general lolled for a moment, looking as though he might faint, but gradually steadied himself, rubbing the back of his head.

'It goes well?'

Fronto and Plancus looked at one another and then back to the general. 'A little *too* well now. Some of the troops are ignoring the commands to fall back to the standards. The moment the enemy broke, the legions roared and chased after them like hunting dogs.'

'The enemy have broken? We have won?'

'The battle is won,' Plancus confirmed. 'The elephants were driven away, with a combination of your strategy and that of the great Scipio at Zama. They left a great hole in the right wing which Fronto and Galronus exploited, and in short order the Numidians were broken. Juba left the field first, leaving the cavalry at that flank trapped and exposed. They fled soon after, and the moment that happened we completely flanked the rebel army.'

'They tried to rally at the camp,' Fronto went on, 'but it was a shambles. There was no one there above the rank of tribune to take command, and none of the legionaries would listen to the junior officers of another legion. The defence they pulled together was paltry, and our men swarmed over the ramparts and put them to flight.'

'And the enemy commanders?'

Plancus huffed. 'We have taken a few lessers, but the important leaders all managed to flee in the chaos. Common rumour has it that Petreius left with Juba, who was running for home. Labienus is said to have rallied his cavalry some way to the west and headed for Hadrumetum.'

Caesar shook his head. 'Labienus is cleverer than that. He cannot defend Hadrumetum with cavalry, and the garrison there will have been committed in the battle. He will make for

Utica and Cato, the only man left who can take control of Africa. What of Scipio?'

'No idea, I'm afraid,' Fronto admitted. 'Of he, Piso, Considius, Afranius and the rest there is no sign. They all fled. But they cannot have fled with much more than a small personal guard, for the army was in total disarray. Even now our senior officers are attempting to stop the slaughter, but the troops are not listening. That is why we need you. It is bordering on mutiny, and I fear only their general's command will halt the killing and looting.'

Caesar's face hardened. 'Let them have their rapine and vengeful slaughter.'

'What?'

The general straightened a little more. 'We dragged them from their last mutiny with the promise of loot, and they have been patient and loyal, enduring much these past three months. They are due whatever they can take from Scipio's camp, and they vent months of frustration on the enemy. Let them kill and loot until night falls.'

Plancus' face filled with disapproval. 'General, those men that are being butchered are *Romans*.'

'No, Lucius, they are not. Most of them are recent native levies formed into legions, and those few who are veterans are rebels against the senate and the people of Rome. They have forfeited their rights of citizenship by standing against us. I will not rein in the men. Let them annihilate Scipio's army. Let there be few enough left after this that none can re-form them to stand against us.'

Fronto frowned. 'I don't much like this, sir.'

'Noted. Now leave me. I am not fully recovered yet. When the sun sets have the ad signum blown from every horn and pull the men back. Until then, leave them to their victory.'

The two officers saluted stiffly and departed into the open. Salvius Cursor was standing by the medical tent door, his praetorians in evidence. Clearly he had overheard. 'Trying to save the world again, Fronto?'

'Just my little corner of it, Salvius. The general wasn't having it, though.'

Salvius Cursor fell in alongside the pair as they walked away from the tent. In the distance the roar of the ongoing struggle was still audible, and the army could be seen across the enemy camp and beyond, moving in units and swamping what was left of Scipio's force. 'The general is right, Fronto,' Salvius Cursor said. 'This is an antidote to mutiny, but most importantly we need the beaten enemy to stay beaten.'

'Yes, corpses don't fight back,' Fronto said acidly.

'You cannot have sympathy. Look at what they've done.'

'Where do *you* draw the line, Salvius?' Fronto spat. 'How do you separate out the good men that are being butchered, eh?'

'Good men? Who stood with the rebels?'

Fronto stopped and jabbed a finger into Salvius' chest. 'Tullius Rufus. I remember him from more peaceful days in Rome. A good man, who spent his life in service to the state. I met his wife and children a few years ago before we ended up on different sides. Two boys and a girl. And I watched him die an hour ago. He was holding out his arms in surrender and some oaf put a pilum through him. Pompeius Rufus took a bloody wound in the arm that he was holding up in peace and he only lives because one of my centurions got between him and the legionary who was about to finish him off.'

Salvius shook his head. 'You are being sentimental, Fronto. Our officers have children, and do you think Scipio would have been kinder? Both of those men would yet have stood against us. Look at Petreius and Afranius. We spent months winkling them out of Ilerda, and Caesar's clemency resulted in them going free, only to come here and build a new army while we were in Greece and Aegyptus. This might be unsavoury, but it is necessary. The enemy has to be destroyed to such an extent that Africa can no longer stand against us.'

Fronto lapsed into unhappy silence. He didn't like it, but there was logic to Salvius' words. Taking a deep breath, he turned to the other two. 'I feel the need to look for reason at the bottom of a wine jar. Let's find Galronus and celebrate this nightmare being over.'

* * *

Thapsus, 7ᵗʰ April 46 BC

The officers stood in a small group at the centre of the siege lines, the highest point and with the best overall view of the city. The garrison remained resolutely shut up in Thapsus, rebel banners fluttering all around, and Caesar's army, now sated and once more under control, remained in garrison in droves, like an army of ants surrounding the city.

Caesar had decided, in the lee of the afternoon's unparalleled violence, to offer clemency to Thapsus. The rebel stronghold was now, along with Thysdrus and Hadrumetum, one of the only three cities in the east that were still held for Cato, and Thysdrus would fall without issue, for it lacked adequate defences to stop the Caesarian army. Similarly, Hadrumetum, while it boasted strong walls, lacked much of a garrison to defend it, since those men had been called to battle and then defeated. Only Thapsus remained a potential thorn in their side.

The looting had lasted until sundown, when the men were finally reined in, though Postumus had once more earned his growing reputation by taking Juba's camp and holding it, preventing the place being ransacked. The Numidian king had fled without returning to his camp, and the opulence of the place had been staggering. Postumus had run an inventory and had reported that they would be able to pay the wages and bonuses for two legions from Juba's goods alone, for among the treasures in the king's tent had been three chests of gold coins.

The estimated figures of enemy dead approached ten thousand in the end, a figure that most of the officers had heard in abject horror. Caesarian losses had been far fewer, thank the gods. A few enemy soldiers and officers had been taken captive, but most of the men had been allowed to flee for their lives and return to the obscurity from which they had been levied, the senior officers having vanished from the scene.

The next morning, an enterprising centurion had presented Caesar with twenty-five elephants that had been recovered from the surrounding area, and these the general had paraded in front of the walls of Thapsus. Now, several hours later, those elephants were penned and calm, and the general had had all those men singled out for their actions during the battle arrayed before the siege lines in full sight of the defenders. As the garrison of Thapsus listened on, each of the heroes was announced, his part in the victory made clear to those atop the walls, and his prize, decoration or promotion bestowed.

Once the ceremony was complete, Caesar, with his senior officers and praetorians at his back, rode forth from the lines and halted just out of missile shot of the walls. There Caesar rose in the saddle, hands crossed on the reins.

'Gaius Vergilius Clarus, commander of Thapsus, do you hear me?'

A small figure appeared on the battlements, between officers, banners fluttering above. He called back in response. 'I hear you, Caesar. Say your piece and be gone'

'Vergilius, it is time to surrender your command, as you must now realise. Scipio is beaten and the remnants of his force scattered. No army or commander of note stands between us and Utica, and Africa is poised to fall. You will find neither support nor succour henceforth. I am, however, of a mind for mercy. All the republic knows of my legendary clemency.'

Fronto felt a twitch at that, remembering watching noble Romans being run through on behalf of Caesar's clemency the previous afternoon.

'Surrender Thapsus,' Caesar went on, 'and every man will be granted his freedom, those soldiers in your charge given their honesta missio and retired from service with honour, the officers allowed to return to their estates in Africa and Italia with only the proviso that they will be forbidden from political office henceforth. There will be no sacking or looting of the city. These terms are generous, as you will understand, and I offer them only once, for Utica and Cato beckon. What is your answer?'

There came no word in reply from the wall, but a moment later there was a thud, and a ballista bolt slammed into the dirt a few dozen paces in front of the general's horse, an answer in itself. Caesar's face hardened.

'Very well, Gaius Rebilus will remain here with two legions, and Quintus Aquila with a fleet. Thapsus will be squeezed until it bleeds and expires in their care. The damage to the city and its population and garrison will be on your head, Vergilius, for I have offered clemency and you have refused it.'

The general turned to the men behind him.

'Messalla, take the cavalry and ride ahead. Check out Utica, for that is our destination. I and the army will follow on at a steady pace.' He turned to Rebilus and Aquila. 'Take Thapsus with as few casualties as possible. Give no quarter. They have made their decision.'

* * *

Utica, 9th April 46 BC

Scipio rode through the gate of Utica to a sombre greeting. For months he had imagined returning here in triumph to hand Cato a settled and secure Africa. Instead, he was limping in on an exhausted horse with just a handful of dejected cavalry and officers. The welcoming party that waited in the street consisted only of a handful of Gallic cavalry, headed by the stalwart Labienus, whose face radiated disapproval and what looked suspiciously to Scipio like hatred.

'How many men do you have?' he asked with no preamble as he approached the waiting officer.

'A few hundred. No more. The entire right flank disappeared and have not been heard from since. We lost a tenth of the left flank to the elephants, more than a quarter to Caesar's horse, nearing another quarter to a naval barrage that prevented us from leaving safely, and many of the rest have fallen by the wayside in the last three days. I cannot blame them after the way they were treated at Thapsus.'

Scipio ignored the vague insult. 'A few hundred is not enough. Precious few escaped the battlefield.'

'Perhaps if they had been told to withdraw while there was still time...' snapped Labienus.

'This is no time for recriminations. We must prepare. Caesar will be on the way. Where is Cato?'

Labienus' face did not change from his grave expression. 'Upon the tidings from Thapsus, he shut himself away in his palace and has not reappeared.'

'Who commands here then?'

Labienus' eyebrow rose. 'Of the paltry handful of soldiers, I do. Of the city, the corporation of the Three Hundred once more manage their own affairs.'

They were moving through the street now, heading for the forum. 'Garrison?'

'Negligible. Not enough to provide more than a hurdle for the enemy. If Caesar comes to Utica he will take it without a fight.'

Scipio roared his anger. 'Then we must persuade the Three Hundred to do what they can. Can you call them?'

'There is no need. They are already in the council chamber deliberating on whether or not to raise a Taurus standard and throw themselves on Caesar's mercy.'

'Cowards,' snapped Scipio. 'Come on,' and began to ride harder again for the forum.

'If you had only listened,' Labienus snarled, 'we would have enough men to make a fight of it here.'

'And if you had not run, we may still have won at Thapsus.'

Reaching the forum, Scipio and Labienus dismounted, their escort following suit. They marched purposefully for the door of the council chamber, two of their riders flinging it open to allow access. Perhaps two thirds of Utica's ruling council sat in the chamber on stepped seats according to rank, all attired in togas as befitted rich men on official business. The orator who had been addressing them stumbled to a halt and turned in surprise.

Scipio marched over and stood close to the man, turning to the assembly.

'Famed and esteemed councillors, our great enemy comes. Victorious at Thapsus through sheer fortune, he remains strong while our army is scattered across the landscape of Africa. As loyal sons of the republic, for whom I and my officers and men have fought and bled and ensured so much hardship, I now call upon you to aid us in our final defence. We still have allies in Spain, and forces can still be rallied in Africa given time, but Caesar comes within days, and Utica must hold long enough for that to happen.'

'How?' called a voice.

'What?'

'How are we to defend Utica?'

Scipio threw out his arms. 'Free and arm your slaves. Arm yourselves. Use what funds you have to hire mercenaries and to entreat your neighbours to send help. It will take several days for Caesar to reach Utica and we must be ready for him.'

'Foolishness,' called an old voice. 'Cato assured us that you were undefeatable in the field. You assured us that our money would buy an undefeatable army. And now you and that army are both defeated. If you cannot beat Caesar with a hundred thousand men, a city's worth of gold, a season's grain stores and a year to train your army, do you really believe you can beat him here with a few slaves and old men waving sticks? You fool yourself, Scipio Nasica.'

Scipio felt his lip twitching. 'You would simply hand Utica to Caesar and hope?'

'At least that way there *is* hope,' another man countered in acid tones.

'And what of all those loyal warriors who have done all they can to defend you and yet who Caesar will see broken for what they have done? You will hand them over?'

'Fear not for your skin, failed general,' called another voice, causing Scipio to bristle with anger, 'there are ships in the harbour. You can still flee Utica before Caesar arrives. Find a safe haven far from here, for Utica will no longer stand against Caesar.'

Scipio glared at the assembled councillors, aware that he was utterly impotent in this. Between he and Labienus they could barely rustle up enough men to defend this chamber, let alone the city. And without the support of the Three Hundred, Utica was lost. With a last scowl at the room, he turned and stomped away. Labienus paused for a long moment, regarding the scared old men, and then followed, to find the general outside with his shoulders slumped.

'Africa is lost,' Scipio muttered. 'All upon which I had pinned my hopes to stop the would-be king of Rome.'

'Africa is lost,' Labienus agreed, 'but not the cause. As long as men like us live, Caesar will not reign unopposed.'

'I should find Cato.'

'Cato is lost to us now. He will have to find his own path. We must forge on and fight anew.'

'Where? Spain?'

Labienus shrugged. 'Spain is our last bastion against him. We still have allies there and it is the only place left with adequate manpower upon which to draw.'

Scipio nodded. 'We must take everyone who will go, and every ship in the harbour to discourage pursuit and make our trail hard to discern.'

Labienus agreed. The war here was lost. They would build the cause anew in the last place possible…

Spain.

EPILOGUE

Utica, 15th May 46 BC

Fronto sat in a waterfront tavern in a reflective mood. The spring sun played off the waves in the harbour, glittering in the most charming manner. The city, untouched by war despite being the rebels' political hub for years, was a lively place, the shouts of sailors mixing with the laughter of content children and the calls of street vendors. It could have been any port city in the world, any tavern in the world. But it wasn't. And every day they remained here served to remind them of what had happened. Victories and defeats, highs and lows, gains and losses.

Caesar's army, including Fronto, Plancus and Galronus, had arrived at Utica on the sixteenth of April and had encamped outside, carefully keeping the defences to a mere temporary stake-born solution so as not to appear to the people of Utica a besieging force. Messalla had ridden out to meet them, alongside representatives of the Three Hundred, offering the shelter and loyalty of their city, once the greatest in Africa.

The war had been over in Africa, with just small pockets of resistance to mop up. They had secured Uzitta and Hadrumetum on the journey, though most cities simply threw open their gates to the general as though they had never for a moment borne the flags of the rebels. Yet while the war here was over, elsewhere it was clearly going to go on. The two most dangerous of the enemy leaders had slipped out of Utica by ship, making for Spain, where their allies Attius and Gnaeus Pompey, the great general's son, continued to hold out. But the power of the great African army was broken, at least, and Spain would be a shadow of what had awaited them here.

He was pondering on the subject of loss in particular this morning, of endings, in contrast with the brightness and cheerfulness of the city morning. It was a season of endings, and it had begun with Cato.

The general had been insistent that Cato should not be killed. He was a Roman of the old order. He would have to stand trial for his part in all of this back in Rome, but he was too high profile to simply do away with. Yet Cato had eluded them in a different manner to Scipio and Labienus. The master of Africa, who had pulled the generals' strings and planned a campaign that should have seen the end of Caesar, had realised when news of Thapsus arrived that Africa was lost.

Upon their arrival in Utica reports of Cato's fate had come from various sources, but since at least one was from the great senator's body slave there seemed no reason to doubt their veracity. Cato had sent his children to his questor, put his affairs in order and retired to his rooms for the night, ostensibly to ponder the importance of the day's tidings and the next steps to be taken. There he took a knife and stabbed himself in the chest, in the old manner of a defeated general throwing himself upon his sword. Sadly, Cato was a politician not a soldier, and the blow had not been fatal. Medics had been called and had attempted to staunch the flow and bind the wound, but Cato had found a last reserve of strength, had fought them off and had managed to retrieve the knife once more, finishing the job before plenty of witnesses. Thus had passed the architect of 'Fortress Africa' before Caesar could take him.

The general had tarried in the city only as long as necessary for the sake of appearances, and had then begun a brief tour of the local sites of importance and resistance, bringing the settlement of the republic to them, bringing them back into the fold. Indeed, this very morning he was at Zama, the site of the ancient Scipio's great victory over Hannibal, though he would be back soon. Caesar planned to depart Africa in the next month and return to Italia briefly, putting things there in order before moving on to finish the war in Spain.

Fronto had voiced his intention to depart properly this time, to return to the bosom of his family, but it was hard to avoid the fact that his family were also currently in Spain. Besides, in his heart of hearts, he knew damn well that he was not going to walk away until this was finished. Until Labienus and Scipio were done for.

They were more or less all that was left of the enemy command. The season of loss had claimed many, even since the victory at Thapsus. King Juba had fled as far as Zama, only to be turned away by a city who now declared for Caesar. He, and Marcus Petreius who had accompanied him since the flight from Thapsus, and moved hither and thither for days between towns theoretically loyal to the Numidian king, all of whom turned him away. Finally, they had fallen foul of a unit of cavalry who decided that the two leaders would make a fine gift for the conquering general, and had fled to one of Juba's country villas, there to take refuge as enemy forces closed in upon them.

With hungry cavalry, mercenaries and desperate citizens all coming for them, believing their heads would buy Caesar's favour, the Numidian king and the Roman commander had stepped out into his garden with sombre expressions and sharp swords, and there fought one another to the death, both men expiring in the manner of a soldier, and robbing the screaming locals of the opportunity to make sport of them.

Considius, the man who had first greeted them in Africa, who had held Hadrumetum against them, had watched

Caesar's forces coming for him at Thysdrus, and had fled the city with only a handful of native mercenaries, carrying off a sizeable fund from the city's vaults in an attempt to find somewhere quiet to disappear. Unfortunately, the Gaetuli he chose to accompany him had swiftly changed their allegiance, enhanced by the presence of a large sum of gold, and had cut Considius down on the journey, leaving him ravaged and torn on a dusty roadside for the carrion eaters. Thus had the defender of Hadrumetum passed.

Afranius had fared no better. Fleeing Thapsus with his aide, he had fallen in with a surviving unit of Juba's cavalry and accompanied them west, only to fall into the hands of Sittius, Caesar's mercenary who had been ravaging the Numidian's kingdom for the past few months. Sittius had tried to convey the two men to Caesar, but one night on the road a fight had broken out, and Afranius had been knifed in the dark.

Of the survivors of the battle, the only important name who fared well was Vergilius, the garrison commander of Thapsus town itself. Upon learning of Cato's death and the departure of Scipio and Labienus, he had agreed terms with the besieging force, surrendering the town and himself. He had been escorted to a ship and had set sail for Italia to retire to a country life.

Africa, then, was secure. Not a single city of importance now remained in support of the rebel cause, and Caesar had carefully installed loyal men in the most influential positions to ensure that the province remained settled and faithful.

'Only Spain,' Fronto muttered.

'What?'

He turned to see Galronus and Plancus standing in the street.

'I was musing over the war. Only Spain remains.'

Plancus nodded and the two men slipped into seats at the table, gesturing for wine. The proprietor hurried over with two jars and several expensive looking glasses, bowing obsequiously to these three senior Roman noblemen.

'What will you do when this is over?' Plancus asked, pouring the wine for them all.

'Me?' Fronto said. 'That's complicated. I'd like to retire. I've a family to look after, and I've missed years of my sons growing already. I'm far too old for this kind of thing now. I'll see out Spain, and then stay there, I think. Raise my boys and teach them why this sort of thing should never happen again.'

And try not to think of a promise I made to a dying man years ago...

'And you?' he asked Plancus.

'For my part, I think I would like to see what Gaul becomes now it is part of the republic. With Caesar's favour, perhaps I can secure the governorship. The land is said to be in a poor state, and I hear speculation that it will take generations to make Gaul a viable land again. Well, I like a challenge, and I think I'd like to see if I can prove that wrong.'

Fronto laughed, partly at Plancus' grand plans, but mostly at the variety of expressions that crossed Galronus' face in response.

'And you?' Plancus turned to the Remi.

'Me? I don't know. I am pulled in every direction. Back home I still have family, and my people will be looking to their nobles to help rebuild the world, albeit a lesser job for the Remi, who have supported Caesar at all times. But Caesar has told me flatly that he needs people of provincial blood but with republican ideals to fill the new senate. He believes Rome can only benefit from the wisdom of all of its constituent parts. The argument is persuasive. And last, but far from least, I would hate to spend my latter days absent from friends. I must stay in contact with the men with whom I have shared a decade of war.'

'So what of Caesar?'

Now all three fell silent. Caesar would continue to focus on the security of the republic, but once that was done with? Well, there may no longer be an armed resistance to the general, but there would always be dissenters. Fronto himself had had plenty of disagreements with the man, and Balbus, his father in law, outright defied Caesar, naming him a would-be monarch. And now that the man had a son with his dangerous Aegyptian queen, there would be plenty of men like Cassius who saw this as unacceptable. The future for Caesar was at best written in sand.

'Caesar is Caesar,' he said in the end. 'He will endure and he will succeed, as he always does.'

And yet his mind filled with an image of a broken friend at the bottom of a quarry, desperation filling his eyes.

Caesar has to die. The boatman will not take me with an unfulfilled oath. Take on my vow and let me pass in peace. I've done ten years as a ghost. Don't make me go on longer.

Yes, the future for them *all* was at best written in sand…

The end.

AUTHOR'S NOTE

The first seven or eight books in this series were to some extent a straightforward proposition, based largely upon Caesar's own war diary with nods here and there to other ancient sources of information. The continuation of this great saga across the Rubicon and to Pharsalus was similarly simple in essence, for Caesar's diaries continued as a source for these events.

Everything changed when I came to the previous book, number 12 in the series, which is based upon the text 'The Alexandrian War', by the author known as the 'pseudo-Caesar'. That book, which is most often believed to have been written by Caesar's secretary Aulus Hirtius, was a more complex, troublesome, confused and generally less-well-written tale than those known to have been written by Caesar himself, and translating that work into a legible, exciting and feasible work of fiction was a much harder proposition than earlier ones.

Cue 'The African War'. The source text for this, also 'pseudo-Caesar', moves a step further into difficulty. It is often self-contradictory, glosses over critical events in mere vague paragraphs, while going into unbearable detail of total non-events, and is quite simply a mess. Tacitus would have hated it. I did. Unravelling the text and using it to form the basis of this story was a fresh challenge, though I must give due credit to the translators of the Loeb Classics edition, whose work in trying to locate the events in the text in their geographical context and in mapping such was invaluable to me.

The toughest challenge came from the content of the story, though, not from the dreadful form of the source. In Gaul and even in Greece, Caesars strategies are provided in excellent clarity, and show him to be a capable general. The African War, on the other hand, is little more than a catalogue of strategic errors and narrow escapes, culminating in a victory that really should have gone the other way. When writing these tales, I have each story planned out by the chapter, and the contents of those chapters already noted. At the head of each chapter in my plan, I will have a short sentence describing said chapter. By two thirds of the way through *this* book, I was sick of those chapter headings saying 'yet another skirmish'.

The main challenge then was to take a series of seemingly non-strategic manoeuvres, skirmishes and non-battles that smacks of a complete lack of tactical thought and make them make sense, and to make them interesting and varied too. And the funny thing is that though the writer of 'The African War' relates the events and occasionally takes guesses as to Caesar's motives, reading it through several times provides clues that there is more to this than the author suggests. In the source book, for example, Caesar retrains his troops like gladiators, and no mention is made of the effects of this elsewhere. Yet in TAW, Caesar also counters Labienus at one point by keeping cohorts in light order so that they can surprise the enemy with an attack. These two things seem inextricably linked in retrospect, and I formed them into cause and effect in my book.

One event I have tweaked unashamedly is the challenge by the veteran during the battle of Ruspina when Labienus is unhorsed. In the original text this is a veteran of the Tenth Legion. I have made this a veteran of the Fifth, purely because the Tenth have not yet arrived in Africa at this time, and while it is possible for a veteran of the Tenth to be serving in a different legion is seems to complicate the issue in an unnecessary manner.

I had likened the enemy in my head to the evil characters from Star Wars before I even began, and this despite the fact that in this book the rebels are the bad guys. In fact, I had a private snigger every time I wrote about the rebel force and rebel strongholds, and had to fight myself not to use the phrases 'rebel alliance' and 'rebel scum'. In my head Cato, who sits in Utica and drives the whole affair, is the emperor Palpatine, while Scipio, who storms around the battlefield looking impressive, but is ultimately flawed, is Darth Vader. For those of you familiar with the extended Star Wars universe, Labienus is my Grand Admiral Thrawn, an undervalued and overlooked brilliant tactician on the periphery of most of it.

The African war of Caesar was, in essence, a hasty and badly-planned affair. It is a testament to luck that Caesar achieved what he did. It certainly does not appear to be the fruit of brilliance in the theatre of war. I have attempted to put purpose to everything Caesar decides, but even in fiction I cannot explain everything, and the inevitable conclusion is that the general was distracted and did not 'have his head in the game'.

We all know it's Cleo's fault, don't we?

I have chosen to gloss over large portions of the history of this year and concentrate instead upon the war itself, which takes place over just four months. Events in Italy beforehand are of great importance and value, and so I have spoken of them in the text in retrospect and have alluded to their significance, in particular the mutiny of the legions. Despite the value and interest of this event, relating it in sequence would detract from the flow of this tale, and so I chose to start on the beach of Lilybaeum. Similarly, two months of faffing around in Africa after the battle of Thapsus I have condensed largely into a series of death scenes, they being the pertinent factor. One thing I do regret is not having had the opportunity to go into the history of Sittius the Roman mercenary, who had been sent by Caesar to keep the Numidians busy. His would have been an interesting tale.

Still, this is always the story of Caesar and of his stalwart officer Fronto. And while we are closing on the end of this great saga, there are two more tales to tell. Fronto will be back next year, attempting to bring an end to the civil war in Spain. Until then *vale*, and beware the ides of March.

Simon Turney, July 2020

If you enjoyed Marius' Mules XII, please do leave a review online, and also checkout other books by the same author:

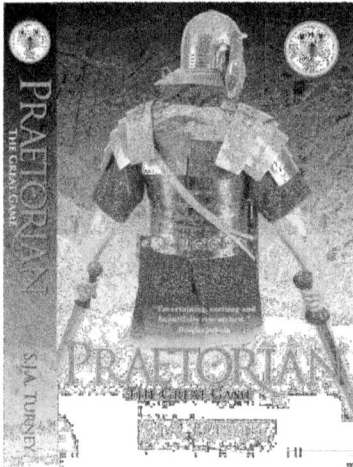

Praetorian: The Great Game

By S.J.A. Turney

Promoted to the elite Praetorian Guard in the thick of battle, a young legionary is thrust into a seedy world of imperial politics and corruption. Tasked with uncovering a plot against the newly-crowned emperor Commodus, his mission takes him from the cold Danubian border all the way to the heart of Rome, the villa of the emperor's scheming sister, and the great Colosseum.

What seems a straightforward, if terrifying, assignment soon descends into Machiavellian treachery and peril as everything in which young Rufinus trusts and believes is called into question and he faces warring commanders, Sarmatian cannibals, vicious dogs, mercenary killers and even a clandestine Imperial agent. In a race against time to save the Emperor, Rufinus will be introduced, willing or not, to the great game.

"Entertaining, exciting and beautifully researched" - Douglas Jackson

"From the Legion to the Guard, from battles to the deep intrigue of court, Praetorian: The Great Game is packed with great characters, wonderfully researched locations and a powerful plot." - Robin Carter

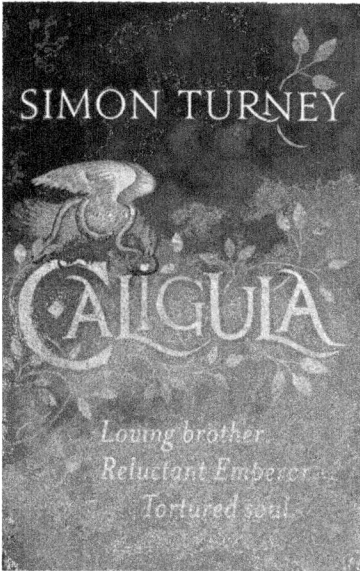

The Damned Emperors: Caligula

By Simon Turney

'An engrossing new spin on a well-known tale' Antonia Senior, *The Times*

'Caligula as you've never seen him before! A powerfully moving read from one of the best ancient world authors in the business' Kate Quinn, author of *The Alice Network*

Everyone knows his name.
Everyone *thinks* they know his story.

Rome 37AD. The emperor is dying. No-one knows how long he has left. The power struggle has begun.

When the ailing Tiberius thrusts Caligula's family into the imperial succession in a bid to restore order, he will change the fate of the empire and create one of history's most infamous tyrants, Caligula.
But was he *really* a monster?

Forget everything you think you know. Let Livilla, Caligula's youngest sister and confidante, tell you what really happened. How her quiet, caring brother became the most powerful man on earth. And how, with lies, murder and betrayal, Rome was changed for ever . . .

'**A truly different take on one of history's villains** . . . All through this **I am seeing Al Pacino in *The Godfather***, slowly stained darker and darker by power and blood' Robert Low, author of The Oathsworn series

'**Enthralling and original, brutal and lyrical by turns.** With powerful imagery and carefully considered history Simon Turney provides a credible alternative to the Caligula myth that **will have the reader questioning everything they believe they know about the period**' Anthony Riches, author of the Empire series

Printed in Great Britain
by Amazon